The Uncontinented Stars

Haden Cross

Contents

ONE

AT QUARTER TO FOUR in the morning, Noah Starbuck was knocked back to Earth with all the ceremony of a swatted fly.

His half-lucid daydreams crested on the peak of a nebula, gold-burnt, before gravity latched around his ankle and yanked him awake at his desk—first blinded by the bright screen of his tablet, then scrambling to find where his flailing hand had sent it flying. The buzz rattled against the floor, at the foot of the sofa he'd been calling his bed for the last three weeks, the caller's contact photo half-obscured by the print copy of last year's *Xenozoology Review*.

"Hey!" he said, breathless. "Savannah—"

"I wasn't actually expecting you to answer. I told him as much, you know. Wait—did I not wake you up? Please tell me I interrupted some dream you'll never know the ending of—"

Noah sighed, sprawling out on his back and hoping the hardwood would dig something close to coherence directly through the back of his skull. "What, and lie to you?"

"Again?"

"I was asleep at my desk, if that makes you feel any better."

"It doesn't," she said. "I still can't believe you let Justin have the bed in the breakup."

"Not that I don't love you—"

"Right. It *is* late. Early? Is four in the morning when it starts to be early? Whatever," she said. "Not the point. The point is that you need to get on your bike and pedal to campus right now. Noah—" At this, she cut herself off, and he instinctively pulled himself to his feet. "Noah," she started again, "they found Abelard. He's alive."

The last thing anyone at the University of Rassawek had heard of Abelard Cousteau came from the ship's black box—a hasty SOS, a timestamp for its critical power failure. Every department conducting fieldwork off-planet had, over the years, honed the protocol for when missions went awry. The email templates came pre-installed for the administration, crafted to balance on the atom-thin line of offering sympathy and delivering the mountains of red tape to which the recipient would have to take their scissors once the initial shock wore off.

In retrospect, Noah had come to accept that he'd received the deluxe package when the news about Abelard had to be disseminated. The xenosciences department was already wracked with enough guilt that his dissertation advisor was spending a year on assignment for another university and conducting check-ins over satcall—no, he had a phone call before the official notice was distributed to the rest of the department listserv writ large.

"I'm so sorry, Mr. Starbuck. This is the worst kind of news we can deliver to any of our resident scholars. If there is another advisor you would like to request, paperwork must be submitted by the end of the month, or one will be chosen on your behalf. Furthermore, university counseling services—"

He couldn't remember if he blocked out the rest of the call or merely hung up. When Justin found him later, the floor of his office was papered in every stray note that had towered around the perimeter of his desk, him sitting in the eye of it all. The tablet had landed on a bit of carpet, thankfully unscathed, but Justin's gaze fell upon the wad of paper held in Noah's fist with a grip that strained at his knuckles. He knelt before him, peeled open his fingers. *I just talked to Savannah, she told me what happened,* he said, smoothing out the wrinkled page on his knee—questions scribbled in shorthand ahead of the next satcall, lines of thought pleading for direction they were now never going to get.

As Noah coasted his bicycle down the road to the xenosciences complex, he tried to recall what those questions had been, dredging up that piece of paper before his mind's eye and taking care to edit out the bits of Justin's hands hovering at the borders. Not that it would matter now, with his doctorate approaching its second birthday; but it was the principle of it, the closing of a door that had remained ajar with a distinct air of recalcitrance long enough.

The roads at this hour were deserted, the divots of the tramlines empty for at least another hour until service restarted for the day. He'd taken this route so often that the specific path of the rail in the wider stretch of road had carved itself into his memory; as the hill bottomed out, he let himself veer out of the bike lane, close his eyes against the whipping gust of wind underneath which, for a moment, he could trace back to that open door as it finally started to swing shut.

As the bike rack rushed up to greet him, the silhouette drawn by the nearby lit window waved him down.

"Just us so far?" he said, half-jogging to the stoop of the building.

"Come on…" Savannah sighed. "Where is your helmet?"

He didn't own one. "You call me to say Abelard is alive after all this time, and I'm supposed to remember my helmet? It's a miracle I put on shoes."

Savannah's scowl faded after a beat. By the time her face tilted back toward the light, the pointed look in her eye was fully fond, and she hugged the ends of her worn cardigan against her hips. "Well… to answer your first question—yes, it's just us. You know how long it takes good ol' Bill to commute in from the farm."

Noah stared out toward the road. A lone undergrad biked by on their way to the freshman dorms a few blocks down, where the subtle bass of a pop hit thumped into the ground.

"What were *you* doing up so late?" he asked.

"Overnight shift at the engineering library." Savannah's hand drifted to her pocket, procuring a pen as thick as a sausage. She squeezed the jelly grip above the nib, bringing it up to her mouth and holding it between her teeth like a cigar. "Really exciting stuff, as always."

"You hear back from that grant yet?"

"Noah…"

Before he had the chance to push back, a car squealed to a stop under the streetlamp, directly in front of the public tram stop. Four in the morning had its perks, after all, particularly for one of the co-heads of the university's flagship department—and in this iteration, it manifested in Bill Abraham arriving in one of the region's three personal vehicles, wearing bedroom slippers and a navy bathrobe.

"Brown, Starbuck—hello. Follow me," he grumbled overtop the clanking of his key fob against the front door. "Quite a day, quite a day…"

Overnight, the hallways were lit by every third bulb, the shadows exaggerating the worn paths in the tiles. Talks of renovations had been circling for ages, never acted upon; graduate students especially were known to complain, but the wear on the building—scars, some would say—still had a certain charm that could only arise from the dogged pursuit of science. It was a nice speech to give to new students, at least. When Abelard had given Noah and Savannah's cohort their first tour of the lab facilities, he'd stood beside a selection of bricks in the wall that had been eaten away, a wide grin obvious even beneath his fluffy white mustache. *My demonstration in the inaugural undergrad lab went a little awry. Isn't it wonderful?*

Abraham's office door creaked as he swung it open. "Go on in," he said. "Take a seat… goodness, what a day…"

"Is, um—" Savannah stopped herself and hastily shoved the pen back in her pocket. "Is Dr. Eber joining us?"

"Not tonight." He half-heartedly rubbed at his brow as his desk tablet booted up. "He's down at Cape Guacara consulting on some returning ship they threw in quarantine… a right mess, as if anything from Europa warrants such a to-do."

Noah nodded as Abraham caught his eye. "Quarantine for what?"

"Someone was worried about mildew in the galley sink, I think. No one else on hand, typical TerraCosmos nonsense. Patrick said he'd be on the first train back up in the morning." He checked the clock. "Perhaps he's already on it."

Turning back to the screen, Abraham sifted through a long list of unread emails, minimized the open windows of academic articles—finally at his desktop, he found the file he'd been searching for, a video overlaid with the distinct graininess of long-distance satcalls.

In the thumbnail, frozen mid-wave, was Abelard Cousteau.

Abraham glanced at both of them in turn, allowing them a moment to prepare, before tapping *play*.

"Greetings, my esteemed colleagues!" Dropped frames rendered his movement jerky, and an odd buzz curled under the lower tones of his voice, but there was no mistaking it was him. "I do apologize for my—oh, what should I call it, surprise sabbatical? Good news, though, is that it's wrapped up. I assume my teaching post is right where I left it, Billy-boy—"

Abraham swiftly paused the video right as Abelard tilted toward a wink.

"'Billy-boy?'" Savannah barely kept the snort in her throat.

"I'm not getting into it," he said, adjusting his posture like a ruffled bird. "Now, I could let you watch the rest of that, but it's over half an hour long and frankly a bit… you know how he gets. Still, I wanted to prove to you that he is indeed alive, as it is quite the premise to wrap one's head around. Patrick must have blustered for a straight twenty minutes without letting me get a word in."

Noah let out a low whistle. "Sounds like a new record."

Savannah's snort escaped as Abraham moved on without acknowledging the comment—a tacit agreement, Noah assumed.

"Look," Abraham sighed. "It's late. We all have a full slate of classes and meetings starting up in a few hours, and I don't want to keep you. But…"

The questions, too many to gather and collate, landed on the desk between them with a smothering weight. Abelard was still alive, and in all of the *hows* wrapped around that one short statement, Noah grasped onto the image of the wreckage he'd constructed in his head years ago. Stray pieces of his ship had been picked up by deep-space cargo haulers a year after his signal went dark, twisted with the apparent ease of aluminum foil and singed with a patina that shone in the starlight like bismuth. Whatever could do that to a standard transport ship would leave a human body little more than a splatter.

The assumption, as Abraham explained, wasn't unfounded. It seemed that another cargo hauler had stumbled upon the ship in the immediate aftermath —amid the crumpled scrap, Abelard clung to existence with brain waves so weak they barely lapped against the monitor. They brought him to the closest TerraCosmos outpost, a station in the Epsilon Eridani system, where doctors were able to upload his consciousness into a Constructed Body; after all the years of calibrations and testing, they could officially bring him online and discover who this John Doe actually was.

"If I were one to believe in miracles," Abraham said, "I would certainly count this among them."

"What are you calling it instead, then?" Noah wrenched his eyes from the freeze-frame of Abelard under Abraham's steepled fingers. The floor seemed to shift under his chair with even that minor of a movement.

"Dr. Starbuck, you're the specialist who illuminates the life of deep space for us here on Earth," said Abraham, massaging his temple. He, too, had turned his attention back to the video. "Why don't you tell me?"

Not long after the tail lights of Abraham's car disappeared around the corner, after a worn back-alley shortcut with Savannah perched on the bike's back axle pegs, she and Noah sat outside the all-hours pizza joint just off-campus, jumbo slices dwarfing the compost plates already half-soaked with grease.

"If you're not hungry…"

He turned back to Savannah and the piece of pepperoni she held between two fingers, clearly stolen from his slice. "It's just a lot to take in."

Savannah nodded, popping the pepperoni in her mouth. Since the bike ride over, a few strands of her wide-curled hair had pulled loose from whatever manipulation of physics held the rest in place, hickory ringlets she didn't bother to blow out of her face.

"Was your shift done at the library?"

She rolled her eyes. "The way I ran out of there, I don't think my boss was expecting me to come back. I'll probably get an earful next shift, which won't be fun, but it's not like he can fire me. I mean, that's what I keep telling myself since no one else there seems to have any technical background—and sure, I'm not an engineer, but I at least know the basic difference between mechanical and civil—"

Noah tapped his hands together in a time-out sign. "Sav, whoa. I'm sure you're fine."

"Sorry."

"There's nothing to apologize—

"S—right. Right." Her eyes fell on the half slice left on her plate, and she folded it up for another bite before she could say anything further. Her light brown skin flushed with a tint that almost matched the neon-red *OPEN* sign in the window. "So… you say it's a lot to take in. What are you thinking?"

"About what, exactly?"

She shrugged, drew circles in the air with her remaining piece of crust. The end of the semester was fast approaching, enough so that drafts of his classes' final exams had already taken prime space on his tablet's desktop. His inbox had at least three unanswered, week-old messages from Abraham and Eber asking to confirm which courses he'd be teaching in the spring—and by the time he arrived home, there would be another, this one offering an alternative to a cavernous lecture hall merely trying to fulfill their interstellar science requirement.

Their meeting with Abraham had concluded with a quick overview: just after the New Year, Abelard would be arriving at Natocke Station, orbiting Ganymede, to make preparations for his first official venture post-return. As soon as Abraham said *Project Khepri*, the air in his office started to buzz—one of TerraCosmos' two jewels of research and exploration. The first phase of Project Khepri's exoplanet bases was up for their mid-tour check-ins, nothing the agency's top brass considered too taxing. Abelard would need a small host of scientists to assist in the effort, and his stated first picks consisted of anyone he'd already worked with, former doctoral candidates included.

"I've never been outside the Asteroid Belt," Noah said after a few moments.

"Right."

"Neither have you."

"Never been off-planet," Savannah said, rolling the crust into a dough-like ball. "But I don't think Abraham was thinking about me when he started going off about Abelard's big comeback tour."

"Why not?"

She clasped both of his hands between her own, and the late-night angles of fluorescent bulbs and streetlamps rendered his an unhealthy sort of pasty. "It's very kind of you to pretend you forgot about the *Journal of Xenobotany*'s mishap of the decade, but I'm sure everyone—even orbiting Epsilon Eridani—heard about that one."

"Abelard's been in the equivalent of a coma," Noah said. "You're still the golden girl of space plants as far as he's concerned." He cut off her impending huff by wriggling his hands from her grasp and taking it in his own. "Plus, Abraham called you first. Not me."

"Fine. Still going to have to run it by Tracy, though," she said. "Three years is a long time to be away. *That* far away, too. 'Hey, babe, why don't you come visit us while we're near Rigil Kentaurus'—come on."

With dawn starting to stretch over the rooftops and spindly bare trees, they took the rest of their pizza to go. The cheese on Noah's slice had mostly congealed, and Savannah walked his bike as he tried to get a few bites in before it cooled completely. The joggers already out for the morning side-stepped him without a second glance.

"I wonder what it's like," Savannah said after a stretch of silence. They were standing on a corner waiting for the tram line to cross, and on the opposite corner another jogger hopped in place, trying to spot the last car in the larger train.

"I don't," Noah said. He tossed the last third of his pizza into a nearby bin —the jumbo slices were always a little too much. "What good does being able to run that much do anyway?"

"Ooh, close. I was talking about the whole Constructed Body thing. To your thought process, though," she said, eyeing the jogger as they passed him in the crosswalk, "I agree. Wholly unnecessary."

The dewy morning quiet fell over them once more as they kept on, unconsciously opting for the longer route back to the street where they both lived. Nursing and medical students in wrinkled scrubs flitted to and from clinical shifts at the hospital. It was all the regular background set of campus at this hour, familiar enough that Noah had managed to all but tune it out—

this morning, his attention circled all the ways medical personnel had to hold the functions of a body above water until it could swim on its own again.

And also: an old man made delicate by age flung against the forces of the vacuum of space.

"I bet having a ConBod isn't that different," Noah said. "Swap out, what, IBS for dealing with software updates… it's not like it gets rid of the potential to have a problem."

In undergrad, Noah's organic chemistry TA had to use a specific fabric for her hijabs to keep her ConBod's brainware processor from overheating, lest she spend a week offline in maintenance. *Still,* she'd said, *beats terminal cancer.*

"Did I ever tell you…" Savannah said as they turned down their street. "When I came out to my family, they asked if I wanted to look into that, uploading myself. They even offered to pay the non-fatal circumstances fee."

"Seriously?"

"Yeah." She waved away the ghost of the idea like a gnat. "In their minds it was easier to just build the body I wanted instead of getting… their word was 'messy.' I don't know. I guess I can get where they were coming from, but it's not my meat suit's fault she didn't get everything right. I wasn't going to kick her to the curb for it."

They'd come to a stop in front of the stout apartment building that Noah shared with three other young adjuncts and an old man with five cats, and Savannah rolled his bike forward until he could take the handlebars. She leaped from the sidewalk, long limbs flung wide in an uneven pirouette delivering her back to the path. Beyond her, behind a gnarled half-dead oak, was the large house-turned-apartments where her wife was likely starting to stir with the sun. She didn't spare it more attention than it needed, just a check to ensure she was walking in the right direction before searching out the moon hanging over the tree line.

As much as Noah felt the call to cancel his noon lecture, his conscience kicked and screamed at the very thought this close to finals. He still had to close out the last unit, and the loopy dramatics of sleep deprivation insisted that *this* was the lecture that could make a difference in a student's life, convince them to shift their path up past the boundary of the atmosphere. The textbook was dry on its own; the slidedeck, peripheral at most. The lecture had sold it for Noah as an undergrad, and who was he to deny his students that same moment of revelation?

"Please relax," he grumbled to himself. "Embarrassing." Half the collar of his button-down stuck up against his neck as he shuffled to the lecture hall, and his eyes hadn't stopped stinging with every blink. The detour to the coffee stand in the physics department lobby delivered him an extra-strength concoction that was doing little more than expanding the frequency at which he could vibrate at a skeletal level—not that he didn't believe there weren't benefits to this, but most of said benefits were ones he hadn't yet discovered.

Fifteen seconds to noon, the title card to his slidedeck lit up the wall behind him: *Introduction to Non-Carbon-Based Lifeforms.*

When he gazed out over the wide berth of the lecture hall, the prepared introduction collapsed on his tongue; after half a beat, he was able to stop gaping.

A raised hand jutted up over the heads of the surrounding students. A first.

"Hi—um, yes, you have a… uh, question before we begin?"

The hand remained in the air as they craned their head in an attempt to make eye contact across the distance. "Is it true that Cousteau guy we've talked so much about isn't actually dead anymore?"

"Yes—I mean, he was never actually dead at all, but… semantics—"

"And didn't you work with him on deep-space xenozoology?"

Noah swallowed his hesitant stammering and glanced around to the other students for some sense of reassurance he wasn't hallucinating the encounter. "I did, yes, at least until his presumed death—"

"On vacuum leviathans, right? Is that what killed… or…" the student sighed.

"Yes to the first, still very much don't know to the second. Why the sudden interest?" He surveyed the rest of the class again, but their faces betrayed only the current stage of the semester, under-eye bags visible for even a few in the back row. "I planned on ending class today with some trivia about leviathans just for fun but…" Quickly he tapped through the rest of the slides to the one in question, an artist's dramatic rendition taking center stage. "It's obviously not going to be on the exam," he added. "I—"

The student held up a tablet open to a garishly teal website. "This guy's blog post about Cousteau not being dead went viral this morning. It's… what's a nice way to put it—"

"It's an experience," another girl said in the front row.

The diversion had sopped up enough of the allotted fifty minutes. After asking the curious student to stay after class, Noah dove right into the lecture without any preamble. He knew the case study on Io's silicon- and sulfur-based ecosystem almost as well as he knew the subject of his own research; with half his attention focused on the outlining the key conceptual differences between carbon and silicon photosyntheses, he let the other half roll back to an early research huddle with Abelard the first semester of his doctorate. Abelard's office wasn't much larger than a modest walk-in closet, and the climate control wheezed against the summer heat as they squinted, focused, at some abnormal radiation readings picked up around Wolf-359. Not even a guess on the matter had been formulated before the university and the rest of the world had assumed Abelard had met his end as a frozen corpse in space.

As the class drew closer to its end, the slide on vacuum leviathans made its reappearance.

"And back to the topic of the hour," he said, gesturing up toward the display. "Vacuum leviathans, as they've been called, are large theoretical xeno-organisms that live in the void of deep space rather than a planet, moon, or other solid body. None to date has ever been observed directly—hence 'theoretical'—but studying the anomalies picked up around various interstellar outposts has indicated the existence of *something*. As my mentor —yes, that one—told me once, it's like studying the ripples on a pond trying to find the rock. But sometimes it's a dragonfly, or a frog, or the rain, and often there's a hundred other ripples happening at the same time, so it feels impossible to say much of anything definite about a single rock. But..."

He paused, and the rows and rows of students leaned forward almost in unison—aside from a few at the back, who had started to pack up. Glancing at the clock, he saw it was already 12:52. Over his shoulder, the professor for the next hour cleared her throat.

"Next time," he said, waving the lecture to an end. He shouted over the clamor about a coming study guide for the final and office hours for the rest of the semester; the other professor quickly took his place at the podium, and he made his way toward the back of the hall, where the student from the beginning of class hovered, a tablet clutched to her chest.

The door to the corridor outside thudded shut behind them, and they pulled off to the side as a steady stream of students for the next class began to file in.

"So about this blog post you mentioned," Noah said. "I'm just having a hard time imagining anything about Abelard Cousteau reaching outside academic circles. He doesn't have that kind of…"

"Name recognition, yeah," the student said. "Not yet, at least."

Noah raised an eyebrow, and soon found himself staring at the post in question, squinting against the glaring teal background. As he started to skim the first paragraph, she elaborated on other key elements of the post, the less academic bits that likely snapped up the larger public's attention.

"I'm going to pretend I know what all that means," Noah sighed. No one had ever told him he would feel this old at the tender age of thirty-three.

The first part started off measured, but by the end of the fourth most of the punctuation had been flung into the ether, unspooling the rest into long run-on sentences. Abelard's name, as he expected, was everywhere. At the sixth paragraph, he began to spot his own name with increasing frequency.

"Interesting." Noah tapped back to the main feed of the blog and scrolled through the rest of the posts—while all of them focused on vacuum leviathans, there was otherwise little cohesion to the wider subject matter. Links to journal articles bookended long treatises on the latest depiction of leviathans in a film or piece of art, and still Noah kept spotting references to himself beside the likes of Abelard and other renowned deep-space xenozoologists like Chen Yuxuan and Renata Wood. "Could you email me a link to this when you get a chance?"

"Absolutely." She took her tablet and tucked it back in her bag, and they began to meander down toward the central atrium, the chatter there a distant mumble. "Sorry if this is… too personal," she said suddenly. "But it must be pretty wild for Cousteau to basically rise from the dead like this."

"No apologies necessary," he said. "It *is* weird. Abelard's barely been back a full day and he's already trying to recruit me to a TerraCosmos fieldwork mission."

"Are you going to go?"

He opened his mouth to answer, and found he didn't have one to give. In all the flurry since Abraham first mentioned the offer, he hadn't spared a single thought to the fact that said offer required a decision. "Haven't decided yet."

"I know I'm not you, but it seems like an easy sell. 'I thought my mentor was dead, but he's not, and now he wants to do an interstellar research trip with me'—that's the stuff of delusional daydreaming, but you get to live it."

Before either of them could say anything further, they arrived at the atrium, and she was flagged down by a group of friends on the opposite wall. She threw Noah a wave over her shoulder and he half returned it, most of his thoughts swiveling around the question of the hour—week, or year, really— with a deadline unspoken but certainly short.

As he tugged his bike from the rack outside, he squinted up toward the sky, as if the solid sheet of blue would momentarily part to allow him a view of Ganymede, the potential trailhead and where in the stars it could possibly lead.

Opening the front door to his apartment building, Noah was greeted by a chorus of his neighbor's cats on the other side of the wall. "No, it's not him," he called as he trudged up the stairs. They only whined louder. "I promise. Hang in there a little longer."

In his own living room, latch bolted, his messenger bag fell from his shoulder with a dull thud. If he'd made an effort to aim, it would have landed on the end of the shoe rack, but it had missed spectacularly. He stared at it down the length of his arm, the top flap open and releasing dead pens and bits of debris onto the floor.

Surveying the apartment, he listed his options. A nap ran to the top spot, shoving lunch out of the way. Taking another pass at the final exam barely tried to catch up, but Noah could still appreciate the effort; he stooped down long enough to pull his tablet from his bag and tossed it onto the hideous orange armchair that Justin had snuck into the moving crates when he wasn't looking. "You're lucky you're comfortable," Noah reminded it.

Lunch could wait, but he was starting to crash from the concoction he downed before class. He set a mug in the mimeo to make a coffee, and its hum rattled the small bit of counter space around it—a fitting arrangement given that the kitchen wasn't a separate room but a strip along the living room wall. Fitting, but not the worst. He'd heard horror stories throughout graduate school of classmates needing to find new accommodations after breakups, and the pickings offered by the local housing board on quick turnarounds were rarely ideal.

The mimeo chimed in time with a ping on his tablet—new coffee, new emails. More pings followed, an avalanche. The warmth against his palm was grounding, and he took care to balance the mug on the chair's arm as he settled in to face the latest plea for his attention.

The bunching pain in his lower back eased as he saw most of the new messages could be deleted immediately. He hovered over one, a forwarded screed from his father railing against Base Materials, idly wondering if his parents had also considered pushing a ConBod when they discovered he was on testosterone and planning top surgery.

Sighing, he pulled up the file labeled *XBIO101 FINAL - FALL 2776* and stared at the first three questions through a blurred, unfocused haze. Gulping down a third of the coffee hardly helped. How was he supposed to focus on an impending exam, or the latest edits on his journal submission, or even what he was going to eat for dinner? Over all of that loomed the question of the year.

Are you going to follow Abelard into the great beyond?

There was an impulse to insist that his life was here, in Rassawek, at the university.

His job was here, sure. The position wasn't tenure track, and the stipend meant he was still six months out from buying a proper mattress, much less a bed frame.

Savannah was here, but she could also be beside him off in the stars, under the heading of Project Khepri.

Justin was here, but as of a month ago, that no longer mattered.

He tapped back over to his inbox, staring at the unopened message from his father. He let himself consider a scenario where he shot off a rebuttal to the predictable hole-pocked argument, but the scene cut off right after he presented a version of his finances mangled by the inclusion of expenses Base Materials had covered for centuries.

He deleted the email, pushed the thought of his father and the tense, burning knot at the center of his chest away, out the window, smashed into nothing on the baked slab of earth below.

"Come on," he muttered. "Just read over section three of the exam and then you can pass out all you want."

Review the descriptions of xeno-organisms below. Determine whether they would be classified as animal, plant, fungus, or miscellaneous microbe. Justify your answer using Suwannarat's Taxonomy Principles.

"Nope, too much… what's section one?"

The multiple-choice questions gelled into a single, incomprehensible block of text.

The tablet fell flat against his lap, catching a glare from the sunbeam shining through the corner of the window; he followed the angle of it up, shielding his eyes lest he trigger his long-dormant migraines. It tilted him back to the earliest days of grad school, Abelard's insistence on pedagogy courses despite the department having dropped the requirement years ago.

Noah's transcript was absent of them; Abelard's supposed death preempted that. And maybe that class could have taught him how to write an exam, and maybe that was far beneath its concern. Maybe the fact he was asking at all underlined the need for it in the first place.

Where was Abelard now? He'd recorded the video sent to Abraham and Eber at Njord Station, where his unidentified body had first been delivered. Was he still there? Had he already boarded a shuttle to Natocke Station, awaiting the assembly of his crew?

"Screw it." Noah tapped over to dial Savannah but was only met with her voicemail.

Vaguely he was aware of his footsteps rattling back down the stairs, echoing over the continued plaints of his neighbor's cats—into the lobby, through the front garden tamped down by the coming winter, and finally at the base of the ancient oak whose limbs shaded the window to the living room of Savannah and Tracy's second-floor unit. It was open.

"Savannah!" he called. "Savannah!"

Tracy appeared at the window instead, shoving the swinging pane wider for a better view. "You have a key."

"I do. Yes." In his apartment, in one of the pockets of his bag. "But…"

"Okay, okay, should've known…"

A moment later, Savannah joined her at the window, her hair spilling out of a dark green silk scarf. "I was going to call you back. Only been up ten minutes."

"Clearly I wasn't thinking," he said.

"Not about some things," said Tracy, "but obviously about something else."

"Right, right…"

Savannah squinted down at him. "You didn't teach your whole class with your collar like that, did you?"

His hand flew to his neck—the collar had been jostled into a slightly more acceptable position during the bike ride back from campus, but not by much. "First of all, we all know it's been a weird… not even twelve hours—"

"Oh man, half those kids probably didn't register a word you said," Tracy laughed.

"The hopelessness of my teaching today aside…" He sighed, and it rolled through his whole body as if one good push could get him to finally stop reeling, align himself in the world that seemed to have shifted two inches to the left overnight. "Did you decide yet?"

"About the Abelard TerraCosmos thing? I mean—right, duh," she said. "What else would it be? I just…"

Tracy leaned over and pressed a kiss to her temple. "Are you asking because *you* decided?"

"I think so? But…" he sighed. "I'm not going to go if you don't, Savannah."

Her face had fallen into her hands, barely propped up against the sill—at this she glanced up, brow furrowed, chewing against the inside of her cheek without the pen to occupy the impulse. "That seems a little silly."

"Does it?"

"You won't let me embarrass myself?"

"If I haven't by now," he said, "then I think you're safe."

The thick breeze that had curled around the branches overhead died, and without the rushing hiss of it, Noah could almost hear Savannah rotating the idea in her head, watching its orbit from all angles. A new thing to factor into the calculations of the everyday, something that could accommodate her from the inside this time, not staring through the bay windows of the engineering library while it streaked through the sky like a comet, there and gone.

"Yeah," she said, nodding at Tracy, then down at him. "Yeah! If TerraCosmos wants us so bad, let 'em have us!"

Somewhere beyond the opaque blue overhead, Jupiter held Ganymede and Natocke Station in wait; and beyond that, lightyears past the edge of the Kuiper Belt, further than anyone could truly comprehend, the galaxy would open up for them, a welcome so many had dreamed of for centuries and they would now get to live.

TWO

WITHIN MINUTES OF DISEMBARKING onto Natocke Station, Noah and Savannah found themselves whisked away by a TerraCosmos cadet to a conference room far from the gleaming bustle of the central promenade. Interviews for the final two support staff, she said. A formality, mostly. Abraham and Eber would be holoprojecting in from Rassawek to supplement —and that was the last detail she offered before running off to the next errand.

The room's porthole boasted one of the best views on Natocke Station: a narrow slice of Ganymede's curve laid against Jupiter's restless agate storms, the Red Spot raging into view more by the second. Even from the door, it was enough to prevent them from catching their breaths, though the pale woman perched beneath it seemed unimpressed. Her thick black braids were pulling loose from the coils keeping them off the back of her neck with the way she tilted her head, staring through the porthole's corner. As Noah approached, the hand-drawn star chart came into focus on the open page of the notebook in her lap.

"Are you sure we're in the right spot?" Savannah whispered. "Where is everyone?"

"Project Khepri, right? With Cousteau?" the woman said. She paused her drawing to assess them both, the nib of her pen tapping against a thin tattooed line running from her bottom lip to her chin. "This is it."

Savannah said nothing, directed her nerves to chewing the inside of her cheek as the stranger turned back to Jupiter. Her hand dug into a pocket for her pen while she studied the array of clocks on the wall: one for each of TerraCosmos' three regional headquarters, and a fourth larger one for Interstellar Standard Time, aligned with the primary office in Cairo.

"Everyone else is probably running late. We're fine," said Noah. He motioned for her to sit beside him in one of the empty chairs, and the table soon muffled her rapid pen clicking.

As if on cue, a loud conversation down the hall began to sharpen into actual words. The woman by the porthole muttered to herself in a language Noah didn't immediately recognize.

"...don't understand, how does TerraCosmos not have the right medical release forms?"

The door slammed open to reveal a short redhead midway through smudging her analog glasses, followed closely by a Black woman fighting to cling to her last dreg of patience.

"When I explained your physician's office only speaks Quechua, they said there hadn't been a need yet to translate them in that direction. Plus, personal translation software won't—"

The redhead skidded to a halt. "Dr. Oyekan," she sighed, and a pinch of a South Britain drawl bled through. "Adedayo...we're going to be crewmates, after all."

"Just 'Dayo' is fine."

"Brilliant." She kicked out the sole chair on the other side of the table and fell into it, running a hand through her short messy hair. "You know, most of Cornwall's been underwater for centuries and they've still got every form in Cornish, but sure, screw the Greater Andes. That's fine—"

"Interesting thing to complain about with that accent," said the woman by the porthole without glancing up from her notebook.

The redhead begrudgingly accepted the point with an eyeroll, which finally landed her attention on Savannah and Noah.

"Oh. You two are new," she said. "Assuming you're the xenos botany and zoology to my mycology, then." Without waiting for an answer, she pulled a small tablet from her pocket and retreated to the far corner to wait for a satcall to connect, presumably to her doctor wherever she called home.

Removed from the hurdle of the moment, Dayo's disposition took on a newfound sunniness. She rounded the table to sit on Savannah's other side, going on about how they'd been cooped up in this wing of the station since that morning. Nerves and a touch of cabin fever, she concluded with a grin.

"Bodes well for the next few years," the woman behind them muttered.

The small talk fizzled almost immediately, the room falling into silence once the redhead finished her call with a huff. She flashed Dayo a halfhearted thumbs up, and the clock ticked closer to 1600 IST.

The atmosphere threatened to clog Noah's throat and had already wound Savannah's normal jitters into a taut spring, which grew more contagious by the second. They were all waiting on Abelard—still an odd concept to grasp, that not only was he alive somewhere in the galaxy but that he would be alive *here*, a solid thing who could actually answer the questions Noah had posed to his ceiling in the intervening years.

When the door finally opened, his startled yelp failed to dislodge.

Abelard strode inside with an ease once curtailed by the arthritis of old age and a poorly-mended knee, a mismatch with Noah's memory that stuttered his attempt to rise from his seat. But this was the same man, he reminded himself. The same man: pale and bald with an errantly-combed white mustache, now with seams along his wrists and collarbone where synthetic skin met matte-bronze casing.

"My crew! And my old protégés!" He rounded the table, beaming far past the ends of his mustache. "My goodness… *Doctors* Brown and Starbuck, what a delight it is to greet you with your proper titles—your dissertations… incredible! Noah, I do apologize for being absent so long, as your official advisor, but you hardly needed me at all. To think we live in a world where we can all be together again given everything that's happened… entropy has been very kind to us."

There was hardly room to respond before he swiveled his attention around to check on the rest of the room with a familiarity steeper than was warranted. A flood of information—the xenomycologist's name was Frida, he'd just come from a talk on Project Aker's progress to the Polaris system, had they heard of the avian-like species around Gliese-1061?

Dizziness warped the edges of Noah's vision, and he gripped the table's edge as an anchor. This was going to be his life for the next few years. New people, new soil—or nothing at all—under his feet. The surrounding conversation fuzzed into nothing, only pieces leaking through. The holoprojector booting up. The click of a tablet connecting to a wall monitor, displaying Project Khepri's mission (*Healing the Earth in the Post-Climate-Catastrophe Age!*). Savannah, testing the lock on an emergency exit

—

"I wasn't sure you'd actually want me on this mission," she said. "Considering…"

"That was *you?*" Frida said.

Abelard ignored her. "As I said before, I read your dissertation. The incident was what led to your discovery of the unique qualities of that Chironese fern, wasn't it?"

"Sure, but—"

"So they had to quarantine and exhume the whole building. The fresh—"

It was barely half a second. Like all ConBods, Abelard's eyes were digital displays meant to imitate their organic counterparts, the actual camera enabling sight tucked away above the bridge of his nose in a pinprick no larger than a pore. It was half a second, a flicker, the cosmetic pupils and irises shuddering as his grin held steady.

"—knowledge is worth the price. Hm, apologies." He knocked his fist against his skull, the metal clang a much more solid thing than Noah expected. "Still getting calibrated, I think. If I could remember what it was like learning to walk, I'd expect this would feel very much the same."

Noah's attempts to process the last couple hours could benefit from the comparison as well. The dizziness had mostly subsided, but he was half out of himself helping Dayo fix the holoprojector configurations keeping Abraham and Eber muted, so by the time the interview candidate was sitting across from their hodgepodge of a panel, he felt like a whole week had passed, and also no time at all.

The candidate was oblivious to how the eager trill humming under his skin fought to skitter them all into the hallway and down to the nearest airlock. Both sides stared in a kind of stalemate.

"Call me Esmail."

Abelard opened then very quickly closed his mouth. "Yes. That is the name on your application, Mr. Rostami."

"Right. Of course." The line of Esmail's grin strained to keep from bursting wide open. "As you already know, I am Esmail Rostami. I've got twenty years' experience as a merchant pilot—currently out of Aotearoa, mostly contracted by TerraCosmos for local transport of goods mimeos aren't fond of, raw materials from recycling plants and the African Mining Board, though that's dropped off a lot lately in favor of pre-assembled gadgets. Anyway, not to sound over-eager, but I believe I am the best candidate for this position for a number of reasons, the first of which being—"

Eber's hologram halfway tripped over himself in his attempt to cut across Esmail's speech, landing the projection of his body in the middle of the conference table; being a short man, the surface sliced right through his waistline. He held up his hands to quiet an already-silent room, aside from Frida's stifled snort from the far end.

"Thank you, Mr. Rostami—"

"You can call me—"

"I know." Eber rubbed a tight circle at the center of his brow, and Esmail proceeded to give the whole of his attention—or at least his eye contact—to a seam in the table that hinted at an ability to fold itself out of the way. "If you could do me a personal favor, just... don't mention the merchant work."

As Eber retreated to his hologram seat, Esmail remained focused on the table seam. "That's... um. It's all of my experience."

"Don't mind him," Abraham said with a long sigh. "Tell us what you think we ought to know. Just don't contextualize it on that axis. We'll strike your last answer from the record. "

Slowly Esmail pulled his gaze up from the table, taking a few steadying breaths as he flexed his hands in and out of fists. His fingers fluttered in a wave, and after five or so of these flexes, he shoved them back out of sight. "Sure, absolutely. Can do. So…" Another deep breath followed, and as soon as he exhaled, that same enthusiastic near-bursting grin returned to his face. "I think I'm a perfect match for this. As I've detailed in my application, I've navigated through numerous precarious incidents, including run-ins with space debris and colliding asteroids, and also one time when our engines had failed and I helped engineer a solution that kept us from falling into Saturn's atmosphere and being crushed to death."

At this, Esmail's grin rose to its full toothy potential.

"Is that so?" Abelard said after a beat.

"It is!" He waited a moment, carefully watching Eber to see if he would react at even a sideways reference to merchant contracting. "Also, xenobiology is one of my primary interests. I may not have a degree or anything, but I've read every article published by everyone in this room. There wasn't anywhere on the application to mention that, so—"

This time it was Abelard who held up a hand for a pause, waiting a solid moment after Esmail fell quiet before speaking. "Have you ever worked with an astronavigator before? If you've only flown within the Solar System, then I'd suspect not."

Esmail stared at a point just over Savannah's head. One of his hands had balled into a fist, but with the thumb tucked between the first two fingers, rhythmically digging his nails into his palm. "You suspect correctly," he said, tentative. "I do know the theory of how that arrangement works, and… is the astronavigator here?"

From the far end of the table, the woman from the porthole gave a small wave. "Hi."

Eber was starting to fidget in his seat, low mumbling growing louder despite the toe of Abraham's shoe tapping against his ankle. Abelard cleared his throat—or merely made the sound of it, since he had no actual throat to clear. "Yes, Dr. Irene Tuuluq is one of the most—"

"Do you listen well?" she asked.

"You mean… following orders?" Esmail said.

"I guess."

"I'm great at it, and—"

Irene turned to Abelard as well as the spatting holograms. "I like him."

They'd found themselves a pilot. Esmail flushed with an infectious glow and leaped to his feet, insisting on thanking them all individually in a continuous run-on sentence. Before Abelard could give him any further details about paperwork or the ever-shifting departure timeline, he shouldered his way back into the corridor.

"Woof," Frida mumbled. "You're sure about this guy?" she asked Irene, then turning toward Abelard and the holograms.

"Dr. Wick, his records rank him as one of the highest-rated contract pilots working today," Abraham said.

Abelard chuckled to himself. "I can't say it made any note about his enthusiasm, but—"

The door flung back open, slamming against the wall spring. Esmail stood in the frame and pointed, half out of breath, to the man behind him. He was a full foot taller and met them with a grimace as he ran a hand over his bald head.

"On the listing you said you still needed a chief of operations, right?" Esmail said. "I got one for you."

As much as Esmail's buoyant demeanor had spread mere moments ago, the silence that followed this announcement rivaled the pressing nothingness of a spacewalk. Beside Noah, Savannah's foot jiggled, fighting the tense hold of the rest of her body. While he couldn't read the rest of the room as precisely, the air still thickened around him, thickening further when Frida pointedly shot a glance toward Abelard at the center.

He ignored her, and Esmail stood oblivious to it all.

"And… where did you find him?" Dayo said.

"He was right outside—"

"Oh boy," Frida muttered.

"He was waiting for me. He's my husband," Esmail said. "I probably should have led with that."

Abraham and Eber waved the two of them in, and without Esmail or the door jamb in the way, Noah could get a better look at the newcomer. Each facet of him that Noah could discern lay at the opposite end of the spectrum from Esmail—solid where he was bony, the tan hue of his skin holding warmer undertones, his mannerisms closer to a comma while Esmail embodied an exclamation point.

"He's not springing this on me," the man said. "The original thought was that he'd mention me in his own interview but…"

"We were all there. Except you, obviously," said Esmail.

"Technically. The walls here aren't that thick."

Pacing behind the table, Eber's hologram was primed to pop a digital blood vessel, and Abraham's warning stares could only tamp it down so much. Abelard sat immune to the projected commotion at his back, the hands that passed through his skull, as he leaned ever so gently forward with an eager grin coaxing the conversation further.

"*Heoi…*" he sighed, as he fell into the closest seat. He offered a winding summary of his experience, waiting to introduce himself as Quinn Kaiwhakatere at the very end, and within half a breath, Quinn found himself embroiled in a highly-technical conversation with Abraham over the specs of the type of ship they'd been assigned. With the discussion revolving around light-barrier engines and internal gravity modulators, it was nothing Noah could follow, and by the looks on everyone else's faces, he wasn't alone.

Abelard caught his eye then, flesh to digital, organic pupil contractions working opposite the aesthetic estimate. The corner of Abelard's mouth curled upward, a private showing just for the two of them. *I don't want you to take this lightly,* Abelard had said. *I think we can make a lot of progress together.*

"Under my watch," Quinn said, "our ship could make it to the edge of the next galaxy."

"Good," said Eber, and Abelard slid over the official offers for him and Esmail to sign, hitching themselves to an empty research vessel docked on the underside of Natocke Station, far off in the maintenance bay, that would soon carry the eight of them off to the farthest reaches the human species had achieved.

The Gamma-class research vessel *TCS Amihaf,* upon first boarding, was not so small as to immediately prod at a sense of claustrophobia. Photos of earlier spacecraft, from the cramped bulb of *Vostok 1* and narrow passages of the International Space Station to TerraCosmos' own Alpha-class ships, dug their phantom fingers into whatever walls surrounded Noah in the moment, dragging them inward until the walls squeezed into his bones. Depictions of caving or being buried alive never left his brow damp and palms clammy. There was something, though, about how very little space existed that was safe against the unfathomable vastness of the universe and all its apathetic hostility.

While only built for a crew of eight, the *Amihaf* stood ready to ease the apprehension, its limited floor plan designed to imitate a far larger vessel. The main corridors effortlessly accommodated three walking abreast, the lab space wouldn't force them to tango around each other, and even Quinn—the tallest among them—didn't have to duck in doorways.

With Natocke Station and Ganymede shrinking in the ship's proverbial rearview mirror, the mission was technically underway. Among the crew, only Esmail and Irene had truly settled into their respective stations, using the few days of travel ahead within the Solar System as a trial run for the sorts of vector calculations they would face once outside the Kuiper Belt. Quinn and Dayo made their own rounds, taking stock of the med bay or touring the tech keeping the ship fully functional.

Noah whittled through the first few hours after departure trying to pull his bunk into something that could reasonably pass as home for the next few years. He shoved his clothes into the provided dresser, threw his favorite pillow over the crunchy piece provided, and tried to arrange a few trinkets on the small set of shelves facing the end of the bed. Pulled from the crowded perches in his apartment back on Earth, they shrank in the bare space afforded to them now. Even his Spock figurine appeared to droop, a five-hundredth-anniversary issue whose features had long been worn away, sagging in some uncharacteristic display of emotion.

"Not bad, just different," he muttered to himself, repeating it again after splashing his face with some water in the bunk's private washroom. "No use sulking."

A short distance from his door, the section housing the bunks opened up into the communal living quarters, a small lounge tucked into an alcove beside a galley and mess hall, though calling it a hall was more than generous. It was closer to an upscale cafeteria table, an eight-seater awaiting the crew's take on a family dinner.

"Good, you're here!"

Savannah sat around the lounge's stout table with Dayo and Frida, their heads looming over a larger-model tablet with an incomplete crossword puzzle. None of them looked up but they beckoned him over with an oddly dire sense of urgency.

"There's nothing else we need to do right now?" he asked.

"I already checked everything in the med bay," Dayo said.

"And what the hell is there to research right now?" Frida tore her eyes up from the puzzle with a look that answered the question for him. "Anyway, please tell me you're good at Terrestrial geography—"

"Or history," Savannah added.

"That too." She pointed to a nine-letter vertical stretch of squares, all blank aside from an *E* in the last spot. It was the primary link to the final corner left to complete. "The hint is 'American border.' Vague *and* something I haven't a clue about."

"Not too vague," Dayo said. She tapped a finger against her close-shorn hair. "It's a *historical* border. 'American' gives it away."

Frida huffed low in her throat. "I know more about Ancient Greece than the United States."

"Also… I don't want to be a nag…" Savannah grimaced in a way that told Noah she very much wanted to be a nag. "'American' could refer to any of the old borders in the Testudines. I just—Noah, help."

Sighing, he knelt near an empty spot at the table and skimmed over the clues attached to the current mystery. The first dealt with horses, which was even more of a lost cause than geographic history, and the rest were just as hopeless. "Maybe we'd have better luck with a new one?"

"Absolutely not," said Frida. "I will never let a puzzle defeat me."

Dwelling in the stalemate, Noah sat back against his heels, listening to the hum of the ship—still as omnipresent as when they first boarded, but it was sinking into his bones, and through it, he could discern the sound of footsteps clanging up the spiral stairwell from the ship's lower floor. The tones grated together like two mistuned horns, slowly revealing Quinn as it kept on.

"Hard at work, I see." The sweater he'd been caught in during his impromptu interview had hidden his toned arms and their intricate sprawl of tattoos, the lines there tensing as he pulled open a service panel.

"Is there a name you could put to 'American border?'" asked Dayo.

Quinn hummed to himself as his fingers wove through the delicate assembly of wires and blinking lights embedded in the wall. "I make it a point not to know anything more than necessary about that sort of thing. I got better use for my brain space." He shrugged. "I know Tāmaki Makaurau's former name, but I grew up there. Rassawek or Ychma? No chance."

He continued to tease through the tangles deeper in the wall, and Savannah and Dayo turned back to some of the other clues yet to be deciphered. Still Frida glowered at that long line of empty squares, and with little else to hold onto, Noah tried to enjoy the simple matter of company, the way this kind of quiet settled around him without the threat of suffocation. The ship sped toward the Kuiper Belt at its buzzing clip, and through the porthole against the mess' wall, Saturn's gentle yellow was beginning to step forward from the speckled backdrop.

"What about horses?" Savannah's head popped out of the huddle, a stray coil of hair bouncing down the center of her forehead. "Four-letter word for a kind of coloration—"

"Oh sure," Quinn said. He secured the wall panel with a gentle click. "I know tons about horses. Such as—"

He promptly turned on his heel and hopped down the stairs to the main deck.

"Something tells me he doesn't actually know anything about horses," Dayo said.

Before Frida could pick up her grumbling about another clue—"BLANK von Bismarck," still as unfamiliar as it was ten minutes ago—Quinn's head reappeared over the threshold of the stairwell. "Noah, right? Cousteau wants to see you down in the lab."

He answered the question Savannah held in the quirk of her eyebrow with a shrug and followed Quinn below. The staircase deposited them in the corner of the large central node of the ship's lower level, opposite the portside wall attached to the airlock and the landing ramp. Emblazoned at the intersection of the corridors was the TerraCosmos emblem—thin gold line art of Earth with seven sunbeams shining from behind.

Chatter from the cockpit lured Quinn away from whatever he'd listed next on his agenda; he disappeared around a corner to the right, leaving Noah alone with the low buzz of the engines underfoot as he turned left toward the lab.

The door slid open when he approached. Abelard was perched on a stool at the center black-top lab table, tablet open to a journal article full of graphs and figures, and holding a microscope slide close to his ConBod's visual lens above the bridge of his nose.

"I hope I'm not interrupting anything," Noah said. "Quinn said you wanted to see me?"

"How much do you know about xenomycology?"

"Not as much as I'd like, but that's why Frida's here."

Without any indication that he'd looked away from the slide, he motioned for Noah to come closer. "She brought some of her samples as potential comparison points." Only then did Noah spot the long cardboard box at the other end of the table, the long edges of slides in neat, ordered rows. "Look at this—it's a specimen from Ceres with remarkable similarities to our Geoglossaceae family of fungus."

Noah was juggling the sample before he registered Abelard had tossed it to him, barely catching it between his ring and little fingers.

"I don't understand the organization system they use here." The speed at which Abelard had gone from the stool to the cabinet at the far corner was so far out of bounds from Noah's memory that it was almost alien. "Standard TerraCosmos methods, et cetera. Silly if you ask me. Which I know you didn't, but—aha!" The metallic clangs of his rummaging fell off as he bent down to the bottom shelf. The edge of his shirt slipped up his back to reveal a sliver of the ConBod's bronze casing.

"What type of fungus is the Geog… Geoglast—"

"Geoglossaceae," said Abelard. He stationed the newly-procured microscope, assumedly meant to compensate for Noah's organic sight, at the corner of the table and switched on the power. "In the vernacular, the Terrestrial varieties are known as 'Earth tongues.'"

"That's… terrible."

"I'm sure Dr. Wick would say the same thing about very deep sea creatures. What about the anglerfish?"

"It's the name."

"Right, right. Of course." He plucked the slide from Noah's fingers and secured it under the lens. "Come look at this structure in the cell walls…"

While Noah peered at the slide, Abelard hopped up on a stool on the other side of the table, grinning at him and pointedly flicking his digital eyes between Noah and the other empty seat. "So," he said, hoisting himself up. "You didn't call me down here to talk—uh, Earth tongues?"

"Heavens around us, no. I simply got curious in the interim after running into Mr. Kaiwhakatere." His hand slipped back toward Frida's box and secured another slide. This one had a vibrant blotch of pink at the center hemmed in by red biohazard nanotape, and while the duller sheen of the slide meant it wouldn't shatter if dropped, Noah's stomach still clenched as Abelard flipped it between his fingers. "I must confess that I am still reeling from… dear Billy-boy called it a 'miraculous return,' and I suppose he's right. You know, my internal calendar hasn't quite realized so many years have passed. Part of me is still eager for our next satcall conference, and I have to remind myself that you are long past that point."

The slide hovered at his brow, though his eyes remained fixed on Noah. Queued up at the back of his throat were the staples he once relied on to buoy himself through situations that made his nerves pull too tight. Dust had gathered where he'd white-knuckle gripped them through reviews and conferences and interviews, and it left him more prone to slip, both from the physics and general disuse; but old habits died hard, and they died harder when their ecosystem found itself suddenly restored.

"You said you read my dissertation," he said after a moment. "What'd you think?"

"That was what I was hoping to discuss with you. I have so much to catch up on, but I do feel this is what's most immediately owed. Not that I..." Abelard sighed. "I'm not doing this merely out of a sense of obligation. I hope you know that."

"I get what you're saying, but... " Noah rested his chin atop the knuckles of his fist. "'A sense of obligation' isn't a bad thing, necessarily. Could be a different form of—Justin... you remember, from department events, he sidestepped anything about science. Still sat front row at my defense."

"You two are still seeing each other? That's lovely. How is he taking your being away for so long?"

"Um. We aren't—"

"Oh."

"You couldn't have known. It wasn't even two months ago—"

"I'm terribly sorry, Noah."

He ran a hand through his hair, tried to wave the whole topic away. "It is what it is."

Abelard nodded. "Yes, I suppose so."

The lab entrance hadn't slid shut behind him; beyond the corridor, through the central space Noah had started thinking of as the foyer, rang an odd series of clunks that rattled through the walls. Irene and Esmail's voices rose between them, indecipherable.

"Still," Abelard said, clasping his hands together. "Even if I had not been your advisor, I would still want to discuss your research. Because it is good work, and because it is yours."

"I…"

"Didn't you say you understood what I was trying to convey?"

"I did, yeah."

"Yet you seem surprised."

Hearing it laid out so plainly made the nibs of it impossible to ignore, and he'd never learned how to hold it all comfortably. Something always sank wrong into his gut. "It's just been a long day."

Again Abelard nodded, slotting the slide back into its box and securing another, this time without the biohazard markings. The blot at the center resembled mashed orange pulp. "Has it been too long of a day for us to return to the topic at hand? New methods of detecting potential vacuum leviathans in deep interstellar space? I can't quite recall the exact title. And I hope I won't further embarrass you by calling it brilliant."

"I—thank you," he said. "That means a lot."

"You know I'm not one for embellishments—it *is* brilliant. I read it through a few times, poured over all your data… but I'd like to hear about this research of yours from *you*, not the stilted propriety the academy demands."

"Which parts, exactly?"

Abelard returned the slide to its proper slot, replacing the lid and letting it sink under the gentle press of a finger. "There was a section on radiation that sparked my curiosity. It read as if you were omitting a few remarks here and there." His shoulders rose and fell like a sigh, just short of becoming a shrug. "Conjecture that reached too far beyond what would be permissible for your defense?"

"Like what?"

Abelard cast his gaze—the digital representation of it, at least—around the lab, then toward the door. Irene could be heard quizzing Esmail on some protocol of piloting with an astronavigator. "I tried to tease out the potentials for myself with the data that you did include, but I was unsuccessful. I wonder if it would have saved me some trouble. There weren't..." He frowned, but quickly swallowed it. "There weren't any readings from anything that could have been an *actual* leviathan, were there?"

The hum of the *Amihaf*'s engines rose in Noah's ears with all the pressing insistence of tinnitus. He stared at Abelard, first at his ocular displays, then up toward the dot of the camera. He placed both hands on the lab table, the smooth black surface a touchstone to Earth, to every science class he could recall—a much-needed sturdiness. "You're working up to tell me your ship got attacked by a leviathan, aren't you?"

"Astute as always," he said. "Not even a pebble left unturned when you're around!"

He was so *casual* about it, being the first witness to a theoretical, one that would blow their field wide open. Noah stuttered trying to get his words out. "Did you get a good look at it?"

It wasn't like Abelard deflated at the question, but rather he appeared to momentarily forget the augments afforded by his ConBod, how time hadn't had the chance to pull at his bones; the hold of his back curled on itself, hunched, and his mustache twitched in a way that betrayed it was hiding a grimace. "I may have. I don't know, but... I think so?" he said, quiet. "They told me that some memories are so flooded with adrenaline that it's akin to a corrupted file. I get flashes of it, sometimes. Not much context. The lecture series I was recording for Sichuan University... on the way back I reviewed the last one I got to make. Only half of it found its way to Earth before—and I couldn't remember recording it. I couldn't even bring myself to accept that the man onscreen was me."

The degree of the doubt on Abelard's face stepped past what Noah had come to expect, past his reputation among students as a font of knowledge.

"Let me see…" Abelard reached for his tablet, flicking the stylus out of its casing. With a notes app pulled up between them, he began to draw, curves made angular by a halting hand. His other held the tablet still. "Sometimes, if I concentrate on the moment, the gap where it should be… there's a—Noah, take it away."

"What?"

"Take it." He spoke through gritted teeth, suddenly frozen.

Noah swiped the tablet away from his hands, and it slid down the table, stopping just short of Frida's box of slides. When he reached for the stylus, Abelard's fist flexed and the dense ecoplastic snapped in two.

A quiet whir rose from the base of his neck, there and gone, leaving them with the ship's ambient noise and the broken piece of stylus rolling to the floor with a dull clink. Abelard regained some sense of motion in slow, jerky tests of his joints.

"As you might guess," he said, forcing a chuckle, "I don't try to do that very often."

"What was that? I mean—sorry, that was blunt. Are you okay?"

Abelard rolled the remaining bit of stylus between his fingers, his fluidity returned. "Never better!" he said with a contented hum. "Now, do tell me about your current research."

"We can talk about that at literally any time," said Noah. "I—"

Overhead, the ship-wide intercom chimed for their attention: Esmail, with a rambling announcement of a potential exit vector from the Solar System that would pass by Neptune and Ushuaia Station, in case anyone had discovered something they'd forgotten to pack.

For a moment, Noah cycled through the items in his duffel bag, and it was a moment long enough for Abelard to scrape his stool back from the table, tossing a remark over his shoulder about a crew meeting in the mess hall before they passed through the Kuiper Belt. Alone with the spared tablet and Frida's samples, the bustle of the rest of the crew muted by the walls and now-closed door, he let himself breathe in the quiet. It was probably nothing, that moment with Abelard. Noah wasn't an engineer, much less one that specialized in the interface of the organic and mechanical. For all he knew, this could have been normal.

Still—he hopped to his feet and exited the lab, passing through the foyer and straight on toward the antechamber of the cockpit. Even more maintenance access panels lined the walls here before the entrance proper, and Quinn hovered at an open one in the corner, staring into and also past it. Noah waved, had it returned, then settled into the jamb of the open cockpit door, gazing out toward the shimmering starscape.

"...so if we were going to use this process to travel from here to Pluto," Irene said, "what would be the first thing you'd do?"

"I would double check the—oh, hi Noah!" Esmail said, turning around in his seat. "What's going on? You need that pit stop?"

"Has anyone else mentioned anything?"

"Dayo said she wanted to check for a spare part for some device that interfaces with ConBods, but..." he sighed.

"She didn't want to be the one person holding us up," Irene finished.

"Good news for her, then," said Noah, melding together the beginnings of an excuse as fast as he could manage. "I've got something to pick up, too."

He didn't, of course, but he had a few days to figure out how to prevent that from coming to light. Surely there was something he could drum up a sudden need for, crucial but easily overlooked. He just wanted to get a second opinion on Abelard without any chance of him catching wind of the conversation; but as the ship began its final approach toward Neptune and the rocky orb of Triton, he still had no options, and he tried to tell himself that it didn't matter, that he merely had to step off the ship and be grateful that it was Dayo who had an errand, that he could play it by ear despite it being made of tin.

When they docked, Dayo carried the conversation through the space bridge —it was more talking to herself than conversation, however, as Noah offered little aside from the occasional hum of acknowledgement.

"I don't blame medical schools for not always having the resources to offer training about ConBods, but it's an increasingly common reality for the population," she said. "There's a whole generation of physicians out there without any background in engineering or computer science, and they're the same people who give the *Amihaf*'s diagnostic machines a passing grade on inspection when it's barely functional…"

Her monologue kept on as they entered Ushuaia Station's promenade, a far less impressive spectacle than Natocke's, as if TerraCosmos hadn't spared the funding strip to keep Ushuaia's sparkle up to code. Who bothered to stop at Neptune, anyway? Only the desperate, crawling their way inside the Kuiper Belt like the heat-stroked collapsing at a Saharan oasis—and the absentminded, and Dayo did not want to count herself among the latter.

"And I'd rather not be desperate either, but…" she sighed, staring down the stretch of shop signs in the nearby hall. "Prana Technologies' parts are proprietary. Have you ever seen a troubleshooting session using off-brand components? You don't want to. Trust me."

A question was starting to form in the hold of her mouth as she double-checked the directory on the corner, so Noah cut back in. "You have a lot of experience working with ConBods?" he asked. Savannah would have laughed at his attempt at sounding casual.

"Relative to some doctors, I think so," she said, motioning down the hall and not paying Noah's odd affect any mind. "There are a lot more bad accidents and weird diseases when you're practicing off Earth..." She trailed off while peering in the window of a shop displaying metallic obelisks of Neptune's core and various sizes of dull white shards from the planet's diamond rain. "'Deepen your connection to the cosmos and ethereal plane with these authentic pieces from the planet of mysticism itself,'" she read. "What do you think the chances are that they're real?"

"At those prices? Pretty low."

"Is that something you're into?" Dayo flashed him a curious grin as they continued down the hall. "Last thing I would expect from someone in your field."

"Ah... no. My, um..." Justin's face wasn't the only one Noah had tried to smudge out of his memories. "My ex was good friends with this art history professor whose partner was very..." He waved the rest of the remark away. "It doesn't matter."

"Sure it does."

"Not anymore."

She nodded, mostly to herself. "Fair enough."

The sign for Prana Technologies was approaching faster than Noah anticipated, and the topic of conversation had been steered from its previous path, and—his face pinched as he let loose a mental string of curses. Nothing in any of the shops they'd already passed had anything he could wrap his lie around, and now he was left with a faint tinge of incense hovering at the edge of his senses from the last time he was ever in that professor's condo, showing up with Justin, without their promised pie and without a resolution to the fight they'd had about whose fault it was that it burned. And the professor's partner, a reedy woman with a Venusian rock set in silver around her neck, greeted them at the door with a serenity that ignored the flush of the argument still glowing under their skin.

When they reached their destination, Dayo paused as she reached for the handle. The corridor light caught in her dark eyes in a knowing twinkle. "You didn't actually need to come into the station did you? It's fine!" she added, just as Noah's heart seized in his chest. "That just makes two things you've been weirdly cagey about, and I don't know you well enough yet to talk about unpacking anything."

She tilted her head, waiting.

"Thank... you? I think?"

Her head tilted further.

"Oh, this is my cue to tell you, isn't it? Okay," he sighed. "I'm probably being too cautious or—I don't know, paranoid. Probably paranoid. But something strange happened with Abelard right after we left Natocke Station and I don't know if it's normal."

"And you were worried about him overhearing you talking about it on the ship," she said.

"Basically."

"Yeah, there's a lot to unpack there." She told him to wait outside while she picked up the part, and five minutes later, she was enabling his tongue-tripping, weaving recount. With her arms hugging the part's large box to her chest, her chin tapped against the top whenever she offered an encouraging nod.

"So is he fine?"

"Physio-mechanically? Probably," she said. She'd paused across from the crystal shop to give her arms a rest, having refused Noah's offer to carry it the rest of the way. "Psychologically, though, he did experience something pretty traumatic, and there's a lot we don't know about how that manifests in a Constructed Body's brainware. The initial theory was that it wouldn't, but you know science."

However optimistic she sounded now, it did little to push away Noah's hold on the sight of her grimace when he mentioned the nearly-broken tablet. "Intimately."

Hands on her hips, Dayo surveyed what was visible of the atrium bar and turned toward the shop, then to Noah. "We've got time to kill. Let's check this place out." She didn't wait for a reply, hoisting up the box and tapping the lower of the door's mechanisms with her foot.

Noah fought a grumble as he slipped in after Dayo before the door swung shut, bracing for a heavy fog of incense that didn't come. The shop was cramped, sets of glass-bottomed shelves forming aisles that could fit two people only in their wildest fantasies. The walls sat bare aside from a large tapestry with the zodiac signs in a circle, an imprecise design that spoke of hand embroidery.

"Come look at this," Dayo called from one corner. "It's a mineral from Chiron. I've never seen a stone so yellow before!"

"That there's lennikite."

How Noah managed to miss the shopkeeper, he couldn't say; gripping his chest, he took another glance at the man with his unkempt gray hair and leathery skin that, on Earth, would betray a long life spent at sea. He stared straight ahead, right at the door.

"Named for Giles Lennik," he continued. "Part of the first survey team they sent out to Proxima Centauri way back when. Keep that stuff on hand if you're trying to manifest personal insight."

They both mumbled some acknowledgement and continued perusing. The wares ranged from the more Terrestrial fare to polished stones of the Solar System at large and raw slabs of rock labeled with an exoplanet and a scribbled chemical composition.

Dayo gazed at the selection with wide eyes, a finger tracing the rocks' varying shapes from a few inches away.

Something twisted in Noah's stomach as he followed behind her, a thread that wove around his ribs, up his throat, and through to the back of his neck, heavy. It dug like a hook into his skin, begged him to turn around—so he did, searching, and still only found the shopkeeper with his steady gaze ahead toward the door, a cane pressed into the box Dayo had left there upon arrival. The hook returned whenever Noah focused back on the latest stone on display, barbed sharp like the lethal end of a fishing wire but darker, more expansive, a pupil dilating in the dimming light.

Most of the items claiming to be from Neptune took up the opposite side of the shop, and Noah meandered his way over as Dayo lingered on a pile of gravel supposedly from a planet orbiting Wolf-1061. The shopkeeper sat as still as a wax statue aside from his breathing, a careful steady thing that tugged at his bony shoulders.

But as he passed to the other side, Noah noticed his eyes. They were clouded, but instead of the pale blue of cataracts there was a swirl of lilac, lines of deeper purple webbing through the helix.

The man smirked, a coffee-stained canine peeking out over his bottom lip. "You there, boy," he said. "Engaged in Cousteau's latest little venture, are you?"

Noah froze. The thing in his stomach clenched, and he found his gaze yanked to meet the haze of violet. "You know Abelard?" He tried pretending to examine the nearby display of diamond rain, but the whole of his head was locked in place.

"Of a sort, if you believe that kind of thing." The man reached into his coat pocket, retrieving a piece of thick cardstock held between his index and middle finger. It sat sideways, the face of it staring straight into Noah's wearying eyes—tarot, Earth's moon hemmed in by other satellites throughout the Solar System. "That sort of thing is thinking you've got quite the storm coming."

"I, um… okay." He slid between two shelves to reach the back wall and the hook stopped him cold. When he glanced over his shoulder, the shopkeeper still stared straight ahead. "Hey Dayo, we should probably go."

"Are you sure?" She headed toward the center of the store, giving the inventory a final once-over, until she was standing before the box from Prana Technologies.

"What about you, miss?" the shopkeeper said. His bulging knuckles held the tarot card in place so tightly that they were one good squeeze from creasing it. "Your medicine-learning keep you from embracing the unknown sciences?"

Dayo shot Noah a quick frown. "You know what, I just need to get that box
—"

"Sure, sure."

"We're on a schedule, you know—"

"Oh, I do."

Noah's hip knocked against one of the shelves, the panes rattling on their
supports. "Thanks for your time, sir," he said, grabbing the opposite side of
the package from Dayo, tugging it up so suddenly that the man's cane didn't
have time to move. The end slipped to the floor with a slight bounce of its
rubber tip. "Interesting place you've got here."

His palms suddenly slick with sweat, he nearly dropped his end of the box
as they shuffled to the exit, Dayo's foot already reaching for the door
mechanism. Noah tried to focus on not tripping over his ankles walking
backwards, but the man's lavender gaze bore into him and also through, that
same hook weaving in the empty spaces between his atoms.

"You ever seen a wagon with a fifth wheel? How about one of them bots
with a soul? Don't you say Elijah didn't warn you, don't you say it—" the
shopkeeper called after them, his voice silenced as the door swung to a
close.

"He said *what?*"

Savannah spoke for the rest of the crew's unnerved winces after Dayo and
Noah relayed the incident at the station. At first, they'd gathered around the
mess hall table with time to spare before Abelard's mysterious all-hands
meeting to speculate what he'd spent the past few days doing holed up in his
bunk, and the lone empty seat had no way of answering on his behalf. Noah
hadn't even planned on bringing up Elijah and the crystal shop at all—

encountering odd people, by itself, wasn't a momentous occasion—but then Quinn mentioned some awful pun Abelard made about a wagon not long after leaving Natocke Station, and Noah must have made a face because otherwise Dayo wouldn't have laughed like she did, and then everyone had to know.

"Yeah," Dayo said. "I've never actually met anyone who had such a problem with Constructed Bodies before."

"I think she was talking about literally everything else," said Frida, chin in hand and already halfway to an eyeroll.

Nodding, Savannah added, "But the ConBod thing is also not great, obviously."

"It also might not mean anything! The rest of it, as a whole, not just that piece," Esmail said. "The box has 'Prana Technologies' on the side, so he might've just inferred you were a doctor that way."

Frida groaned toward the ceiling. "Just because you were able to 'infer' your way into finishing that fresh crossword in three minutes *does not mean* anyone else could do something like that."

"Hey." Quinn pointed at Frida from across the table. "Don't talk to him like that."

"*Azizam*, I can stand up for myself—"

"If you thought that was bad, then you're not ready for when I'm *actually* pissed off—"

Noah took a quick survey of the rest of those present not flinging the decibel level out of Neptune's gravity well: Savannah's head had fallen to the table, laced fingers bridged across the back of her neck, while Dayo sat frozen, perpetually halfway to butting in, and Irene continued to draw on the piece of scrap paper she'd found in the galley. Behind her, the clock read 1858 IST, and though the telltale sound of an opening bunk door hadn't yet come, Abelard was punctual enough that it would be soon, and the thought landed in his stomach like one of those Neptunian obelisks. It hadn't even been a week. The *Amihaf* hadn't even made it out of the Solar System yet. Elijah's clouded eyes stared toward him, just out of frame, there and not, look-and-you'd-miss-it—

He'd never whistled that loudly before. It left his own ears ringing as he held up his hands, Frida and Quinn halting their spat mid-syllable. Esmail's own hands kept flexing in and out of fists, and Noah waited until they slowed before speaking.

"If we're going to have a big blow-up fight, maybe we should save that energy for something other than a crossword puzzle."

"It's not the crossword puzzle I have a problem with," Quinn muttered.

"Obviously." Irene looked up from her drawing, flipping the pen around her fingers. She brushed the hair out of her eyes and left a smudge of black ink across her forehead. "And he knew that, and you knew that he knew. So…"

The clock clicked forward to 1900 hours, and before Irene could formulate an end to her thought, Abelard emerged from the dark hall of the bunks. The tablet Noah had saved from destruction peeked out from his shirt pocket, this time with a projection lens attached. "I feel as if I've missed something." If there were any lingering effects from the conversation in the lab earlier that week, he was doing an expert job at shoving it past where anyone would think to search.

"Um…" Savannah said as he filled the last empty chair. "I wouldn't say it's important."

"Well, what would you say it was?"

The phrase brought a grim smile to her face, and Noah's as well—if they were to stack every instance of that sentence in the first year of their doctorates on top of each other, even accounting for the intangible thickness of memory, each of their piles would be as tall as they were.

"I would say," she said slowly, "that it was unimportant."

Abelard clasped his hands together, then setting the tablet upon the table with the projector facing this ceiling. "Right then. We might as well dive in!" He hopped back to his feet, positioning himself at the head of the table. "My dear crew—thank you so much for joining me this evening. Tonight, we will be undocking from Ushuaia Station and entering interstellar space, that great new frontier, in order to carry out... the folks at TerraCosmos called it a survey, but I believe it's closer to a check-up, see. As you're all aware, TerraCosmos and various scholarly institutions across Earth initiated Project Khepri over a century ago in order to investigate how extraterrestrial life might further aid the healing of our planet. Just over three years ago, the first research posts were established on various exoplanets that were deemed not completely hostile to human life, and now they want to pay them a visit— check on the research, how they've acclimated to the new environment, essentially corroborate the reports that have been coming back to Earth since they first left. Every year, a new wave of outposts has been established, but we have been tasked with just the initial round. Our first stop is the system around Ross 128."

With a couple taps on the tablet screen, the projector displayed a rotating hologram of the star and its three planets, the first of which was illuminated with a glowing green aura. "Ross 128b," Abelard continued, "officially known as Shala, is remarkably similar to Earth in size, gravity, and the amount of sunlight it receives. Despite its close orbit, it is not tidally-locked, and the research team assigned there has created a bustling little community in the jungle ecosystem along the planet's equator. That is where we are headed for the maiden leg of our journey!" He clasped his hands together again, and at the point of impact, his digital eyes seemed to flicker.

"All that being said," Abelard sighed. "TerraCosmos has their asks. With how they control funding, we of course have to heed their directions. But..."

The rest of the crew leaned forward in their seats almost imperceptibly. The same man that taste-tested a newly discovered xenoflora delivered them a *but* in the face of one of Earth's highest global authorities. That single syllable held all the potential of the universe drawn down to the single, infinitely-dense point before the Big Bang, and they all were caught there, toes curling over the lip of it.

"I must confess... the details of what happened in my accident are mostly lost to me. One moment I'm trying to get a better look at the bizarre unknown body looming in the distance, and the next I'm coming online at Njord Station. The rumors are true: I know it was a vacuum leviathan that attacked my ship and nearly killed me. A creature I'd dedicated my life to documenting and studying, hopefully discovering, and it tried to make my death... ironic, in its own way."

Whatever strain that had wracked Abelard's system before in the lab was notably absent as he met the gaze of each of the crew in turn, holding there long enough to form a connection, lay out exactly what they each needed to see in that moment.

"So," Abelard said after a pause. "We will be going to Shala, and then on to the rest of the list provided to us. We will do what is asked of us. However..."

He paused again, and the angle at which they all leaned forward deepened another degree.

"We're going to find that leviathan." His digital eyes landed on Noah then, a wave of pixels blackening in the irises. "And we're going to kill it."

There was a moment when all sound on the ship bottomed out into nothing, but it was too short-lived for the ringing to start up in Noah's ears. Barely two seconds passed, and Esmail's hand shot up like an eager student's; when Abelard failed to acknowledge him with even a glance, that enormous grin they'd all seen on Natocke Station reappeared, his fingers fluttering in the air.

Under the table, Quinn's hand came to rest on his Esmail's knee, a wordless plea to, for the moment, stand down. This did little to dissuade him, and the creases lining Quinn's face revealed themselves as practiced worry lines with how easily they folded at the slightest nudge.

Finally the silence was broken by Savannah, her throat squeezing a drawn-out *um* into a strained pitch. "If we did find it, wouldn't we want to—I mean, hypothetically… it would be more useful for research purposes alive." She caught Abelard's eye, then glanced to Noah, and then all of the crew was looking to him for a response.

It was only fitting. There was so little they knew about these creatures, assuming they actually did exist, from basic physiology to their size to how they could thrive in the least hospitable environment in existence. The theories could guess at some of it, Noah's dissertation among the proposals—perhaps all those odd radiation readings in their quadrant of the Milky Way were leviathans communicating, perhaps their cell structures incorporated new chemical compounds that withstood the strain of the vacuum. What they could learn from them was tied directly to the living examples—living and breathing, Noah was always tempted to say, as if all the universe's children needed an atmosphere.

"Why would I want to kill what I've dedicated my life to studying?"

Noah felt the words shrill through his vocal cords before they registered in his head. And shrill they did—his voice hadn't snapped and broken like that since his first few months on testosterone.

"It nearly killed me. Look at how I exist now," Abelard said. "State of the art, yes, but I miss the body I was born with, lived with. I was robbed of it. What kind of biologist exists as a machine?" He was quieter now. "What would we lose studying a dead leviathan?" Again, he met Noah's eyes. His own were increasingly speckled with black. "What else could it possibly give us alive?"

Abelard waved away the possibility of an answer, ending the meeting with little more than a muttered *dismissed*. He retreated to the ship's lower level, the hiss of the lab door opening for him beneath their feet; and the crew at the table could only consult their hands, then those next to them, and whomever they'd formed some kind of connection with since Jupiter narrowed to a point of light beyond the *Amihaf*'s stern.

"If we're going to get past Pluto…" Irene said, her voice halting.

"We should start working that out, huh?" Esmail stood, planted a kiss on Quinn's forehead, and followed Irene down to the cockpit.

Noah focused on his breathing, used it to fight the encroaching—he couldn't put a name to it, but the pressure of its approach forced him out of himself until the thread of his focus narrowed to a stifling afternoon in Abelard's office late in the spring semester of his first year. A spider landing on the scratch pad of notes in his lap. The heel of his palm leaving it a brown smear in the margins, and the gentle admonishing that had followed. *The ecosystem is still recovering*, Abelard had said. *We need to let the spiders flourish. No living thing in the universe is deserving of disrespect.*

The spell broke under the sharp tines of Frida's grumbling. "This ship's not exactly armed. What the fuck is he thinking?"

Savannah made a face. "*That's* your objection?"

"No, but no one else was saying anything!" She leaped up from her seat and disappeared toward the bunks.

Only then did Noah register how Dayo chewed at her bottom lip, and when she caught his glance, it was evident she was considering how much of the information he presented to her on Ushuaia Station needed reevaluation.

Frida strode back into the mess hall with the forceful stomping of someone a foot taller. She had a hand around the neck of a handle of clear liquor and bypassed the mess table in favor of the galley's mimeo. After a few beeps, a mechanized voice confirmed the imminent creation of a gallon of soda water. "What?"

Quinn sighed. "I didn't say anything."

"I know you wanted to—"

"*Please* can it, you two," said Savannah. "But really, Frida, what's—"

"I don't know, all right? *Bon voyage* or whatever." As the soda water announced its completion with a high-pitched beep, she rose to her tip-toes to fetch enough glasses for everyone still present. "Liquid courage to face a future more unknown than we originally anticipated? Cut me some slack. I was saving this. You know mimeos don't do booze, much less authentic *pisco.*"

She mixed them each a drink, and the sweating glasses quickly left rings in their wake. The silence was punctuated by table-thuds and throats cradling the alcohol as it descended hot down their chests, as if it could sense the infinite depth of space just beyond the hull of the *Amihaf* and wanted to spare it that fate.

THREE

THE ONLY SIGN THAT the *Amihaf* had passed the Kuiper Belt was the jolt that followed soon after. That night—or the interstellar equivalent—sleep deftly slid away every time Noah tried to sink into it; he'd pulled up the newest issue of *Xenozoology Review* on his tablet, and then his head slammed back into the pillow as the ship launched into the unimaginable velocity of turbolight. The threshold demanded a regalia of recognition: you left the Solar System, you entered humanity's last frontier, you counted among the species' vanguards. At that hour, though, Noah's eyes stung with fatigue. The only acknowledgment the moment would receive from him was shutting down the tablet and flicking it to the end of his bed. Shala was lightyears away, and he was keener than ever to lop off however many hours of the journey he could to sleep.

The initial number ended up being far fewer than he wanted. Once the clock glared a neon green 0600 IST, he painstakingly tugged himself to standing, retrieving the discarded tablet, and tried not to think about what the University of Rassawek campus faced at that very moment. The beginning of the semester, not yet midnight—even back on Earth, Noah could have been shaken awake by his undergrad neighbors.

"Not bad," he reminded himself again. "Just different."

When he exited his bunk, he found himself squinting against the lounge lights—somehow, he wasn't the first one up. He fought a yawn as he shuffled in, spotting Esmail facing a wall over a colorful prayer rug.

"I hope I'm not interrupting anything," Noah said, making a beeline toward the mimeo for a coffee. "I can take this back to my bunk."

"Just about to start, so you're fine." Esmail's voice popped as if he hadn't spoken in a few years instead of a few hours. "As long as you don't mind a side of mumbling over breakfast."

"Not at all."

The thumbs-up he received in reply held none of the groggy sluggishness of the rest of him. Soon the mimeo chime was bolstered by a murmur of nothing Noah could understand but a lilt he could recognize, the tones and rhythms rolling like a sine wave through the morning haze. With coffee in hand, he fell into one of the lounge chairs and opened up the article from the night before, a piece on the feeding habits of a worm-like species on Enceladus, a moon of Saturn. One of the co-authors was in his and Savannah's cohort, which he would be sure not to mention to her later.

The morning ticked onward. Esmail joined him with an enormous mug of chai once his prayers were finished, and one by one the rest of the crew slunk bleary-eyed from the bunks. Conversation was minimal, no matter how much Esmail initiated, and then they would disappear back into their rooms and reemerge, ready to tackle the day, whatever that meant in this liminal period.

As the ship rocketed closer to Shala, they settled into a routine: Noah sat with Esmail during his prayers, and Irene would grab the largest mug of coffee to retreat to the side of the cockpit's navigation computer, and Quinn would begin his maintenance rounds with a peck on the top of Esmail's head, and then the bottleneck arose as the rest of them filed out and fought for control of the mimeo. For dinner, one of the crew would commandeer control of the galley and mimeo the raw ingredients for a dish that would help boost the ongoing first impressions, and when Ramadan started, more hands chipped in to make a proper iftar, leaving Esmail leftovers for suhoor the next morning. Toward the evening, Frida would pull up the latest incomplete crossword puzzle, or Savannah would initiate another teaching game of spades, and eventually everyone would trickle off to bed. Abelard, who required neither sleep nor food in the same way as the rest of them, still made a point to participate as if he did, and he made no mention of the speech before they departed Ushuaia Station. It was almost as if that crew meeting hadn't happened at all.

But it had—and Noah knew better than to chalk an odd one-off moment to a collective fever dream. Savannah stopped by his bunk late one night after the rest of the crew had left the lounge's lights to dim in their absence.

"I talked to Tracy about it yesterday," she said. "She's not *not* worried, but…"

"But what?" said Noah.

"You know better than almost anyone alive. How likely is it that we're going to be able to find one of these vacuum leviathans on this assignment? Much less the exact one that supposedly attacked him?"

That night, he'd pulled up the data he'd been examining when she first called him about Abelard's return, recent compilations of gravitational and radiation anomalies picked up by TerraCosmos, all in hopes of securing more a concrete direction in the search for leviathans in this arm of the galaxy. There were still so many unanswered questions.

"None of the latest abnormal readings are anywhere near where we're headed. Half of them are out of range of Project Khepri altogether," he said. "Besides, the size they'd be… if a research base couldn't see them from their planet's surface, they'd pick them up in daily monitoring. I don't know." He swallowed his sigh and bunched up the ship-supplied comforter in his fists. "The galaxy is unfathomably enormous, and this is one single organism. It's not going to come to anything."

"You mean you hope it doesn't come to anything."

Noah didn't answer. Of course that was what he meant. Saying it out loud was allowing too much uncertainty into an already wobbling future.

Ross 128, one of the countless red dwarf stars in the Milky Way, sharpened into view as Esmail brought the *Amihaf* down to intrasystem speeds. It was by far the brightest object in the vicinity, and with nothing else present to compare it to, Noah failed every time he tried to imagine how much brighter the Sun was. About ten nonillion times brighter, Irene supplied. One followed by thirty-one zeroes. Abelard nodded, cosigning her math as the rest of the crew crowded behind the two seats in the cockpit for a glance at this sun and its brave new worlds.

"This Body's brainware is really quite something," he said. He hovered against the jamb of the cockpit's entrance, behind the rest of them. "I've never been able to truly grasp how much a nonillion actually is."

"That's a plus, right?" said Savannah. She was the closest to him and gave him a playful elbow jab that she immediately seemed to regret.

The Ross 128 system was among the smaller ones TerraCosmos had folded into its influence—Shala held the honor of being the star's only planet without the risk of being misfiled as a large asteroid. Once its terrain could be discerned beyond splotches of color, browns and purples sharpening with texture, Esmail shooed people out of the cockpit. "You know I love the company but it *is* regulation," he said, nudging Frida a few times where she sat crouched between him and Irene. "Not allowed to enter atmo with an audience."

Noah passed the entry holed up in his bunk, willing himself to ignore the shuddering vibrato of the wall beside his bed. The ship's insulation kept the interior from growing more than a few degrees warmer than normal, but it was just enough for his attention to splutter and die as he re-skimmed the official briefing on the research base. His gaze slid over personal blurbs. No matter how many times he reviewed the specific mission objective, he could only retain the notion that, among other topics, they were trying to determine if a native rodent-like species was a suitable candidate to fill one of the countless niches razed by the Climate Catastrophe. Every xenobiologist knew the transplant theory behind Project Khepri, and xenozoology was his specialty, and still he found himself rereading and rereading the same sentence about potential viability on the northern Testudines' Great Plains.

Just as his pulse and sweaty palms shot into overdrive, Esmail landed the ship and brought the ever-encompassing hum and rattle to a close.

"We're disembarking in ten minutes," Abelard called up and down the ship's limited corridors. "Get what you need for an oxygenated tropical atmosphere!"

When they descended the exit ramp, the soupy miasma was hot enough to make Irene groan at first contact. To Noah, it was about as intense as a

Rassawek heat wave at the height of August.

Dayo placed a hand at Abelard's elbow. "Do you need to run a system scan with this heat?"

"I'm quite all right, Dr. Oyekan," he said, patting her hand until she withdrew it. "What a lovely planet this is…" He trailed off, gazing around the reaching branches of native trees.

At the bottom of the *Amihaf*'s exit ramp stood a wiry man with a close buzz cut, the thin layer of black hovering over his scalp like a fog. According to the personnel files, Rohit Tripathi had spent his career in systems engineering positions before being assigned to Project Khepri, and the TerraCosmos notes worried if his lack of experience off Earth would undercut the managerial strengths he'd shown in Cape Guacara. It had been years since the base was established, so if complaints were to be had, they were long overdue.

"Dr. Cousteau, welcome to Camp Bachelor! We are honored to have you and your team visit our humble outpost," said Rohit. His arms spread wide in welcome, held there just a moment longer than he intended to—retracting them was a halting, jerky business, fingers crooking into the grimace he wouldn't let cross his face. "Our resident xenozoologists are more than ready to answer any questions you have about our rodent studies or any other research endeavors currently underway—"

Abelard laid a hand on Rohit's shoulder, and he was half a step from jumping out of his skin from shock. "It's been a long journey. This is the first time my crew and I have set foot on good old-fashioned soil in a while. There will be time."

"Of course, my apologies, of course. Let me show you around, then."

Rohit steered Abelard off toward the crescent of small metal trailers that made up the central part of the base; most of the crew followed after them with a moment's pause, but Noah stayed behind. Savannah stared wide-eyed across the rest of the Shalan jungle canopy.

"I've never seen anything like this," she whispered.

The wall of foliage at the edge of the base was comprised of life that could slot itself into the categories Earth provided before humanity turned its gaze beyond the planetary border: trees and ferns and vines, flowers and spurts of grasses. They could sort them but had no name for the particulars, the odd ways leaves spread their fronds toward the pale light of a red dwarf, the bark patterns, the misshapen particulars of the organs reaching up from a spread of petals. Above it all, however, was the plant life basking in the rays of their sun in a deep violet.

"I thought all the purple we saw in the approach was a trick of the atmosphere," Noah said.

"Not unreasonable." Still a few yards from where the jungle growth started up in earnest, Savannah knelt and rubbed a blade of plum-colored grass between her fingers. "Whatever their chlorophyll equivalent is here could've ended up this color because of the different radiation levels." She stepped toward one of the trees on the outskirts of the jungle, a tall specimen whose trunk supported a mauve vine as thick as her own calf. "You have to imagine so much when you can't be there. The pictures… it always seems like they've been recolored. And it's one thing to work with a preserved sample in a lab…"

Further off, where Rohit had led the others, a garbled hubbub of voices rose above the normal chatter of the planet, bodies clad in cut-off shorts and tank tops eager to greet a new face. Noah and Savannah meandered their way to the loose knot congregating in the base's center square as Rohit unfurled another small speech about the *Amihaf* crew making themselves at home, a potential time to circle back, the deliverables the pilot-turned-administrator was currently pulling together from the last month—"If that's something you're interested in," he said. "With the timing of your trip coinciding with the end of our quarter, I thought some sort of audit might be involved, or—"

"I think those fine folks in Cairo are the only ones who care about that kind of paperwork," Abelard said. "So not to worry."

"Excellent, good to know." Behind him, in the open window of one of the trailers, a Black woman sighed with relief and dropped back to her desk. "Alisha, did you—okay, yes, she heard. Good, good…"

"Hey-ho, Tripathi!"

The voice came from the far end of the base, near wide overhanging branches laden with more of the vines, offering shade for a makeshift patio area outside what was marked as the medical trailer. One of the xenobiologists, Noah assumed—the man whisked his hoverchair into the circle where the rest of them had gathered, leaving the base's doctor glowering in the doorway.

"I thought you said the home crew was coming tomorrow," he said. "Maria and I still have to check on a few things with the bloodwork and fix up that busted water purifier—"

"Excuse Trevor," said the woman Trevor had gestured toward, likely the Maria in question. "They just got here. We can rope them into the real work starting tomorrow. Right?" She cast a raised eyebrow toward Rohit, who shrugged into a nod.

"Awesome," said another one of the researchers, whom Noah had overheard introduce themself as Tal. "Luz and I were planning on trekking back toward that new river we found last week. It's a long haul, coming out this way," they said to the *Amihaf* crew. "You should explore a little. Stretch your legs."

They nodded toward a gap in the foliage on the opposite side of the arc from the medical trailer and the whittled branch covered in peeling yellow paint standing beside it. The trailhead marked the results of a base-wide blazing venture their first year on-planet, a means of carving out space for the operations that needed a more natural environment than the heavily-trafficked clearing could provide.

"That sounds like a fantastic idea," Dayo said. "We stay out of your way, our xenobiologists get introduced to the planet... win-win."

Frida and Savannah led the procession to the trail marker, Noah bringing up the rear staring at the nape of Abelard's neck, one of the several lines where synthetic skin met metal. A curling roll of nausea laid in his stomach, like he was waiting for the other Constructed Foot to drop.

"Hey! Before you go—hold on!" Trevor sped his hoverchair up beside them, stopping so suddenly that a small spray of dirt cast itself over Irene's boots. "Not sure if you're going to go that far, but—anyway, there's a really nice-looking pond at the end of the trail. It's fine to drink from, even if it smells kind of off, but *definitely* don't swim in it. I didn't always use one of these." He tapped the side of his chair. "There's some kind of aquatic scorpion that lives there, or that's our best guess. Haven't been able to actually snag one after I got stung, so..."

He ended his warning with a double thumbs-up, which only Esmail returned in any discernible form.

The flora swallowed up all signs of the base within the first curve of the path, and the quick clip Frida opted for was abandoned by the third.

Savannah brought the procession to a halt admiring the first of many newly-spotted stretches of leaves, and Frida may have complained if Savannah hadn't nudged her toward a pocket of violently yellow mushrooms lining a section of tree roots looping in and out of the soil. The rest of the crew milled about until everyone was up from bended knee, samples tucked away for closer inspection.

Irene tended to wander. Despite the warnings of toxic aquatic life implying a planet rife with similar dangers, she traipsed through the underbrush during the lulls indulging the others' curiosity, crouching among the violet grasses so that only the crest of her long dark hair could be seen from the trail. She returned in a half-skip, teeth securing the cap on her pen, a finger playing bookmark in her notebook.

An hour passed like this, and even though Noah hadn't spotted any xeno-organisms under his own specialty, the buzz running through the rest of them caught easily. For that hour, they were untethered from TerraCosmos, university deadlines, department politics—fifteen again, on a biology field trip to the nature center just outside town, at least until a research station revealed itself through the underbrush.

With the primary subject of the base's research being the local rodents, Noah expected the facility to be more robust. Dense fencing made of local materials cordoned off a sizable clearing, a long storage shed lining the edge perpendicular to the trail. The creatures themselves were far from the rats he'd pictured. Their stout, stocky bodies resembled a cross between a cow calf and a capybara, the wiry fur a muddy purple camouflage.

One of the small herd caught sight of Quinn and Dayo hovering near the fence—or it noticed them in some way, as Noah was too far to properly locate its eyes. Its attempts at hopping to where they stood were closer to a full-body wriggle, and as it vocalized, the rest of the herd followed after. A harmony rose, low and reedy, as they gathered close against the barrier, a progressing stretch of notes that resolved into a bone-rattling chord.

Beside him, Irene choked back something thick in her throat.

"Didn't see anything about this this in the briefing," Frida said.

Noah eyed the shed, the path of trampled grass connecting it to the main trail. It was barely a footstep wide, and the fern-like sprouts curled away from his ankles as he shuffled through it, exposing a darker purple underbelly toward the faint rays filtered through the canopy.

"I think they're cute," Savannah said. She and the rest of the crew stayed on the main path, and their conversation softened in the humid air between them. "Look at how their ears twitch! I mean, I think they're ears."

"Still can't get over the whole purple thing here," said Quinn.

"They'd probably say the same thing about all the green if we plopped them in the middle of New Amazonia," she said. "If they could talk."

"They're talking."

The voice was directly behind him. Noah's body clenched so tightly that it held his shriek at bay.

"Irene, shit, you scared me…" He caught his breath and replayed what she'd said. "Wait—what do you mean?"

"The… I just…" Both of her fists were balled at her side, white-knuckled. "You're the xenozoologist, aren't you? Don't wildlife behavior and communication fall under your field?"

"Sorry… yeah, you're right. I just mostly work in the theoretical, so I haven't had many chances to work with living specimens—but!" he added hurriedly as Irene's face pinched into a frown. "That's obviously changing, given that I'm here and not back in my office pouring over spreadsheets—"

"You were headed to the shed." It was pointedly not a question.

"I was, yeah."

"Let's go."

"Are you waiting for me to—"

"I'd rather not go alone. So, yes."

Neither of them was willing to walk on the ferns already balking at their presence, so Irene remained behind him. The chatter from the others had fallen to a murmur, beneath the crunch of rocks and twigs under their boots. Irene reappeared beside him once he was able to step inside; it wasn't fully enclosed, only offering two and a half walls as shelter from the elements, and every surface was covered in a thin layer of grime.

He absorbed the sight one object at a time. The first: a clipboard holding a weathered piece of paper, an ancient ballpoint pen on a string. It was a feeding schedule for the rodents, morning and evening, marked by hastily-scribbled initials. The clipboard laid on the wooden counter bolted to the back wall, unremarkable, until its far end concluded with a squat piece of earthenware. Noah and Irene approached it together—air-dried, a few inches shy of the *Amihaf*'s bed frames in each dimension. He prodded it with his foot, and he sensed it was far too heavy for even the whole crew to move.

Irene's eyes were fixed, drilling into the thin seam beside the lid.

"Not a lot of documentation around here," Noah said, glancing back around the sparse counter. "You'd think—"

"Open it."

She didn't need to specify. Something dank settled into his bones.

He grabbed the long end of the ceramic lid and gingerly lifted it up until it could lean against the back wall. Inside sat a slightly smaller piece of ceramic, the gap between them filled with damp black sand; and inside that, chilled, were piles of wax paper packages, the corners tinged with the drip of raw meat.

Beside the makeshift refrigerator stood a collection of logs and purple twine, unassembled fencing, and when Noah glanced beyond the wall of the shed, there was another whole swathe of cleared jungle, raw empty soil with plucked stems of vegetation gasping for breath.

"I knew it."

Something caught in Irene's throat again, maybe tears, but she rubbed any evidence away on her wrists, stomping back to the trail.

It didn't make sense. If Camp Bachelor, or whatever they called themselves, were supposed to be studying these xeno-organisms as part of Project Khepri, why would they harvest them for meat? And if their mimeos were working, why harvest any local fauna at all?

"Irene! Wait—"

He stopped himself. She hadn't gone far, just past the edge of the shed, where the fencing met into a clumsy construction of a gate. He waited for her to turn around, but she stared instead where one of the creatures had stuck its nose through a gap. A snuffling followed, though the assumed snout it pressed forward didn't twitch in time, and then finally its rear flumped to the ground.

Irene knelt before it, murmuring softly under her breath in what he'd learned was Inuktitut.

There was a blot of fear Noah had to step over before he could crouch beside Irene at the fence. The few living xeno-organisms he'd worked with in his career had been confined to a petri dish, tiny writhing creatures without parts analogous to any *windows to the soul*. Europan flatworms, Tritonian algae polyps, nervous systems narrowed to points. So he held his breath, pressed his knees into the damp soil, and stared up the snout to—

Not two eyes, but four, tiny beady things recessed deep in its skull, shrouded by the mass of fur. This close, he could spot other cavities in the bone structure, deep furrows along the top and bottom of the snout. Away from the herd, it played them a solo, humming in those bony hollows and through the tips of each sprig of fur, and the longer it hummed, the hairs surrounding the cavities grew tauter, straightening, vibrating in time with the sound. Noah inched forward. The note jumped up a half step. Irene put a hand on his shoulder, a firmness advising caution; he leaned forward another inch. Another half step higher, the humming rattled through the barriers between them until it spilled out of his own ears, a gentle coolness in the jungle air.

And then it was over. The creature bounded back toward the trail to the rest of its herd, leaving him and his soiled knees in the dirt.

Irene had already stood. "Come on," she said, nodding after it. She didn't wait for him; by the time he got back on his feet she was already halfway to the rest of the crew and scribbling something in her notebook.

He took a moment to assess his bearings. The jungle didn't swing and shift in vertigo as he'd expected. It was sharper, somehow, as if the dials on his senses had been recalibrated, and he tucked the observation aside for a moment when he wasn't at risk of being left behind in a new exoplanet's wilderness.

"—and, ugh," Frida grumbled as he approached. She hopped up from a crouch, watching one of the creatures sink its paw into a glob of mud. "I know I don't deal with specimens with this kind of mobility and basic sentience, but you'd think the keystone project of this place would be a little more… monitored? Not looking like it came from the back of beyond?"

On the other side of the group, Noah caught Irene's eye.

Abelard spoke first. "Because it's not. On Earth, we would certainly classify these animals under the Rodentia order, yes, but TerraCosmos is focused elsewhere." One of his digital eyes winked at Noah, and Noah responded with a hesitant grin that turned his stomach, an acrid burn crawling up his throat.

"Livestock," Irene said, barely audible.

"That they are! I'm sure we'll find Shala's star rodents if we press on."

That first step farther into the jungle fell at their feet, and Dayo took on the mantle with little fanfare. A crest of chirping far off in the canopy drowned out their footfalls until it was just Abelard and Noah again bringing up the rear. Noah kept his head down, focused on the toe of his boots and the jutting rocks dreaming of twisted ankles. The path wound forward in tight curves even when the trees didn't dictate it, to the point that Noah could only ever see two people ahead of him at any given time. All of it came to him with an eerily-high definition, the mystery rodent's three-note progression still coating the inside of his skull.

The next turn in the trail veered sharply left, and as soon as Savannah's head was out of sight, Abelard spun around, grabbed him at the elbow.

"Noah."

"Do you know how strong your hands are? Worth looking into if you can get it adjusted, I think—"

"Why are you here?"

"What?"

"Why... are you... here?"

Abelard's hold on his elbow only tightened, and the question of the oncoming bruise was less existential and more a guess of its color and size.

His eye displays flickered, or maybe it was just an illusion from a cloud passing over the dim light already filtered from the canopy.

"On this mission?" When Abelard nodded, he took a steadying breath. "You asked me to come. You wanted me here."

"I did want you here, but I didn't force you."

"I wouldn't be where I am in my career without you, even if you weren't around for the last half of my degree."

"An obligation, then?" He raised an eyebrow. "Of which sense? A debt? Or the one you spoke of before? It can't have been easy to decide to step away from your own research with all the security Earth and Rassawek provide."

He was starting to lose feeling in his fingers, the metal joints in Abelard's digging down against bone as the grip shifted perilously close to the crevice sheltering his ulnar nerve. "Eber said he'd send me any relevant readings from the department's scanners, so I'm covered there," he said. "But—I don't see this as repaying a debt, no. It's…"

If debt factored in anywhere, it was in the ledger of Abelard's accident. Making up for lost time, then, could count as repayment. But Noah couldn't get his tongue around the sentiment, not without other pieces trying to shoulder their way in from those millions and millions of miles away, long beyond any point where they could hope to reach him.

"Did you really think there was any chance I would say no?"

His chest clenched, cold. The tone wasn't right. Too sharp for an authority figure, begging for him to fold into that familiar position, into the shadow of one of those figures removed from this spot of soil at an impossible distance. His elbow was already laced with pain, and he couldn't stop picturing it as a tablet stylus—ecoplastic and bone, a race to see which would be the first to fold.

"I wanted to be sure that we were on the same page, is all," Abelard said, a sincere smile undercutting any threat Noah might have read.

"Awesome, great, can we finish this conversation when you're not cutting off circulation to half my arm?"

"Oh! I'm dreadfully sorry!" His hand retracted from Noah's arm like he'd been shocked.

They stood together on the path, the grating wail of a local bug filling the lapse in conversation. Beneath it, Noah could almost hear the buzz of a countermelody rising behind them through the trees.

"Why are you asking after my research again?" he asked, stretching his arm as the feeling returned. It wasn't like he didn't have a likely theory on the matter, but he'd rather not be left to his thoughts as they hiked to catch up to the rest of the crew.

"Oh, you know…" Abelard gazed up at the tangle of tree branches and their umbrella of violet. "We're a good team, you and I. We can help each other."

Down the trail, Frida and Esmail's voices rose above the group's hike back, clumsily loud on all counts, from the snapping twigs underfoot to the argument that, judging by his tone, Esmail may not have realized he was in. As their words sharpened in the closing distance, Abelard stopped, turned, reached for Noah's arm; and with a metallic snap, he retracted it.

Noah's heart settled from where it had jumped in the back of his throat.

"What I mean is, I hope you'll assist me in my quest for the leviathan. I know you were hesitant when the subject was first broached."

The gaze he fixed upon Noah landed like the open arms of an overly-touchy aunt at a family reunion: warm at first, impatient as time lagged on without giving into the invitation. With the options before him, Noah froze, and for a moment he could almost see the branching web of potentialities—the yes and no and maybe, the refusal to answer, the answer as action. He wasn't a coward; the life he had led, the one that flung him eleven lightyears from Earth, stood as a testament to that. There was something to be said, however, for the approachability of known unknowns, the predictable mysteries of transitioning and interstellar space travel.

And Abelard, this new form of him, was anything but predictable.

The bruise on his elbow had started to throb.

"Of course I'll help," Noah said finally. "Like you said, we're a team."

The beaming grin his received turned his gut sour, but then Savannah appeared over Abelard's shoulder leading the brigade back to Camp Bachelor. "Where'd you two get off to?" she asked, more to Noah than the both of them. The corners of her eyes strained as threads of Frida and Esmail's latest clash reasserted itself—a look Noah knew how to diffuse.

"Oh, you know," he sighed, then asking Frida directly if they went far enough to see the rodents that were actually part of the study, and she had plenty to say on the matter, not the least of which being that the two xenozoologists of the group didn't join them.

"Couldn't do much more than look down at them and say, 'yep, those sure could be rats,' could we?" she said, sliding through them and trudging back toward the base. "The documentation there was indecipherable. What is it with xenozoology, everyone in that field does the same thing... waste of time..."

As the rest of them slowly fell in line behind her on the path, Esmail held back with Noah at the rear, waiting until the glow of Frida's red hair disappeared behind a tree trunk.

"I thought that was the point. You know," he added just before Noah could ask what he meant. "Wasting time. That's what they told us to do. And we've still got a week here ahead of us."

"Yeah, well…" Noah nodded ahead and they set off to catch up. "That's probably not the main issue."

"She doesn't like me, does she?"

Noah didn't know what to say to that, so the question dropped at their feet among their boot prints in the soil, fading into the collective backdrop of the landscape. They reattached themselves to the snaking line, and Noah let Esmail slip ahead between him and Dayo, as if offering up his own unguarded back to the alien jungle around them could make up for the unanswered and unsaid.

Camp Bachelor served burgers for their first group dinner, and no one asked if the meat came from a mimeo.

Irene remained on the *Amihaf*.

The conversation skirted around her absence, carving out the shape of it. Savannah alluded to an allergy flare-up on the hike that left Irene sneezing for a minute straight, a minor detail in her discussion with Maria. Dayo, positioned beside the base's doctor, sprinkled in something about treating heat exhaustion in exoplanet climates. At the other end of the table, Quinn shut a potential line of questioning down by making up an Inuit holiday on the spot, nodding along as Esmail wove a whole net of lies about closed practices and how Quinn still didn't know, even after ten years of marriage, all the secrets of Nowruz. None among the other crew caught in said net noticed anything amiss.

Eventually, the separate pockets of chatter melded together as Luz and Tal relayed what they'd encountered at the river that day. "You new lot don't know," Luz said, "but I'm a geologist by trade. We hadn't seen many weird rocks among all the weird trees and animals and such, but! But!"

A tale of expanding plumes of disintegrated rocks followed, Tal and Luz illustrating the chemistry with swinging arms, sound effects that no one would think to pin on the subject at hand. The details of the science shrunk behind the spectacle; there would be time for that later, but still Rohit pulled out his tablet to take notes, highlight points to return to in the calm of morning.

Once the dishes were cleared and every salient detail of the day's rocks had been laid bare, Abelard straightened his back, imitated the clearing of a throat, and took in the eyes turned his way. "I do hate to change the subject so suddenly," he said. "See—I have a question, and you might consider it an odd one, and you might have to consult your monitoring equipment to be sure and that's quite all right with me, but..."

By the galley sink, Maria had retreated to fix some drinks with a bottle of liquor the local crew had stashed away for a special occasion. The clinking of glasses passed uninterrupted, Rohit hopping up to help her.

"You've been here for a few years... have you detected any signs of vacuum leviathans near this system?"

The trailer's ambient noise dropped to nothing almost instantly.

"I don't... I don't believe so?" Rohit said slowly.

"Oh, absolutely not." Trevor reversed his hoverchair from the table and maneuvered beside where Maria stood. He retrieved the pair of elbow crutches strapped to the chair's back, hoisting himself up to procure one of the drinks. "No way. We do monitor the system, before you ask, but... look,

Dr. Cousteau, you're a giant in this field and I've read everything you've ever published, including on leviathans—you and Chen Yuxuan both. I respect you more than I can put into words. But I don't buy it." He took a deep swig of the cocktail and shifted back to his chair.

"Yeah…" Tal said, rubbing the back of their neck. "Don't get me wrong! It's a really interesting theory, but the general consensus here is that whatever readings you're picking up are astronomical anomalies. The chances favor weird physics over weird biology, at least on that scale."

"General consensus here at Camp Bachelor is what they mean," said Rohit. "All I can personally say is it's been a bit of a debate since the announcement of your return. I can't always follow the discussion—"

"Starbuck, right?" Trevor nodded toward Noah as he steered himself back to his slot at the table. "You're of Cousteau's school of thought."

"I am, yes."

"So you buy it?"

"That's what being in that 'school of thought' means, doesn't it?"

Trevor bit back a sigh. "Fine. Wouldn't we have seen one by now? TerraCosmos' system of bases and probes—"

"Big universe," Noah said quickly. Beside him, Abelard's ConBod fan whirred. "Half of what came out of the first wave of exploring Europa rewrote biology textbooks, and that's basically our next-door neighbor."

The ongoing debate that Rohit had referenced was not keen to continue that night in particular; Trevor shrugged it off, and Abelard didn't push the matter, and a stray remark from Alisha about Mars flung everyone's thoughts in the opposite direction. It was as good a time as any to attempt a graceful exit, Noah mentioning something to Savannah about not being able to sit with his sweat-tacky skin any longer.

Outside, the metal siding of the mess trailer muffled the chatter until it was little more than another layer of the jungle's nocturnal ambience. He closed his eyes, and for a moment, he could picture himself standing on the quad at Rassawek, or in the courtyard of the apartment building where he grew up, anywhere but a planet over sixty trillion miles away from the only chunk of rock he'd ever called home. This far away, the night shouldn't have trilled such a familiar tune, or that was the instinct.

The hull of the *Amihaf* muted it all once he hiked up the ramp and into the foyer. He didn't search for Irene, though the idea crossed his mind, and instead headed up to his bunk, sliding to the floor once the door shut behind him. Tomorrow morning he would have to pull Dayo aside to examine his arm. He would have to decide how much truth he wanted to spread in the quick-catching tinder of gossip in a crew this small.

This was the sort of thing Justin knew how to navigate on instinct, and months past the breakup, Noah still hadn't learned to stop reaching into those worn divots of habit, even knowing they had grown thick with briars.

Idly he calculated what time it would be on the northern Testudines' Atlantic coast, fighting the urge to base it off the local Shala time Camp Bachelor had adopted in place of IST. Instead of checking the clock around the corner, he conjured up a half-memory of Luz mentioning they were about six hours ahead of Cairo—six hours ahead of Cairo was twelve hours ahead of Rassawek, probably a reasonable hour of the morning when reasonable people would be awake. If he booted up a satcall to Earth, no one had to know, even Savannah, because this was an endeavor for the reasonable and the reasonable alone.

This far from the central satellite relays, the call took an extra fifteen minutes to properly connect, and he propped his head against the cool metal door as the monotone chimed in the limbo.

"Nngh… hello?"

Noah refocused on the screen so quickly that something in his neck popped —between his hands was a choppy feed of Justin squinting into his own tablet screen, the only source of light aside from the smudge of the Moon in the window. A few stray locs fell across his face, a gold cuff throwing a glare across the picture.

"Yikes… um, hi—"

"Noah," he sighed. "Do you know what time it is?"

"Apparently not."

"So you're not local. How much not local?"

"Well…" said Noah. "Not local in the same way Vulcan wouldn't be local —"

"Jesus Christ, okay then." The picture froze and jumped trying to keep pace. Once it settled, Justin had propped himself up against the headboard, the bedside lamp casting his dark skin in a sheen of bronze. Beside his head, the edges soft from the video quality, sat a nick in the wood carved by one of the cats they'd fostered together.

"I obviously missed the mark on the time. You can go back to bed."

"Unfortunately you've made me curious."

At this angle, he could see the ratty shirt Justin had worn to bed that night, a faded screen print of the TerraCosmos Moon base that Noah thought he'd misplaced over a year ago. "You heard about Abelard?"

"My grapevine out that way is slow without you in it, but I caught wind eventually. I—" Justin's eyes widened. "You're out there on that assignment they gave him to—that's cool, man!"

"Gave him to what?"

"Anyone else I know out there with you?"

"Savannah is, actually. The resident xenobotanist."

"That's fantastic!" Justin's smile spread wide with that charming gap between his two front teeth, and it all glowed like the last three months hadn't happened. "Good for her, tell her I said hi."

He wouldn't. "Yeah, of course, but what were you saying about Abelard and this assignment? Is there talk around campus?"

Justin shrugged. "Word around the literature department is the mission's supposed to be a real softball. You know, something easy just to keep him busy and give them extra time to strategize."

He held back the follow-up, a question about what exactly they would need to strategize. Justin wouldn't know. Any relevant technical details would have been shaved off by the time the rumor hit the humanities offices.

Distantly in Justin's feed, a clock rang for four AM.

"I shouldn't keep you," said Noah.

"It's fine. I'm glad you called." The smirk, weighed down by the hour, still managed to tease whatever else he was eager to say, clutched close to his chest.

"I'm not going to play a guessing game. It's been a long day."

"I bet. Long enough for you to get all twisted around about exoplanets and time zones."

"As if you've never fumbled the pronunciation of Dostov—Dostoy—you know. Those guys."

"Okay, okay…" The connection fritzed, freezing Justin as he was tucking a couple locs behind his ear.

For a moment, a half-thought's worth, Noah couldn't remember why they broke up.

Then outside his bunk door, Savannah and Dayo's conversation rose from the stairwell, loud and tilted from Camp Bachelor's liquor. It wasn't egregious, but it was enough to signal the end of their call, just before Noah's tablet was close to wailing about its dwindling battery.

"Don't be such a stranger," Justin said before hanging up.

For another moment, Noah couldn't remember who broke up with who.

The first few days on Shala passed by in chunks, skittering blurs broken up by long, thick stretches where time melted into the haze of the jungle's high noon. While Frida shut herself away in the *Amihaf*'s labs with piles of local fungus samples, the rest of the xenobiology contingent dragged themselves to the research enclosure every morning just before the dense air roiled itself into a sauna. Abelard and Noah held lengthy discussions with Trevor and Tal, swapping out tablets full of graphs and statistics for handling the rodents themselves—wriggling masses of violet-black fur twice the size of a guinea pig and with a long tail too fuzzy to resemble a rat's. While they attached themselves to the enclosure, Maria guided Savannah through a network of more loosely-blazed trails through the underbrush, a thick file folder of tests and conjectures on the creature's plant-based diet under her arm. Miscalculations in the original century-old scouting reports meant they weren't assigned a xenobotanist, so it had been slow work determining whether Terrestrial plants would be able to supply the nutrients found in their Shalan biochemistry.

They subsisted on canteens of bath-warm water and sandwiches bruised with jam. The water was never enough to fight the dry tinge of want hovering at the back of the throat—of dehydration, yes, but that first full day Noah also couldn't fight the memory of Justin perched over one of the Rassawek campus water fountains in the middle of an autumn heat wave, a moment that sat snug between their first date and when things started to get serious; and when he blinked his way back to Shala and the squeaking expanse of rodents, the dry scratch as he swallowed begged louder for his attention.

At sunset, Ross 128 burned over the canopy with tendrils that streaked across the sky in a deep blood-red, living up to its classification. It cast the entire base in an alien crimson glow until it sank under the horizon, and the center square buzzed in anticipation of mealtime. And while Irene wasn't buzzing, she was in attendance, popping into the mess trailer to talk to Luz about a vegetarian diet that hadn't appeared once during the prior weeks of turbolight travel. Still, no one asked after the source of the meat in the adobo Luz served up, but the *Amihaf* crew glanced away from Irene whenever fork tines pressed into the threads of flesh, acutely aware of the lack in Irene's own bowl.

The next night, Quinn began to eat around the meat. The night after that, a vague nausea haunted Noah as he tried to fall asleep. In the hazy realm of half-consciousness, his ears rang with the chords that rose every time their group passed that first enclosure, how they grew darker as the days rolled on.

"I've done some reading on linguistic theory," said Esmail late on the morning of the fourth day. He'd tagged along to the research enclosure, eager to see more of the rodents first-hand, and he'd made a seat for himself on a half-rotten stump out of the way. "Has anyone studied the... those other animals? Or named them?"

The outpost was quieter than usual that morning, with Abelard and most of Camp Bachelor's other xenobiologists tied up in an important satcall. Trevor had stayed behind to accompany them out to the jungle, but he didn't seem to hear Esmail's question—he braced one of his crutches against his shoulder, trying to pull down a bag on a high shelf through the arm-support loops.

Noah shrugged. "I haven't heard anything."

"Have you asked?" Esmail said, staring at the back of Trevor's head.

"Not quite," said Noah.

"Hm?" Esmail cocked his head, tapping against his knee in a rhythmic, repetitive beat. "How do you 'not quite' ask?"

"Not quite ask what?" Trevor twisted halfway in his hoverchair, his targeted bag now swinging from the end of the crutch.

"What do you call the animals in the other pen?"

Esmail's question hung in the air for a moment before thudding to the ground.

"It's nothing, y'know, codified or whatever." The length of the crutch slid through Trevor's hands until he could reach the bag and take it into his lap. "Alisha and Tal got popped one night that first year off some fermented cornberries… made a mash-up of a name. 'Musicow.' I hate it, honestly, but it stuck."

He found what he wanted in the bag—a roll of twine—and zipped around toward the other side of the enclosure without another word.

"Popped?" Esmail said. "I haven't heard that before."

"Probably just meant 'drunk.'"

"That makes sense." The soil crunched under his feet as he hopped off the log and joined Noah at the counter, peering over his shoulder at the last physical exam the rodents received.

Further crunching soil announced Abelard and Luz coming up the trail; a weathered palette hung between them, lifted by a complicated weave of purple rope. A palanquin, almost, with the quarry as bound bundles of the rats' food. "Hauling this out here is normally an all-day thing," Luz said as the palette settled beside a shed.

"I am more than happy to put my enhancements to good use," Abelard said. "Though I won't be staying…" Trevor was needed for the satcall after all, and if someone needed to trek into the jungle to fetch him, they might as well knock out a chore—or so he'd rattled off to Rohit. He and Trevor disappeared into the thicket, conversation fading.

Luz collapsed onto the empty stump.

"Not going back with them?" Noah said.

"Ugh, no…" She pulled out a tablet from her hip bag. "McGowan's in one of his moods and I wasn't getting any of my reading done—wait…"

Only then did Noah realize he'd made a face in time with his mental question marks.

"Ugh, he didn't bother to introduce himself, did he?" Luz groaned. "Our physician. Real sour piece of work, that one. Anyway, I was in our lab waiting for some results on that mineral we found at the river, trying to play catch up"—she waved her tablet in the air—"and he came in every fifteen minutes with more questions about the thing than even I'd thought of at this point and got grumpy when I said I didn't know. I can't work like that…"

Esmail nodded along even as she trailed off, and Noah let himself swivel back to the data at hand. The latest spreadsheet was from the base's first year, less numbers than qualitative notes on the rats' health after McGowan administered the veterinary xenopathogen vaccine.

"I've never seen anyone try so hard to get along with that man as your doctor," Luz said. "Even Rohit gave up by the time we landed here. But Dayo's followed him around camp trying to talk about the horseshoe scorpions every day while you lot have been out here."

If she had more to say, it fell to the wayside as Savannah's head popped up among the stretch of violet ferns, having recognized Luz's voice. She'd found a weird-looking rock, electric orange, and before she could ask if Luz wanted to check it out, she'd flown off the stump, tablet tossed to the length of counter at Noah's side.

He glanced down at the page onscreen—a news article out of Marrakech reporting on trends of TerraCosmos material usage over the last two centuries. Luz had zoomed in on a chart listing quantities of metals recycled versus mined versus consumed for headliner endeavors like Projects Khepri and Aker. The numbers implied a tight squeeze; the paragraph below the chart referenced untapped resources in the far northern Testudines before the bottom of the tablet cut off the thought.

Not the kind of thing Noah knew anything about. He frowned and returned to the rats, nodding along to the rolling tune Esmail started humming, keeping the beat with his hands tapping against his chest. Idly he wondered after what about those aquatic xeno-organisms had captured Dayo's fascination, but it was a wonder that burned away as Shala spun on, as Savannah and Luz headed the trek back to base with a new gleaming rock in tow.

Of course, though, there was the resurgence. The end of the *Amihaf*'s stay on Shala was fast approaching, and over dinner that night—Maria had fixed vatapá, a favorite among her crew, and Dayo was keen to take advantage of the quiet of a good meal.

"Before we leave, I would like to get a sample of the horseshoe scorpion venom to study."

Spoons paused against their bowls mid-scrape, all eyes fixed on the sparkle in Dayo's own.

"Traveling between planets, we have a lot of spare time," she continued. "We could figure out an antivenom, at the very least! And who knows what uses it might have in Terrestrial medicine."

Her enthusiasm wasn't mirrored by anyone at the table aside from Abelard, and McGowan swung decidedly in the opposite direction. Glowering, he fished out a bottle of pills from his coat and pressed two cream-colored capsules into Trevor's hand beside him, which he swallowed dry.

"One try. Three hours, max." She turned to Rohit with a silent plea.

"Well…" Rohit rubbed his palm over his hair, back and forth, the pulse of his jaw chewing a reply into place. "You need to know the risks—"

"Of course," she said.

"She won't be going alone," Abelard added, "I will certainly be there. Noah, you'll be coming along as well, yes?"

"Sure," said Noah, before his mouth could catch up with the rest of him— not that it would have made much of a difference.

"I guess that means I should go too." Trevor chased his remark with a swig from his canteen, squinting over the lip of it at the silent protests raised by his colleagues. "I'm the one who almost ended their tour early because of this thing. Why wouldn't I come along? Okay, look," he said, swiveling to face McGowan head-on. "You'd keep me out of the carpenter rat enclosure if you had your way. Can I at least do *one* thing to help you earn your high blood pressure?"

McGowan took a long, measured breath, muttering something under his breath before stealing a gulp from a flask at his hip.

"Look, Dayo," Trevor said. "You're their doctor. You're who wants this. You go in there, get unknowingly stung, leave… see, because it doesn't hurt like anything back home. It's sneaky. The venom takes a little over forty hours to kick in. McGowan saved my ass, but who would save you once you're off at turbolight to wherever the hell next?"

To Dayo's credit, her grin hardly wavered. "I trust my colleagues. But that doesn't mean I don't see your point."

They shook on the matter, and by the morning of the last full day on Shala, dew beading thick on the grasses and ferns, Trevor and Dayo found themselves staring out at the pond at the end of the trail, the entire *Amihaf* crew hovering behind them. The reasons everyone had given varied: Frida and Savannah had shrugs of *just in case*, while Quinn offered himself up as muscle in case of emergency, and where Quinn went, Esmail was sure to follow. Irene, on the other hand, wordlessly perched herself on a large rock where the path shifted into the silty stretch of shore. Her notebook had come with her, and she focused on the right-hand page, let the other fall over the side of her leg.

Trevor pointedly cleared his throat and steered his hoverchair around in a tight loop to face them all. "I want to reiterate once again that we know far less about these things than the other xeno-organisms we've documented in this ecosystem. They're aquatic. They're venomous. They're carnivorous." He held up a slab of mimeo chicken breast in wax paper. "And that's where the list ends. There is a risk of threat-activated pack dynamics. There is a risk that, much like Terrestrial crabs, they can thrive outside water. If that sounds like too much, you can head back. No judgment. Trying to get it from the pond into there…" He nodded toward a sizable glass tank sitting on the same rope-borne palette from earlier in the week. "You might not be able to just be a spectator."

No one moved. Even the brush around them momentarily stilled until the loudest sound in the clearing was the fluttering of Esmail's fingers tight at his side.

"All right then. On we go." Trevor reached around to the back pocket of his hoverchair, pulling out a crude fishing pole. It was carved from the same dark wood as the poles of his crutches, but far thinner; a line of transparent wire wove up the length, braided through a line of drilled holes, and as Trevor shook it, the full line of it fell loose, the dented metal hook landing on the ground.

"What is that supposed to do?" Irene asked without looking up from her notebook.

"It's going to catch the thing, obviously?"

"And who told you that?"

"The wood here is a lot sturdier than Earth wood, first of all."

"Okay." Still she concentrated on the notebook, tongue held between her front teeth as a slow arc of ink colored the page.

A single, low squawk from the underbrush punctuated the beat where Trevor waited for her to say anything else. "Anyway." He held out the pole to Dayo. "I assume you'll be doing the honors, Doc?"

"Been a while since I've been fishing... though this would probably be something else right?" She glanced toward Noah and Abelard, clutching the pole to her chest. "Because they're not fish?"

"Watch the hook." Quinn hopped forward to pluck the dull metal away from where it had set its sights on the exposed skin of her knee, tucking the curved end between her awaiting thumb and forefinger for safekeeping.

"I was fine, but thank you all the same." She held up the hook just in front of her nose, going cross-eyed. "If it's so similar to a scorpion that it's part of the name, shouldn't we be using a net? Or something closer to a crabbing contraption? That's what my baba used fishing on the Yewa."

Trevor sighed. "It's scorpion-*like*. It's got a soft underbelly. You ever seen a picture of a horseshoe crab? Same thing."

Nodding to herself, Dayo strode confidently to the pond's edge, Noah and Quinn following close behind on either side. What role Noah expected himself to fill was a mystery, but he was the only xenozoologist present without accommodations that water could send into a fit of sparks.

The pond lapped gently at the toes of their boots as they approached. The silty bottom clouded only the farthest depths, leaving a border where the clear blue suddenly closed ranks. Dayo let the rod swing down from its vertical hold, gripping it to a stop just as the hook grazed the surface. "Were you going to give me any of that chicken as bait, or what?"

"I was getting there," Trevor said. The wrapping ripped as he grabbed for it, soft from the humidity and sweat on his fingers, and the chicken slipped to the ground beyond his reach. "Can you—thanks," he said as Frida stepped forward to retrieve it, even as she paused to examine the goods.

"See…" Frida tugged off the remaining paper and flicked away the larger chunks of dirt. "Bait usually works better when it's on the hook."

"It's not that kind of fishing pole." As soon as Frida dropped the chicken into his hand, he lobbed it over the pond with the kind of force that spoke of sports trophies crowding a childhood bedroom.

The chicken's arc wobbled, the rush of air as it started to fall toward the water drowning out the rest of the jungle. They all held their breath at the distant *plonk* of it breaking the surface, just a moment's worth, but Noah's lungs still burned in anticipation, burned sharper when an inky black body crested out of the water in a spray.

The creature appeared to hover in slow motion as Noah and the rest of the crew took it in—an oval dome with eight thick legs, claws at each end. A long sectioned tail curled up behind it, tapering to a needle-thin point that caught a stray beam of sunlight with a glare. Noah had seen life-size models of horseshoe crabs, and this was easily twice as large, four times as dense.

Savannah's hand covered Esmail's where it had latched onto her at the sight. "I'm not feeling great about this pole of yours, Trevor."

"I'm sure it's fine!" Dayo's normally sunny grin angled itself steeper on one end. Noah and Quinn ducked out of the way as she swung the pole forward, the hook barely an inch above the center of the pond when the creature heaved forth once more. Its path aimed toward the shore, exposing the thinner, lighter membrane of its underbelly. The longer Noah stared at its shell, the more he thought of deep space, black holes, a kind of unknown that dug into his stomach with a cold grip. And Dayo, taking in that same sight, simply laughed, quick and low, and with a swift jerk up, the hook pierced into the soft flesh between the chitinous plates lining its underside.

A high, thin screech shook the clearing, the hidden creatures in the brush scattering.

The pole bent. Noah stared at the end of it, waiting for the gentle curve to start groaning or the fishing line to slice through the wood. The pole was no thicker than a sausage link, and yet it held against the boiling spray where the scorpion's limbs thrashed, the screeching ticking up a half step, out of tune.

"Ooh—we got this," said Dayo. She locked her arms at her side, a steel grip on the pole, but the heels of her boots were sinking into the slimy silt, the creature dragging her forward in short spurts. "We definitely got this."

The short spurts gave way into a long, sustained jerk; Dayo's body was halfway to horizontal the way she leveraged herself, and anyone within a few steps' distance rushed forward to grab onto her—Noah adding his hands to her grip, Quinn muddying his knees to latch around her waist, Savannah and

Frida locking arms on either side. The power behind its legs and flailing body was closer to a cinder block with a mean streak than any horseshoe crab, and Noah's focus narrowed to the burning friction between his hands and the pole, his hands and Dayo's.

Behind them, Esmail was shouting something at Trevor, a mix of English and Persian, the buffering silences filled by a dull, rapid tapping; Abelard was trying to calm him, and from what Noah could pick out in the roiling knot of noise, Esmail must have been slapping his palms against the wavy cushion of his hair.

"Dayo," said Quinn, "if I get ahold your wrists and help do a final yank, d'you think we can—"

"Yeah, yeah, go for it—"

Quinn was a tall man, and his arms stretched long. He only had to shift the stance of his crouch in the muck to latch his hands on the target, fingers spreading up to where Noah's own grip added a measly extra ounce of support. "We're going for it on the count of three, okay? Not one-two-three-go, but—"

"*Just go!*" Savannah yelled.

The edges of their boots were inching into the water where shadowy blots shifted against the pond floor in wait. Another meter and they'd all be in range of their stingers.

"Fine—pull!"

The force of their collective strength sent them stumbling back the first few steps, but they settled into a rhythm, one step after another. Off to the other side of the shore, Abelard and Trevor were throwing rocks into the pond to stave off the rest of the pack; the closest shadows to their feet had retreated into the deeper reaches against the weight of the stones breaking through the surface overhead. Every muscle in Noah's body wailed once the hooked creature was fully pulled out of the water, his chest-tightened gasping lost among the others crowded around him.

The horseshoe scorpion fought and slung its stinger as far as it could manage, but with Irene's deft herding, its struggle came to a solid close, deposited into the tank with the lid latched and locked.

The whole of their contingent caught their breath as the creature's thrashing ebbed.

"You'll send us whatever you find on the thing, right?" Trevor asked no one in particular.

When he turned his gaze to the crew of the *Amihaf*, he landed on Noah first, and there was a plea tucked into his brow, narrow enough that he doubted anyone else could have spotted it from where they stood. "Of course," he said, and again he repeated to Maria and Tal and Rohit, to all of the base, to the tall stretch of violet breaking into the dull high noon.

The next day, two hours after the *Amihaf* broke through Shala's atmosphere, the ship received an inquiry from Camp Bachelor asking after their pen of musicows, if they knew anything about the splintered line of fencing that had been trampled into the dirt.

"Sounds like a personal problem," Noah said, and Irene trashed the message with a tight and vibrant smirk.

FOUR

THE CREW HADN'T BEEN together long enough for them to be squeezed so close together—a rat king of limbs and faces and bunched-up clothing in front of the lab, shifting this way and that for a position allowing them all to peer through the small square window in the door.

No more than five at a time could manage it, Frida and Noah inevitably finding any favorable angle lost as soon as anyone taller so much as adjusted their footing; and neither Irene nor Savannah pressed back against the competition with any real gusto. Still, they all glimpsed enough snippets of the spectacle before them, one way or another, for a uniform grimace to sink onto each of their faces.

Inside the lab, the horseshoe scorpion thrashed and pounded against the sides of its tank without any sign of relenting, and as much as Rohit had assured them that the glass was reinforced at the grade just below that of spaceship portholes, no one had yet rationalized trusting him with their lives. So: they watched, they winced, and they waited for someone else to break the silence on their side of the door.

"We should name it," Esmail said. "How about Tristan? It feels like a Tristan."

They paused to consider alternatives, but the thoughtful silence kept them immobile too long, joints left to complain. All at once the cluster of bodies separated into its constituent parts, drifting off to the cockpit or a maintenance closet or whatever destination drew their footfalls upwards. Noah found himself behind Frida as she clanged up the stairs, muttering to herself about Shalan mushroom samples and the impediment their new guest imposed.

"It won't be able to maintain that stress for long," Noah said as they emerged onto the second floor. "You'll be able to get back in way before we get to the Luyten system."

"That your professional xenozoological opinion, is it?" She whirled around on him so quickly that he almost walked straight into her.

"I'm not sure what you're getting at here."

Her hand reached out like it was aiming for a folded point of his shirt, retracting at the last moment in a slow, finger-by-finger curl. "Something's wrong. Something somewhere, and if anyone was going to start the freak-out, it'd be you. Call it a hunch."

"Not to repeat myself," Noah said carefully, "but I'm not sure what you're getting at."

There was a moment when he was sure the issue would drop, but it passed as soon as Frida's gaze landed on his bruised elbow, the odd way he held it under the cover of his sweater, and he'd never had a face for poker.

Approaching feet on the stairs curled her back toward the galley, an impossible distance covered in the beat Noah took to reorient himself. By the time Esmail's head appeared at floor level, Frida had already engrossed herself in the contents of the fridge.

"This kubideh still good?" she called.

"Oh! Um…" Esmail's face squinted in concentration. "No, probably not. It's been in there almost ten days."

"Damn shame."

"You… liked it?"

Frida shrugged at him over her shoulder. "Of course. It was good—"

Noah retreated into the bunk corridor, then his own room, collapsing face-first on the bed. The bruise at his elbow pulsed at a dull ache that still managed to reach the back of his throat. Tomorrow Dayo would want to follow up on how it was healing, and tomorrow he and Savannah and Frida would have to determine how to continue their research if their newest passenger hadn't yet settled; and even before tomorrow rose over the horizon of Cairo and thus over most of humanity hanging in the great emptiness of space, the question of Abelard sagged against the crew's shoulders with an unnatural gravity.

At some point lying there he stumbled into sleep. Stumbling back out was a murky matter, a smear of the clock's green digits obscuring the rest of his room, and the tendrils of a dream fought to remain present. However ardent their efforts, they slid away as Noah reached for them, retaining only the suggestions of scenes ringing with a dim musicow chord—a Neptunian obelisk mired in a muddy field, a rowboat landing on a choppy sea, a smudge of a body echoing the curve of an unknown planet just above the line of its atmosphere. He blinked. The images dissipated and the clock, now clear, read 0530.

The wakefulness landed on his chest in a shock, the sort that wouldn't allow him to simply turn over and tuck back into the shroud of sleep. The hint of the chord settled just out of earshot, begging him to strain for it as his socked feet padded toward the lounge. For a moment the only illumination rose up through the stairwell, a column of sterile white-blue absorbed into the greater mass of light as soon as Noah tripped the motion sensors.

He stood at the center of the common area, seeing it and not seeing it, some part of himself willing his feet back on solid earth, in Rassawek or Erie or wherever else his roots had woven into the soil. The idea of a trillion miles tried and failed to manifest in his head. There was a version of that mission years ago where Abelard's research vessel had not been torn to scrap, and that version saw Abelard sitting behind his desk on campus, trudging to department meetings on arthritic limbs, and the only contact he'd have with the *Amihaf* came in glitchy satcalls and emails tossed out at odd hours.

What time was it in Rassawek? He could call Justin again, relay the latest news, tie another line between himself and that chunk of rock beyond the barrier of visible stars. 0545 IST now—six hours behind that was still too late given the hour the last time he called.

"Pathetic," he mumbled to himself.

"Not sleepwalking, are we?"

Quinn had silently appeared just outside the bunk hall, still blinking sleep from his eyes.

"The opposite actually. I think," he added.

"Yeah, you were just kind of standing there, so. Worth asking." He headed toward the galley, tucking his tablet into the waistband at the small of his back. "Esmail doesn't normally wake me up when he goes for prayers, but this morning he was very keen to finish his train of thought from last night, so…"

He trailed off into the absent early-hour mumbling of someone less than pleased to be up at that hour, wondering if there was such a thing as being *too* early for coffee, or what time was supposed to mean while turbolight was stomping on the laws of physics.

"I can fix a gravity modulator," he said, at least settling on an enormous mug of grapefruit juice from the mimeo. "Doesn't mean I understand how it *really* works."

By this point, Noah had coaxed his feet into dragging him toward the mess table, if only to appear less like a haze-brained husk. "Don't tell me you're bringing this up because there's something wrong with ours."

"Nah, nah, you'd know if it was something that bad. Wouldn't have stopped for juice and a chat, for one." He leaned against the galley counter, half a head short of dwarfing the fridge beside him. "Just figured while I was up that I should check on a couple systems… y'know, see if the logging errors from last night were just a fluke."

Noah nodded as if he understood what a logging error was.

"It's probably nothing," Quinn said, placing his mug in the sink with a *clank.* "Some of our internal databases like to act up, and that can set off alarm bells elsewhere in our system. But better safe, yeah?"

"Yeah," Noah echoed as Quinn hopped down to the lower level two steps at a time.

A few minutes later, Esmail appeared in his pajamas, face and hair damp, fumbling for his prayer rug behind the lounge's armchairs. His nodded acknowledgment of Noah was heavy, weighted, half out of himself as he mumbled on about Irene and calculations she'd made for him before leaving

Shala. "Mecca's this way," he said finally, pointing his knees toward the port-side of the ship's aft.

Unconsciously, Noah found himself plodding down the stairs. Quinn's head was buried in one of the service panels just outside the cockpit, and Noah's gaze didn't linger—the screen had been left off overnight, and the spaceshield displayed the jet-black void of turbolight, the occasional flickers of passing astral bodies reflecting off the dashboard. Staring too long at it left him queasy in the best of states, and the irregular strobe effect swung his stomach around in a lasso.

So he was left with the horseshoe scorpion on the other side of the lab door. Without the multiple bodies vying for space, he could get a better look at it through the window—the overhead lights outlined the puddles from its continued thrashing, and it had drawn back into a pacing loop around the tank. Clockwise one lap, a turn, counterclockwise the next, and its sharp spindly claws clicked in the space against its underbelly. If the worst it could do after a full standard day was fling water through the latched, grated lid of the tank, that counted as a win, however desperate. Some instinct insisted that they should take what they could get.

On the lab tables, abandoned, sat scrap notes and cartons of samples.

The journey to the next exoplanet was another weeks-long expanse, closer to a month by Irene's estimation, and if they had to spend all of it crowded around Frida's crossword puzzles, at least one of them would be landing on Lulal with a black eye.

"Take what we can get," he muttered to himself. "I can get this."

When the door slid open, it felt loud enough to wake the rest of the ship. Noah retracted his hand and stole a quick glance at Quinn, whose face remained buried in a dense set of electronics. Tristan, however, stopped pacing, tugging its body up until the underside laid vertical against the glass. The eyes were there, as dictated by all the evidence provided in his education, but they blended in too seamlessly to tell for sure this far away.

Noah took a step, paused. Tristan remained flush against the tank wall, hardly twitched when he took another step, another two steps. "Okay, buddy… are you going to behave?"

He slowly guided himself toward the far table. Savannah's tray of cuttings laid in the corner of his vision as he maintained eye contact with Tristan, hands in clear view. One step, and again. Its body crawled against the plane of the tank like it was following his progress. "I'm not here for you." He tilted his head toward the tray, and the scorpion tilted with him. "We don't want to bother you."

Three steps followed, unhurried but fluid, and Tristan did little but let its clawed legs wave gently in the water.

"Yeah," he said. "Just here for the other stuff. We're curious about a lot of things from your home. And we're curious about you, too, but… I know we didn't make a great first impression."

His trek toward Savannah's table remained measured, and the sole change in the scorpion's mien laid in the legs. Their waving had grown more pronounced, though nothing about it appeared threatening. Eber would kick himself halfway across campus and back if he knew what he was missing— the one class he still consistently taught, graduate-level behavioral xenozoology, always opened with a centuries-old video of a mariachi band serenading a tank of beluga whales. *Pretend you know nothing about the kind of creature they are, them or their still-living relatives*, he'd said. *Notice how they react to the stimulus. What could you conclude from it?*

The first response, both in Noah's own class and in those he attended as the TA, was *intelligence*; and to Eber, that alone was a non-answer. *Intelligence about what?* he'd say. *Qualify it. The beings we study here evolved in ecosystems potentially far beyond our imaginations, and there is a type of intelligence for every niche we both can and cannot envision.*

"I know you don't understand English." He finally reached the table and began slotting the notes and pencils in the viable space between the plants. "Then again…" He glanced up. Tristan had moved itself to the shorter pane of the rectangular tank, still staring. "Who knows? Long-term exposure to Camp Bachelor and a developed equivalent of a Broca's center, yadda yadda…" he said in his best impression of Eber.

A buzzing rattled against his hip, the telltale alert of his tablet registering an email pre-labeled with high importance. He reached for it on instinct—a hand swept behind a curtain.

The scorpion erupted, its screeching from the jungle piercing in the closed space, the water doing little to muffle the distress. Cursing, Noah bundled Savannah's materials into his arms and dashed to the door as fast as the added luggage would allow. "I'm sorry, I'm sorry—"

He was five steps short when the door seemingly slid open by itself—but it was Abelard, stepping in toward Frida's messier station, slides and vials swept into a nearby box. Noah squeezed himself between Abelard and the wall on his way into the hall beyond, tripping over his ankle and skidding on his shoulder blade to a stop near the foyer.

"Ceasefire, ceasefire!" Abelard yelled as he retreated backwards, the door shutting in his wake. He deposited the precariously-loaded box against the wall to catch the ConBod's equivalent of his breath.

"I really caused that much of a ruckus?"

"Oh... not really," he said, uncurling himself to his full height. "I was already up and about, and Esmail mentioned you'd come downstairs. Good thing I caught you when I did."

The eye displays tracked over to the window in the lab door, where Tristan's clawed legs and sharp, venomous tail crashed in protest against the barriers locking him in.

"I had it under control," said Noah, even though he couldn't be completely sure.

Tristan continued to bash itself against the tank without success.

"Of course." He offered Noah a hand and pulled him to his feet. "I wasn't thinking of that as a rescue, just... a helping hand, as it were." His grip on Noah's own released with a nod of his head that had come to replace his eyes' inability to wink.

"Right. Well, thanks."

The rest of the crew had trickled out into the common area by the time the two of them ascended the stairs, the air laced with the aromas of breakfast fresh from the mimeo. Savannah and Frida both leapt to their feet seeing their research materials emerge from below, and they all asked how the horseshoe scorpion was acting this morning, and someone offered to fix Noah something fancy for his efforts—but despite the adrenaline still rolling through his veins in aftershocks, all he could focus on was his bunk on the other side of the floor and its promise of solitude.

He handed them an excuse about wanting to log his observations before the memory eroded. It wasn't a lie. Sometime later in the dark of the arbitrary early afternoon, he would reappear among the crew with a memo, an email with it attached already rocketing back toward Shala and the inbox of one Trevor St. John. Now, he collapsed back on his cot. The banging of Tristan's shell against the tank ricocheted in his head no matter how much he tried to stifle it.

He still had the offending email to check, after all.

The light of the tablet screen dug into his eyes as he held it overhead, highlighting one unread message from Justin Patterson.

Hey Noah,

I went up to the research telescope the other night on one of its public sessions. I don't think I ever believed you when you said it could fight through the light pollution, which is why I always made so many excuses. But I went, better late than never, and asked them to show me Ross 128. (Your itinerary is publicly listed on TerraCosmos' website, not hard to find.) They said that type of star isn't visible from Earth unless I accessed something like the facilities up in the Andes.

Just know I looked for you, trillions of miles away. I had an image in my head of spotting a shadow against the dot of light, and maybe it was the planet, or maybe it was your ship heading off to Luyten's Star.

Be well.

J

Noah tossed the tablet to the end of the bed, conjuring up an alternate iteration of a year-old night, a deliberation taking a different turn where he took Justin by the hand to the observatory, sharing the lens as the attendant rattled off facts they both already knew about the rings guarding Saturn against the rest of the universe.

Five days after Noah's incursion into the lab, no one else had dared attempt to tread on what was quickly becoming solely Tristan's domain. The lounge table had been divided for Savannah and Frida to examine their respective samples as best they could without the microscopes and other equipment that hadn't been part of the initial recovery effort. Five days, and Noah was no closer to figuring out how to right the situation.

"It has trust to give," said Dayo late that night around the mess table with Noah and Irene. "We need to find a way to earn it, especially if we're going to get a sample of its venom."

The parameters, as far as Noah had laid them out, were these: the horseshoe scorpion has the means of recognizing language, and it understood hands as a means of infliction. Hands could carry new variables into the equation. Hands could only be trusted when they were visible.

"So you establish a rapport," said Irene. "If it's trust you're after, start with respect."

"That makes sense," Noah said as Dayo typed some shorthand notes on her tablet. "Should be simple enough—"

The noise Irene made straddled the line between a snort and a hesitant grumble. "What? We're working in a deficit as far as respect goes. Even without the kidnapping and diet of mimeo shrimp, that…" Her fist hit the table, slow to unfurl. "Camp Bachelor doesn't strike me as a shining beacon of humanity to the local fauna."

Dayo frowned to herself and tapped another few lines of notes, the only sound on the ship aside from the engines and a faint, muffled voice with Savannah's unmistakable cadence. "Well… I'm obviously going to need some help with this."

"Yeah, of course," Noah said. "You're a doctor, not a zoologist. Should we bring in—"

"More people are just going to stress the thing out further, don't you think?" Her eyes didn't have to flick to his elbow for him to know she held it close in mind, even as its purple had started to ebb.

"Fair point."

Despite their best efforts, the next morning Abelard inserted himself into their cohort anyway. All of the unknowns surrounding the horseshoe scorpion grew more daunting with Abelard peering over Noah's shoulder, as if the blank pockets wanted to reach forward and swallow him whole.

"This is so exciting," Abelard whispered as Tristan paused its laps around the tank. "Noah, you haven't had much field experience, have you?"

"Well…" he trailed off, watching the scorpion swim up to press its undershell against the pane—a recognition. "TerraCosmos is pretty reluctant to give out that kind of grant money for the theoretical."

With Tristan's eight legs curling in and out, still at a gentle rhythm, Noah directed Abelard and Dayo to slowly pull apart the two lab tables closest to the tank, allowing all three of them the room to sit at its eye level. He crept at a painstaking pace up the middle, hands spread before him. A bead of sweat tickled rolling down his back. Another nervously followed as the noise narrowed to his own breathing rattling in his ears. A longer pause, a slow breath, and he forced himself to tune back into the conversation around him over the scraping table legs—a story of Abelard's youth, a stint of fieldwork on Chiron's sister planet, a standoff with an enormous furred snake-like creature whose single eye had bored into his soul.

"*Ólúwá ò*," said Dayo as she slunk back to Noah's side. "That's the stuff of nightmares."

"I don't think you ever told me about that," Noah said.

"As you said, though…" Abelard rejoined them, then stepped past with seeming abandon until he was a mere foot and a half from the tank.

"Hey, careful—"

He made no acknowledgment that he'd heard him, instead kneeling down to the floor. "...not that relevant when you're working in theories." He lobbed his nod-wink over his shoulder, and with Tristan still resting placidly against the tank, Noah and Dayo followed him to his perch.

"We should really be more cautious," Noah said. A tinge of frustration edged into his voice, and he shook the kneejerk panic away. It could be expected given their current circumstances, no one there would latch onto the nub of it angrily seeking his penance, he was fine—

"I brought up my encounter with the Pholusian adder for a reason, you know. I have a certain instinct with these fellows honed from my career."

"And I respect that," Noah said, weighing each syllable. "But Pholus isn't Shala isn't… any other exoplanet—"

"If I could cut in here for a sec?" Dayo's sunny grin had returned, a bit forced, as she leaned around to catch their attention. "As the crew member who would be responsible for treating anyone stung by the lovely Tristan, I too would like to err on the side of caution, please."

Dayo continued on before Abelard could slip in any rebuttal, citing everything from the limited capacity of the med bay to the *Amihaf*'s lack of accessibility if afterward someone required any of the mobility devices down in storage. Noah tracked the larger points of it, but Tristan had edged closer to his side of the tank, all the surface anatomical details legible. Four eyes like whole peppercorns laid in an arch across the top end of the underbelly, a shallow V connecting the two end points. The V wafted open and closed in time with its legs—a mouth, probably. Below were the legs, lining a surprisingly fleshy body, with a half-inch-wide line of shell running down the center; as it approached the eyes and mouth, it split, folding at each side under a plane that reminded Noah of cartilage.

At a certain angle, the horseshoe scorpion was almost cute.

"Are you having a moment?" From anyone other than Dayo, it would have come with a palpable film of snark.

"Maybe." He sat up, stretched his posture. "And what did I miss while having my moment?" He made a show of swiveling his head toward Abelard, expectant.

"I'm going to… think before I act," he said, his tone a step away from a petulant teenager. "And… respect that consequences of my actions can affect those around me. You see? We're fine." He grinned wide enough that Noah almost missed how the ConBod's eye displays stuttered, a half-second frame of static edging in from the left. "Shall we begin the peace summit with our new crewmate?"

They began with the tiniest of baby steps, offering up their empty hands, their clothes free of pockets. No danger here, no hidden threats. Noah spotted where the fishing hook had pierced muscle, the scar tissue an ash-gray, a gorge they had to crawl out of before progressing any distance forward. He crawled with them, but he couldn't help but mentally pace circles around the looming question of Abelard and the vacuum leviathans. He recalled an incident relayed to him his first year by another graduate student a month out from defending her dissertation—*Abelard views spontaneity as a cardinal virtue, full stop, no caveats*. A lecture hall full of Essentials of Xenozoology students, a venomous Chironese beetle raised in the nursery labs, a demonstration ill-conceived and acted upon regardless: she told the tale less as a precaution and more to help manage expectations.

Noah imagined one of Abelard's strobing eyes gazing out of a porthole, the pinprick of the ConBod's lens focusing on a distant shadow amid the stars, a hand twitching with want, desperate to send them all hurtling toward some far-off unmapped fate. The scenarios born from the rich loam of anxiety grew wild. There was the *Amihaf*, and then there was the enormous vague specter of the leviathan, and in Abelard's mind somehow their little hunk of metal would stand a chance.

"Would you look at that…" Dayo's hand splayed against the glass beside Tristan, and it reached its nearest claw toward her palm, two dull thunks following as it tapped there against the tank. "You think that's a good sign?"

"It's a sign of something," Noah said, returning her grin despite the spiraling chasm of worry in his head. "But it's just one data point."

"So we keep at it," said Abelard. "You remember what I like to say about pointillism, correct? The art in the science!"

Electron clouds and scatter plot graphs—squint at them hard enough and they could discern their findings sunbathing on the banks of the Seine. There, or drowning just out of frame. The bright, waterlogged burning crawled up his sinuses as Abelard patted his knee.

Days passed in the whirl of turbolight, as they were prone to, and after those days were filled with Frida spinning tales of the kinds of traditional American cuisine offered around the TerraCosmos Occidental headquarters, someone had to act. What qualified as a *someone* was limited, so the crew handed Noah and Savannah breakfast-for-dinner duty on their northern Testudines bona fides alone, even if Erie and Nacotchtank were far flung from the Gulf Coast.

"I don't think most of these ingredients are programmed in the mimeo," Noah muttered.

"*I* don't think Frida knows what scrapple is made of." Savannah frowned at the end of her spoon where a mix of flour, milk, and bacon grease congealed into the start of a gravy. "Might not notice your substitutions if my end's a disaster."

"Here's hoping. It's not happening otherwise."

The mimeo whirred, churning out the closest available alternatives to what the recipe demanded. The clumsy slabs smelled enticing enough after he slapped them into the pan, but the gray-brown color did its best to counteract.

"Talked to Tracy this morning," Savannah said.

"Oh?" Noah tried to match her exceedingly casual tone. "How's she doing?"

"I'd say she was doing grand," she said, "except she ran into a certain Mr. Patterson at the pharmacy and he mentioned something about having spoken to you... *recently.*"

The scrapple had already started to smoke at the edges, and Noah couldn't decide if he'd rather endure the wrath of a hungry Frida or the concerned curiosity hovering at the crown of Savannah's head. A jerk of his wrist turned the stove down to a simmer, and he faced her with a long sigh. "What do you want me to say?"

She shook her head. Beside the galley, the rest of the crew were piled nearly on top of each other in the lounge, deep into a game of charades. Underneath all the shouting and the grumble of their collective stomachs was the clicking of Quinn's knitting needles.

"Look, I don't want to be... I don't know, callous," she said, "but when you showed up at my door that night, you gave me a lot more tears than details."

"I was there. I remember."

"Excuse my creeping doubts, then. I just thought the version of you that would be speaking to him... oh, what is it now, three or four months later would also be the version that had forgotten." She'd pulled her spoon out of the fledgling gravy and aimed it at his nose, close enough that he could sense the heat. "You still haven't told me what happened."

"Do I smell burning?"

She jumped back to the pot, scraping any hardened bits from the bottom before they turned to pure carbon. "You didn't smell anything."

"Easy mistake." He eyed the timer propped up against the wall and threw the raw biscuits for Savannah's gravy into the oven, then chiseling at the edge of the scrapple with a spatula in an attempt to flip it.

"You know I'm only bugging you about this because I worry," said Savannah. "And you know how I worry."

"I do." He frowned at the crispy ends blocking the spatula's leverage. "Look, it was one call. We're not due back on Earth for years. And what am I going to do, leap trillion of miles through space for some ill-thought hook-up?"

"Satcalls have video, Noah!"

"Yeah, that frame rate is *really* hot."

"You're lucky I love you, because you're a pain in my ass."

"Right where I should be."

The galley condensed to the hissing grease and the contentious round of charades on the other side of the half-wall. Frida was having trouble guiding them to the right answer—Abelard seemed stuck on various political leaders from the twenty-third century, no matter how many times Dayo or Quinn tried to push the group in any other direction.

"Um… sorry to interrupt…?"

They both turned to find Esmail hovering a few feet behind them, his hands flexing in and out of fists just under his chest.

"How long were you standing there?" asked Noah.

"Ah… well… a little bit. I'm not great at charades," he added. "I've been trying to do Quinn a favor by getting everyone's favorite color. He's knitting sweaters in his off time."

Esmail nodded at their answers as if he should have known as much all along. His hands had broken away from their flexing, now wriggling into the bun at the back of his head. Most of his hair fell around his ears in a wavy bob, but he'd been adamant in trying to maintain that small knot. "Also, not to eavesdrop," he said, "but I think Savannah makes a lot of good points. Anyway… I'm going to, uh…" He pointed back toward the lounge and slinked away.

"Two to one," Savannah said after a beat. "I win."

"Yeah, yeah, yeah…"

Finally he got each piece of scrapple to flip, and the gravy under Savannah's watch started to amass into something not only edible, but potentially appetizing.

"Holy shit, *thank you*," Frida groaned after Irene finally got it right. "Do none of you read?"

The charades rolled through another couple rounds as dinner balanced on the line of edibility, finally collapsing with a leg on either side—the gravy was a little runny and one side of the scrapple was a tough sheet of black. No one complained, either out of mercy or because they assumed it was part of the rustic charm. Noah leaned toward the latter from Frida's lack of commentary, hesitant to commit because she had become engrossed in a debate about the last round of the game with Abelard and Quinn.

"Well, I think environmental 'doomsday-ism' made sense back then. It was the middle of the Climate Catastrophe, for fuck's sake," Frida said.

Quinn rolled his eyes. "The guy was from Europe. Of course he thought that was the only sensible outlook—"

"Now, now," Abelard said, oddly nonplussed. "Let's not—"

At this, Quinn held up both of his hands in a makeshift wall between him and Abelard, leaning toward her across the table. "And do I need to remind you that the fact we're sitting where we are means he wasn't right? And who made that possible?"

She mirrored his pose, taking a moment to force herself to ignore Esmail's commentary about how Quinn didn't know how to whisper. "It's not like he could've known that!"

"He also wasn't listening, was he?"

Noah cast a glance around the rest of the table. Savannah and Dayo exchanged various degrees of grimaces, and Esmail consciously focused on using his fork to carve out a design in the most charred sections of his hash browns. At the other corner of the table, Irene was locked in on her notebook, blank spaces slowly filling with simple doodles of mushroom clouds. She only paid attention to the paper under her pen, taking time to study Frida and Quinn as they argued the larger points of econihilism.

Eventually, Frida threw her hands up. "You're impossible."

"Me?" said Quinn. "Have you ever done even an *ounce* of introspection in your life?"

They fumed silently at each other until Esmail cleared his throat. "I think it's funny," he said carefully, "that you two can be so alike and not be friends."

Frida's frown flattened, thinned. She reached for where she'd set her tablet on the table, an odd angular motion that flung her fork to the ground with a clang that ate up all the empty space on the ship. They waited for her to start swearing, a single held breath split across all their lungs. Her glance fell to her partially-eaten dinner, and then she retreated to her bunk with the plate without a word.

Abelard craned his head to follow the path of her exit. "I wonder what that was all about."

"Is she mad at me?" Esmail received only hesitant half-starts to answers, then glanced at Quinn. "Are *you* mad at me?"

"*E aroha*, no," he said. "Whatever it was, it's not..." He motioned for the two of them to start on the dishes, drowning out the rest of the wordless table in a din of clattering plates and flatware.

A new page had turned in Irene's notebook, her pen tapping against the warped ridges of the drawings on the other side. "You know," she said, "when she got up with the food, my first thought was about attracting ants. Ants... while flying at turbolight... as if I've never done this before." She looked up and caught Abelard's eye displays locked on her. "Space ants don't exist, right?"

He shrugged—it was the shrug that grad students came to understand meant *sounds like you have something to investigate*, not that Irene would know.

"Right?" She turned to face Noah.

"I mean—"

"Actually!" Esmail called over a dishtowel-draped shoulder. "Research suggests that larger organisms are more capable of maintaining the specific cellular structure that could withstand a vacuum—oh!" The heel of his palm thudded against his head. "Abelard, you and Chen Yuxuan co-wrote that paper. Obviously you knew that. Anyway, dishes..."

The way Abelard stared at the back of Esmail's head lit a twinge up Noah's bruised elbow, but he didn't have time to think about it before Irene raised her eyebrows, waiting for any kind of confirmation.

"Not something to worry about," he said.

Her relief was a solid weight sliding off tensed shoulders. "Good. I thought so, but… good. Thanks," she added, quieter.

One by one, the rest of them started to tread in Frida's wake toward the bunks. Irene went first, claiming a stress headache, then Dayo wondering if the latest issue of a Constructed Body medical journal had finished downloading. Esmail and Quinn left with dishwater-pruned hands, then Savannah—she ruffled Noah's hair with a smirk, and as he mussed it back into place, it set in that he and Abelard had been left alone.

"We've got a special crew here, don't we, Noah?"

He could have meant any number of things by that, and there were still too many variables to solve for a proper reply. "You could say that, yeah." Noncommittal. Safe.

Abelard's body hoisted itself up from its seat, an odd bending pattern in his limbs that rendered the whole of it unnatural. His digital eyes remained cemented on his the entire time, and Noah fought not to shrink from the pressure.

More than halfway to Luyten's Star, weeks since the logging errors in the ship's system first caught Quinn's attention, he had yet to discover a solution. The severity wasn't up for discussion, but it skirted around the casual chatter in the common areas, deniable enough that Quinn's brow wouldn't immediately fold into knots. Over time, he started to rise even before Esmail, already elbow-deep in a server closet on the bottom floor before the water was drawn for ablutions. With no one using the lab benches properly as the studies on Tristan continued, he nabbed a stool on which to park himself, a sleek laptop propped up on his knees.

"That's when you know it's serious," Esmail said. He loitered just far enough inside the lab entrance for the door to close behind him, a stop in his daily rounds through the ship. Noah suspected the entire routine was an excuse to sit in on the ongoing research with the horseshoe scorpion.

"The amount of raw processing power that you can put in a laptop compared to a tablet is just unreal," he continued. "And he built it himself!"

"So what does that mean for the problem?" asked Noah.

"It means he's frustrated and about... four days away from irate, give or take twelve hours."

Esmail changed the subject with a hard left, asking after the simple language comprehension test Noah and Abelard had spent the last few days designing, eager enough to witness the results that he allowed himself to halve the distance between himself and the tank. "So you think this species might have the cognitive capacity of a human baby?"

When Noah turned to gather the haphazard materials he'd pulled together, he caught Esmail grimace at Tristan's wafting arms, putting more space between them by hopping up on the table. "You good?"

"The view is better here, I think."

"Just checking." Noah handed Abelard the tablet and customized note chart. "To answer your question—that's the idea. The more we've talked to it, the more we've noticed it start to respond to more common words and phrases in... I don't want to say a consistent—"

"Consistent enough to be statistically significant," Abelard finished with a wink-nod.

Noah nodded. "Exactly. Dayo's really excited about the potential insights it could offer into… y'know, child development and recovery from brain injuries. If Tristan is fully grown and still has this sponge-like learning capacity… there's a lot there."

Chin in hands, Esmail focused in on the tank. His gaze over Noah's shoulder was solid against the knot of his spine as he flipped to the page in his notepad where he'd scrawled the words for the test. And where Esmail's eyes were a defined sort of palpable, Abelard's landed like a fritzing live wire, straight to the temple. There was only so much that he could tune out, that and the lingering anxieties of everything else orbiting around his personal gravity well.

"Good afternoon, Tristan," Noah started after a deep breath. "We're going to list out some words to see if you know them. Okay?" he added after a moment.

Its two highest claws knocked against the glass, a gesture they'd inferred was purposeful.

The first word was "left." Tristan appeared to hesitate, its claws curling in against the shell line running down the center of its underside. Beside Noah, Abelard pondered silently, his body's cooling fans ticking up just enough to notice.

"Your left," Esmail blurted.

Noah and Abelard both turned toward him as his hands rushed to cover his mouth, but when they spun back to the tank, Tristan had slid five inches to its left.

"Oh wow…" Noah murmured. It could have been a coincidence, of course, but even the possibility that he was making contact with a sapient xeno-organism was lighting up every inch of him, the giddy buzzing in his chest seeping all the way down to his toes. "*Your* right."

Tristan wriggled another few inches to its right.

"This is big, isn't it? Esmail said, breathless.

"I'd say so." Noah glanced to Abelard for confirmation.

"Incredibly."

Noah's eyes trailed down the length of Tristan's shell as it narrowed to the dormant spine at its tail. The tapering was gradual until it reached the first joint just beyond the shell's lower border; tucked underneath it was the venom sac, ready to shoot through the long segmented needle at a moment's notice. He'd hardly paid it any mind since their sessions with Tristan began.

Again it faded to the back of his head, the test moving forward with the next set of words. "Yes" and "no" questions landed like scattershot guesswork, improving in line with its vocabulary and understanding of the second-person, improving further as it learned Noah and Abelard's names. Tapping out the answers to simple math problems came through almost instinctively. Its legs curled in and out at a faster rate whenever Noah caught himself grinning—and after three hours of scribbled notes with too many exclamation points, that was more often than not. For once, he was even looking forward to transcribing it all.

"That's the end of the list," he said.

"That it is." Abelard glanced between Noah and the tank, a satisfaction coloring his face that Noah had only witnessed when accidentally walking in on his brainstorming sessions with the older grad students, the ones past taking classes, neck-deep in their dissertations. "I don't think I needed to be here at all."

Only then did Noah register that it was just the two of them. Esmail must have moseyed on toward the next crewmates in his rounds ages ago.

"I remember the day I took your cohort on a tour of the xenosciences complex," Abelard said. "That spot in the lab where the bricks were eaten away? You flinched from it… bumped into that one fellow from Dushanbe before you knew what you did. Now look at you."

Noah had forgotten about that specific moment, though he couldn't forget Sergey, the xenomicrobe specialist who shared his lab bench on and off over the whole program.

Still—as Abelard's point alluded to, it was a long time ago.

And also still—the pride Abelard had in him lit a warmth in his chest that flushed up to his face. The bruise at his elbow had receded to a sour green and only ached when something prodded it with purpose; that reminder came too late, after he let the affection for him settle and burrow. Was there any harm in pretending, just for a moment, that all the anomalies he'd tallied since the *Amihaf* left Natocke Station added up to nothing?

"End of the list, end of our test," Abelard said. "Dayo did want us to ask."

A sign of respect, or an attempt at a sign—she and Noah had debated the matter the night before, holed up in the med bay while upstairs the rest of the crew watched Abelard fail to stump Esmail with xenozoological trivia. Whether Tristan would understand the gesture of asking its consent to get a venom sample was the major sticking point, both the concept of what they were after and also that they recognized it as a sapient individual. *How do you communicate that we don't see it as a lab rat when that requires unpacking twenty layers of context?* she'd groaned into her hands.

She'd also reexamined his elbow, biting back a frown she didn't elaborate on—but he was continuing to choose to write that off.

He looked Tristan in its many eyes, spinning up the potential approach. The yes-no questions that had the most success were less actual questions than it confirming or denying facts about itself, with true statements earning a two taps from the top claws.

"Your tail"—he pointed to the needle-like end—"has venom."

Tap tap.

"We… Noah and Abelard do not have venom." He tapped both of his pointer fingers on the tank opposite Tristan's claws, and it responded in kind.

His heart thumped at an angle where he could sense it knocking against the muscles of his throat. He was communicating, actually *communicating*, with a demonstrably intelligent xeno-organism. He was doing so traveling through interstellar space while his mentor sat beside him, back from the dead, the stagnating eddy of Noah's own existence shocked back from a similar brink.

"This is the important part," whispered Abelard.

"Yeah, no pressure, right?"

"*Some* pressure, Noah."

Of course. He swallowed, willed his heart to steady itself as he pulled one of the lab's test tubes from his pile of materials. "You give venom here"—he motioned to the test tube—"to Noah and Abelard."

By the time Noah registered that Tristan's tail was moving, it was already halfway toward a snapping jolt against the glass, stronger than anything they'd seen since catching it on Shala. The force of it scraped the tank forward a few inches, the water sloshing and spilling through the tight mesh top. Noah and Abelard scrambled back, almost climbing over each other to get to their feet. Tristan slammed again, and a third time, and a fourth, and then their backs landed on the corridor wall outside.

"If anything called for a readjusted hypothesis, it would be that, hm?" Abelard was eerily calm as Noah wheezed through his fear-seized windpipe. "You're all right, Noah, you're okay—"

"I know," he rasped, doubling over. "Just trying to get the rest of me to catch up."

Elbows perched on his knees, he took a slow, deliberate breath and surveyed the rest of the corridor. A small crowd had collected over the TerraCosmos emblem, Frida and Irene and Esmail, Quinn still atop his stool in the cockpit's antechamber but peering over Irene's shoulder. Savannah's footfalls rang down the stairwell, and Dayo emerged from the med bay door, tucked in the corner by the airlock. All their individual variants of worry colored the silent, questioning expressions.

"The test was fine, mostly," Noah said. "Until the end… but what can you do?"

Dayo pursed her lips. "It was asking for the venom, wasn't it?"

When he and Abelard confirmed as much and reiterated they were fine, the rest of the crew slowly dispersed. Noah collected what pages of notes he'd managed to scoop into his arms during the retreat. As the nervous sweat on his brow turned clammy, he retreated to draft the report in his bunk, where the adrenaline leaked from his system like oxygen in faulty life support. The scraps of notes he managed to grab were illegible, so he settled for typing up at least an outline, formatting the different headings with bracketed reminders of what should go where. Background on Tristan here, list of tests there, a breakdown of the breakdown between their two parties at the end. A conclusion, pared down to its most clinical.

The room didn't have space for an actual desk, so he yanked out each keystroke from his unmade bed. The prospect of attempting further communication with Tristan bore down like the sheer rock face of a mountain. That the xenosciences hadn't yet branched out to linguistics after almost two hundred years of interstellar exploration and study was something that itched at the back of his head on Earth. Occasionally a student would ask, one per semester across all the undergrad offerings, the answer unsatisfying but bland enough to put the subject to rest.

Now, though—Noah would have eagerly shared a bunk with another crew member if that meant a linguist could sit in front of Tristan's tank to navigate the subtleties swallowed whole in the gap between Earth and Shala. He would have relegated himself to eating every meal on the mess hall floor if that meant a linguist could have parsed the musicows' offerings—the grating harmonies the last hour before the *Amihaf*'s departure that billowed above the tree line in a steady crescendo, resolving in a major chord that drew the scattering bird-like creatures back to their roosts.

Noah glanced up at his Spock figurine as if its inert, dead face could donate anything aside from projected moral support. His email pinged before he had the chance to feel foolish about waiting for a response from a piece of plastic. It was just the one alert, but with two messages landing in his inbox at the same moment, likely even down to the same relay, and he couldn't click away from the flimsy scaffolding of the report fast enough.

"Please be something nice and time consuming…"

The email that sorted itself to the top was from Eber. Subject: *Watch this space*; full text: *Data analysis in process, more to come. Be ready.*

He considered replying with a lone question mark, if only to busy himself imagining the blustering lap it would cause around the lab wing's worn halls. Considered, yes, and decided against. That was a game for the senior undergrads to play, not faculty.

The second email was another forwarded chain message from his father, the subject line so overtaken by *FW*s that he could only read half of the first word after the string came to an end.

Terra.

So—TerraCosmos.

He could assume, without even checking the ten lines of recipients, that this was not necessarily pointed; his father likely opened up his address book and selected anyone who ranked above an acquaintance. He could delete it, but the remnants of adrenaline humming through his bloodstream had given him a streak of—not daring, but something closer to a self-abasing curiosity.

Typically, these kinds of emails only required a skim to grab the basic thesis, but whether it was the lack of forty-point font or the images not surviving the relay journey, Noah was forced to actually engage beyond a surface level. The usual tripe decrying Basic Materials and the dissolution of the pre-Climate-Catastrophe world order littered every paragraph, but when all that was brushed away, there was a story about mining company representatives lobbying—harassing—municipal officials in the Arctic region of the Testudines, which lacked the support of something like the African Mining Board to protect the interests of the local environment and residents. And maybe the story was fabricated as part of some larger call to restore national governments and the borders they implied, but Noah recalled the article Luz had been reading that day by the carpenter rat enclosure, the raw materials shortage plaguing TerraCosmos' manufacturing arms.

Luz's address was written somewhere, and he could dig it up to ask for a link to the article—later. He could ask for it later, when he could dedicate more time to reading it over in full and other reports and tests and expectations weren't breathing hot against his neck.

The first thing Noah registered was the shouting. He stretched out the worst of the knot in his neck as he ran toward the lounge, catching Savannah and Frida leaping up from their workstations, nearly tripping over each other in the rush to the stairwell as the noise expanded below.

"What the *hell* is—oh no." Frida froze at the bottom step.

Noah and Savannah pulled themselves over the side railing to get a better look at what had drained her face of its little color. Esmail stood near the window of the lab, hands cupped over his nose and mouth, while Quinn and Dayo and Abelard propped up the volume in a tight knot of arguing and flying hands.

"Shit," Savannah hissed.

The front panel of the tank had somehow shattered, glass shards littering the spreading puddle of water like ice floes. Tristan scuttled in and out of view, its tail thrashing from side to side—and standing on the center table, primed to leap to any other available surface, was Irene.

"Why was she—I—hey!" Noah shouldered his way between Dayo and Quinn. "Is there some sort of plan here?" he shouted over them, or tried to.

"All I am saying," Abelard said, his ConBod momentarily ticking up the decibels to an unnatural level, "is that as I am inorganic—"

"And as *I've* said, we don't know what that venom could do to your wiring. Stand down, Cousteau, doctor's orders—"

"If we're all repeating ourselves, then I guess it's my turn to remind *you*, Dayo, that your plan would get you both killed." Quinn shoved his palm heels into his cheekbones, nails dragging down the front of his forehead. "Once we get Irene out, *then* we can worry about the damn scorpion. And I can do that."

Over his shoulder, Noah caught the dark blur of Irene's hair and tank top as she jumped to another table. "Good!" He clapped both Quinn and Dayo on the shoulder. "I say we let him."

Without another word, Quinn strode toward the lab, pausing where Savannah, pen in mouth, now hovered behind Esmail, where his own flavors of jitters could meld into newer, more potent forms. Quinn paused, tugged Esmail's hands away from his face to kiss him, murmur something just for that small space. And then the lab door was closing behind him.

Noah's ears rang with the sudden quiet, that piercing tone soon overcome by the engine underfoot, Savannah's teeth squeaking against the pen grip, a sudden rush from the fans at Abelard's neck. The window into the lab could only show them so much, its thick walls muting whatever parts of the scene laid hidden behind them.

A rush, the door opening, waiting feet skittering back—Noah tripped over his ankle, head smacking against the floor. Pain webbed through his skull, down to his teeth. Eyes shut, teeth grinding through it, he fought his way to his knees. Knees first, then standing, then he could take in the scene, blinking away the last vestige of blurriness in his vision. Irene and Quinn were out, but—

His legs buckled. He saw the red streaming down his calf and then his nerves caught up, the rupture a searing throb. Blood dribbled to the floor. He tried to ignore it. He tried to ignore his entire leg, how a wave of pain seized it from ankle to knee when presented with any amount of weight.

"Noah, watch out!"

He couldn't place who spoke or where they were situated; but he glanced down, caught a gleam of black shell and limped away as fast as he could. Toward the cockpit, he realized. The TerraCosmos emblem underfoot was smeared in blood, more than could have leaked from his own leg. He braced himself against the side of the wall that opened into the cockpit's antechamber, and at last the haze cleared.

Most of the crew had drawn back to the edges of the foyer, cradling their own wounds or attending to others'. Frida had climbed her way up Abelard's shoulders, the unruly licks of her hair brushing the ceiling. From their tense holds, however, they were acutely aware of the detente near the lab door, how it could fall apart the second Dayo or Savannah made a wrong move.

"What's the over-under on this thing calling for a truce?" Savannah's pen had disappeared from between her teeth, and her hand started to slip toward her pocket.

"Sav!" Noah called. "Hands—"

"Ah—thanks," she said, eyes firmly staring at Tristan. "So... Dayo..."

"Not a betting woman. But..." She jerked her head toward the lab door. "It's not a tank, but it's still a containment unit. The sensor should pick up its life sign and open if we just... corral it..."

Still facing Tristan's scuttling shell, they each took a gentle, coordinated crab step to the left. Tristan shifted away, Another step, another scuttle to keep the distance. The tail twitched—both Savannah and Dayo hopped back.

"C'mon, work with us here," said Savannah. "We don't want to hurt you—"

Tristan lunged. Screams re-erupted on all sides. They both dove out of the way, Dayo toward the end of the hall and Savannah closer to the lab. It slid open behind her and caught on the splay of curls that had cushioned her head. She couldn't roll away or get back on her feet. Tristan's tail snapped toward her neck—

Her reflexes were faster, grabbing it at the joint closest to the spine and angling it away from her, both arms fully extended. It thrashed and flailed.

The claws that a few hours ago had facilitated dialogue between their two species were slick with blood and stabbed into any part of Savannah's legs that it could reach.

"Someone—*argh*—come get—"

Dayo sprang to her feet, rushed forward. Tristan had turned itself over in the struggle, exposing its undershell. With Savannah's grip holding, Dayo thrust her hand toward the base of the creature's tail. The tips of her fingers only brushed the crest of the venom sac before Irene tugged her back.

"You pull too hard and it ruptures all over Savannah. Have some sense—"

Savannah's arms shook, Tristan's relentless attempts to escape gaining more ground with every desperate swing of its body. Noah limped forward. He couldn't fight Tristan but maybe he could untangle her hair caught in the door, let the struggle barrel forward with her on two feet, because that was only fair and she was his best friend and—

Frida hit the ground with a thud. Abelard had shrugged her off, and he strode toward the center of the melee with a level of urgency that did little to ease the sick curdling in Noah's stomach. Abelard swooped down, snatched the end of Tristan's tail in one hand and braced the other against the underbelly, pulling it away from Savannah. They were going to be fine. Noah's entire leg was starting to burn from the pain but they were going to be fine, and Savannah would be fine. Dayo and Irene flocked to her side, ripping tourniquets from the bottoms of their shirts as an immediate stop-gap, and Noah dragged himself to join them. He could still coax her hair from the door, now without the looming danger.

As he crossed the border of the blood-strewn foyer, a glint of bronze in the corner of his eye turned his attention toward the airlock. Abelard stood before the inner door, unfazed by the onslaught of all eight of Tristan's claws into his synthetic skin as he held its body high. The angle hid his face from Noah, but the tilt of his head as he ran a finger along the stretch of shell running down the underside of its body was a studious sort, calculating.

"Abelard, we can put it back in the lab," he said.

"Hm."

"There's still—"

A sickening crunch clenched his words in his throat. And then there was the high-pitched agonized wail as Abelard's hand squeezed further into Tristan's soft underbelly. Its tail drooped, lifeless, and then the piercing screech pitched up further, warbling toward the inaudible.

Noah's throat closed further as he tried to call out. Translucent brown liquid oozed down Abelard's wrist. It didn't have to happen this way. It didn't have to, but he couldn't limp fast enough on his injured leg. The inner door to the airlock hissed open. Tristan landed inside with another cracking thud. The atmosphere inside the *Amihaf* turned sour as doors shut and others opened, shunting a broken body into the unforgiving void.

The blip of it passed the nearest porthole, ripped apart by the forces of turbolight.

"Well!" Clapping his hands together, Abelard's cheerful grin surveyed the silent, bloody scene before him. "I'd say in the relative view of things that this was decently successful. Dr. Oyekan, what support do you—"

"I'm fine," she said, curt. "You go… recharge."

"Are you—"

"I can handle it."

Whatever else passed between them, Noah missed; his injured leg had started to wobble terribly, and he let himself sink to the floor. Abelard walked around him, veered away from the first aid station Esmail had set up for Quinn at the bottom of the stairwell, and once he was gone, the rest of them found they had little else to say to each other to fill the sudden vacuum.

Dayo insisted on keeping everyone near the med bay for observation, whether they'd been clawed or not. No one had seen Tristan's tail come close enough to break skin with the venom, but given the stealth nature of its sting, they couldn't be certain—that, and they had no way of knowing if the venom could be injected through the claws as well. Noah's theory that it was a diversion from the real threat of the tail spine did little to dissuade Dayo. "Esmail's getting all the pillows from the lounge and your bunks. No ex— well, *fewer* excuses. You'll all be free to go at the forty-hour mark."

By 0300 IST, Esmail and Frida—the least scathed aside from Dayo—had mopped up the blood and claimed their own pillow and stretch of wall. Both of them snored like they were drowning, but Noah couldn't blame either of them for why he was still conscious.

Irene sat awake as well, laid on her back at the center of the foyer.

"What were you doing in the lab by yourself?" asked Noah.

Her head turned toward him on the couch pillow she'd commandeered. "Hm?"

"I guess I just wanted to know what happened."

"Oh." She glanced back up toward the ceiling, squinting against the harsh light. "I talked to Abelard after the incident this afternoon. It happened after you asked after Tristan's venom. I was... we were obviously missing something. I just wanted to see if I could understand them... or where they were coming from."

She stretched her injured arm from where it laid at her side, a solid three inches of skin below the wrist wrapped in gauze. It landed on her stomach, riding the easy rise and fall.

"You're not going to ask me what I learned?" she said.

"Figured you would've already said something about it."

"Maybe." She sighed, ran the hand from her uninjured arm through her hair. "This is your area, though. What are you thinking?"

What Noah was thinking was how heavy fatigue weighed down on all parts of him from all angles, even the impossible ones, and how the pain in his leg had shifted from a sharp needling to an ache that left him queasy. And still, there was one more thought caught in the eddy—"The report on this is going to be such a fucking ordeal."

He'd glanced over to Savannah, curled around the bunched comforter of her bed as if it were a pillow itself, the glow of her skin offering no hint that mere hours ago she'd lost a significant amount of blood.

"There are worse things than paperwork."

Noah turned back to Irene. She offered up her palm, where the rust of drying blood left a clumsy smiley face, her own mouth tilting up to mimic it.

FIVE

WITH SCABS TURNING TO scar tissue and Dayo no longer dragging the injured crew to the med bay for daily checkups, the air on the *Amihaf* had started to buzz. Any movement or glance too sharp threatened to ignite whatever crackling fizzed in the air among them. Three days they existed like that, thrifty with words, fidgeting confined to tight bubbles, all interspersed with regular visits to the cockpit where Irene sat with her electronic counterpart. Embedded in the right wall of the room, the navigation computer featured a display for the more visually-minded travelers—a crude assembly of pictograms, a ship gradually sliding along a dotted line to the eventual destination, an ETA counting down in the corner.

A watched pot never boiled, and a watched ship never magically broke through its velocity limitations.

Even before Dayo had given his wound the all-clear, Noah had started dreaming of land. Different iterations cropped up every night, from the specific crunch of dried earth behind the Rassawek xenosciences complex at the height of summer to the unsteady gravel-stoned path that connected

Abraham's farm to the main road. He dreamt of damp-packed sand at the shore of Lake Erie, mud drifts leftover from the spring floods. When he woke in the morning and pressed his feet against the metal floor of his bunk, the cold there slithered up his body, unnatural. The closer the ship flew toward the Luyten system, the larger the group would be in the early hours of the day, crowding the cockpit with coffee and tea and fruit juice in hand, fighting the heavy pall of the hour for just a glimpse at how much longer they had until touchdown.

They whittled the time away in the newly-cleaned lab, or nodding along to Quinn as he talked through his latest idea in the ongoing struggle with the system logs. Esmail's prayer rug vanished from its usual spot in the lounge, and Noah followed his cue, opting to spend most of his time outside of meals in the confines of his bunk.

In the sizzling static atmosphere, Abelard was a fire hazard the way he couldn't read the room—or refused to. Tense muscles strained to stone when he loped to the mess table halfway through lunch, breathless with excitement over an article he'd read about something-or-other of interest to one among them. He spoke on end over the clinks of silverware.

That was enough to contend with.

It wasn't as if he didn't have work—Eber and Abraham hounded his inbox once they received the full report, and if responding to their continuous follow-ups meant that Justin's reply to his impulsive BCC got buried in the deluge, so be it. There was also the brief for the next exoplanet base to study, other stray input requests from the larger Rassawek xenosciences community. He didn't ignore them, but if they tugged at his sleeve while he curled up around his tablet, rewatching *Star Trek: The Voyage Home* for the umpteenth time, they would have to wait.

Even a watched ship had to arrive at its destination eventually.

Abelard reiterated the major points of the TerraCosmos brief after Esmail brought them out of turbolight—another red dwarf system, the planet tidally-locked in accordance with the oldest predictive models. Only the thin border between Lulal's day and night sides was habitable; the base sat in a realm of perpetual twilight where the forested mountains transitioned to grassland. This specific set of factors, he warned, translated into a climate that hovered around a frigid thirteen degrees Celsius.

"I would layer if you don't have the proper attire," said Abelard, heading up the staircase. "It does more good than you think!"

The *Amihaf* landed in an empty stretch of the grasslands, facing a collection of trailers identical to what they saw on Shala. In the magenta tint of Luyten's Star shining over the mountains, the scene was far more alien, aided by the lack of human bustle that had defined every moment at Camp Bachelor. The base, as far as Noah could tell, was little more than a ghost town, yet Abelard bounded down the exit ramp as soon as it had fully unfurled.

"Something's wrong here," Quinn said.

Noah followed with cautious steps, hoping that no one picked up on how Abelard didn't deny Quinn's gut observation. He hadn't read through the entire brief, but he had come across a section on how it had been two years since anyone at TerraCosmos had made any significant contact with the base, a qualifier that was never expanded upon. The tall grasses lining the *Amihaf*'s landing zone waved in the wind with an edge of menace, perhaps imagined, perhaps not. Noah studied the warped equivalent of trees towering over the trailers, looking for any further hint of people.

"Don't you think we should maybe… take it slow?"

"Why?" Abelard turned, eyed the rest of the crew huddled at the bottom of the ramp and then to Noah halfway between them. "They could very well just be asleep, what with the planet's tidal locking. Who knows what the local time is! So quick to assume the worst!"

Behind them, Savannah muttered something about the last time they gave something the benefit of the doubt, but Abelard pressed on. Swallowing a grumble, Noah ran forward and caught his wrist; while he could never match the strength of a ConBod, the gesture still made him pause.

"Noah…"

"Look," he said, stepping closer. He lowered his voice below the rumbling bass of croaking that had started up around their feet. "You're the closest thing we have to a captain. The crew—*your* crew—is uneasy. Afraid, even. Whether you think it makes sense doesn't make it *not* your responsibility."

His stomach flipped and twisted waiting for Abelard to react. A beat passed, then two, and then Abelard's face beamed at just the right angle to catch the perpetually waning light. "You've become so much more assertive since we first met. I'm very proud of—"

"Abelard…"

"Point taken that this was not your point." He pulled his wrist from Noah's hand and waved down the rest of the crew. "Shall we make a more nuanced plan?" He didn't appear to recognize the heaving sag of their shoulders as the strain lifted.

He waited for them to join him outside the ship before continuing on, but he barely made it five yards before the camp sprung alive—a buzzing alarm, metallic clangs of trailer doors slamming open, a flurry of bodies, a shouted string of rapid Mandarin.

The rest of the crew shrunk back, instinctively clinging to each other. "Well," Esmail murmured. "At least they're alive!"

The view of the base was still murky through the twilight, as unadjusted as their eyes were; Noah could only make out silhouettes of people ahead of Abelard, and whatever the lead of the other crew was saying flew so far over his head that it left orbit.

"Huang *Bóshì*," Abelard said calmly, "we're here with TerraCosmos. You can put the gun down—"

"The *what*?" Irene hissed.

Noah squinted at the head figure, who was indeed holding a gun. The shape of it hinted at a model an interstellar marauding gang would wield in a forgettable action movie, cobbled together from spare parts and a patchy schematic file.

"You're not going to get me that easily," the figure continued in English. "If you were going to fake us out, you shouldn't have chosen someone I knew was dead."

"It's funny, actually!" Abelard chuckled like he was at a department holiday party instead of being held at gunpoint. "I was probably the most surprised out of everyone to find that I didn't actually die."

There was a pause, and then he added something in Mandarin.

The gun remained up, but Huang signaled something over her shoulder—a set of floodlights fixed atop each of the trailers shot straight into their pupils, already blown wide by the twilight. The *Amihaf* crew yelped, half in alarm and half in pain, ducking out of the glare. Noah strained through his hand's makeshift shield. Abelard hadn't budged; Huang's sharper silhouette finally lowered the gun, the lamps cutting off.

"Constructed Body?" she asked, stepping forward to meet him.

"Is it that obvious?"

"You didn't flinch in the lights like the rest of them. I wanted to be sure."

They trailed behind Abelard, vision re-readjusting to Lulal's twilight, and Huang was revealed as an older woman with a tight braid, clad in a tank top and high-waisted shorts that had long abandoned their original colors. A thick pink scar ran down the side of her nose to her chin.

"Mingyu..." Abelard took a step forward, extending his arm when she didn't pull back. "We're checking on all the first-wave Project Khepri bases. That's it. You don't need the gun."

"Well..." She tucked it into the waistband with a huff. "I do. But thankfully not for you." She shouted another bit of Mandarin over her shoulder, and five more figures emerged from the shadows. "Come to the mess hall. We can catch you up to speed there."

At one point, their mess trailer was identical to the model found in Camp Bachelor, but the last few years had taken a much harsher toll. The galley counter was piled high with home-crafted cooking implements that couldn't fit in the cabinets, and most of the chairs around the main table had been repaired so many times that the legs were no longer balanced. If Noah were to check under the sink, he wouldn't have been surprised to see his and Justin's own solution to a leaky pipe in their apartment—a thick layer of duct tape and a prayer.

Whatever the state, Huang Mingyu surveyed it like her personal war room. Leaning against the wall, arms crossed, she cast a heavy pall with the slightest effort. The rest of the base gathered around the far edges of the trailer, focused anywhere but where she had perched herself.

"So..." Mingyu shuffled toward the head of the table, rapping her knuckles against the surface. "TerraCosmos finally decided to check what was going on here. The short of it is… two years in, there was a major solar storm. It fried our mimeos and most of our communication arrays. There's enough juice left in a backup that lets us get our quarterly paperwork in on time, at least. I can't help but wonder if they would have sent for help sooner if we were late on deliverables. Tch."

One of her crew commented in accented Mandarin—his tone was halfway joking but layered with a thick slab of fatigue, and whatever he said earned a wry smile from Mingyu.

"We have research to show," said the woman beside him. "We know it's what you're looking for. We…"

"What Thuy means is," Mingyu sighed, "is that we've been preoccupied."

"Clearly," Dayo said. "Mimeos broken… even the AutoChemist?"

"Deader than the Moon."

"Ours is functional, so—who's your doctor?" She was already hopping out of her seat and rewrapping her scarf before Mingyu could point to the man who'd just spoken. "Okay! Great, let's get you restocked—"

"Sovann doesn't speak English," said Thuy.

"And I don't speak Mandarin. We'll manage."

Thuy translated the situation for him, and then he and Dayo were jogging across the field to the *Amihaf*—Noah watched through the window, tuning out Quinn as he inquired further after the base's attempts at repairs. Sovann and Dayo's communication consisted mostly of elaborate gestures, then only partly once they found a language in common.

Within the trailer, the conversation had escalated, and Mingyu pared it back to silence with one sharp whistle. "I don't care what problems on your ship Mr. Kaiwhakatere has or hasn't fixed yet… I assume it's 'doctor'? What's your name?"

Frida's entire face flushed with the same shade as the light outside as she met Mingyu's gaze. "Uh, um… Frida. Frida Wick."

"Noted. Dr. Wick, your opinion on Mr. Kaiwhakatere's task list is irrelevant at the current juncture. Hinata?" She turned toward the lanky man who had slotted himself on the far corner of the galley countertop. "Go see if you can make any headway with our new friends."

Quinn and Hinata departed for another trailer at the camp, and the terse remark Mingyu gave to the rest of her personnel dismissed them back to wherever they needed to be at the current hour.

When it was just them, Mingyu and the remaining crew of the *Amihaf*, she let her shoulders droop, an air of weariness creeping into her joints. "We've been without help for a long time," she said after a heavy couple moments. "What's the prognosis, Doctor Back From the Dead?"

"Well…" Abelard heaved his chest through a fake sigh, landing his chin in his hand. "The more information we have, the better the odds that we can help."

The rest of them might as well have disappeared with how Mingyu stared off over their heads, winding a finger around a loose tress of hair she'd left tucked behind her ear, a solid slat of gray easily missed in the lighting outdoors; once he noticed it, Noah caught more streaks of silver in the length of her braid.

"I for one," Esmail said suddenly, "would like to know about the gun."

Mingyu sighed. "It's a good enough place to start."

Offering little else but a nod silently asking them to follow, she led them to the back of the base, where the same vegetation in the landing field grew noticeably wilder. It rose above Noah's shoulders and tickled his face with wide-reaching blooms, one of which Savannah plucked in passing to examine as they hiked onward. Croaking creatures hid in the dirt among the grasses, tendrils weaving up and down the base of the stalks while a thicker appendage writhed at the center.

The trail eventually delivered them to a lakeshore. No one dared step past where Mingyu settled her stance in the sand, a full four feet beyond the edge of the lapping waves. Arms crossed, she glared at the far-off tree line. "Lulal is a real gem of a planet," she said. "Carbon *and* silicon-based life existing in harmony… it's not every day you get handed a lake of sulfuric acid with a full ecosystem." She stared at Abelard, and then at Noah, as if she could sense who among them was his most direct successor. "TerraCosmos is interested, of course. It's why they sent us here. We dedicate what resources we can when we're not trying to keep ourselves alive."

They forage and hunt, she explained. The grasses in the field where the *Amihaf* landed were an odd cross between wheat and corn, and they'd been able to use some of the local fauna both for nutrition and supplies. With the mimeos down, they had to use whatever was available.

"Many of the local species are resistant to sulfuric acid, in varying degrees," she said. "It's helped ease the logistical nightmare, research-wise… protecting the functional equipment we have."

"Esmail did ask about the gun," said Irene.

"Indulge me my preamble."

As Mingyu massaged her brow, further collecting her thoughts, Savannah and Irene both put a few extra steps between themselves and the lake. Noah had a sudden vision, perhaps collective, of a lake monster breaking through the murky depths and scalding them all with acid before anyone could think to reach for a firearm.

"When I say Lulal is a gem of a planet, I don't just mean for science," she said finally. "The initial geological survey... untold abundance no matter where they took samples. Beryllium, manganese, tungsten, cobalt, lithium, every raw material Earth has ever drooled over... and that's just in this section of the habitable strip. To cut straight to the point"—she glanced at Irene—"not long after the solar storm, we got some new Terrestrial neighbors. They weren't friendly."

Noah peered across the lake; he was just able to make out against the shifting haze of grasses the outlines of more trailers, as well as a smaller-model commercial cargo ship. A flag, little more than a fluttering black rectangle this far off, rose over the largest of the trailers.

He turned to ask Savannah about the flag but found everyone else staring expectantly at Mingyu, who in turn leveled Abelard with a rare kind of intensity reserved for the desperate moments when language failed to materialize. And Abelard met it, held it, the dawn of his understanding rising in time with her deepening frown.

"Wait. Where's..." His digital eyes flicked to the silhouettes across the lake and back. "Where's Chen *Bóshì*?"

"Like I said..." Mingyu turned away. "They weren't friendly."

If there was anything else to be said on the matter, no one dared to voice it.

Shēngdì, as the base had been named, was quiet upon their return. They spied Dayo and Quinn deep in conversation through the mess trailer window, the rest of them having returned to their bunks as it pushed closer to 0300 in time with Beijing. Mingyu gave Abelard a nod, murmuring something to him, low, before turning in herself. There was a further splintering after her— Esmail and Savannah to the mess trailer, Abelard and Frida back to the *Amihaf*. With nothing much to work with, Noah took a seat where he stood, the ship and the rest of the flat fields opening up to the sky. Irene soon joined him.

Lulal's habitable strip wasn't dark enough to let the starscape shine through, and Noah could pin down little else for why she decided to dirty the seat of her jeans in this precise spot. Still, he appreciated her presence. None of the conclusions he could draw around the limited pieces of information from Mingyu trended toward anything good, and factoring in a potential bright side shut the whole exercise down. As if she could sense the snaggle in his head, Irene pulled the notebook and pen from her inside jacket pocket, flipping to a blank page.

"Hey." She tapped the cover against his knee, a pen tucked inside.

"What?"

"Doodle something."

"Huh?"

"It's boring if it's only my drawings. Look." She flipped back a couple pages, opening to a spread—the left side a detailed sketch of Quinn knitting with Esmail sitting at his feet, the right an oddly-proportioned llama balancing a teapot on its head. "That one's from Frida."

She all but shoved the notebook into his hands. The next open page sat opposite another one of Irene's sketches, this one of Savannah and her favorite pen held square between her molars. The rendering of the particular way her fingers wove into her hair, how she studied a puzzling specimen or block of data—Noah could almost hear the frustrated litany of mumbling rise from the ink.

"I can't draw, though."

"Frida said the same thing."

"No... *really*," he said. "An art teacher once told my mom it was like I forgot most of my motor skills whenever I picked up a crayon."

"Okay."

"What do you mean, 'okay?'"

"I *mean*," she said, "okay!"

His mouth pinched into a tight frown as he turned back notebook. It hardly felt right marring a page with something like a stick figure or the long train of a squiggle; he snuck a glance at her and caught her eyes immediately, keenly intent. His face burned as he buried his attention in the open space below the pen nib.

The ground around them croaked.

That was an idea.

His drawing had only grown into a vertical line with the hint of a curve toward the end when Irene spoke again. "Do you know who this Dr. Chen was?" she asked.

He finished the bottom of the creature's theoretical bottom, chewing at the inside of his lip. "I didn't read through the brief's personnel blurbs before we landed, but there's really only one person it could be. Xenozoology isn't a huge field, and the way Mingyu... anyway, Abelard coauthored a lot of papers with him early in their careers."

"Not lately?"

The outline he'd drawn looked more like a warped test tube than any sort of burrowing xeno-organism, but it would have to do. "If they did work together later, it's not well known. That might be the kind of information I could've unlocked later in my doctoral program if he hadn't... y'know."

Irene hummed under her breath.

"Chen Yuxuan's work was foundational in expanding the concept of what xenological life might look like," he said, wondering how long he should draw the creature's tendrils in the cross section. "He went beyond ideas like silicon-based organisms or blurred taxonomical borders... theories of expression for sentience and sapience, mostly, but also challenging what it meant for an environment to be truly inhospitable."

"So... the basis of those leviathans you and Abelard are so keen on—what is that?"

"Hey!" He swatted away her pointing hand that had secreted its way over his shoulder. "I'm not done yet!"

"Is it the thing making all that noise?"

"I told you, I'm not done!"

She thankfully let the matter settle, the lull in conversation carried on by the creatures' croaks bubbling through the field. The furthest of them sat just at the edge of his perception, a vague, low itch just inside his ear.

"To answer your other question," Noah said, clearing his throat, "Chen's work did set the stage for vacuum leviathans."

"Oh. Neat," she added, almost as an afterthought.

"And..."

At this, Irene straightened her back.

"Here." He held up his terrible little doodle of the creature. "It is indeed what you guessed."

For less than a second, her face crumpled into a grimace, reverting back by the time she took the notebook and slotted it back inside her jacket. "Whatever it is, I hate that it has a tongue."

"Yeah, me too."

A metallic creak rang from the other side of Shēngdì. One of the other local researchers that Mingyu hadn't yet introduced wandered blearily down the trailer steps, knuckles rubbing at the corner of his eye. Noah and Irene watched him as he cast his gaze out beyond the edge of the parked *Amihaf*, then to the two of them, a course now apparently set. A yard from where they sat, he crouched down and dug a cupped hand, spade-like, into the soil. It reemerged with one of the creatures held close, just by the grip of his thumb. It was smaller than Noah imagined, two inches long at most, and the man popped it into his mouth with all the fanfare of a daily vitamin.

It wasn't long before he noticed Noah and Irene staring. "Can't sleep," he said. "And also... hungry."

"Um. Of course," said Noah. He gave the man a thumbs up, which was returned after a pause.

The man started his return back to his bunk trailer, a slow shuffle that kicked up stray bits of dirt with every step. "Not much your lot can do here," he said.

The door of the trailer clanged behind him, as good a sign as any for Noah and Irene to follow suit to the confines of their own bunks.

Breakfast the next morning was a crowded affair with the residents of Shēngdì joining the line for the *Amihaf*'s mimeo, and the break from the meals they'd improvised for themselves since that fateful solar storm shot them through with a newfound energy. The ship had never been so loud. Noah picked an empty spot of floor closer to the stairwell away from the center of it all and was soon joined by Dayo once the lounge reached capacity.

Neither of them seemed too hungry, so as they picked at their food, Noah tried to eavesdrop on Abelard and Mingyu through the noise—the way

Abelard said *vacuum leviathan* always had an odd lilt, which poked it up over the rest of the garbled conversation. At his current rate, the chatter had been poked enough to leave it in tatters.

Mingyu was less than pleased.

"I am *not* talking about this here," she hissed, and then she was leading the two of them down the staircase to the empty rooms below.

Dayo grimaced. "Great." When Noah didn't say anything, she prodded his knee.

"I don't want to think about it," he sighed. "If enough people like Mingyu slap him on the wrist over this whole thing, maybe he'll drop—I know, okay," he said to Dayo's raised eyebrow. "I can dream."

"So can we all."

The rest of his appetite withered into a husk, the mimeo strawberry in his mouth souring until he fought back a gag. He forced it down, blinking away reflex tears and the memory of Tristan's entrails dripping down Abelard's arms.

Dayo hardly seemed to notice. "Let's take a walk."

"What?"

But she had already stood, Quinn and Esmail making excuses to those around them a few moments later to follow her below. His curiosity raged, though not loudly enough to keep him from returning their abandoned plates to the sink.

"Sorry, I should probably go too," Savannah said as Noah hopped down the stairs. "It's been nice, um—anyway—sorry!"

Noah was waiting for her at the bottom step. "You good?"

"Shut up," she grumbled. "Where's everyone going?"

"A walk, apparently." At the window in the lab door, he caught a flash of Mingyu in a heated but muted conversation. *Not right now*, he thought. *I am not going to worry about this right now.*

"A walk where?"

They spun around just as they stepped onto the exit ramp. A member of the local crew, the one who had translated for their doctor, had followed them down with a lidded mug of tea.

"I was about to ask the same thing," Savannah said. "Sorry, what's your name again?"

"Oh—Nguyen Nhu Thuy. Xenozoologist," she added. "If you're leaving camp, I should probably come with you."

Noah couldn't argue against that, and neither could the rest of the group that were waiting on the edge of the central square. Thuy didn't explicitly say as much, but the way she kept peering out over the tall grasses and to the tips of the tree line spoke to some earned instinct toward caution. One of her own had already died, after all.

Sensing her unease, Dayo explained that she didn't want to go too far, just to the edge of the lakeshore where Mingyu had led them the night before. "I'm curious about something I saw, and we weren't given much information. Also thought it was a good excuse to stretch my legs."

Thuy took a long swig of her tea, eyes slipping shut as she tucked the mug into a makeshift sling on her pants. "I used to hate mimeo green tea. The stuff we've brewed here is…" She made a face. "Anyway. You want to go, let's go."

The trek was silent aside from their footsteps and the occasional bubble from Thuy's mug. Though it was no brighter than the night before, when they arrived at the lakeshore, Noah could now make out more of the mining camp.

The trailer materials gleamed expensively in the twilight, and a few even had a second story. The side of one of the larger ones read *AMC, INC.* in flecking paint.

"Hey, um…" Savannah slid behind Noah as if she were trying to hide behind his far shorter frame. "These guys killed that other guy. And we're just, what, standing out in the open nearby?"

"Mingyu said yesterday that they weren't friendly," Quinn said. "*Weren't.* Past tense." He glanced to Thuy, who sat on a large rock jutting into the lake.

She stared at the toe of her boots on the rock's edge, the thin distance between them and the lapping crests of acid splashing up from the breeze. Her tea had run dry, but her hands clamped around it like a life raft. "They didn't last long," she said finally.

A second solar storm—smaller, an aftershock—drenched the planet a month after the miners had killed Chen Yuxuan for wandering too close to their camp, and none of them knew how to fend for themselves off Earth without a mimeo.

"Three days after, we stopped hearing them," she said. "Iseul and Eun-sook find a new poisonous plant every week… not hard to guess what happened."

This only turned Savannah's worries to a new target—Thuy reassured her that Luyten's Star hadn't acted up since, that the *Amihaf* had no risk of being stranded with them.

Dayo and Quinn had turned their attention back across the lake. They huddled around her tablet, using the camera function to zoom in on identifying bits of information visible at a distance. "Ikemba's got an in with the African Mining Board," she said. "He'll be able to figure out who this lot is."

Filling the silence, she continued on about this contact, on old friend of her partner's from university, all sorts of irrelevant asides to help ease

Savannah's nerves as Quinn took the tablet to fiddle with it further.

After a few minutes, he sighed and handed the tablet back to Dayo. "Try these configs. The exposure timing should help, but it's still pretty far."

"It'll have to do. Thank you," she added with a half-bow. "All right… what do you have for me…"

Thuy looked between the two of them and frowned. "Wait—"

A flash shone across the lake as Dayo snapped the photo, the scene momentarily rid of its magenta filter. "This is better than I expected," she said, turning the screen to Quinn.

"We need to go," said Thuy. "Now."

"Oh no. Someone's still alive over there, aren't they?" Savannah collapsed on a nearby rock. "I'm going to be sick."

Esmail rushed forward with Noah to help hoist her to her feet. Ahead, Thuy was all but pushing Dayo and Quinn back toward the path to base, ignoring their stream of questions. They made it just inside the reed line when a loud splash cut through the garbled crosstalk.

"Um. What was that?" asked Dayo.

Thuy swore under her breath in Vietnamese. "Nothing you want to meet in its current state. *Move*."

There wasn't a need to run, at least, just put another ten meters between them and the lake, and Thuy wouldn't let them stop once they'd passed the threshold. "It's an estimate, anyway," she said. Behind them rose a growl, then a thick slap against the surface as the xeno-organism sprayed the shore in acid—and several of Dayo and Quinn's questions answered themselves.

No one said anything until they were almost back at Shēngdì. Esmail broached the silence by first clearing his throat. "So… is that what you need Mingyu's gun for?"

Thuy shook her head. "It was only startled. Temporarily blinded, maybe."

The rest of the group peeled off toward the trailers as they arrived at the clearing, Dayo wondering about properly visiting the abandoned camp in the coming days and Savannah already opting out. Noah didn't follow, pausing to search the sky for signs of where the sun hid under the horizon. Of course the Lulalan fauna reacted like that to the flash; it was likely the brightest thing they would ever see.

As he headed toward the ship to retrieve his own tablet, he picked up Mingyu and Abelard's voices from the shadow of the bow, apparently having been kicked out of the lab, still neck-deep in the argument from breakfast.

"This is my life's work, Mingyu. My life *and* death's work, if you want to get technical—"

"You're still not hearing me. No, stop for a minute. My people have such limited resources and time, and you want us to use it for this little vanity project? Don't make that face at me—"

"This would be an unfathomable breakthrough in xenobiology!"

"How would that breakthrough help us not starve after you leave? How will it bring Yuxuan back to life?"

"I… this isn't about him—"

"Deny it all you want. Sure, it's probably not all about him, but are you going to look me of all people in the eye and try to tell me he hasn't been a factor?"

Abelard said nothing, and Noah hovered a quarter-way up the entrance ramp.

"Give it a rest, at least while you're here. For me," Mingyu added, the rest of her remark falling out of earshot and ushering Noah back inside the ship.

Once Noah re-emerged from his bunk, there was no sign that the morning's excited diversion had happened at all. Iseul and Eun-sook, the resident xenobotanists, swooped to his sides as soon as he descended the stairs, stealing him away to a meeting at their lab, where a contraption he couldn't begin to describe took up most of the main table.

The only discernible facets of the mass of material were that it was broken and that it was built with locally-sourced materials. Thuy and Iseul took turns explaining the function and various pieces—leaves from this tree and that fern, bones from one of the pack species living in the bush, all highly resistant to lake's acid in ways that their research equipment wasn't, and far more renewable than glass or titanium.

"What about these xeno-organisms makes them resistant?" asked Savannah as she rubbed one of the leaves between her fingers.

Iseul sighed. "When would we have had the time to figure it out? We spend long enough making sure the shit here wouldn't poison us if we eat it."

At that, Eun-Sook signed something at him, earning a cynical snort. He didn't translate.

So the week's agenda was settled: procure substitute material for the protective device, and begin to look into aspects of Lulal's xenobiochemistry previously unexamined.

Noah snatched a segment of broken bone that had fallen from the device to take back to the ship's lab, which he hoped would be empty. He turned it over in his hands as he shuffled across the base square to the ship ramp—there was little to differentiate it from a normal human shin bone upon first examination, aside from its iron hue and deceptive weight.

Just as he realized that he hadn't asked Thuy about the animal the bone belonged to, he found himself knocking heads with Mingyu herself.

"I'm so sorry, I wasn't—"

She didn't so much cut across him as merely point a finger in his general direction—regardless, it had the same effect. Hours had passed, tilting closer to dinner than the morning's to-do, but that didn't matter to the flaring ache belted around his lungs.

"Abelard speaks very highly of you," she said.

"I—oh. Um—sorry, I wasn't expecting... uh, thank you."

She smirked, but it didn't last. "Keep him in line, would you?"

"I'm trying."

"There's an English idiom about doing more than trying right? An old one?"

That was the sort of thing Justin could speak to, if anyone. Noah shrugged and stepped around her to the empty lab. The bone landed with a heavy *clack* on the center table, barely lighter than the black resin it laid upon.

"You're not the first person to decide that I'm his... I don't know, minder," he said as she followed him to the opposite side of the bench.

"So others think he needs one?" she said, knocking a knuckle against the bone.

"Never heard anyone say as much explicitly—"

"Do *you* think he needs one?"

Her arms crossed tightly against her chest, across a thick line of splattered orange stains, faded among the embedded dirt. He'd only just noticed it— that, and how the ship's lighting lit up the angry edges of her scar, the darker grays that hid better in the twilight, the hazy arcs of indigo under her eyes.

Noah ran his hand along the length of the bone fragment and its unnaturally smooth surface. "I don't know what to think. I've never done fieldwork with him. My gauge of what counts as concerning is very Earth-centric." Which was a true, if not complete, assessment of where things stood.

"You don't have to hedge."

"I'm—"

"I know that man. I know him very well." She stared him down, let the meat of those two simple statements lie thick and heavy between them. "I… when Yuxuan died, the one bright side was that I didn't have to tell Abelard. He beat him to it. And now he's—same as always, I guess."

"You guess?"

She ground her teeth, chewing something over, but not to share. Eventually, she tutted under her breath. "And what do you think about this vendetta against the leviathan?"

He let the segue drop. "We're never going to find it," he said. "It's easier to indulge him whenever it comes up. I don't see the harm."

Her only reply was leaving the lab with a shallow smile colored in something resembling pity. She relented enough on the taut composure the planet kept wrapped around the whole of her for it to leak through, snatched back as soon as she passed the threshold into the rest of the ship. Outside, Sovann caught her attention and the steely exterior returned.

Noah split his time between the ship lab studying the bone and sitting in on the other pockets of activity lighting up the rest of the base when his synapses crashed into a roadblock. Sometimes it was enough to take a couple laps around the trailers' perimeter, catching sight of Esmail prodding at one of the buried croaking creatures with a blade of grass. Quinn and Hinata, having given up on the fried circuit boards of Shēngdì's mimeos, dedicated their energies to the persistent logging issue once the quarterly ship check wrapped up. Sitting at the top of the *Amihaf*'s stairwell, Noah listened in on their debates rife with technical jargon, letting it wash over him to clear his head. The longer he listened, the more issues Hinata seemed to uncover, mysteries that orbited his muttering about file types and testing scripts. Later, Quinn's crow's feet appeared deeper, freshly-creased, in search of Esmail to hoist his spirits up from the depth of futility.

In the ship's med bay, Dayo and Sovann babysat the AutoChemist as it produced enough medical supplies to last Shēngdì ten years past the duration of their assignment. Whatever language they shared had been gladly cast aside—the foyer outside the cracked door leaked the lessons in Yoruba and Khmer, and while Noah never allowed himself to interrupt, the unfamiliar roll of phrases slowed his step, begged him to dawdle. And he would indulge, at least until the cadre of xenobotanists, with their freshly-adopted xenomycologist, would barrel up the ramp to raid the lab for their current pursuit. When he did take up a corner in the base's lab trailer, merely existing around the unending store of frenetic energy was exhausting; with a fungus expert finally on-planet, the creatures in the dirt could finally exist as more than just a staple food, and Frida's volume increased exponentially with her excitement.

Most of Noah's hovering was allotted toward the quick partnership between Thuy and Irene. The necessities of survival had overshadowed mission-relevant research, and what extra time they did have had been directed at the lake. With no formal surveys of the forest fauna on hand, Thuy spent a couple hours every evening describing her memories of the species they'd encountered as Irene brought shape to them in her notebook. Page after page filled with the possible cousins of these xeno-organisms as Thuy clarified and backtracked, honing the specifics while sanding off the mess of mental mistranslations. Odd crosses straddling the disparate lands of bird and insect, burrowing bodies that would be considered plants if not for their teeth and eyes, shining globular masses roping around the limbs of what passed as trees—Thuy never gave the closest sketch anything higher than a *close enough,* but in Noah's head, each monochrome image peeled up from the paper and into something lifelike, breathing, peering at him through Lulal's twilight.

"This one has the bones we use for the lake research," Thuy said.

Irene had just circled the finalized depiction of the creature in question: the hairless, muscular body with six jointed limbs ending in thumbed feet drew in his attention first, but the snout and its protruding canine teeth sank into his stomach with a piercing unease.

"You hunt this?" Irene asked, frowning.

"No! No way. We've seen it only once, to be honest," Thuy sighed, collapsing in one of the lounge's armchairs. "It was already dead. All the bones we've used came from that one. The meat was good, better than the bush lizards we normally eat now… very bitter."

From where he sat, Noah studied the various sketches of Irene made of the xeno-organism, not just the final iteration; a through-line wove through all of them, recalling ghouls that crawled out of mirrors in horror films.

"It was right after our mimeos broke. We still had rice and some vegetables left, so Eun-Sook made bibimbap with it."

"You're talking about the creature with the resistant bones, correct?" No one had noticed Abelard's appearance at the bunk hall entrance, and he didn't wait for an answer nor an invitation to join them. He strode up to the coffee table and plucked Irene's notebook from her grasp. "Oh, this is an excellent rendering! I was having a solid bit of trouble picturing the feet. How fascinating! The evolutionary trail must be quite the trip…"

He made a sound like he was clearing his throat, as if suddenly aware that the rest of them were staring, but he only met Noah's gaze—the disquiet from Irene's drawing tensed with a cold pang, with nothing in Abelard's digital stare to prompt it.

"Mingyu said the bones in your equipment's protective contraption were what needed repairing, yes?"

"Um, yes," said Thuy. "We just haven't found another way that can survive in the lake. We had some industrial glues and tapes left from our original supplies, but—"

"What if we got you new bones?"

Thuy stuttered for a moment. "What?"

"Yes." Irene pointed at her, raising an eyebrow at Abelard. "I second this. Weren't we supposed to be finding alternatives?"

"We're supplemental hands," said Abelard, snapping the notebook shut. "Let us fix the problem, not merely bandage it."

When Thuy nudged in the fact that these xeno-organisms' teeth were of a concerning size, Noah excused himself from the conversation. There was an email from one of his xenozoology colleagues that had gone unanswered since before the mishap with Tristan, and that was a fine enough excuse. As he passed Abelard, he tugged the notebook from his vise grip and tossed it back to Irene, not pausing to catch the glance she spared his way as the pages fluttered in the air.

At least Abelard was keeping to Mingyu's plea to let the issue of leviathans drop, Noah told himself. Kept telling himself, even as they found other issues to warrant closed-door meetings that increasingly bled past those boundaries as the week wore on. Politics, Sovann relayed through Hinata, though the translation was several sentences shorter than what he'd originally said.

"It's got to be about repairs, right?" Quinn said at the mess trailer table. "Coordinate a cargo run with some spare mimeos and parts for your ship's backup life support, and you're set. They can't expect you to finish out your tour like this."

Hinata shrugged, rubbed the corner of his eye. "They've known, though. The only reason coordination would take so long is…" He trailed off, picking at the leftover mapo tofu from the night before.

There was a particular way, Noah had noticed, that Quinn pulled back a thought upon second guessing it, and he did so four times in a row. He went in for a fifth when the trailer door slammed open.

"Absolutely unacceptable!" Mingyu said. Abelard followed a steady two steps behind her as she paced around the table, toward the counters, and back again, finally pausing at the farthest corner from the door. "You satcall her office right now. I don't care what time it is on Natocke Station—"

"Rassawek, actually," said Abelard.

"Rassawek?" She tossed a glance toward Quinn and Noah before turning back. "You mean the person 'too busy to meet' isn't Petra Glenning, Colonel of TerraCosmos Special Projects, but—"

"Abraham and Eber, yes. Our mission reports to them."

"They're blowing us off!" she shouted. "Too busy? I swear—" She switched to Mandarin too rapid, apparently, for Abelard to track, though Sovann and Hinata nodded along. "Those two aren't even officially part of Khepri," she said in English. "Did you know that?"

She directed the question to Noah. "Maybe they are now…?" he ventured, but she'd pushed past Abelard, heading toward the door.

"I can try them again," Abelard said, and she paused with a hand on the doorknob.

"Don't bother…" She chuckled, humorless. "For all I know, those two have a hand in what those miners were doing here… and will send their replacements." Her hand slipped toward the rail gun at the small of her back, just for a moment, and then she stomped out into the twilight, Abelard following after a beat.

"You see?" Hinata said. "Politics."

"We made a promise, you know."

"*You* made a promise. You, by yourself."

On the second-to-last full day on Lulal, Noah found himself in the bowels of the *Amihaf*'s cargo hold, scanning the handwritten notes the Shēngdì staff had made on the wildlife as well as the samples they hadn't found uses for. It was the only space large enough with the right lighting and out of the way of the most trafficked thoroughfares; and while the ceiling was lower than Noah would have liked, it held onto the heat better than anywhere else at the camp.

"I spoke on behalf of the whole crew. Wasn't it you who said I was as close as we had to a captain?"

Noah swallowed the bubbling grumble. The tag of the sample he was logging was labeled with a writing system he couldn't locate in the spreadsheet software's presets, much less identify himself. He sighed, tugging the stylus from its slot, and it carried the last bits of the grumble before it turned flat.

"It *was* you, and not seven days ago. We both know this. And we both know it's in the best interest of—"

"I don't disagree, all right?" Noah's first pass at approximating the leftmost symbol had twice as many lumps in the curve than it needed. He tapped the undo button. "I just share the crew's… y'know, continued apprehension?"

"I thought you'd be more excited to encounter more xenofauna in their natural habitat."

"Abelard…"

"Noah." He waved a hand at the tablet waiting beside the mystery sample. "Put that away for a moment. Please. Come sit." He settled himself atop a large metal trunk opposite a box with refills of space-safe fire retardant. The box was just barely too tall for Noah to hop up without making it an ordeal, though Abelard's face betrayed nothing of the scramble.

They could have been seated in one of the lab storage rooms at Rassawek, surrounded by semi-organized mess and poor lighting fanning the fatigued ache in their marrow. The next trial would yield significant results, the next reading would uncover an anomaly, the next moment would shine upon the overlooked connection.

The next planet would soothe the anxieties still gnawing at his soft spots that refused to be named.

"Do you remember the first time we met?"

Classes wouldn't start for another week and the greater Rassawek area strained under drought, parched earth spitting up dust since mid-March. Climate control fizzled and choked in the older buildings, the xenosciences complex included. The window unit behind Abelard's desk moved air but didn't cool it, circulating the stain of stale body odor.

"Hard to forget a day that hot."

"But do you remember what you told me?"

At twenty-five years old, Noah still placed himself behind a pane of romanticism whenever he looked out toward the larger universe, aligning his footsteps in the prints left behind by the likes of Neil Armstrong and Laila Bhaduri. One first leap to the Moon, another first leap beyond the Kuiper

Belt. And then another leap beyond them, in step with an unknown footprint unlike anything seen on Earth. The details of that conversation had washed out of his memory in the years since, leaving only the shape of it, cavernous.

"I wanted to help push Earth forward to the next great milestone in xenobiology. And…" he sighed. "You took me at face value."

"Of course," said Abelard. "It's the best way to take anyone. Who was—or am—I to say otherwise?"

That day, as Noah sweated into the chair before Abelard's desk, the sun had crept into the window over his shoulder, pressing gold through the blinds that demanded he look anywhere else.

And what, Abelard had said, *does that 'next great milestone' look like? I doubt it's what you wrote about in your statement of purpose applying here.*

He was right of course. It wasn't that he found the mechanics and applications of Europan eel bioluminescence boring as much as a ghost of his childhood self was tugging on his pants leg, pointing at Abelard sitting mere feet away, attentive and genuinely invested.

"We're not bringing a live one back on the ship this time, right?" Noah asked, rolling a knuckle along the burgeoning line of a headache.

"Heavens, no. Just an excursion," he said, and his neck vents whirred with a short spike. "We retrieve the supplies Mingyu needs and our own set of samples, and we hike right back to base."

The proposition, as Noah relayed it to the rest of the *Amihaf,* was received about as well as Abelard could have hoped, at least with realistic expectations applied. Quinn insisted on staying behind to continue troubleshooting with Hinata, while Frida had already arranged for Iseul to show her around some other mycological mysteries Shēngdì hadn't had time to do more than acknowledge.

And so it came to be that the six remaining among them stood on the faintest hint of a path winding into the forest at whatever counted as high noon on a planet squeezed too tightly by gravity to spin. The shadows cast by the angled light painted the scene before them in patches of dark plum among the sunspotted magentas. The exposed metal of Abelard's ConBod glinted with a narrow spark of bronze where he stood, where the Lulalan canopy pulled apart to a natural skylight. Hands on hips, he stared into the dark, paying no mind to the underbrush crunched by jittering feet or the tapping of Dayo's fingers against the first aid kit or Irene's teeth pressing into the casing of her pen.

"Did Dr. Thuy say what this creature had been named?" he asked.

"She didn't, no." Noah exchanged a glance with Savannah as he chose his next words. "Another issue of resources, I think."

On his other side, Esmail stood on his tiptoes to peer over Irene's shoulder —she had started sketching some angular form evoking the description Thuy had given.

"Did she say how, um… big it was?" Savannah asked.

"Nope," said Irene.

"It's just—I've seen your drawings, and I've seen the broken bones in the lab and… you're sure? No hint at the size?"

"Nope."

"Great. Wonderful."

The path forward was far less defined than the trail they'd used on Shala, with towering ferns leaning over the narrow line of tamped soil winding deeper into the thicket. It forced them into single file, Abelard leading the charge; he insisted that Noah take the second spot, and Savannah was liable to bite through her favorite pen if she couldn't latch onto the strap of Noah's knapsack.

"You didn't have to come," he murmured over his shoulder after half an hour. "Everyone would have understood."

"No way. I want to see the plant with eyes that Eun-Sook was going on about."

Behind her, Dayo sucked at her teeth. "I sure don't."

"Ooh," said Esmail, further to the back. "What about that globby animal? Do you think it'd feel like gelatin? Or would it poison you before you could register the jiggle?"

From the rear, a position they chose only to cut short the argument over it, Irene sighed loud enough to give herself room to speak. "Thuy said nothing about poison."

"Lost opportunity, then!"

"Not how that works," called Noah.

Savannah swore under her breath and grabbed at his knapsack with a renewed strength.

Through it all, voiced frets and odd musings and everything in between, Abelard remained silent while his haphazard steps landed on every brittle twig and rock in his path. The baseline level of apprehension simmering under Noah's skin since Jupiter crested and ebbed in waves, even now—the bruise at his elbow had disappeared, but if he squinted in the right light, the discoloration rose again along the edges of bone.

The path soon delivered them to a small clearing, an oval carpet of mosses dotted with ferns and grasses that rose to an abrupt, jagged end far shorter than the thickness of the leaves implied. The trees along the edges grew closer together, and the more wiry specimens looped around the trunks and branches of their thicker neighbors. If the trail continued on through the clearing, the head of it had been overgrown.

"I want to take some pictures of the trees," Savannah said, tugging on Noah's knapsack. "Could you—"

"Sure, yeah." He let her guide him toward the largest truck at the clearing's border while keeping an eye on Abelard, who strode through the sparse shoots of grass with his hands clasped behind his back, every so often reaching down to inspect the broken tips and leaving it to everyone else to uncover the next leg of the hike.

"This is wild." Savannah gently prodded at the trunk of one of the curving trees with her thumbnail—leaves further down the specimen rustled at the pressure, but the structure of the trunk didn't visibly give, even despite its narrow diameter. "It's not touching the larger tree at all. Completely unattached, and it still keeps a consistent distance…"

Her grin spread wide around the pen she'd stuck back between her molars, an uncomplicated sense of focused awe he'd only seen during dissertation breakthroughs. Her hold on his backpack dropped without hesitation to direct the tablet camera, scribble notes in the margin—

And then Savannah shrieked.

She jumped back into Noah, who only kept his footing thanks to a lucky patch of moss that could support his weight. When he looked toward the trees, a gelatinous oozing creature had wrapped its body along the coiling path of the trunk, stretched thin like taffy. The head, or at least the frontmost part of its body, held its position as the rear traveled over the loops. The final, condensed result was about the size of a shoebox.

"I'm easily startled, okay?" Savannah said to the barrage of imagined questions.

The creature stretched the front of its body toward them through the closest gap, twisting this way and that as if it were examining them with a curious head tilt.

"Touch it!" Esmail called from the other end of the clearing.

Noah spotted a twig near the toe of his boot but nudged it away. "Considering how our last major encounter with a xeno-organism went…"

"Good point. Don't touch it!"

Dayo's shoulders sagged in relief.

If he wasn't going to touch it, all that was left was for Noah to attempt some diplomacy. "Hi there." His wave was hesitant, and the ooze didn't react. He took a quick survey—in the tinted light, the creature appeared a shade of violet-magenta like most of the biome, the curves shining in a matte finish. "Your home is lovely."

Something rippled through its body, its front stretching another few inches closer to where Noah stood—but a cry warbled up from the underbrush, and a blink later, the creature had disappeared.

Noah scanned the scene before them for any signs of where it might have slithered off to. The forest held its breath, the quiet broken once more with the distant snapping of twigs and another wail, louder this time, strained, the sound tearing against vocal cords as it climbed toward the open air.

Esmail kept his gaze fixed on the tree border as they all slowly gathered together at the center of the clearing. "Did Thuy mention if this creature we're after made a noise?"

"We all remember her saying they found it dead, right?" Irene's voice didn't waver, but she was making slow deliberate work securing her notebook back in her bag.

Even the ambient chorus of the ecosystem around them had fallen silent; that, or Noah's own shallow, hushed breathing had condensed the reach of his hearing to the bodies huddled around him. Dayo's feet against the moss, Irene's intermittent gulps, Esmail's hands flexing in and out of fists, Savannah's—

"My pen!" she whispered. "Where's my pen?"

The moment played back in slow motion, her scream at the sudden appearance of the ooze, mouth flung wide, pen tumbling down to the moss bed until it landed like a tilted stake among the rhizoids.

Sure enough, he spotted the pen buried in the moss halfway up the jelly grip. His first step out from their huddle squelched louder than he liked, but the planet was far from collapsing under its weight. He bounded across the clearing, never allowing his feet more contact with the earth than was necessary to propel him farther forward. Squelching fell to a minimum. Savannah's pen found its place in his grasp.

And then the cry returned—the cry, and then a dramatic rustle of leaves, nails digging and dragging into wood. Louder and louder, it slid closer to the clearing until the reverberations were shaking the last ferns still intact at the edge.

While he still had his wits about him, Noah shoved the pen in his knapsack.

He cut the moment close. As the zipper shut, the ferns at the rightmost edge of his vision parted to reveal a pale, wrinkled snout with one of its protruding black teeth broken in half. Its front limbs spread wide—one propped high against the thick trunk, the other latched tight around the ropy stretch wrapped around a wider branch—and the eyeless face surveyed the clearing, all the people staring back.

Its breathing came in heavy puffs, working up to more of its plaints. A gluey burble of blood dripped down its broken tooth as it howled, limbs spidering it up the border of the ferns, just inside the clearing, and then scuttling under an umbrella of foliage draped over—

"The trail head!" Abelard gasped. "The chase is on!"

He ran after it, bursting through a curtain of ferns and leaving half-broken stems in his wake.

"Abelard!" Noah took a couple stuttering steps, paused, turned back toward the gallery of shocked faces.

"He's coming back, right?" Esmail said.

"I don't—*fuck*, stay here, okay?"

"Noah, wait—"

Whatever else Savannah yelled at him died under the sudden resurgence of sound, all the croaks and buzzes and melodic arias that were three steps too removed to pass as anything familiar. As he ran after Abelard on the narrowing path, the noise fought to stifle his thoughts, bury them with their wrongness, as if the planet had trapped Noah in the nadir of the uncanny valley and started to dig.

He was left with two discrete thoughts rattling in his head: *get to Abelard, stay on the path.* They could survive under the cacophonous onslaught—until the trail tapered further, barely spanning the width of a single boot. This might not have been the path at all, just some aberrant stretch of soil too blighted for anything to grow. And if that were the case—

"Shit..." As he slowed, his breathing came in wheezing gasps; he crouched, tucked in on himself, pressing the heels of his palms over his ears. His side clenched in pain—a stitch from being out of shape, or old rib damage from binding, or a nasty Lulalan bug bite? No time to investigate now. When his knees began to complain, he unfurled himself, and not even the forest could hide their crackling as he regained his bearings.

The trees were denser this far in, roots roping over each other and tangling around the stalks of other plants claiming the dwindling empty space. The gaps between the trunks that he could peer through were too thin to do more than hint at what laid beyond what he'd assumed was the trail. Thin stretches of bare soil sat wherever he looked, maybe another path, maybe not.

You could die here.

It was the same sneering voice that used to creep in after the worst nights in Erie finally ebbed and left his ears ringing. A new refrain for a new age, a new planet.

Now it only made him realize he no longer knew which direction on the trail led back to the clearing.

You will likely die here.

"No. No. That's not going to happen."

The forest answered him with a grating screech that seemed to come from every direction at once.

"There is only so far I can get on foot. There'd be, what… thirteen people in my search party? That's a lot, right?" He nodded to himself. "It's definitely not nothing."

The longer he waited for the heading to announce itself, the closer the noise pressed against his eardrums. It pressed against his eardrums and it pressed at his very bones. Something at the corner of his eye shifted, maybe another ooze, maybe something else that no one on the planet had been able to document yet.

Noah waited, and his chest burned.

He waited longer, tense.

And then winding through the leafy canopy came Abelard's voice, trying to soothe some unknown force—off to the left, and the path underfoot leaned in that direction. So he ran, wincing every time his breath shot through with pain until it was something he could ignore.

He rounded a curve hugging the border of an enormous tree and found himself in another clearing, smaller than the one he'd left by half, and his boots uprooted the moss underfoot as he stumbled to avoid running directly into Abelard's back.

"Abelard—"

"Shh…"

Biting his tongue, Noah surveyed the rest of the clearing and found the creature collapsed on the forest floor, writhing in pain, blood oozing from a long gash in its torso as well as an orifice that might have approximated a nose. "You followed it all the way here, then?"

"I did. You know, the most ancient humans were endurance hunters. Our ancestors could track and follow prey until it was too exhausted to do little more than crumple and wait to die."

The creature's breathing came in labored huffs as its head turned toward them. Another trill rose up its throat; when it sounded, pitch tilted up in agony, Noah thought of Tristan, their own screeching pleas as Abelard escorted them to their death.

"What's your angle here?" Noah asked after a moment.

"Well… the bones are intact, from what I can tell. The injuries didn't arise from anything breaking."

"Wh—no, that's not…" He took a few tentative steps toward the creature, waiting for its hackles to raise or its claws to dig into the soil and moss.

"The plan wasn't to find one and wait for it to die. This… it could still recover. We don't know—"

Abelard spun on his heels, bursting Noah's bubble of space with little warning. The hot whirring of his ConBod crossed the narrow gap between them. "Noah, Noah…" He grinned, his body aligning itself, straightening, as if the mechanics were trying to imitate breathing. "Dr. Starbuck," he finally sighed. "Everything is fine."

His hands hovered over Noah's shoulders for a moment before settling. Each finger pressed one by one into his flesh—not as forcefully as Noah knew they could, but enough to flare up a reminder. Not necessarily on purpose, he told himself.

"Our friend over there isn't exactly having a *fine* time."

"I'm tangible proof that occasionally our work can be messy."

"Are we part of the same conversation right now?"

"Of course!" Abelard's hands squeezed, earning a flicker of a wince he didn't appear to register.

Behind him, the creature cried—a gasping, desperate thing that sent whatever lived in the canopy scrambling for cover. It lasted longer than the weary body should have been capable of, until it subsumed every other sound in its own, until every atom struck by the clamoring waves rang with a resonance that turned Noah's stomach on end.

And then it stopped.

"Exciting, isn't it?" Abelard released his hold and sauntered to where the creature laid among the moss.

Noah half-collapsed, propping himself on his knees as the dry heaves clenched up his throat. "Can we please head back to base? Thuy will understand."

"Look at the musculature…" A single finger traced a line down the creature's pale body, smearing through the blood instead of weaving around it. "The limbs… and—my word, how do you suppose its sensory system operates? I see a potential nose but no eyes or ears…you remember the encounter earlier, of course. It could clearly register its surroundings…"

From the underbrush ahead, past any point that could be considered a continuation of the trail, came the unmistakable percussion of twigs cracking under the weight of footsteps. Gradually the foliage began to shiver.

"Abelard, we need to go."

He didn't glance up from his careful consideration of the body before him, the trembling twitching sinew under the skin, as he rounded the creature's rear and re-approached its head from the other side. Noah stepped closer, then again, hesitant. He still hadn't grown totally accustomed to the lighting, and he couldn't tell if Abelard's digital eye displays had turned their irises black or if it was just a bad angle, a bad shadow, a bad thesis tricking itself into existence.

"*Abelard.*"

Again ignored. As the bodiless rumbling grew ever closer, Noah rushed forward, meeting Abelard on the other side of the creature. His arms stuttered in aborted attempts to gesture him away.

"Watch your eyes," said Abelard.

Noah hardly had time to consider the words before Abelard's hand rose from behind his back with Mingyu's rail gun. The barrel of it landed at a pulsing spot of its neck—*bang!*—and then at the crown of its skull—*bang!*

Searing heat rose across Noah's face in a gushing, roiling anger like he'd rarely felt, pushing his limbs forward with unthinking recklessness. Only after he'd wrenched the gun from Abelard's grasp could he absorb the full breadth of the scene. The creature, dead, its head leaking blood and bits of brain matter into the moss; Abelard staring at him with a bemused slant of an expression; the rest of the creature's herd or pack or family slotting their heads forward through the flora, quiet, taking in the rising stink of gore.

"What the fuck," Noah murmured. "Why?"

Abelard maneuvered over to the other side of the dead body with the grin Noah had come to associate with the friendly discourse of office hours. "What do you mean?"

Noah stomped after him. "What do I—you killed it! You killed it and it didn't need to die!"

As soon as Abelard had put sufficient distance between the two of them and the body, the rest of the creature's clan nudged forth into the clearing. They poked at the corpse with their feet, the ends of their snouts. Low whimpers rose from deep in their chests, some nestling against the bloody torso as others unfurled talons to strip the nearby trees of bark. The feeblest of the newcomers lifted the deceased's skull with its frontmost foot and began a low rhythmic melody that the others idle among them recognized with a snout tilted toward the sky.

Noah's knees shook as he took it all in—the creatures' ritual, and Abelard's inert, inquisitive smile.

"Science, as you should well know," Abelard said, "demands sacrifices."

"No! No—do you remember before you left Rassawek, you scolded me for killing a tiny little spider that had gotten into your office. You said every living being matters—"

"On Earth, Noah! On *Earth.*" His grip reasserted itself on his shoulders, digging in with abandon as the plaintive cry of the herd shot through the canopy. "Our planet almost died, us along with it. That we managed to stabilize it at all was a miracle, and that feat isn't even four hundred fifty years old. 'Stable' isn't 'thriving.' We could backslide into extinction at any moment—"

"What did this have to do with—"

"Consider this: would you rather live forever or die? That is what is at stake here. You and your name, the bastion of our species—"

"This animal didn't need to die!"

"What if it did?"

"I—" Noah choked on the jam of words fighting their way to the front of the queue. "No."

"It dies. We deliver the bones to Thuy and the rest of the base. They make a discovery that revolutionizes the status of Project Khepri across the globe and returns hope to a blighted region in Europe or the Testudines—"

"You can't believe that," Noah said, voice trembling. A pressure had settled on his breastbone, relentless, the pain radiating to every extremity. "You're a biologist. You value life."

Over Abelard's shoulder, the creature's clan gathered around its body, pressing hands to its stilled form. Curled strips of tree bark, now adorned in careful markings, laid across its spine.

"It's one life," he said. "One against all humans. One against the fate of our planet."

An atonal chord rumbled from the gathering beside them.

"It's not that dramatic. It's never—I won't be a part of this." Noah's fists tightened, dull fingernails digging into his palms. Glancing away from Abelard's eye displays, he snagged the attention of one of the mourners; eyeless, it still zeroed in on where Noah stood, the hold of its head indicating some level of recognition. Noah nodded to it, nodded again to the whole of the gathering, and followed the trail back to Shēngdì alone.

The path took him through the first clearing, to where he'd left much of the *Amihaf* crew to wait. They cheered his arrival, however short, and he tried to ignore how quickly they fell quiet.

"Hey, hey," said Dayo. "What happened?"

Esmail cupped his hands over his mouth. "*Ay khoda,* Noah-*joon*—"

"Okay, so maybe things didn't go according to plan," Savannah murmured, grabbing his elbow with Irene close behind. "Spill."

He searched for words and none came. Savannah's warm brown eyes implored, shining with worry, so he did what he could—he reached around to the zipper of his knapsack and clasped her pen into her awaiting palm. He nodded. He tried to shake away the strained questions held in the press of her brow.

With another nod, he turned back toward the path to Shēngdì.

However long later, the trees and ferns retreated from his side. The trailers and the *Amihaf* loomed ahead. His feet rang on the entrance ramp, in the lower-level foyer between the cockpit and lab, and then finally on the rungs of stairs to the upper floor. He operated on autopilot, deftly ignoring Frida and her latest crossword puzzle in the lounge.

Noah dragged himself into his bunk, then to the cramped corner that comprised his personal bathroom.

The man staring back at him in the mirror had a face splattered with blood.

SIX

FROM: BROWN, SAVANNAH

To: Starbuck, Noah

Subject: I started watching Star Trek

You were right! It's old as hell but it's a really great—okay yes, I baited you. Esmail helped me figure out the exact number of characters before the text preview cut off, but since you've already opened this... I know you know what I want to say, I won't waste time saying it. Anyway, Dayo wants to do an exam and she wasn't sure if you'd open a message from her.

A few other paragraphs continued below, but Noah minimized the window without even skimming them, uncovering the baseball episode of *Deep Space Nine* on pause. Not even one full rotation through his playlist of personal favorites since leaving Lulal and already someone was banging on his virtual door.

It was a good trick, the particular tweaks in the email: a solid hook with the right sender overriding any self-imposed email ban he could conjure. Dozens of other messages languished unread in his inbox, from department newsletters to journal subscriptions to well-meaning undergrads asking after office hours, unaware he was off-planet. The breadth of the ban covered wide swaths of territory. It was enough for certain sorts of messages to be swept up in the crowd, a plausibly-deniable oversight until he decided how to play it off.

Three such emails, as it turned out, were three too many.

And those three too many, not even counting Savannah's, turned the neutral gaze of Captain Sisko on his tablet screen into something accusatory.

The clock in his bunk read 2245 IST, but Noah ventured forth into the lounge. An excuse hovered behind his teeth about having missed dinner in case of an interrogation.

The only person lingering in the garlicky post-meal miasma was Dayo, scrolling through some article that was quickly abandoned when he emerged from the dark of the bunk hall. "Hey, stranger."

"Quite the ruse with the email."

She shrugged, entirely betrayed by the smirk inching its way across her face. The golden yellow of her pajama shirt and bonnet left her glowing like the ship's personal sun. "Pretty good, wasn't it? Come on." She hopped up and headed toward the stairs. "The exam part wasn't a lie. I do actually want to check some things."

Her slippers padded down the steps as she led him to the med bay, and she busied herself with preparing equipment, securing gloves, and then triple checking that the door, after it slid shut, was locked from the inside.

"Okay, so the exam is maybe overkill, but we can do two things at once," she said, fatigue leaking into her voice. "It was *definitely* overkill for Savannah, but…"

"This is the only way to hide that you're having a secure conversation, isn't it?"

Dayo nodded, then launched into an explanation on the numerous studies on the effects of xenobiological materials on humans if they make it into the bloodstream or past a mucus membrane. "I didn't have a chance to catch all the places the blood got you," she said. "Most of the time there weren't any noticeable issues, but that wasn't the case with the transgender participants with hormone replacement devices."

A blip of panic lumped in his throat, and he instinctively coughed to try to dislodge it. "I don't think that's overkill," he finally managed. "Wasn't exactly paying attention if any went in my mouth or nose."

"Don't worry. It's a simple check, and catching it early makes it easier to flush out."

Noah forced himself to focus on the white-tinted sheen of her bonnet under the lights as the hemograph scanned the base of his skull. Her other hand checked the lymph nodes in his neck, and after fixing the device in the crook of his elbow to take a blood sample, she set it aside and flopped into the room's only other chair.

"Am I good?"

"We'll know in a few minutes." The long sleeves of her sleep shirt were stretched from age, a few steps short of threadbare, easily tugged over her hands. She bundled the pulled fabric into her fists, staring at the many corners of the oddly-shaped room.

"Dayo?"

She didn't look away from the farthest end of the ceiling, just to the side of Noah's head.

"Did Abelard say anything when he came back? Did he bring anything with him?"

When their eyes met, it landed like a kick in his stomach. "He had nothing. No bones, no updates. Just headed the charge back to base. He did pull Mingyu and Thuy aside for a chat, not sure what about exactly, but in a general sense it wasn't hard to guess."

Around them sang the hum of turbolight, punctuated by the beeping hemograph on the counter.

"Right."

"Noah…"

So he told her—the chase, the scene as he found it, the wails and the clan hemming in the ailing body they were called to, Abelard's insistence and the ammo shredding veins. The more he spoke, a numbness crept through his limbs, chills settling into his fingertips even as the core of him flushed against the—what? He couldn't readily identify it, its heat churning as he sat, motionless, before Dayo's expectant gaze.

"We need to tell the rest of the crew about this," she said.

"I know. It's just…" He sighed, all the troubles following them from Lulal sprouting up around them all like toadstools—too many to cradle in his arms at once, so he plucked the ones in reach. "We should discuss it in person, together. The medical exam excuse isn't going to work for seven of us at the same time. I don't know if we'd even fit."

"Agreed on all counts." The hemograph trilled on the counter, and she rose to retrieve it. "At least nothing's wrong with you physically," she said, waving the device. "A win in a sea of—well, garbage. But to your point…"

She leaned against the counter, elbows balanced against the dull metal surface as she paused to consider a flickering overhead light. There was a hint of dark circles under her eyes that definitely didn't feature in his memories of her on Natocke or Ushuaia Station, before the mission burst into a thousand different threads.

"Are you all right?"

"Oh... you know, dandy." The only downside of her smile's usual brilliance was that it was impossible to fake. "Just about as well as anyone else is."

"I've been a hermit the past few days. I can guess, but my frame of reference is a little outdated."

She nodded, slowly, mostly to herself. "Mingyu and I had a long satcall with Ikemba about the mining camp. They'd hit a five-year ban from the Board for violating a contract's environmental clauses, turns out. But he seemed... it was weird." Further details as she chewed at her lip. If he wanted to press, he could look elsewhere. "Anyway," she said, "do you think Quinn would know where else on the ship might be secure?'"

Out of all of them, he was the best bet, and Noah told her as much. At that point, the exam was over. They could whisper and plan later without the grit of fatigue under their eyelids.

Noah's bed held no residual warmth from his earlier burrowing. He powered down his tablet and threw it aside without any care toward the files pleading for attention he couldn't give.

Sleep came fitfully, if at all, for the rest of the night, leaving him stinging-eyed and groggy during the normal morning bustle. As much as the basest parts of his brain begged him, Noah knew he couldn't hide out in his bunk the entire journey to the Tau Ceti system. Those parts could be reasoned with, were amenable to compromise, so with half a half hour of morning to spare, Noah dragged himself into the galley for a mimeo coffee. A dense fog had settled into his thought space, a state perfectly content to watch the edges of two sugar cubes recede through the steam. The entire upper level of the ship and its emptiness enveloped him in its silence, a slow transition back into existing among the crew.

"Wow, you look *awful*. Can I ask you a question?"

Or not.

He took a few steps backward to crane his head around the corner into the lounge, where Frida sat on the armchair with her legs thrown over the back, a tablet propped up in her lap. The chair's upholstery was a sickly sort of blue that camouflaged her jeans and navy t-shirt enough that Noah didn't kick himself for not spotting her.

"Is the question related to me looking awful?"

"Oh. No," she said, frowning and twisting herself around to standing. The shirt was another odd screenprint job, this time featuring yellow line art of a potato with *HINALLATAPAS* arced above it. "With you nowhere to be found and Savannah consulting on the live fungus sample I took from Lulal, she's been telling me things more personal than usual—she always have weird dreams?"

"Um." He retrieved his mug and returned to his station at the dividing wall, sipping at the coffee even though the sugar was still mostly undissolved. The acrid taste clenched at this tongue but pieces from the web of fog started to break apart. "Not any weirder than anyone else's, based on what she's told me. If you want a better sample size, ask her wife."

Her frown indicated she would not be making a satcall to Tracy Liu any time soon. "You're the next best thing. I'm sure you've heard that before."

"No comment."

"What do you have to say about Abelard turning into a pyramid and then Savannah kicking the shit out of him?"

"Uh—"

"Yeah, exactly. That's what I said."

There was a lot else Frida had to say, and Noah managed to excuse himself just as Esmail emerged to retrieve his prayer rug from the corner. His feet shepherded him to the stairs before the sniping could started in earnest. Not that he or any of them could escape it—the *Amihaf* was too small for that, but they'd all learned to pretend otherwise.

The first face he spotted was Quinn's, turned briefly toward his footfalls as he descended. He returned to the laptop balanced on the ends of his knees by that same maintenance closet, waving in Noah's general direction. On the other side of the ship's foyer, through the lab door window, Savannah and Dayo huddled together over some unseen specimen on the table before them.

"That same thing's still giving you trouble?"

Quinn grumbled, a hand rising to fiddle with his earlobe, where Noah spotted an old, unfilled piercing hole as he came to lean against the jamb to the antechamber. "It shouldn't be this hard to track down."

The laptop screen was split between two windows, one dark with block white text of gibberish, and the other crowded with lists and lists of menus. He scrolled through the lists, expanding and collapsing sections seemingly at random, then jumping over to the other window to type another few lines of nonsense, hitting enter, breath held by a bitter tense of his jaw.

The laptop beeped in error, and Quinn's worry lines folded over themselves.

"It's not even the logging issue I'm concerned about anymore," he said after swallowing whatever string of curses had rushed up his throat. "Not directly.

There's something larger going on behind the scenes, and that's what's playing hard to get."

He elaborated with the kinds of technical details Noah couldn't hope to follow, tossing around obscure types of files and scripts, third-party software tools whose version numbers ranged from betas to quadruple digits. "Even with the clear errors, my smoke tests aren't failing, and I would run one of those new timber scripts but it doesn't work with this OS…" He sighed. "I might as well be speaking Te Reo to you, *nē*?"

Noah shrugged. "I knew some of those words."

"That's something."

"I guess." He stepped toward the wall just behind Quinn's perch. "You've got to have at least some suspects, though. Right?" he added.

Quinn sighed again. His hands tapped across the keyboard, sifting through the slew of open windows on-screen. "Hard to find any in all this mess," he said. "The security architecture did have a weird alert a while back, but I was in the middle of reconfiguring some of the local servers. I was thinking the file it had in quarantine had been there before we took off and the configs reactivated the ping on it, but… there's ten other things tugging at my sleeve, y'know?"

Closer to the cockpit, Noah heard Irene puttering around near the navigation computer, murmuring under her breath—which meant the only one of the crew unaccounted for was Abelard. Amid all the definites and provens reinforcing the chokehold on Noah's lungs, not knowing where Abelard was lurking on the ship was what burned deepest.

"Got another question for you," Noah said. "Unrelated this time."

"All right. Hit me."

"Privacy mandates mean that the ship's med bay is extra soundproofed and also unconnected from most of the comms tech, right?"

"Yeah." He shifted in his seat to shoot him a questioning frown. "Why?"

"Are there any other spots on the ship like that?"

Quinn let out a noise that was a cross between a sigh and a low whistle, sneaking glances at another window that had sprung up on the laptop screen, strings of text jetting down and down and down until it was rendered a choppy blur. "Maybe. Why?"

"I was talking to Dayo," he said. Quinn's gaze sat expectant, and the *Amihaf* with all its bells and whistles and open-channeled, hackable ears trained in on him, just as expectant, pressure threatening to spill over into a migraine. "And she was telling me how the med bay can only hold so many people."

"Uh-huh."

"It's, um…" A wheel in his head spun uselessly. He hadn't anticipated that last hint not spelling out what he was trying to communicate. "We—"

"No offense, mate, but I've really got to drill down on this while I'm in a groove." He motioned to a few particular lines of code, or whatever it was. "There's a few more tests I want to run before breaking out the battering rams, some debugging plug-ins stashed in the cargo hold."

His eyebrows rose a half inch straight up his forehead, holding Noah's gaze in a vise grip.

"All right?" Quinn said after a moment.

"Oh—uh, yeah, yeah." Noah flashed two thumbs-up that collapsed into half-hearted pointing in Quinn's general direction, all as he tried to lean into a retreat. "I understand."

"You do?" It shouldn't have been possible for his eyebrows to reach any higher, but apparently no one had ever told them no.

"Absolutely."

His first real step backward nearly sent him tripping over his own ankle, the flush of unbalanced panic shifting seamlessly into plain old embarrassment the way Quinn fought to stifle his grimace. At least Savannah couldn't witness the spectacle from the lab.

Tossing a thank you over his shoulder, Noah spun on his tiptoes and leapt up the stairs, hopefully before the flush settled into something that more closely resembled a sunburn. Frida and Esmail hadn't moved from where he left them—the subject had shifted to the use of vacuum leviathans in some art house film from twenty years ago. Neither of them paid him any mind, hidden as he was behind either the gleam of enthusiasm or agonized ennui.

It was just as well. Something in his stomach had started to curdle; he fixed himself another mug of coffee by the mimeo and secured himself in the relative peace behind his bunk door.

Sweetheart, I know you told me not to do this, but after going so long without hearing from you, I called up Justin to see if you were just too buried in your research... When were you going to tell us that you two had broken up? And more importantly, when were you going to tell us that you were going to be spending the next few years off-planet? It's one thing that you moved halfway down the coast, but lightyears away? What is it now? Your father and I deserve some answers.

Still, I hope you're well, as far away as you are. Your father's back is acting up again, and you know how Major doesn't listen to anyone but him. It's been an ordeal trying to get him outside with how old he is, but I've managed. The building's also had some work done after the winter rains so the lobby flooding shouldn't be so bad this year.

If you can spare a moment from your interstellar adventures, we'd love to hear from our son.

Love you,

Mom

If anyone else on the crew had eyes inside his bunk at that moment, Noah would have fed them a story about how he'd meant to toss the tablet to the end corner of his bed, how he misjudged the distance. It wasn't his intention to send it spinning into the shelves on the far wall, folding a dent into the corner. He'd played softball in high school, and sometimes his fingers reverted to old habits, weaving in a boost where it was better off without them.

But he was alone. There was no one to hold out a tray for a spoonful of placating lies, only himself and the memory of gym class softball games when he found himself pitching and the girl at bat shrank from the zipping approach of the ball.

Maybe history repeated itself, maybe it mirrored. The tablet landed on one of the empty shelves below Spock's roost, the end of a pitch with no one to flinch away.

Something like that.

He was tired. The thought didn't have to make perfect sense.

In the hall, Esmail and Quinn chatted about a hike they'd taken together years back. The fondness in their voices poured through the door; his eyes slid out of focus and his ears couldn't follow. Couldn't, and refused to—so when their warmth faded, he knew they'd stepped into the lounge.

"I had a good run, Spock."

The figurine had fallen to its side from the impact of the tablet, but was otherwise perfectly stoic.

"I mean, yes, aside from calling Justin before Lulal and BCC'ing him on those emails. You're right."

Spock's eyes bored into him, unblinking. Noah stared back, his throat catching as he once again saw the dying creature in the forest, its six legs shuddering against the planet's gravity.

"Okay, okay... fine." Noah shoved the tablet into his back pocket and repositioned the figurine in its corner so it was sitting upright.

As soon as he entered the common area, the bustle of activity around the mess table froze—the rest of the crew, aside from Abelard and Irene, huddled over Frida's dedicated crossword tablet, various kitchen utensils tucked under their arms.

"Good!" Dayo said over her shoulder. "You finally showed up!"

"What did I miss?"

"A birthday," Quinn said. He stood the furthest from the huddle's center. "I've been able to figure out that much."

Irene's thirty-fourth, apparently, and it was imperative they baked her a surprise cake during her daily rounds in the cockpit with the navigation computer. They hadn't yet agreed on a recipe, much less if the two-hour window was enough time.

"Don't you think she can hear all this from the cockpit?" Esmail wondered aloud. "The stairs aren't that soundproof—"

Groaning, Frida dragged her hands over her face and streaking lenses of her glasses. "That's not the point!"

"You just said it *needs* to be a surprise!"

Noah quickly edged away from the unspooling argument and its now-familiar beats of escalation. Savannah, too, pulled back and soon barricaded herself behind a wall of supplies, muttering about the need for frosting no matter the cake. She squinted down at her own tablet and the dozens of open tabs in the browser while her trusty pen held its vigil between her teeth. She didn't notice him sit down beside her.

"You good?"

"Did you know," she said, "that mimeos can't make powdered sugar? Regular sugar, brown sugar, sugar substitutes, all fine. Powdered? Nope. Not happening. It's because it's not pure sugar, technically—"

"Savannah."

"—it's part cornstarch too, which we can get, but you know what we don't have on this ship? Something to cut the mimeo sugar grains down to the right size. And every kind of frosting uses powdered sugar, and I am *not* telling Frida before I come up with a backup plan." Her head flopped onto the table, hair settling in a curly halo, muffling her voice as she grumbled back to life. "Is a jelly or jam a good substitute?"

"You know I'm the last person to ask about diverting from a recipe." He patted her shoulder, then again when she lifted her head to shoot him a petulant scowl. "What? You do."

She sighed. "You didn't come here to relieve my sugar woes, did you?"

"Well, no. But I can multitask." He poured out a mound of sugar in front of him and laid the flat end of a spoon on a thin layer of it. He brought his palm down with a crunch, again and again until there was nothing left to audibly crack. "We can powder it manually."

"Debatable," said Savannah. But she still reached for a shallow ladle, scooping away half the sugar pile between them. "We need three cups, by the way."

"Of course we do." He could already tell his arms were going to be sore the next morning.

"Also, if you don't fess up why you're still lingering when…"

The background argument had tumbled into new territory, one defined by Frida's gesticulating toward Quinn with a thick, unwinding skein of his yarn. Esmail watched on, mouth pressed thin, having slotted a few extra feet of distance between him and it all.

Savannah didn't look up but still cocked an eyebrow.

"Yeah, so…" sighed Noah. "My parents emailed me."

The crunch under Savannah's ladle hesitated, a pause so slight he almost missed it. "Go on."

"Justin got the honor of dropping the double bombshell of our breakup and my current whereabouts, so it's not my *favorite* thing in my inbox."

"Mhm."

"I guess it's better than more of that forwarded bullshit about loosening weapons bans or this summer's march on Nacotchtank or whatever else the neotrads are going on about now…" He sighed again, grinding down more of the sugar under his spoon. "I mean…"

He cast a sidelong glance toward Savannah and her laser-keen concentration on the angle of her ladle against the sugar. They were sitting in the galley of the *Amihaf,* but also in the late-night cafe in the undergrad dorms, and a secluded corner of the library's lowest level of old stacks, and the sagging sofa in Savannah and Tracy's living room—the same conversation stamped across all their overlapping years.

"It's not like they can hop on the train and show up at your door now," she said after a few moments.

"I just don't know—"

"Noah. Listen." She gently set down the ladle and stared him straight in the eyes. "We're in space. I love you. Both stupidly obvious. But you and your parents have had this same basic conflict so many times that I don't know how you don't know what to—this isn't new."

On the other side of the galley, the mimeo beeped for Dayo's attention, begging after a third hand she didn't have. Frida and Quinn had skewered their yarn argument with an odd political bent that wove so tacitly between the lines that it tangled up in his head. Suddenly his mouth was a tacky sort of dry. "I left the Solar System on a years-long mission without telling them. That's new."

"It's a wonky branch out of the same tree, my friend."

He needed to take a walk, the kind that the *Amihaf* couldn't allow, but he shot to his feet anyway, banging his knees on the underside of the table on the way up, and then more pairs of eyes settled on him as the noise faded to nothing.

"You too, huh?" Frida said with a jerk of her chin. "The fuck's going on with you?"

He tried clearing his throat, but even that was too loud. "Fight with my parents. Didn't tell them I was doing this."

"Hm!" She tossed the yarn skein at Quinn with a casual flip of the wrist, and he scrambled to catch it. "A fight with your parents! Oh, *boo hoo*, join the fucking crowd—"

Behind her, Esmail frowned. "Frida…"

If Noah's face hadn't gone numb, surely he would have sensed it burning.

"Shit, who goes on an assignment like this if they've a good thing going with the rock we call home?" Her arms flung wide, stretched to the very limit. "Maybe I'm just projecting, but on the other hand—" She caught sight of Quinn holding his thumb and first finger close together in a wince. "Sod off, Kaiwhakatere."

Noah was halfway down the stairs before Quinn had time to react.

The noise cranked back up within seconds, little of it muffled by the layer of metal and wires and pipes between them; and while it wasn't the calm afforded by his bunk he let himself stand before the ship's foyer and sink into the emptiness of the surrounding halls. Trillions of miles away from Earth, a distance further than any flesh-and-blood human could ever hope to conceptualize, with the vast nothingness of deep space stretching on past the borders of the ship reducing the inconceivable trek back to Earth to the likes of an atom. Trillions of miles narrowed to a pinprick. His own body rolled into a quark.

To call the looming specter of his parents a supermassive black hole felt like regressing to some adolescent instinct for trite, overwrought metaphor, but it wasn't as if he had a backup.

A backup was something he sorely wanted at this moment, at least to present to Savannah as an explanation—because he knew, at the basest level of the matter, that she was right. It was a story as old as Noah's consciousness, all the ways he kicked past his parents' borders of permissibility, how he had to be dragged back to repair the damage with fingernails bloody from digging into the ground in protest. The same story, again and again, and yet the plot twist still rang with the bright peal of surprise.

The memory of the smell of a Rassawek summer bloomed faintly in the deepest hollow of his nose. By the time the *Amihaf* reached the Tau Ceti system, summer would have already settled in for the long haul, regardless of the equinox. Nothing on Shala or Lulal that he'd seen could compare. He ached for it and the ache had nowhere to go, no pre-settled spot where it could wait for him to comb out the knots.

And when he thought of Erie, his parents' top-floor condo—his childhood home—high above downtown with its view of the lake, his breath stung, sharp and metallic along the cartilage. When the winter lake-effect rain poured down on the city, it wasn't the earthy loam he remembered, but the mildew, the slimy black fringe creeping along the inside of the windows.

"Hey."

Noah jumped. Irene was leaning against the jamb of the cockpit door when he unclenched.

"Oh! Um, happy birthday, by the way."

"It's not my birthday." Her mouth quirked like it was fighting a smile.

"So why is everyone—"

"Because I said it was my birthday."

"But it's not."

"Correct."

She slunk back into the cockpit without the door sliding shut behind her, as good an invitation as any. He took Esmail's empty pilot's seat, careful not to bump any stray buttons or knobs, a consideration Irene had turned second-nature with the casual way her gangly legs hung off the arm of her chair. The navigation computer hummed against the wall with an occasional beep, nothing that could pull her from the notebook propped up against her lap.

"The leg to the Tau Ceti system is twice as long as the last two," she said, chewing the end of her pen.

Noah glanced at the spaceshield, a tint muting the nauseating strobe effect. "I'm not following."

"Twenty-three lightyears instead of eleven-and-change," she said. "Do biologists not have to know math?"

"What? No—" He cut himself off at the sight of Irene's barely-there smirk. "What does this have to do with the scene upstairs?"

"You don't know because you spent the first few days after Lulal in your bunk." Her pen clicked, and the thick strokes of the nib left an emerald green weaving around the tips of pine trees. "Something was going to give if the energy wasn't redirected. We might as well get cake out of it."

"Not sure if it's going to be a very good cake."

Irene shrugged, taking a moment to color in more swathes of green. "I've been thinking about home a lot lately," she said. "All the people who first taught me how to read the stars." Her pen clicked again. The thinner black lines reappeared, filling out more of the spiny needles of the trees, spears of grass breaking through a slushy layer of snow. "Where are you from again?"

"Lake Erie."

She nodded. "You've never seen the Northern Lights, then, have you?"

He hadn't, and her tone colored the question as a formality. She already knew. The pines grew sharper points the longer her pen laved attention on that side of the page.

"Haven't seen much of anything, honestly."

The Starbuck family latched close to the lakeshore as if it would save them from being flung into space—or a big city, and Noah could never tell which one his parents considered a worse fate. Nacotchtank never counted among the dreaded urban threat waiting at the other node of the railway; most years, July would click into place and they would gladly head south to sweat in the boggy air, gathering before relics of a bygone era. Battered sandstone, enormous half-cracked domes flecked with bone-white paint and rust— mourned for, wished whole again. Noah never accompanied them, never traveled further than fifty miles from the lake until undergrad, then further still until he landed in Rassawek. Whatever he'd seen of the northern Testudines, most of it had passed by in the blur of a train window.

Irene brought the nib of the pen to her tongue, leaving a blot of ink to spread like watercolors.

"What's it like?" he asked, nodding toward the drawing.

She paused, the thumb of her free hand tracing the tattooed line down her chin. "Grounding," she said. "Like I'm right where I'm meant to be." She held up the two-page spread up for Noah to see. The lights absorbed the whole of the night sky, streaming through the breaks in the pine needles and coloring the snow a pale, glowing mint. It dominated the landscape in a way that Noah had tied to Lulal and its single, perpetual sunset.

"Is Lake Erie nice?"

"I haven't gone back since I left for undergrad."

"Hm." Irene pulled the notebook back to her lap and flipped to the next fresh page, tapping the back end of the pen along the center seam. "I did hear Frida say something about you and your parents not getting along."

"Yeah, well…" Noah curled his arms around his stomach. "Frida's an asshole."

"Hey…"

"She is!"

"Okay, let's clear this up." She methodically closed the notebook and swiveled the chair to face him. "Frida is not an asshole. She's a prickly personality with some anger management issues."

"That's the same thing." He waited for her to respond, even acknowledge that he'd said anything, but her stare remained resolute.

The navigation computer trilled a discordant tone. Lights flashed between the monitors. Irene jumped up, hands latching onto dials and buttons and keyboards. Or, at some points, just one hand, the other tracing out some calculation in the air before numbers could be punched in with any certainty. The noise dropped moments after she stepped away.

"Should I be worried?"

"We're fine," she sighed. "Just a weird blip… I'll have to run it by Quinn in case it's related to his pet problem but…" She shook her head as if to dispel the pessimistic threads. "Back to your parents."

"Oh. Uh. I need to call them—"

"So call them."

"I—"

"Right now," she said, waving at the pocket bulging with his tablet. "In my experience an outside presence will temper any difficulties."

"I mean… you don't have to. Really, it's…"

Irene hopped to her feet, his voice trailing off as she slid the cockpit door closed and deftly plucked his tablet from his hand.

The notebook had fallen to the floor in the hurry, ignored as she paced and dug for the satcall program. Noah nicked it, flipped back a few pages from the aurora piece. One side was blank—but the other side of the spread was a drawing of a man. Abelard, the whole of his Constructed Body unfurled, legs together and wingspan extended, with his flesh limbs, overlaid, stretched in a spread-eagle.

The Constructed hands both ended in fists, smashing through the square.

"What's this?" Noah asked just as Irene said—

"It's dialing."

"Hey—"

"What are you doing with my notebook? I—fine, swap."

The tablet and notebook arced past each other and landed in each other's awaiting hands.

"I'm not prepared for this conversation," Noah grumbled.

"And that drawing wasn't done. I think we're even."

The tablet hummed with a low drone as it reached for the nearest satellite relay, coiling itself up to be flung back to the tighter network inside Neptune's orbit. Five minutes passed, and Noah tried not to watch too closely as Irene opened up to that same page, pen in hand. Ten minutes passed and her pen still hadn't touched down to the paper, hovering over Abelard's head, his torso, the knobby curve on either set of knees. At the fifteen minute mark, they'd both ignored the clattering of pans from the galley, and finally Irene's pen dug into the Constructed thigh at a soldered metal seam.

Eighteen and a half minutes, as Noah was opening his mouth to ask after the drawing, the satcall clicked in the connection.

"Noah! There you are!" His mother's voice filled the cockpit, static and all, and then the video stuttered into view. She sat beside his father, far more animated than he would ever deign to be, and even with the poor resolution, something turned over and ground sharply into his gut. "I was beginning to worry my email hadn't reached you."

"Nope," said Noah with a forced grin. "Just busy—*ah!*"

Irene had kicked his chair with more force than her wiry legs should have allowed.

"Everything all right on the ship, son?" His father's beard obscured the bottom half of his face, but the twitch of a frown was unmistakable.

"Yeah, yeah, it's fine. Actually," he said, meeting Irene's gaze, "I wanted to introduce you to one of my crewmates." He tapped the screen to flip the camera and caught Irene as she reached for one of the flickering lights on the dashboard. "This is Irene Tuuluq, our astronavigator."

A wave, a wider grin than Noah had ever seen—Irene offered it all, a convincing show that everything was fine and dandy. He switched the camera back, spinning his chair away from that side of the cockpit, and Irene's posture slumped back to normal.

"It's a small ship, so I hope you're okay with... y'know," said Noah, cautious. "An audience."

"That so?" His father *tsk*ed under his breath. "Not even your own quarters?"

"Oh—no, yeah, all communal space," he said, forcing himself to ignore Irene's full-body tilt at the lie. "It's like those pictures you have from summer camp. The bunk beds?"

"All those resources," his father sighed, "and those border razers still can't make suitable transport for the folks on the front lines—"

"Dad."

"All I'm saying is—"

"*Dad.*"

"Noah, honey, remember what we talked about." His mother's voice fell into that cloying lilt, the fuzzed-out smile on the screen broad, showing teeth, but tight in a way that tugged the rest of her face out of alignment. There was a script to these moments, and they'd long been off book. "Let's not make things an issue when we don't have to."

"Right. Sorry." Noah craned his neck to stretch out a sudden cramp. He caught Irene's eye and all the invisible question marks that had attached to the fly-aways lining her braids.

She closed the notebook with a snap, clapping it between her hands.

"Speaking of being sorry, I did want to say that me not telling you about Justin or this…" He waved his hand around the cockpit. "It was the end of the semester and I had some journal deadlines, and Dr. Cousteau's return definitely didn't help calm things down. Keeping you out of the loop wasn't intentional."

Half-lies were also, at their cores, half-truths. He achieved greatest personal peace by pushing all thoughts of his parents and Lake Erie and the torrential rain storms rolling in for New Year's Eve to the furthest edge of his awareness. Roped into the minutiae of family matters, Noah would miss conference deadlines, grade exams weeks late, find himself buffering before a lecture hall of underclassmen because the words *Proxima Centauri* dropped from his tongue in the same cadence he'd heard from his father.

"Mom," he said, clearing his throat. "How's the, um…" He reached for the date. Just the month even, as a reference. No one had been actively keeping track, but he could guess it was probably sometime in late spring for the northern hemisphere. "…summer plans?"

"Oh! Noah, it's *so* exciting." One of her hands busied itself with twirling her fingers around the end of the braid draped over her shoulder. "You know how last year Hurricane Dawson disrupted the Millennium March? Well, it's back on this year, just belated, and we've got tickets! We'll be headed down to Washington in a couple weeks. We're going with the Johnsons, should be a great time!"

Over the top of the tablet, Irene mouthed, *Washington?*

Nacotchtank, Noah mouthed back, and she nodded, a slow gesture as the pieces connected. And then her lips pursed against the instinctual frown.

"What was that? Did the audio drop?" asked his father.

"No, um… Irene was…" The initial thread of a lie kept slipping from between his fingers, oily. It wisped further and further out of reach the more he focused on pinning it down. "It's not important. How's Major doing?"

"Who's Major?" asked Irene.

And at the same time, his father: "We haven't spoken in months. Everything is important."

"Major is the family dog," Noah said. "Big fluffy guy."

Her eyes popped wide, a beat of stillness passing before she scrambled around behind the pilot seat. "I would love to see the dog," she said over Noah's shoulder.

His mother went to fetch him from the living room, leaving his father to study the tableau before him. A finger dug into the space where his mustache met the greater mass of his beard, rolling a thin section around the knuckle.

"So what was that you two were talking about a second ago?"

"I'd just never heard that name for Nacotchtank," Irene said, "so Noah clarified for me."

He squeezed the tablet harder, fighting against the sudden bloom of sweat in his palms. He wished the video resolution were better just to check if the joints in his father's temple were flexing, grinding down his molars. There were so many fewer ways to determine the right angle to dig his heels in.

"Really? You haven't?"

"Nope. Geography trivia isn't a strength of mine."

There was a version of this moment where Noah had to swallow back the tides of nausea. Those tides could still roll in, every moment of unbroken silence another opportunity.

"Hm." Off-camera, his mother engaged in a one-sided negotiation with Major, the sound too choppy to make out. His father paid it no mind. "Guess you're not from the area."

"Couple thousand miles north," she said. "Give or take."

"No kidding. So you're from Canada?"

His mother's voice, however garbled, grew closer. Noah had practiced this, the even-tempered breath, the still face, stoic, reactions flattened, subsurface, lest the careful calm crack open like a bomb.

"Uh…" Irene said. "Nope."

"Okay—what, Greenland, then? Siberia?"

"No."

"What's the larger region around your hometown called? I'm lost."

"Nunavut."

"So it *is* Canada!"

"It's not."

A worrisome flush crept up his father's face, a new hue Noah had never brought about, much less witnessed. In an instant he was thirty-three hurtling through space, and he was twenty-five packing for Rassawek, and he was nineteen saying in Dionde:gâ for the summer, and he was also eighteen seventeen sixteen fifteen all the way down to the haziest moments where the only touchstones were the sunny summer heat and the rage overhead that made his ears ring.

"Fine." The control in the huff that followed was tenuous at best. "It *was* Canada."

"To some."

Noah's mother returned with Major in tow, and the sudden burning curl in his chest dissolved.

"Had to bribe the sweet boy with a biscuit, but here he is!" his mother cooed.

Major loped into view, the black fur around his snout streaked with gray. His tongue lolled from a panting mouth, one ear flopped inside-out. A string of drool dripped down out of frame, undoubtedly onto the toe of his father's shoe.

"Gerard, is everything okay?" she asked.

He glanced at Irene, then to Noah, and finally back at her. "Just peachy."

The conversation turned toward the usual agenda, a cursory survey of all the base elements his parents had decided comprised a life. When they tried to prod about Justin, Irene butted in with a question about Major, spinning off into a tale of the Tuuluq family dogs.

All the while, his father's eyes barely seemed to leave the center of Noah's forehead. His questions, terse and dense, dropped heavily. He could almost hear them landing in the splat of Major's drool. Polite inquiries about planetary destinations, Savannah's role in the mission—it was leading to Abelard, whose name neither of his parents could ever remember correctly.

The crashes in the galley had grown more frequent, the shouting more legible despite the cockpit's closed door. Savannah's distinct alto rose over the clatter, one word sharper than all the rest.

Abelard.

"What in the blazes is going on in your ship, Noah?" his mother asked.

"Nothing good," Irene said, reaching across Noah toward the call controls. "We should go check up on them. It was nice to meet you."

The call ended before his father could choke out a protest. The beeping of the navigation computer grated up against his eardrums.

"I'm sorry about my dad," he said suddenly.

Irene had shuffled back to her side of the cockpit, picking up her notebook from where it had fallen to the floor. She said nothing, only stared, acknowledging him with the slightest tilt of her head.

"I never know when he's going to… pull something like that." He sighed. "It's one thing if he's an ass to me. I'm used to it—"

"Noah."

"—and it doesn't matter that this was him being relatively well-behaved…" He jumped to his feet and crossed the cockpit. "It's hard for me to push back with him, but I still should have. And I'm sorry."

His hands clasped around hers gripping the notebook, and he fought to keep the surprise at his own actions off his face as Irene hit him with one perked eyebrow.

"I appreciate that," she said, gently pulling her hands free. "Thank you." Beside them, the empty expanse of the galaxy flickered by through the spaceshield. Irene stared into it as if she hoped to decipher it, some astronomical Morse code. "I do like acting oblivious, though. You people never know how to react."

Her face glowed, fueled by the thought of a man trillions of miles away fuming silently over her refusal to cede what he still considered his due, centuries after the fact.

Another clanging crash echoed from the galley.

"Do you think anyone has ever died from a baking accident?" asked Irene.

"That's not the journal article anyone wants coming out of this mission."

When the two of them arrived, Abelard was nowhere to be found; instead, in the eye of a flour-cloud hurricane, sat a lopsided cake. The vanilla icing globbed across the top with the grainy consistency of concrete and proudly held a single unlit candle aloft at the center. Patches of Esmail's face were coated in a thin film of dried batter, and more sprays of it sank into Dayo's hair.

And on the floor, Frida: her shirt sporting a brown stain, her glasses rendered a gritty matte opaque. "Ta-da...!"

"Quinn says lighting the candle is a major fire hazard," Savannah said. "So —"

"I love it." Slowly Irene offered a rare grin where her teeth shone through; and as the cake was cut and shared and dissected, no one dared broach the one missing member of the crew, wherever he lurked in those hours he melted away into the fabric of the *Amihaf*.

That night, Noah dreamt of snow banks drifting into chipped and crumbling relics, of a silhouette standing on a far-off dune craning her neck to gaze up into the wild abyss beyond.

From: Patterson, Justin

To: Starbuck, Noah

Subject: Thinking about that pie again

You know the one, the burnt strawberry rhubarb we were supposed to take to the potluck. I wish it hadn't happened like that. It doesn't matter who messed with the oven settings or the timer, or whatever the issue ended up being. It's been almost a year, and I can't even remember anymore.

I used to say I didn't hold grudges long enough to matter. Can't after that. Another thing burnt. There was a nub of it still there when your family came to town. We should have been able to talk it out better than we did. Or not. That's what Terrance said. And I agree with him a lot of the time, but then you call me from who-knows-where and got me typing all this out.

I don't even know if I'm going to hit send. If you're reading this, it'll be a surprise for both of us.

-J

The timestamp, translated to Rassawek's time zone, was just after three in the morning on a Saturday, and the particular style of the email lit a neon sign pointing straight at Justin's stash of bourbon. This wasn't the first of the sort to wind up in his inbox over the years, sometimes after an argument and sometimes while either of them was at a conference, the other half of the bed empty and the alcohol tipping Justin's head toward the rhapsodic. Those times when they reunited, the apartment door clicked shut at the press of a back, *I missed you*s passing unvoiced, mouth to mouth.

Noah flushed at the stack of memories that shuffled to the surface, shoved them back down as he clicked away from the email.

That awful pie—Noah had wanted to stick to something familiar, but the rhubarb at the boutique grocer had been on sale. Even then, the cost was outrageous, but Justin insisted. The mimeo strawberries appeared when Noah turned his back, and what other use for rhubarb was there? He'd been frustrated, and Justin had been distracted by the latest goings-on in his own department—gas and flame coming together to char the end result. Soil-grown produce wasted, a fodder for an economy of hurtful words.

Two days later, Justin left for a Catastrophe-era literature symposium. When he returned, there was none of the pent-up ardor whistling for release as he passed through the door.

The beginning of the end, all laid out in mushy, overcooked rhubarb.

Still, the corner where his neck met his shoulder twinged with the phantom imprint of Justin's teeth.

Stupid, stupid, stupid,

The clock in his bunk read 0243 IST. The ship had to be abandoned enough for a few winding laps around the halls. He was *not* going to call Justin. It was a reasonable hour in Rassawek, and an itch scrambled under his skin, begging him to scratch it with something impulsive.

"Nope. Nope, not today," he muttered to himself. "Enough to worry about."

Such as: the upcoming crew meeting behind Abelard's back. After Irene's non-birthday, Noah made up some concern about his horseshoe scorpion injury and in the security of the med bay relayed the hint Quinn had passed along: the cargo hold was the next best thing.

"Nice job," Dayo said. "I can make this happen. Keep an eye out."

By the following morning, the arrangements had been made and disseminated—Dayo would schedule a maintenance tune-up for Abelard's ConBod, a lengthy script that required him to power down into sleep mode, and they were in the clear.

The meeting was in four days, and Noah had been able to do nothing about it other than hold his stomach against the frothy waves of nausea. They creeped back as his thoughts orbited in a figure eight around it and the twin planet of Justin.

Was this what it was like to be hurtled into a black hole? Gravity tugging at all ends at different rates, the body straining as toes were yanked forward faster than the rest—the forces trying to tear Noah back to Earth fought his momentum forward within the *Amihaf*. Eventually they would rip him apart, a smaller scale of spaghettification.

If this had to happen, at least it was happening someplace where he couldn't do much about it. The *Amihaf* would continue through space, and Noah would remain in its confines, and the arms of the galaxy would spin on unaware of their insignificant chunk of metal and all the panicked electrical impulses zipping inside each of their skulls.

Surely most researchers that ventured past the border of the Solar System found themselves mired in a similar muck at some point: the sharp thump in the solar plexus realizing just how far away home was, how all the unknowns piled higher around and above their heads the further that distance grew. How they'd dreamed their whole lives of clamoring in the dark for something to pluck out, brush off, illuminate. How a moment would come and they'd long to trade their dream to feel Earth under their feet again, to see a friend without the grainy filter of a satcall.

Nothing felt more like home than whittling away the night pouring over work, so Noah headed down the stairs to the lower level.

The lab door sat ajar, the excited tumble of a monologue drifting into the hall giving away at least one of the current occupants—Esmail was giving a detailed explanation of the role a vacuum leviathan played in a recent action movie, barely taking time to breathe between plot points. One hand flung about widely and occasionally smacked into a nearby cabinet, and the other scribbled on the resin top of the lab bench with a nub from the chalk supply.

Abelard stood on the other side of the table, and when he glanced up to find Noah leaning against the entry, every part of him sparkled, from the eye displays and his porcelain teeth to the metal plates edging into view under his clothes.

"—and that's when my immersion was *really* broken, because if the leviathan was bigger than the Moon, all the gravitational fields would get screwy, right? I mean, there's nothing in the literature that says leviathans are —what's the word—hollow? It would have organs. Mass. And being *that close…*"

On top of his doodle of the movie's leviathan depiction, he drew a lopsided circle and scribbled what Noah assumed was the Persian word for moon.

"What do you think about it, Noah?"

Esmail's hop of surprise twisted him around enough to catch Noah's apologetic grimace. "How long have you been there?"

"Not long enough to answer Abelard's question with any confidence."

He grabbed a stool from one of the other tables and took a seat where Esmail had returned to his drawing, fingers fidgeting in minute, barely-there tics. Noah didn't want to stare, but he doubted he could meet Abelard's gaze without his complexion turning a sickly green.

"What movie were you talking about?" asked Noah after the quiet started to grate.

"It was that big one a couple years ago, you know, *A Mars Divided*?" Registering his blank look, Esmail delved into the plot, bolstered further by Abelard's questions.

Noah forcibly tuned it out. Instead, he studied Esmail's drawing more closely. The shape of the film's leviathan resembled Terrestrial sperm whales, a square-angled head tapering down to the double fan of a tail, though more fins lined the side of its body and the eyes were cribbed from tarantula diagrams.

"I wish you all could have met Yuxuan," Abelard said suddenly. "He was one of the most truly curious people I've ever known. I'd wanted it to be a surprise, meeting him on Lulal." That, he spoke past Esmail, directly to Noah, staring at him for a long moment before turning away to pace around the lab.

Esmail huffed to himself and dug through one of the cabinets for a rag to wipe his canvas clean.

"The surprise part would have been easy," said Noah. "None of us were really looking at the briefing too closely after everything with Tristan."

Abelard nodded to himself, took the corner of the lab with a sharp turn on the ball of his foot. "Mm... yes. Shame about the horseshoe scorpion. Dr. Oyekan was right. The venom could have been quite useful."

Some days, like that moment, a surge of tinnitus crested inside Noah's ears, the same pitch as Tristan's cries as their exoskeleton cracked under Abelard's grip.

"Well... it is what it is." He pulled back from the table so Esmail could finish erasing the chalk. They exchanged a tense glance that Noah wasn't sure how to read.

"It is what it didn't *have* to be," said Abelard.

"That too."

Abelard locked eyes with him, utterly still aside from his slowly pinching brow—the silence between them would have been suffocating had Esmail not started murmuring to himself in Persian trying to scrub some unrelated stain from the table. He readjusted his stance several times as Noah fought the urge to concede by averting his gaze.

"Abelard-*agha*," he said, crouching to eye the stain from a different angle. "Why did you suddenly stop co-authoring papers with Chen Yuxuan after the early 50s? I meant to ask before you started talking about Tristan again." He stole a look at Noah with an inscrutable wrinkle of his nose.

"Oh. It's…"

His eye displays flickered while Esmail refocused on the lab bench. The first eye to reboot swiveled toward some pipettes left on the perimeter counter, lolling back to center by the time the other clicked back.

"I only ask," said Esmail, "because the vacuum leviathan enthusiast community online has *lots* of opinions. But also I'm personally interested, and I'm sure Noah is too. Actually, that's most of it. The internet speculation was mainly flavor text, and I'm also told you shouldn't announce when you're just being nosy."

The lab quieted, the only sound coming from the scrape of another stool against the floor as Abelard fell onto it with a clunk. His shoulders slumped under the weight of the question.

There was so little, Noah realized, that he knew about Abelard's life outside the realm of academia. Where did he grow up? What was his family like? How did he become interested in xenobiology, as new as the field was in his youth? Had he ever been married, did he have children, what had he come home to in the days he still lived and worked in Rassawek? Who outside of the university mourned him in the years before his resurrection?

Had Chen Yuxuan been among them?

"We… disagreed," Abelard said after a stretch of thought. "He thought the leviathans were, at best, a figment of my imagination. The xeno-organisms he posited were… well, I thought they were more fantastical than anything I'd proposed. I never read those papers. It was… I could feel him staring over my shoulder whenever I read his work." He'd picked up a stray pen laying on the table, and his twiddling ended with an abrupt crunch as his fingers tightened on the casing. "We were going to redefine what it meant to exist in interstellar space. And to meet such a pedestrian end…"

He discarded the broken pen and plucked the remaining nub of chalk from the bench, rolling it lightly between the pads of his thumb and forefinger. He held it before the Constructed Body's optical lens and paused to take in the angles at which it had been worn away.

"In our younger years, Yuxuan and I liked to entertain the idea of dying in the field, martyrs at the frontier struck down by the unknowns waiting beyond, our names listed beside the likes of Michael Thorn, Giles Lennik. Mingyu hated it. Still… he used to tell me, 'Abelard, if the force of my fall pushes humanity's progress even a millimeter farther, it will have been worth it.'" Over the dusty remnants of Esmail's original drawing, Abelard began to spool out what Noah could only compare to a spider web, though the lines were jagged, almost electric. "We both fell in our own ways. I was able to recover from it, and he… a senseless death. I never got to tell him that my vision of the leviathans—" The chalk burst into a cloud of dust as his fist clenched, spasming as it curled as tightly as it could go.

Noah carefully rose to his feet, motioning for Esmail to remain where he stood. As he approached, the hum of the ConBod's cooling fan revved to a whine.

Abelard's fist slammed on the lab bench—Noah jumped back, Esmail yelped, and the fan pitched up further. "I was right, you know. I was right… about the leviathans. This… this!" He waved his hand before the drawing. "This is what Yuxuan imagined while he conceptualized the ecosystem of deep space… a sapient web of energy, life unlike anything we'd ever seen, something that could warp our concepts of relativity, tie knots into string theory. And in the end it was my hypothesis that bore out... 'vacuum leviathans,' *tch...*"

"Abelard—"

"I'm still standing, and he's not!" The digital eye displays clicked dark, flickering back to normal after a heavy pall of waiting. "I should have been able to confer with him! He should have been here! The leviathan that took my organic life should have to stare down the *both* of us before it's ripped apart!"

Out of the corner of his eye, Noah saw Esmail glancing between them, a jerkiness to his movement that evoked a trapped animal.

"I'm sorry," said Noah.

A single syllable of a laugh fell from Abelard's waning scowl. "For what, Dr. Starbuck? That the life of an old man has been sadder and less wondrous than he dreamt as a child? It happens to us all. It will happen to you. And to you, too, Mr. Rostami."

There was a pause and then, suddenly calmer, Esmail sighed. "Oh, I don't know about that. The biggest thing I ever imagined for myself when I was little was hiking to the summit of Mount Damavand, and..." He motioned with wiggling fingers to the ship around them.

"How very fortunate for you," Abelard said under his breath.

"I guess, yeah. But!" Esmail added quickly. "But..."

"Maybe we should all just turn in," said Noah. "Call it a night before things... you know—"

"Good idea. I felt my insomnia giving up anyway." Esmail recomposed himself and deftly maneuvered between Noah and the furniture on his way to the door, all on the balls of his feet.

The door slid shit, and then they were alone.

Abelard stared—stared harder at him than anything he'd seen on Earth or since the reunion on Natocke Station. One of his fingers traced through a dune of chalk dust from the stub, but his gaze remained on Noah.

And the *Amihaf* shifted, became the dining room in his family's condo overlooking Lake Erie, his father sitting in silence at the opposite side of the table. Waiting, studying whatever small thing would explode to consume the rest of the afternoon. The hum of the engines was the hum of the dishwasher, a cooling vent turning to a low grumble at the back of his throat.

"Dr. St—Noah…" he said. "Don't you have regrets?"

"Who doesn't?"

"And therein lies my point. I am allowed my regrets. A fair few, too, given my age."

"What do you wish you'd done differently with Dr. Chen, then?"

The bitterness fell away as Abelard turned his attention inward, toward some image pulled to the top of his brainware's memory files. "I'm not sure there's a way to curtail the youthful ego."

Again, the *Amihaf* faded away, farther down the coast this time, from Erie to Rassawek. The foot traffic on 14th Street was dense enough to provide background noise, especially with the bedroom window open; the climate control in the second-floor unit he and Justin shared couldn't keep up with the late-autumn heat wave, so they did what they could. That day, Noah laid back against their bed, bare save for the fitted sheet, himself bare save for an old pair of athletic shorts. Justin straddled his hips, sitting back on his heels. The angle of the sun through the window landed on his loc cuffs and the sheen of sweat on his chest to cast him in a golden halo—one that refused to dull even as the argument dragged on. They argued about—the pie again, sure, but something else had started it, and the pie had only been a detour.

You fight me on shit that doesn't matter, and you wouldn't even push back when your parents casually said all the—the 19th century had a lot going for it? Adding to a personal collection of art by a war criminal? I hope you weren't being polite just because I was there. Christ, are they like that all the time? And do you just let them?

"I wouldn't know," said Noah.

"What does that mean?"

It meant—

That day, lying under Justin, it meant taking it, all of it, uninterrupted by any reply he could muster up. Whatever Noah said wouldn't matter. Even if he could make him understand, he couldn't bring himself to want to. Self-defense, in that moment, at the point where he stood, cast a weak shadow.

Abelard's hand landed on Noah's shoulder, the pressure exerted with a tangible level of self-consciousness, far from the phantom bruises that still panged at his elbow. "I want to remind you, Noah, that I am very glad you're here with me."

Abelard's stare was heavy, landing on his elbow. It twinged out of habit.

A bruise. A bullet to the head.

A hand on a shoulder, too close to his neck.

I am very glad you're here with me.

Noah cleared his throat, nodded. "Me too, Abelard. Me too."

From: Eber, Patrick

To: Starbuck, Noah

Subject: RE: Watch this space

Noah had already read the email at least five times before the clock ticked over to the date of their secret crew meeting. He wasn't going to read it a sixth time. Not yet.

Just after the dinner dishes were placed in the drying rack, Abelard followed Dayo down to the med bay, draped himself across the examination table, and powered down after the appropriate nodes were connected to the larger Prana-brand server. After a few tests to confirm all of his Constructed Body's sensory inputs were offline, Dayo emerged with a double thumbs-up.

"What is it you're actually doing if there's not an emergency patch?" asked Frida.

"Just a thorough system scan," she said with a shrug, stepping back to allow Quinn and Savannah room to hoist open the hatch to the cargo hold. "He was due for one anyway. We might as well use the time. And we could uncover any underlying brainware issue."

Her shining bit of optimism was not mirrored by anyone else.

"Come on, it's the simplest explanation." She followed after Noah, toward the tail end of the procession. "Occam's Razor was not one of the Catastrophe's extinction victims—"

The rest of the crew fell into a grumbling debate as they settled themselves among the various piles of crates.

"Can we please…" Noah tucked his tablet under his arm and tried to bring the noise down to a workable level—tried, and only partially succeeded. So much for his classroom management skills. "We've got a finite amount of time here."

"You said he'd be out all night, yeah?" Quinn asked Dayo, and she nodded. "This isn't going to take that long—"

Frida cut across him: "I'd like to get at least *some* sleep—"

"What, do you get cranky? I wonder what that's like."

"Bloody fucking—"

A sharp whistle pierced the cargo hold: Irene dropped the pinch of her lower lip, finally lifting her attention from the page propped up against her knees. She paused longer on Esmail, waiting until he'd removed his head from between his knees. "I know we're all stressed, but the point of this whole thing was to do something about it."

"Thank you," said Noah. "So…"

The six sets of eyes staring at him in the vacuum-press of quiet clogged his throat. The pressure was too great; instead, he gazed beyond the cluster of boxes to the thick pipes running the water recycling system. This close, the engine couldn't hide the clunks as they shifted and settled—worrying, maybe, if the ship frame wasn't already withstanding the forces of turbolight. Given that, it was a miracle the clunking wasn't more pronounced.

When Noah pulled himself inside the circle of the crew, he found their stares had softened, ebbed to a level that no longer reminded him of an oral exam.

"So," he repeated. "I'm sure by now you've all heard about what happened when Abelard and I split off from the group that last day on Lulal… and we all saw what happened with Tristan." He added further details about the odd glitches from his ConBod, the bruise from Shala, and the reaction when he'd tried to draw a leviathan; others piped up with more strange behavior once he trailed off. Some of it he and Savannah could write off as established habits pre-accident, much to everyone else's surprise, but others cast a thick pall over the room

"One of the things I wanted to share," Noah said after a moment, "is a reassurance that this isn't just in our heads like some, I don't know, space sickness." He held up his tablet. "I got an email from Eber—one of the heads of xenosciences at Rassawek," he added.

"About Abelard?" asked Esmail.

"Well—kind of?" He grimaced, looking over to Savannah for help that, according to the single raised eyebrow, she couldn't give. "Tell you what, I'll just read the whole thing."

The email was heavy with Eber's bureaucratese, drawing out what could have been a short message to several pages: thank you for the continued reports, Abelard's behavior had been noted since his return from Njord Station, the mission could not be aborted. He could barely hear himself as he read, listing out all of the reasoning for closing that door—enormous fines levied against the university as the partner institution, the risk of TerraCosmos blackballing Eber and Abraham on the eve of several other long-term projects, and finally, yes, leaving the remaining research settlements on the docket without their mid-assignment check-up.

"I'd like to go on record," Savannah said, pulling her pen from her pocket. "I never liked Eber all that much."

"Do you know what those other projects are?" Dayo asked. She glanced around the group's deflated shoulders when Noah took too long to reply, then borrowing Irene's notebook and pen. After a moment she revealed a deliberate set of squiggles.

"What are we looking at here?" Quinn ventured.

"It's a pair of hands, and they're holding the wrists of another pair," she said, pointing to what could graciously be labeled fingers. "The circle above is Earth. With continents," she added. "Ikemba said the African Mining Board's found this logo in mining companies' files during contract violation audits."

Noah waited for the rest of them to pipe up with their own commentary, but whatever energy had egged them on for months had found a cliff and tumbled down into oblivion, leaving Mingyu's voice loud in his own head:

For all I know, those two have a hand in what those miners were doing here.

"We don't know for sure that's what this is," Noah said, trying to ignore Quinn's pointed sigh. "And if it is, I don't know what we can do."

"What about helping Shēngdì?"

They all turned toward Esmail's questioning frown, then back to Noah in near unison. His tongue was too dry to wrap around even a fragment of a sentence.

Esmail's pointer fingers tapped in an arrhythmic beat against the pads of his thumbs. "They don't really care, do they?"

The next step in the thought hung unsaid. Earth didn't care about Shēngdì, and Earth didn't care about the *Amihaf*, either. The single filament of thread unspooling from the back of the ship, reaching back all those unfathomable miles into the depths of Cairo, Cape Guacara, Rassawek—all the places they came from—dissolved into atomic space dust as if it had never existed at all.

There was far more to the email, but some details could be spared, reduced to a quick summary as they sat with the rest. Further elaboration on the readings they'd found, how they lined up with the theories Noah had been honing since Abelard had been powered by blood and muscle, and it was too late to get into the details.

"So… they're really thinking it could be a leviathan," said Savannah.

Noah sighed. "The data is remarkable. It's the kind of dataset I'd celebrate with… what kind of alcohol do people use to celebrate? Nice wine?"

"Champagne?" said Frida.

"Well—okay, maybe not splurging *that* much. Which isn't the point," he said. "The point is it lines up with the current scholarship and…"

The crew froze around his pause—all except for Irene, who just barely tilted her head.

"Eber also said TerraCosmos finished compiling all the black box data of the ship where Abelard was attacked. It's as good as an exact match."

"He wasn't copied on this email, was he?" Irene asked.

Once again the crew moved in unison, leaning ever so slightly toward Noah in anticipation of his reply.

"No. Unless it was a BCC, but given what Eber's said… they'd know better. It's—"

"It's a warning," Savannah finished.

Noah tugged one of the lighter crates nearby closer to their misshapen circle, collapsing to a seat. One of the clasps dug into the back of his thigh but he made no effort to move, the low nudge of pain shifting into a vague pressure the longer he stared at his knees. Everyone was still staring at him —waiting for a confirmation of Savannah's assumption, for clarification, for reassurance or a twist he'd held close to the chest out of a sense of duty to dramatics. Any thought he formulated got stuck in his throat, and he threw a helpless wince Savannah's way. She could quell her fretting tremors when presented with someone else's of higher magnitude; he couldn't always gauge where she sat on the scale, but now it was worth the bet.

Their eyes met.

"So what do we do, Noah?" she said finally.

"I…" He shook his head. "Why is this just on me? I'm not—I'm not a… a… what, a *leader*—"

"Would it help if we voted?" asked Frida, deadpan.

"No! That's not—listen." And they did: listened, waited as he tried to string together one coherent idea before it all became hopelessly snarled.

There was a way out of this—that much he knew, whether it was curbing the aberrant flow as it stood or fording through until their feet touched back down on Earth. The path was obscured, but he would find it. They all would.

But it would remain obscured as long as they—*he*—refused to put a feel forward into the dark.

"Listen," he repeated. "It looks bad. This might be as bad as it gets. We don't know a lot of things right now. The most we can do is just—be cognizant of Abelard. Don't mention leviathans. If matters escalate past a certain point, we'll reevaluate."

No one asked aloud where Noah had marked that point, and they didn't need to. The question sank into each of their faces, then the answers they gave themselves, craggy waves that would send seismographs rippling, all because of the man slumped in the med bay with the dead-eyed stare pointed at the flickering stars.

SEVEN

THE LAST NIGHT BEFORE the *Amihaf* was due to arrive at the Tau Ceti system passed just as the rest had since the crew's midnight meeting: uneventful, with a subtle strain in conversation—a half-second pause out of place, a grin that fell open with the rigid hold of a mask. Those with partners on Earth retired to their bunks talking of satcalls as soon as their dinner dishes hit the drying rack, while the rest sat in the lounge, focuses split between their occupations of the night and where Abelard perched himself, parroting discussion starters once the last bit of flaccid chatter finally died. Noah did his best to keep Abelard's latest prompt from splatting open at their feet between articles in his journal backlog.

At the end of those eternal eight weeks, matters were primed to play out the same way. Dayo shifted in her seat, fork scraping the plate she'd emptied of the toroi Quinn had fussed over—the first sign of half the crew's retreat. Savannah shifted toward the galley, poised to hoist herself toward the pots congealing with the leftovers that hadn't yet been stashed in the fridge, and they all wriggled out the knots in their joints, ready to throw in the towel for the day, when Esmail leapt to his feet.

"So while we're all here…" His gaze flickered toward the corner where Abelard sat, the only spot without a plate. "We haven't had a pre-landing briefing yet, and, well—I had something to add, so I figured I might as well say it first thing." He knocked his knuckles together lightly, waiting for input from the table that was unlikely to come.

"Right." He flashed a thumbs-up at Irene, who did little more than purse her mouth into a thinner line. "Tomorrow we enter the Tau Ceti system. The exoplanet where we're headed is the second-to-furthest out, so it won't be a long intrasystem trek, but—you all know TerraCosmos history, don't you? All the troubles they had navigating the Kuiper Belt? The L—"

"The Leroon Disk is in *this* system?" Savannah blurted.

"Well…" Esmail paused. "Yes—"

"So this could've been our last supper?"

"Technically any meal you eat could qualify as—"

"Babe," Quinn said. "You're doing it again."

Esmail took a long breath, nodding as Quinn shot him a wink. "*Bebin…* we're going to be fine! The Leroon Disk shares a lot of properties with the Kuiper Belt, though it isn't mapped or monitored as thoroughly for obvious reasons. I only brought it up in case you were planning on doing yoga or building a house of cards before we landed because it won't be a straightforward trip."

"Answer me this, though," said Frida, masking her gritted teeth with an overly-polite veneer. "Why mention TerraCosmos' history with the Kuiper Belt at all?"

"Oh! In case you were worried about traversing the Leroon Disk. The Kuiper Belt used to be trouble, but they figured it out. And yes," he said, mostly to Savannah, "they did lose the first six or nine or… however many rover probes they sent out here, but—but!" He yanked a tablet from inside his jacket and pointed at something on the screen. "Not only was that years ago, but I checked the manifest for the research base crew, and I am a *much* better pilot than who they have."

Noah had never been particularly good at lip reading, but whatever name Esmail mouthed to Quinn prompted him to reiterate that they'd be fine, and after a few moments Savannah's hands stopped quivering.

"I just think I would've been fine not knowing," she muttered. "One less thing to keep me up tonight."

The next morning Noah woke with a jolt—0724 IST according to his bleary reading of the clock. The ship nearly tossed him to the floor with a second shudder, and he threw on the nearest set of clothes without checking if they were clean and ran out toward the lounge. As soon as he crossed the threshold into the hall, the ship lurched again. He flailed trying to balance on one foot, throwing himself forward just as the floor bucked up to meet him. The room spun as he flipped and tumbled, and when he finally propped himself up, Irene was staring at him from her lifesaver-hold on the stairwell railing.

"Perfect ten. Was just about to get everyone up."

"That's probably been taken care of," he said. "What—"

The overhead speakers crackled to life. "*Good morning, crew of the Amihaf, this is your pilot speaking,*" said Esmail's voice. "*We have officially entered the Leroon Disk and your lovely local astronavigator has informed me that this ride might be a bit bumpier than anticipated. Please make your way down to—"* The ship groaned, and Noah's inner ear sent his stomach churning as the internal gravity modulators fought against the steep angle at which Esmail must have tilted the yoke.

The intercom line remained open for a string of panicked Persian. *"As I was saying, please make your way down to the cockpit antechamber for some completely normal safety measures as we maneuver to Nethuns. Rostami out, and* khoda hafez."

"Just get downstairs," Irene said as soon as Noah opened his mouth. "Quinn's already there."

She dropped to the floor to slide her way toward the rest of the bunk doors, and Noah followed her example as he clambered, crab-like, down the steps. He found Quinn near his usual station outside the cockpit, but without a laptop in sight. Most of the wall paneling was pulled open to produce emergency seating, complete with over-the-shoulder seat belts that crossed over the chest.

"Good morning," Quinn said, strained. "First here, first pick!"

Noah selected a seat in a corner with a view into the open door of the cockpit. Esmail's hair was pulled tight in its usual bun, with the stray strands pinned with an eclectic selection of clasps, the focus taut along all the lines of his body. Just beyond, through the spaceshield, laid a frenetic field of dust and asteroids and debris, and it was all Noah could do to click his seatbelt into place.

"I'm going to throw up." Savannah's voice echoed down the stairwell, followed by Dayo.

"Do I have time to get some anti-nausea pills from the med bay?"

The seatbelt cut into Noah's neck as the ship twisted away from a pitted rock flashing before the *Amihaf*'s nose. A series of thuds followed.

"I guess we don't," Dayo said. "Come on, Sav, we got this—"

Slowly the rest of the seats filled; Quinn clicked himself in last, and then Irene wove back to her station at Esmail's side.

One spot still sat empty. .

"Where's Abelard?"

Everyone strapped in around him twisted his way, their knuckles white.

"Not sure that's my first concern," said Frida. Her pale complexion had turned ashen, brushed with green.

"If we're lucky, his ConBod will break. 'Oh no,'" Savannah said, "'how awful, and we had no way to fix him!' Come on, that's a best-case scenario."

It was.

It was.

His elbow twinged, and he saw forward to the end of the mission, their arrival on the Cape Guacara tarmac. Years had passed without a questionable incident. They collected data and reported back to Cairo without any worrisome caveats. Abelard's powered-down, damaged ConBod was taken to the nearest Prana Technologies lab for repairs; and at the back of his head, Noah wondered, as he had every night in those preceding years as sleep evaded him, if perhaps they had overreacted and let a man sit in broken stasis far longer than brainware engineers recommended.

Another bump jostled Noah to his feet, half-tangled in his unclipped seatbelt.

"Noah, stop," said Savannah. "He's probably fine!"

"Maybe! It's all a lot of 'maybe!' Everything we do here is dealing in 'maybe' and *maybe* I don't want to—" The ship lurched, and he held onto the door jamb to the foyer hard enough for his hands to threaten cramps.

"Just fucking sit back down!" Quinn yelled.

The shouting after him abruptly cut into alarmed yelps as Esmail wove the *Amihaf* around the latest chunks of debris. Noah kept his footing, scrambling up the stairs to the wrecked lounge in the lull. He was staring at the pair of knitting needles stuck in the ceiling when the ship cut sharply starboard, and his feet slipped out from under him. He landed on his yet-uninjured elbow, a stray pack of playing cards digging into a nerve.

"Shit—"

"Noah," Savannah called from below, "are you—"

"I'm fine! I'm... ugh—it's fine!" He winced through the shining, pulsing pain as he stretched both arms out to help his balance on the bucking floor underfoot.

And of course Abelard's bunk was at the far end of the hall.

"Well, you got this far," he muttered, then called louder, "Abelard!"

The ship groaned against Esmail's steering, a low shudder of a scrape rumbling overhead—contact. Below, the rest of the crew shouted over each other, garbled, pitching higher by the second.

"Abelard!" Noah reached the bunk, banging his fist against the door. "Abelard, open up—there's emergency seating downstairs—ah!"

The door slid open barely an inch, just enough for Abelard's nose and the ConBod's optical camera to slot into the gap. Both of his eyes were still hidden behind the door or adjoining wall, and Noah fought the urge to put an extra couple steps between them.

"What was that? I couldn't quite hear you through the door."

"Esmail's navigating us through the—" Again the ship tilted and jumped, testing their centers of gravity. "You know what it is. The ship's got safety features built for this. Let's get you—"

He curled his hand around the edge of the door to shove it the rest of the way open, and Abelard slammed his entire body at the opposite angle.

"I'll be right down. I just need a moment."

"Not sure we have too many of those to spare—"

"Dr. Starbuck," he said. "While I appreciate your concern, it will do little to change my current circumstances. Secure yourself, and I will soon join you."

The door clicked shut.

The ship heaved.

Noah tediously guided himself back to his seat. Within two minutes, Abelard had joined them; within five, the *Amihaf* punched through the inner border of the Leroon Disk, the warmth of the star unblemished by debris.

"Welcome to the Tau Ceti system!" Esmail called over his shoulder, not bothering with the intercom. "We'll be landing on Nethuns in—how long, Irene?"

"An hour."

"You heard her—an hour! The atmosphere on Nethuns is particularly thick, so the ride might get a little bumpy... in case you wanted to remain where you're sitting. Either way, we'll be back on solid ground before you know it."

The ship hummed as if it were channeling their collective relief. Though Noah had his view of the spaceshield to occupy him, he still couldn't avoid Savannah, how the specific tilt of her frown broadcast concern with equal parts frustration and worry, canceling each other out and landing on something new, indecipherable.

Not even Rassawek at the peak of summer could have prepared them for the wrath of Nethuns' humidity. The sun barely leaned over the horizon when the *Amihaf*'s ramp lowered into the sandy soil, and already Noah knew he would have to change into a new shirt by lunch. Bullets of sweat rolled down his back as the air crept closer and closer to a solid thing to be waded through.

"This is foul," Frida grumbled. "My personal space shouldn't feel invaded by the damn oxygen."

Dayo lightly tapped at her arm. "Thought you'd be used to it. Doesn't that part of the southern Testudines get pretty sticky?"

"Still a Londoner at heart. Never quite adjusted… oh man, Irene, you all right?"

Irene had remained at the top of the ramp, her back still holding onto the last remnants of the ship's climate control. Her grimace contorted the whole of her face.

"This is an unnatural temperature."

"Well…" Abelard made a show of placing his hands on his hips and surveying where they'd landed. "I do hate to disagree but it is indeed quite natural. The range of naturally-occurring temperatures in the universe is rather—"

In the distance, the top of a TerraCosmos-issued trailer found the right angle of the cloud-dulled light to catch Abelard's attention; he jumped when Irene appeared beside him, a hand gripping his shoulder.

"Hyperbole," she said.

"Of course, Dr. Tuuluq. My apologies."

In an attempt to ease the toll of the heat, the encampment on Nethuns had been established on the coast of a large inland sea, away from the more unforgiving pattern of tidal waves of the oceans proper. As the *Amihaf* crew crested the dunes stuck full of short, rigid reeds, the dark turquoise expanse of the sea spanned the length of the horizon, and the only factor separating it from Lake Erie was the absence of a city blundering on behind them.

"You have arrived!"

From around the corner of the central trailer emerged a man jogging in a clumsy lope across the sand—another Constructed Body, the metal plates tinted silver instead of bronze, the deep tan of his face and hands glowing against the sheen. His carefully-coiffed hair was unburdened from sweat.

"Abelard Cousteau, as I live and—well, not so much breathe, but you know!" He met Abelard's outstretched hand with his own. "I cannot believe it!"

The rest of the settlement had ventured out to the central parcel of beach, the lot of them barefoot, sporting tank tops and shorts of varying hem lengths. They eyed the *Amihaf* crew with a curiosity more even-keeled than the immediate scene before them.

"Oh, I have been so rude!" The man pulled back from Abelard, running his hands along the permanent haze of stubble afforded by synthetic skin. "I am Captain Henri Bouferma, and I am unimaginably honored to welcome you to Nethuns and Camp Ilunga."

"Ilunga?" said Dayo. "Like—"

"Like Joseph Ilunga, yes," Henri said. "His generosity with his good fortune is the only reason humanity has ventured past the Asteroid Belt, no? Why not give him the honor?" He didn't wait for an answer, beckoning them forward, down the shallow slope of the dunes until they slid, one by one, down to the flat expanse of the beach.

Most of the welcoming party had retreated back inside, the pained whirring of climate control systems drowning out the planet's natural soundscape.

Henri plastered a wide grin that reminded Noah of a panicking tour guide, breaking long enough to call some instruction in Arabic to a face peeking out from a distant trailer door. "The weather here takes some getting used to, so I was hoping to have our opening meeting inside—my crew just needs to wrap up what they were working on, and then we'll be off!"

Once they were inside the main trailer, Henri sputtered out a couple aborted attempts at platitudes before disappearing outside. Abelard's usual upbeat demeanor had tapered, his focus turned not toward idle conversation but the framed photo of Joseph Ilunga hanging near the refrigerator. It was a familiar image, the one typically included in history textbooks: a handsome Black man cradling a model of a TerraCosmos Alpha class ship in his arms. Noah only spared the photo an extra moment of consideration before settling back into the sickly coil in his gut, one he saw mirrored in the others around him. But, he reminded himself, they could have simply sensed something innocuous. An administrative faux pas. A poor result from lab tests.

Or maybe their collective unease was prompted from the awkward mien of another person inhabiting a Constructed Body, some prejudice that had fermented in the time since Neptune blipped out of view.

The silence was cut by a pointed sigh from Savannah, and just as she went to speak, the trailer door slammed open; Henri led the procession, followed by three of his local cohort. "*Ahlan wa sahlan, habari, bonjour*, and all that," said Henri as he strode toward the head of the table, gripping the corners of the seat where Dayo had situated herself. "Everyone here at Camp Ilunga is so very excited to show you what we've accomplished. Isn't that right?"

They all nodded, even one unseen face behind a tablet. Henri continued, introducing them too quickly for Noah to catch anything more than their roles as the resident xenozoologists and xenobotanist.

Abelard nodded to each of them in turn, then pausing at Noah with a raised eyebrow, expecting some unknown interjection—Noah furrowed his brow in reply, and Abelard moved on as if the moment had never happened. "Quite the small group you've got here, *n'est-ce pas?*" he said.

"The others are currently still occupied and I couldn't bear to pull them away. I'd love to meet your staff, though—"

"Henri. Please." Abelard sat forward in his chair, the bundle of his clasped hands landing on the table with a thunk. "We may not have worked much together in the past, but one thing I do know is that you're rarely at any sort of event without your dear doctor at your side. Where *is* Omar?"

The room toggled into a vacuum, suddenly airless, until the xenobotanist broke the seal with a snort. The xenozoologists winced.

"If I misread the manifest and he's actually not on Nethuns, I'll be very disappointed," Abelard continued, unfazed. "Given my current state of existence, I was hoping to discuss your own experiences while I was here, and from my understanding, Omar tells some parts of it better than you. If you don't mind my saying," he added.

Henri sighed, or audibly gestured toward it, dragging it out past any biological lung capacity. "We planned on easing you all into it. I want to make that extremely clear from the start."

Without another word, he wove his way to the trailer door, opening it to the dense heat. A nod of his head ushered his crew onto the awaiting sand, and another nod pulled the rest of them from their seats.

He led them in a single-file line to the other end of the trailers. Noah positioned himself between Abelard and Esmail, searching for any nib of a thought that wasn't wrapped around the heat or whatever Henri was trying to skate over. He forced down one only for another to spring up in its place, over and over in time with the gritty steps on the beach.

The line hung back once they reached the trailer. Henri took the two steps up to the door in one long stride and knocked, a crack opening to reveal a sliver of a tired man with curly salt-and-pepper hair.

"Hello Omar," Henri said, and just a shade too loud to sound natural. "I'm here to brief our guests."

"Okay, in English. That's a *great* sign," he grumbled, and then adding more loudly, "That was quick. They've been here all of half an hour."

"No time like the present, *habibi*."

"Fine. Take it slow."

The door slammed shut. The hot wind off the sea nudged at their backs, unwelcome, as Henri slowly faced his audience. For a long while he said nothing, perhaps contemplating the best approach or giving Omar some unspoken amount of time to prepare.

"Who is your xenomycologist?" he asked at last.

Frida raised her hand with a wary tilt but still followed when he beckoned her forward. "So what's—"

"Remember Omar's words. 'Take it slow.' So—just you."

"Wasn't what I was going to ask."

They stared at each other for a beat until Henri opened the door.

"After you, Doctor."

Without any indication of how long they'd be, their line dissolved into a lopsided oval buzzing with preoccupied small talk. Noah eyed the xenozoologists at the other end of the blob, but his head was teeming with illegible fuzz, nothing that could function in the conversation one of them had already roped Savannah into, half a step from the bounds of casual. Instead, he retreated back toward the edge of the waves, the sharp border where the sand darkened three shades.

It wasn't as hot at Lake Erie but he could lean into old habits, squinting out at the horizon and dropping himself there—far from the shifting surface underfoot, the mechanical churn over the shoulder, the dread pooling at his lower back, tight, begging him to bend over for a moment's relief. He was waiting for Frida to emerge from the trailer with a revelation; he was waiting for a call from his mother to tug him home by the threads of guilt she'd sewn that morning. He gazed toward unseen beaches both like and unlike where his shoes were half-buried, and he lived with a tiny voice curled around the bones of his inner ear murmuring how his survival depended on running to a far-off place as soon as his legs could manage—down the Atlantic coast, out of the Tau Ceti system, both and neither. Voices behind him took shades from his father, the neighbors down the hall, Abelard with a fracturing grip on his arm—

Clang!

Noah jumped and spun around in time to catch Frida fleeing the trailer, her stomping unsteady both from the sand and the livewire hold of her limbs. "What the fucking *fuck* is wrong with you?"

Irene let out a low whistle. "Whoa."

"That's not something you spring on a stranger without warning—just— there are *precautions* you should be—"

"Dr. Wick…" Henri stood in the trailer doorway, holding both hands up in some plea for a ceasefire. "We were going to get to that portion of the briefing, and—I do apologize… I understood it would be a treat for you…?"

Behind him, a twiggy Black man squeezed his way outside, settling on an open rung of the trailer steps a few days from being absorbed into the beach.

He ran his hand through the sparse gray hair clinging to his temples, a grimace refolding well-worn wrinkles.

Frida spotted him and froze.

"Yonas Gashaw… Yonas fucking Gashaw—this is what I get for not reading the briefing, huh?"

"Well—"

"Give me ten minutes. Ten! Minutes!" She marched toward the other end of the beach, closer to the path back to the ship, pausing every few yards to collect herself, steel her composure against the urge to scream.

The man she'd identified as Yonas conferred briefly with Henri before turning to the rest of the *Amihaf*. "Dr. Frida Wick, yes? Her work is very good."

"Maybe wait to tell her that," said Savannah. "She might not be back for a couple hours, otherwise."

With Frida gone, Henri and Yonas called after the ship doctor to replace her; Dayo hiked up the sand, making no effort to hide the suspicion coloring her face. The interrogation she inflicted upon the two of them when she reached the trailer's tiny stoop was too low to be overheard.

Noah slipped toward Savannah in the lull. "What was that about?"

"Oh—you wouldn't have seen one of her, uh… *moments*, would you," she said. "For all the grief she gives Esmail when he goes on one of his tangents —"

The trailer door cut across her with a whine, and when Noah looked up, Henri, Yonas, and Dayo had disappeared on the other side of it. Within seconds, the xenozoologists pulled him into their earlier conversation with Savannah, delighted to have pinned down their equivalent on the *Amihaf*. The older of the two, Nomvula, launched into a summary of the local xeno-organism that could save the Caspian Sea. Skittish and wisp-thin, the net eel consisted of a vaguely rectangular set of flesh clusters held together by a grid of electric currents, just barely visible to the naked eye. "If you know what to look for, of course," said the other, Sanelle. "And it doesn't hurt to have some of these."

She tapped the side of her glasses, a more high-tech model than the pair Frida wore. The thick lenses held not only Sanelle's prescription, but a transparent computer monitor with zoom capabilities.

"It doesn't always help you that much, my dear," said Nomvula. "I spot them twice as often as you do."

Sanelle quipped back in a language that Noah only knew was neither of TerraCosmos Central's operational standards.

More beads of sweat pearled down his back. The damp trails they left seared against his skin in the unrelenting heat, and he wondered after sunblock, how much of Tau Ceti's radiation penetrated the planet's dense atmosphere.

"What are you thinking about?" Savannah asked under her breath.

"How nice it was that red dwarf stars can't sunburn."

"You're far from a tomato. Don't worry."

He finished the unspoken half of her remark in his head: *there is plenty to worry about already to keep us busy.*

The door swung open once more, this time with far less fanfare. Dayo returned to the beach with Omar and Henri following close behind, Yonas hovering just inside the doorframe and blocking the view inside.

"I don't know what you expect me to do by myself," Dayo said. She stopped suddenly, addressing Omar and Henri without facing them. "I may be a physician, but if the last few months have taught me anything, it's that there is a lot about biology I still don't know. If Dr. Gashaw can't offer any leads for me to follow, then I need Frida."

"Okay," Omar said. "Okay. We understand."

Henri winced. "Will she—"

"For you? Absolutely not. Give me five minutes."

Ninety seconds later, Dayo was traipsing back across the beach with Frida beside her, both visibly displeased. Whether the pale pink flush spreading over Frida's face was born of frustration or the start of a sunburn was unclear.

"What the hell do you want from me?" she grumbled. "I haven't any bedside manner—"

"That's fine," Omar sighed.

She ran a hand through her hair, sweat molding its usual unruliness into a ginger mushroom cloud. "And anyway, shouldn't we be using some PPE about this? Tell me you at least have some face masks because I'm not going back in that trailer otherwise."

Henri made like he was about to say something and thought better of it, deferring to Yonas with a pointed glance.

"I understand your concern, Dr. Wick," he said, then paused, circling a knuckle in his first finger over the jaw joint at his sideburns. "We can discuss that facet of it later. Now, though…"

The hand at his temple dropped to his chest, meeting the other in a clasp before dropping down to his waist and dragging his head along with it— drooping down in a moment Noah could only attribute to prayer.

When his gaze became level with the horizon again, Yonas turned to Henri and Omar. "It's time for his grounding, conveniently."

"His what?" Quinn called after all of the Camp Ilunga residents, Sanelle and Nomvula included, returned to the trailer. "What does that mean?" He directed the question to Frida once the door clicked shut.

"Why the fuck would I know?"

Quickly Esmail positioned himself in Quinn's line of sight, holding his face in his hands and tempering down the retort primed at the back of his throat. Noah watched them, how their fingers laced together, how their murmuring tugged them into something intimate that gently guided Noah's eyes away. They instead latched onto the procession now leaving the trailer, to the figure in the folding chair that Yonas and Omar carried like a palanquin, obscured from view, around to a nearby expanse of empty sand. The *Amihaf* crew held their breath, the hot air crackling against soft lung tissue.

The figure in the chair was a man, whose gaunt frame spoke to a heavyset body losing weight at an unnatural and unhealthy pace. His skin was an ashen olive-tan until it neared his eyes. The violet there was a solid four steps past the usual hue of dark circles, and—

All of that was avoiding the point.

The man they paraded into the hazy morning sun was barely lucid. His head lolled, neck slack.

If Noah had chosen to move four steps to his left, he could have seen past the thick stem of a mushroom cap rising from the man's head, seen past the broken shell of his skull to the brain, all the pale white tendrils snaking through the wrinkles.

But Noah's feet were frozen in place. He could only imagine how far the mushroom burrowed, but clearer was the thin netted veil that crept forth from the man's hairline, down over his face, burying itself down into his collarbone. His face stretched in unseeing distress—until his chair was placed upon the ground, his bare feet molding into the sand.

Then it was relief.

Jibril al-Khattab had, until six weeks ago, little reason to frequent Omar in the medical trailer aside from what amounted to Nethuns' take on seasonal allergies. Congestion, headache, the occasional fit of sneezing—they'd all faced bouts of it as the seasons turned, with the biome's life spewing their various pollens and spores and pheromones and all the unknowns they had yet to identify. Zainab, the xenobotanist, fought cases of hives when the inland stone reeds misted in the summer winds. Yonas carried epinephrine in case he stepped on a beach slug buried in the sand and ruptured its lung sacs. The cycles when the sea's algae-like growths bloomed heavy and obscured the glassy surface with bulbous masses of green-black goo, Henri had taken to giving the entire base the week off rather than be the only one standing healthy among his miserable, sniffling colleagues.

But Jibril—he had only ever rasped and coughed through the algae, never anything else.

A persistent ache in his temple and joints failing to ebb after a couple days, and then still after rounds of examinations and routine painkillers: that was the first sign. Then he zapped himself making a basic repair to Nomvula's water meter. His headaches started to confine him to his bunk from the pain, and Omar's scans turned up nothing. Jibril started calling others by names plucked from parts of their lives he'd never been admitted into—he pinned on Henri the name of the man who married his ex-fiancée, on Sanelle the first name she'd tried on early in her transition.

Three days later, as the rising sun lightened the gray tint of the sky, Jibril woke with blood staining his pillow, shards broken off from the seam of his parietal and frontal bones in the smear of red.

"Downhill from there," said Zainab. They had inched their way into the farthest edge of the cluster watching Frida and Dayo circle Jibril, relaying the abbreviated version of events. "Obviously."

"Have you told Cairo?" asked Abelard.

"Haven't even told Kinshasa. Henri wouldn't hear it. So, no." They shrugged. "I think he's trying to save face. The first time he agrees to leave the Solar System after his accident is not going to be marred by whatever this is."

On either side of Noah, both Savannah and Quinn squirmed their feet against the sand.

"Omar disagrees," Zainab continued, "but I don't think it would've done any good."

None of the *Amihaf* said a word, though the air buzzed with it.

Near the medical trailer, the buzzing was closer to a static electricity zapping between the flyaways in Frida's hair and wherever Dayo's finger was pointing.

"So…" said Frida, scrolling through a document on a nature-battered tablet. "Looks like 'grounding' is basically… what, allowing the hyphae in Jibril's feet to reconnect with the larger mycelium?" She looked to Yonas, and he nodded. "That's what's sustaining him, probably. Nutrients-wise, I mean. The fungus has already…"

"It's depleted his body of anything it could use for its own purposes," Dayo said.

"But you knew that already." Frida's voice was empty of its typical grumpiness to the point she sounded like another person altogether. "Dr. Gashaw, you're among the best xenomycologists Earth has, living or dead. And I'm just—what are we supposed to offer here that you couldn't?"

"Firstly," he said, clapping a hand on Frida's shoulder, "call me Yonas."

"I physically cannot do that."

"Please, I insist."

"It's—look," she sighed. "There comes a point when you've cited someone's work in your own too many times to get chummy with them, and I passed that before getting accepted to grad school."

Behind them, Dayo pulled on gloves and armed herself with a pair of long tongue depressors and a penlight from the belt bag strapped across Omar's chest. Using them like chopsticks, she gently maneuvered the thin fleshy netting of the veil to better access Jibril's face.

"What is that magic number?" Yonas asked with the hint of a grin. "For my own reference."

"That's not the point."

"I know, but I am a curious man."

Yonas glanced toward the ongoing medical exam, watching closely as Dayo recruited Omar to shift Jibril's head so the penlight, now clenched between her teeth, could illuminate even a sliver of his eyes.

"You have to understand, Dr. Wick..." he said, still fixated on Dayo and Omar. "I have done nothing but sit with Jibril since he woke with a cracked skull. I have studied the specimen that has taken root in his body. I sampled what I could until it became evident that to even scrape away at the cap put him in considerable pain. I listened as he addressed me as my father, asking after the progress of a painting he never exhibited or even mentioned publicly. I know everything about his condition and yet… also nothing."

The two of them stood in silence for a moment, Frida chewing at the inside of her bottom lip. "Did you figure out what local species infected him, at least?"

"That's the odd part." His fingers worried at a patch of facial hair he'd missed shaving. "You spoke of the mycelium he's connecting to. In all the surveys we've done of the surrounding area, there has been a bizarre absence of any visible fruiting bodies. The samples I did manage to get—I have nothing to compare them to."

"Hm… tell me more about these surveys."

"Of course. The reports are in the lab." He motioned to the line of trailers with a nod, and they set off, their further discussion fading.

By Jibril, Dayo and Omar had contorted themselves trying to examine him around the fungus encasing his body. Dayo's legs had started to shake under the strain of the sharp angles pressed upon her knees.

"Do you… um…" said Esmail. "Do you need an extra hand? I have two."

"No, no." Omar shook his head. "I'd really like to limit the people who get close to him to—just medical and mycological folks. I do appreciate it, though."

"What about me?"

Abelard had situated himself directly behind Dayo, so he couldn't see the pained expression that flew across her face. Omar missed it as well, his eyes firmly fixed over her shoulder on the eager grin half-hidden under his mustache.

"It shouldn't affect his system," said Henri, and at that Omar motioned for him to approach—which he did with all the pageantry of caution.

Jibril's eyes snapped open, wild.

"Mad! Mad! Mad, mad, mad!" His arm not caught between Omar and Dayo flung forward, pointing frantically at Abelard's chest. "Mad, mad! The monomaniacal wave crests high in the heart, driving the tide toward a dark and hollow hell—"

"Back up, back up!" Dayo yelled. "Give him some space!"

"Dr. Oyekan, I am more than ten feet away—"

"That's clearly not enough!"

Wobbling on the uneven surface of the beach, Noah rushed forward, Savannah in step beside him. They each latched onto one of Abelard's elbows, but he held his body firm, statuesque, even as they pleaded.

He stared at Jibril with the same look that would glow across his face watching a student off on a tangent of discovery. Warmth, a fond curiosity, all while the residents of Camp Ilunga took in the sight with horror.

Wincing as the edges of the veil brushed against the bare skin above his gloves, Omar struggled to hold Jibril in his seat even while leveraging all of his weight onto his shoulders. The longer the sermon ran on, the stronger Jibril appeared to become.

"Henri," Omar hissed, *"min fadlik—"*

"—and this realm will never drag itself out of godlessness for your kind, not while you claim—"

A sudden spike of heat rolled through Noah's body as Quinn and Irene grabbed onto Abelard's arms beside him and Savannah. Irene looped her whole arm through Abelard's, positioning herself back-to-back with him, leaning forward to use gravity to her advantage. She locked eyes with Noah, severe but unreadable.

"You are not helping the situation here," said Quinn. "We need to *retreat*."

"But—no, I'm sure…" Abelard shifted his body like he was going to take a step forward, and all four of them yanked back. Even if it couldn't hold him in place, it was enough to make him hesitate, as if he'd merely misread the situation.

"—and, at the end, you shall not even be afforded the prophesied coffin, broken upon the shore of—"

Suddenly Jibril fell silent, slumped in his seat. Henri now stood at Omar's side, and when he pulled an arm back, his hand was gripped around the end of a syringe, assumedly from Omar's pack. Dayo delicately extracted herself from the fungal veil and flopped on the sand to catch her breath, flicking thick beads of sweat from her brow.

Noah fought the urge to collapse himself. The sand burned even through his soles, and he wasn't keen to put his face or vital organs that much closer to the hard toe of Abelard's boot.

"What the hell was that all about?" Dayo said after a moment.

Omar and Henri's muttering in Arabic paused.

"Which part?" asked Omar.

"Are you kidding me? All of it! All of—" She flailed both hands toward Jibril, toward them, all the sweat still clinging to her gloves flinging in a wide spray. "I've seen—I…" With a couple slow breaths, she peeled the gloves off, taking ritualistic care to rub the residual power from her fingers. "I have seen," she repeated, calmer, "so many patients ailing from some unfortunate xenological contact. I have treated submarine crews ill with parasites after nearly drowning on Europa and managed quarantine wards with… wait, is he immunocompromised?"

"No," said Omar. "Jibril was one of the healthiest among us, even got all the optional xenopatho boosters before we shipped out."

"That's…"

"Not great, no." Henri, hands on his hips, gazed down with the concern of a father with an ill child. "It is all very troubling, especially because… Jibril doesn't speak English."

A clammy chill rose up Noah's neck through the ever-thickening heat, one he couldn't fully recognize before Henri dismissed them all—he allowed only Omar to help carry Jibril back inside, and a flurry arose trying to brush away anything related to what they just witnessed. One moment, Abelard and Irene and Savannah were there beside Noah, and then they weren't, and Nomvula was asking him something that he didn't fully hear but nodded along to anyway, and Sanelle conferred with them both before dashing off down the beach, and then Noah found Irene pointing out where Esmail had gotten off to —closer to the lapping waves with Zainab, angled away from the now-vacant ground zero.

Noah watched as Quinn approached them, easing into the bubble they'd created—Esmail spotted him, beamed wide, and then wider still when Quinn dipped down to kiss him. Tension slipped from his shoulders with Quinn's palms against his jawline.

"We're good here."

Irene. She and Savannah flanked the trio at the water from the foreground.

"Oh… okay, yeah—"

"Back on planet, space-walker?" said Savannah.

"Sure."

Irene flashed a thumbs-up and nodded toward the other end of the base. He followed the trajectory to where the sand tapered off against a craggy few feet of chalky rock, upon which Sanelle stood gripping a knot of rope. The other end tied around the tip of a roughshod rowboat.

"Hey! Xenozoology man!" she yelled. "Come on! We are murdering the afternoon!"

"Killing daylight," Nomvula said.

He had agreed to this, whatever it was, so he mumbled an exit and struck a path forward on the strip of sand laid flatter and firmer from the waves. The tips of his ears throbbed, hot to the touch. Ahead, Sanelle and Nomvula were transferring the rowboat down the rocks, arms splayed around the edges of it, shouting over each other, until it finally thumped bow-first into the beach. It barely missed Nomvula's foot, and Sanelle flailed to keep her balance for a precarious few seconds.

"We were not selected for this project for our grace," said Sanelle when he reached them, hopping down the rocks. "What's your name again?"

"Noah Starbuck." He reached down to the vine and began tugging the boat toward the surf.

"Hm. I thought so," said Nomvula.

"And by that you mean…?"

"You and Cousteau are a package deal lately for a lot of people in the field." Sanelle patted his shoulder in passing. "And… well, try not to be worrying."

A humorless chuckle escaped him before he could catch it, though if they noticed, they opted to let it pass.

Noah laid on top of his sheets that night, the astringently-sweet odor of sunburn salve inescapable in the cramped bunk. The state of his skin had only been apparent once he returned to the *Amihaf* after dinner; after Omar had ducked out of dinner early, Dayo procured a tube of the strongest Terrestrial formula in the AutoChemist's files, and it wasn't for nothing. The deep muscle ache had faded, and his knees hadn't buckled under the searing pain of blood pumping against burnt skin when he got up to use the restroom—but the only position in bed that didn't bite was lying on his back, and he would never get to sleep that way.

He stared at the ceiling, then down his nose to Spock on the bookshelf. Hesitant to move against the rough sheets supplied by the ship and battling a time change that put Nethuns' midnight at 1600 IST, there was little else to do but sit with the thoughts his boot heel had been grinding down into the beach all day.

That much effort wasn't required around Nomvula and Sanelle earlier that afternoon. Their chatter rang constant as the three of them took turns rowing to one of the deeper trenches they'd mapped since landing on-planet; and in the moments when they remembered to steer themselves to English for longer than half a sentence, there was so much to untangle that he couldn't have possibly spared one single iota of attention for Abelard or Jibril or the scene that had just passed between them.

Being xenozoologists themselves, Nomvula and Sanelle had followed Abelard's work, his death and also, with the delay born of their spot in the galaxy, his resurrection. The news of it arrived just over two weeks before the *Amihaf* touched down outside Camp Ilunga.

When it was his turn to man the oars, he mentioned Henri offhand, something about how he'd never seen someone with a silver-plated ConBod before in an attempt to wade away from touchy territory—the other two exchanged an inscrutably eager look before launching into a burst of what probably counted as gossip this isolated from the rest of humanity. The silver tone was standard, they explained, for Prana Technologies' Constructed Body models thirty years ago when Henri had his own run-in with the ruinous vectors of space. His first mission outside the orbit of the Moon, fresh off a postdoc at the Sorbonne, and a rogue chunk of rock slammed into the ship—peeling off a layer of the thermal shields like it was a soil-grown carrot, scraping along until it collided with his body, tethered on a spacewalk.

It reduced his bones to gravel.

Dr. Omar Elbaz, also on his first interstellar assignment, transported his body to the med bay with the urgency of someone who, despite his superiors' insistence, refused to accept the apparent futility of the circumstances. Inside the G-suit was a gory mess burying a stubborn heart and brain, which their ship delivered to the battalion of medical staff at Cernunnos Station within the hour. Rigil Kentaurus burned hot as they docked, Toliman and Proxima Centauri winking brightly behind it, and Omar handed off the gurney with multiple voices and accents reassuring him that there was an empty Constructed Body ready to finish saving Henri's life.

Four years later, Omar opened the door to his home in Isdud to a familiar man tinged with silver holding out a tin of makrout so uneven that they could only have been homemade.

From then on, any time either of them was assigned to some mission far-flung from Earth, the other joined him, and for twenty-odd years that never dragged them outside the Kuiper Belt.

Until now, of course. Nomvula had a few theories as to what finally changed his mind. Sanelle's curiosity didn't extend that far, the *why* of it all. She was more concerned with the *what* of Henri's behavior, a phobia acting out when they crossed the border of its comfort zone in the first week of travel. Mostly, she said, it was a matter of him being so cautious that it interfered with their ability to do research—even if the measures he took couldn't prevent what happened with Jibril.

Has he seemed normal otherwise? Noah asked. *Relative to—*

He's an academic past his sixties, said Sanelle. *'Normal' is not… okay, you are clearly thinking about this from another side. So: if Captain Bouferma's behavior was a reason to be worried, Omar would be the first to start the alerts, and he's been quiet for decades.*

And so the nascent theory Noah had harbored since their arrival on Nethuns died, withering under Henri's Constructed feet.

Whatever comfort there was to draw from the moment had long since departed. Surely an older model of a ConBod should have been buggier. Surely the issues they saw—if they were innocuous—were reproducible, evident in other brainware systems in the vast reach of humanity. Newer releases could introduce new problems, of course, but nothing to the scale that they'd witnessed over the last several months. All evidence continued to point to something wrong under Abelard's synthetic skin.

Still, Noah doubted. He doubted despite the phantom bruise at his elbow, the hot spray of blood on his face. He thought back so often to the spider in Abelard's office, the smeared brown stain lined by a lone surviving leg, the mournful pall that settled onto his brow. Consciously and unconsciously he rolled his memory back to that day, until his hand reduced the spider to a smudge of red and the office walls were tree trunks pressing in, and the doubt didn't so much vanish but thin, adjust itself until Noah couldn't make sense of it at all.

Someone screamed.

Started screaming, kept screaming—

Noah fell off his bed in the jolt, hissing at the tight, twinging pull of his sunburn as he slammed against the floor. He clambered to his feet once the worst of the surging pain waned.

His wasn't the only head poking out from behind a bunk door; Irene and Frida both rubbed sleep from their eyes, unfocused gazes latching onto him for lack of anything else distinct in the dark hallway.

Aside from the screaming.

Which, Noah finally pinned down, was coming from behind the door opposite his own—Quinn and Esmail's room.

He got halfway across the hall, arm outstretched to knock, before he stopped himself. No matter which one of them was in distress, the last thing Esmail needed was more sensory overload.

But then, just as suddenly as it began, the screaming cut away to nothing.

A moment later, Quinn came within an inch of ramming straight into Noah. "Shit, sorry—"

"No, no, I should've moved—are you…?"

The door to the bunk slid shut behind him, and Quinn surveyed the small assembly in the hall, now joined by Dayo and her gold bonnet that seemed to glow even in the dim light. "Didn't mean to wake you."

"Try again," said Irene. She slipped around Frida, then between Noah and Quinn into the galley. "What does he need? Water?"

"Uh—yeah, that's…"

She disappeared around the partition before he could get the words out, his shoulders sagging.

"If you want to get back to sleep, I can get you two some meds," Dayo said, and Quinn waved the thought away. "Are you sure?"

"Yeah," he said, nodding. "Not the first time this has happened."

Irene returned with a perilously-full glass of water, and Quinn redirected her to the lounge. They'd both be out in a moment, he said, for anyone who wasn't keen on returning to bed. His eyes lingered on Frida as he said this, and her mouth pinched against an instinctive scowl.

Noah blinked, sharp with fatigue, and then only he and Frida remained in the hall. She stared at him, blank. "Savannah has slept through four separate fire alarms in the past two years. I doubt she'll—"

"Wasn't wondering," she muttered. With her arms wrapped around her sides, she for once appeared as short as she actually was, barely brushing the bottom of five feet and then still shrinking further, as if she were repaying what it took to cast herself a taller shadow.

On the other side of the bunk door beside them, Quinn's murmuring bobbed along, indistinct.

As they all collected around the lounge table, claiming slivers of couch or sections of floor, the mess of the space aligned with how the last dregs of grogginess hung on their shoulders. Someone had attempted a menial bit of tidying since they landed, but Quinn's knitting needles still skewered the ceiling. The stack of papers and tablets mixed Frida's crossword collections, doodle sheets taken from Irene's notebooks, and scraps with shorthand lists that could have belonged to anyone. A few pieces of furniture had swapped cushions.

No one spoke. Quinn and Esmail stepped into the light, claimed the empty spots left for them on the couch. Water dribbled down the side of the glass when Esmail brought it to his lips, both hands rounding the sides in a vise grip. They didn't shake. The glass was half empty before anyone even tried to clear their throat.

"So." Irene gently patted her knees. "So…"

Dayo raised an eyebrow.

"I thought someone else was going to run with that," she sighed. "Broken seal of silence. Or…"

"Do you want to talk about it?" asked Noah, low enough that it was clear he was speaking just to Esmail. "You don't have to, obviously. Um… y'know, you were telling me about this journal article that got published a few weeks after we left Lulal. The one I'm not subscribed to, out of Yerevan? You were saying how this xeno-organism in the Teegarden system —"

"Not right now," Esmail said, mostly to his feet.

"Oh. Okay—"

"My nightmare. It was…" Carefully he set the glass down on the table, then gestured in a wide arc over his head. Over and over he traced the shape of it, his face crumpling in frustration as the words lined up and died before they could be spoken. "Anything else," he finally said. "Frida!"

Curled up in one of the armchairs, she suddenly sprang open, finger-laced latches pulling free. "What?"

"What's your favorite movie?"

And that thread spun out into tangent upon tangent until the route back to the source was untraceable. A hundred subjects in as many minutes pinging between them, at least half of which Esmail must have had an opinion to share, and a lengthy one at that—but he kept quiet, leaned into Quinn when the darker tan of his thumb rubbed at the inside of his knee, listened. He laughed as loud as any of them when Dayo relayed the story of Ikemba's first journey to space.

"Weird hour for a party."

Savannah stood in the entrance to the bunk hall, fully dressed for the day but still squinting against the last remnants of the night, her hair pooling around her face in an unsymmetrical cloud.

"We weren't *that* loud, were we?" asked Noah.

"No way," she said, shuffling toward the mimeo in search of what Noah assumed was coffee. "Zainab is taking me to see a patch of... oh, I don't remember what they called it, but it retracts into the soil at night and resprouts at sunrise. Bit of a hike, too, so..." She gestured toward a wall clock that didn't exist as the mimeo whirred.

"Well," said Frida after a moment, "that does sound more low-stakes than whatever awaits in the land of xenomycology, so color me jealous."

Savannah grinned to herself. "Noted." The mimeo dinged, the aroma slowly seeping into the lounge. A moment later she reappeared at the galley partition, mug in hand. "What did you find out, by the way? Y'know, after you and Gashaw broke off?"

"Just local surveys," she said. "Lots of cataloging and..." She paused, noticing Esmail pulling his knees up to his chest. "The work's not exciting, just checking there was due diligence."

Even with the coffee, Savannah's eyes had fallen shut as she nodded along. The motion of bringing the mug to her mouth appeared automated—until she jerked awake from the voice calling from the level below.

"*Ya* Savannah!" Zainab's boots clunked across the foyer. "You are awake, yes?"

"Yep! Yep, yep, yep—" she threw back the rest of the coffee in a few quick swallows, winced against the still-steaming heat of it. Noah was the closest to where she stood, so she tossed him the emptied mug as she bolted down the stairs. "Ready to go!" she said, distant.

The lounge sat quiet.

Seconds passed, then minutes. Slabs of minutes. As the hour mark approached, Esmail sighed.

"The pilot I said was beneath me when we were approaching the system... that was Jibril," he said.

Irene nudged the toe of his slippered foot. "You didn't know."

"That doesn't help." He buried his face into the cavern lined by his chest and folded legs. "He's... how many planets are we supposed to go to that clearly want us gone?"

"That's not what this is," said Frida. She stared at the corner of the table with a canine digging into her bottom lip. "It's a xeno-organism—in this case, a fungus—reacting with human biochemistry. We don't understand it yet, certainly not enough to ascribe any... what, *motive* to it." She glanced at the porthole and its hint of sunrise, sighing as she pulled herself to her feet. "But... I can, um—understand, at least, that it could feel that way."

Murmuring something about Yonas' own early schedule, she retreated to her bunk; a few minutes later, bedhead somewhat tamed, she jogged to the stairs, taking two at a time. With each clang of footsteps, others drifted away, citing tentative ideas for the day, until Noah was left with Esmail and Quinn.

"Frida's right, you know," he said. "The planet isn't trying to—"

"Well..." Quinn frowned. "I don't—and I'm not just saying this because it's her, all right? I'm not that petty." He waited for him to push, and Noah motioned that he was holding his tongue, even though he hadn't been about to say anything. "I think we're right to be wary of whatever is going on here."

The wide gawp of Jibril as he intoned—mouth stretched open, pulling the skin at angles accustomed to a rounder face—frozen in Noah's memory, laid under speckled light from the fungal veil. His English was impeccable, ripped from nowhere, thick in the throat. Sanelle, rowing the shore under the horizon, had talked to herself through each stroke: Jibril spent all his foreign language credits in the TerraCosmos flight school on Swahili and Kurdish, Jibril's only English was butchered lyrics from a pop band out of Tkaronto and nothing close to the London twang that had settled into his larynx. A man possessed, she'd said. A puppeted finger pointing straight between Abelard's eyes, to his new body's true eye, to the brainware knotting anew with every piece of stimulus.

"Being wary about Jibril doesn't—*I'm* wary of extrapolating the intentions of a planet from one infection," said Noah. "Not to mention that planets can't have intentions. It's a hunk of rock in space."

"Which that fungus helps make up," said Quinn. "Everything on a planet is part of the whole. Humanity trying to live as if it existed outside of that whole instead of as one of its many pieces is what put us on the path to the Climate Catastrophe."

"I don't disagree with you there. But Earth didn't exactly open its mouth and tell us as much."

Quinn stared at him. The joint in his jaw flexed, betraying the effort to maintain the stoic blank of his face. "Didn't it?"

Sighing, he turned away from Noah and squeezed Esmail's knee. He needed someone to help him talk through the latest trials in the ever-present logging problem, he said, and Esmail would be perfect. There had been a breakthrough, an error thrown that he'd never encountered before, and it was promising. His gaze trailed after Esmail as he shuffled to their bunk. The soft thump of an unfurling prayer rug sounded before the door slid shut behind him.

"You know…" Quinn said after a moment. "I didn't want this assignment."

"With Project Khepri?"

Quinn nodded. "Years off-planet was too much. Neither of us ever does anything longer than a few months. Usually it's two, three weeks. We're rarely on the same ship, and I hate being away from him and my sister. But the look on his face when he saw the posting... I don't think he'd ever wanted anything more."

Distantly, beyond the exit ramp, Frida and Yonas talked past each other, bits and pieces of thoughts jostled into white noise.

"I didn't really feel like I had a choice, either," Noah said.

"It's not that." Quinn studied his face, an odd tilt to his mouth. "The only way Esmail would let himself dream of being on this crew is if I came too, and this was—there weren't going to be many other chances like this with a research vessel, if any, and I wanted that for him. Now though..."

They both glanced down at the half-empty glass of water Irene had fetched for Esmail.

"Now I just wonder if all this is going to ruin what he loves most," Quinn said. "Aside from me, of course."

"I was about to ask," said Noah through a thin laugh.

"Yeah, yeah..." He hoisted himself to his feet, hand running along the shade of stubble crowning his head. "Anyway... might as well set up those test scripts while he's getting ready."

Noah waited until he heard the dull scrap of stool legs below at Quinn's station before unfolding his limbs against the achy burn. He dragged his feet returning to his bunk to get properly dressed, eyeing the slit of light under the last closed door in the hall.

Abelard.

A few brief shadows split the thin beam into sections, disappearing, then doubling back as if he were pacing.

It could be something, and it could be nothing.

The verdict, whatever it was, would not be delivered while he stood there, nor as he emerged a few minutes later still tugging on his boots. He heard no footsteps above him as he descended to the foyer and then down into the haze of seashore. The sun blazed, and he could forget about Abelard in the moments that demanded he hasten through ankle-high dunes, Nomvula's silver braids in the lab trailer a veritable rescue beacon.

She and Sanelle took pity on Noah as the worst of his sunburn faded; they sat him in front of stacks of data, graphs, and hand-drawn anatomical diagrams while they ventured back out to survey another grid square of the sea. Two days passed tucked away out of the sun, the rest of their crews popping in and out to check figures, stash field notes, or just give their bodies a chance to dial their temperatures down out of the fever tier. Savannah dropped in more often than anyone when Zainab wasn't leading them through the wetlands.

"Don't ever let me complain about Rassawek's weather ever again," she muttered, wringing out her socks into the sink. "I know I'll try, but you can't let me, okay?"

By the end of day two, as Nomvula and Sanelle briefed him on their latest sets of raw data, Noah found himself picking up a few words of the language they slipped into, which he now knew was Zulu. They were deep in a technical discussion with no signs of English, fingers pointing at various sweat-stained scrap papers as they argued their point like he was some sort of judge, and all he could do was nod thoughtfully at the right lulls.

At least until they both paused, squinting at him.

"What did I miss?" he asked.

"You nodded," said Sanelle, a knuckle pushing up her glasses. "It wasn't a yes or no question."

"Just because I figured out what *ulwandle* translates to doesn't mean I'm fluent."

Nomvula clucked her tongue. "Well, it's inconvenient."

"I've heard that before."

Leaning forward, chin in hand, Sanelle peered at him, grinning. "Oh? Do you really only speak English? The way Frida talked about it, I thought schools in the Testudines required learning the local language."

"Encouraged, sure…" He picked at the folded corner of one of the graphs, the crease turning soft. "I just wasn't very good at the—uh, speaking part of anything. I ended up taking Latin. Maybe it's different on the southern end," he added.

"Typical," Nomvula said, stifling a laugh. She rolled her eyes and motioned widely around her, rolling out some quip Sanelle choked on before she could join in.

Through the blinds of the trailer window, Noah spotted Tau Ceti descending under the horizon with the promise of an easing heat. He jumped up, chair legs screeching against the floor, and he shouldered his way out of the trailer and down to the beach.

The scene was bathed in a gentle peach-purple light, still hot as ever, with a mineral tang in the air.

To his right, Zainab was walking Savannah through the steps of a dance, too slowly for the swing of her hair to match the lagging beat, but their knees bent and hips tilted in sync, the sand clutching the edges of their shifting feet. Crunching footsteps stomped closer from the other side of the trailer, Frida on a tear of thinking out loud while Yonas attempted to slip a remark between breaths.

Noah turned, putting his back to the sea, and squeezed his eyes shut until sparks bloomed from the corners. The same sizzling static as migraine aura, but the wrong shape, stepping out of monochrome. He focused on the melody Zainab hummed low. The whine of the trailer steps under the concentrated weight of a single foot. The sharp scrape of rocks grinding against each other. Layer after layer, until the rumbling bass grasping up from the depths of years gone by was dampened to nothing—or, not nothing, but a sparse collection of frames.

Afternoon light burning through the balcony window. The obstinate stain on the corner of the kitchen table. A tablet displaying abysmal marks in Spanish II hanging on the home's blanket ban on anything Iroquoian. A Krakatoa of a man about to burst, looming, blotting out the sun.

No detail. No sound. Noah sucked in a long breath, enough to stretch the borders of his lungs, released it. Then all of it was gone.

When he opened his eyes, Omar and Henri were guiding Jibril down for his grounding. The edges of the mushroom cap had started to curl into itself, toward the thick ring of gills.

Ten yards separated them. The fungal veil obscured the details of his face. And still—his head whipped toward Noah, and again his voice carried a language that should have been foreign to him.

"The blasphemer's end draws near!"

"I just want to get a second—or, fine, third or fourth opinion."

As she spoke over the crowded breakfast mess table on the *Amihaf*, Frida fiddled with the loose ends of a sun hat woven out of dried sea vines. It had been a gift from Omar and Nomvula on Yonas' last birthday, and he'd loaned it to her out of pity as she started to char.

"A fourth opinion on what?" Savannah asked over the top of her coffee mug.

"Not about to tell Yonas fucking Gashaw that his conclusions don't make any sense. Not without reassurance that I'm not mental, all right?" She shoved the hat out of reach, the brim knocking against Noah's half-eaten plate of eggs. "I just can't square what he's saying with the data and what I've observed sticking out of that poor bloke's brain."

"I don't know anything about fungus," she said.

Noah shrugged. "Neither do I."

"You're still biologists, aren't you? Science, yeah? You're good at it?" She wrinkled her nose in an attempt to nudge up her glasses, huffing when the silence lasted a moment past her liking. "That's what I thought. Just—please come with me out into the marsh. Dr. Gashaw's been roped into some consulting ordeal all day with Bouferma and…"

She trailed off, her fingers' work tying up the frayed threads of the hat slowing until they curled back into fists. "I can think better without the pressure of the world's greatest xenomycologist lurking behind me, but there's no way in hell I'm going out there alone."

Noah and Savannah exchanged a glance; they could save the follow-up *why* on that last remark for later.

"Yeah," said Noah. "Whatever you need."

Muttering thanks, Frida flashed the table's surface a grimace of a grin. "It's not going to get any cooler out there."

Half an hour later, as they made their way to the exit ramp, Irene poked her head out of the cockpit. "Field trip?"

"I guess? Technically?" said Frida, frowning. "Why, do you want to come?"

"Absolutely."

At his usual station near the cockpit wall, Quinn sat hunched over his sleek laptop, Esmail beside him on another stool plucked from the lab. Irene slipped past to grab a few items from their bunk, and neither of them budged.

"I know, Quinn, you're really busy," Savannah said, "but Esmail—if you want to come, we're probably going to see—"

"I'll pass."

"Are you sure?" Noah asked. "I read yesterday that they've found potential evidence of a quadrisexual species of... I don't know what, but it's similar to what you were talking about before we got to Lulal, remember? The—"

"I'll pass."

Quinn glanced up from the laptop with a brief, wordless plea to let the matter go.

"Right." Frida tossed them both a casual salute. "See you later, then."

Irene caught up with the group just as they reached the head of the path. The prickly shoots of grasses broken and trampled still retained the red-black tint of life, unlike those lining the gap abutting Camp Ilunga proper, having turned into a matted mass of gray.

The *Amihaf* cast a long shadow at that hour of the morning, leaving only a thin strip of the sandy soil lit before the grass crowded in. Frida, at the front, paused at that edge and mashed the hat onto the final remaining spikes of bedhead. "Okay. Got the hat—the rest of you got that special sunblock Omar formulated? Great," she said once the rest of them nodded. "Now that melanoma's been thwarted, let's go poke at a different beast!"

She glanced over her shoulder as she beckoned them forward. She wore a toothy smile stretched painfully wide, quivering under the effort.

The sudden blaze of heat as they stepped out of the shade of the ship swept up their trains of thought, narrowed them down to keeping pace with Frida's short legs. The bulk of the ship soon dipped out of sight, taking the rush of the surf with it.

The issue with Yonas' analysis, she said, was that it didn't know what to do with the gap of contradiction, the mismatch of what the data meant and what they could observe. Nethuns' ecosystem was abundant with xenomycological life—not only evidenced by Jibril's condition, but also by the soil samples Yonas and Zainab had taken on a biweekly basis ever since Camp Ilunga became operational. The nitrogen and potassium levels were a footprint, and the cap that broke Jibril's skull open was a severed toe—

"Could you use a different metaphor?" Savannah groaned.

"—but there hasn't been any sign of the actual body. There," said Frida. "All done. But to put it another way, something closer to your wheelhouse, we have an apple far away from any visible apple tree."

When she mentioned this hypothetical apple, her hands mimed pressing against a bulbous mass on the side of her head; Savannah's frown deepened, a hand digging in her pocket for her favorite pen.

She kept miming the motion as her speech ran on—the apple and the mushroom cap both served reproductive purposes for the larger organism. Much like Terrestrial fungi, most of the species that had fallen under the xenomycology umbrella maintained the bulk of their anatomy in the soil. A wide stretch of forest floor dotted with mushrooms after a rainstorm would likely come from the same organism's mycelial network, a network Jibril connected to during the process of his grounding.

"So the originating fungus exists, obviously, but Dr. Gashaw hasn't been able to find any direct physical evidence of the mycelium—the hyphae. The roots. They can be as thin as a spider web, so you can't really have a little party with a trowel. But if we can't find the hyphae, we should be able to find the mushrooms, right? The fucker wrapped around Jibril's brain is enormous! But there's nothing! No caps, no fungal veils, no mold patches or films of mildew. *Nothing.* And Dr. Gashaw doesn't know what to think, especially because the spores had to get to Jibril somehow, and he's not the type to go around swallowing dirt—which, yes, I asked."

The uneven patter of their footfalls bridged the silence.

"You asked Yonas Gashaw if one of his colleagues ate dirt?" Irene said.

"Of course not," she huffed. "I asked Sanelle."

The conversation fell flat after that. The grasses reached higher around them, winnowing to a point just above Noah's temple, their stalks thin and prone to folding when the wind kicked up in the wrong direction. The tips left a cold stinging stripe where they brushed against his face, an itch bubbling to the surface once the chill subsided—that bit was almost pleasant.

Savannah pulled his hand down from where it was idly scratching at his chin. "You're spreading the oils. Stop."

The grasses quit abruptly as the sandy soil melted into something closer to mud, patches of silty water erasing any path the crew of Camp Ilunga may have blazed in the years prior. Instead, the mud birthed a field of stone reeds. Noah had listened in while Zainab gave a crash course to Savannah over lunch the first full day—straddling the line between flora and mineral, they were far more fascinating than any other xenobotanical life on Nethuns, but utterly useless for Project Khepri, so Zainab couldn't study it as much as they would have liked, even when their allergies were lying dormant.

Each of the individual reeds stood between six and a half and seven feet tall. The top of each reed was a flat square, two or three inches to a side, and showed no evidence of weather-softened angles. Against the dark red backdrop of the grasses, their gray-tan hue left the whole scene a sickly sort of drab.

Frida stopped their procession just before the mud overtook the sand. "The way Dr. Gashaw tells it, Zainab wanted a sample from these reed things while they were, uh… what do they call it?"

"Misting," said Savannah. "It's their version of releasing pollen, but it looks more like condensation."

"Right, well, that's what they're allergic to," Frida said, rotating to face them on a single heel. "So they asked Jibril to hike out here, scrape some chips away, and get some of the liquid. Everyone else was busy. And a week later, his headache started up."

The translucent puddles of grime winked against the sun with a new menacing undercurrent as their feet shifted against the silt.

"Don't get like that. He was the last one who hadn't come out this way yet, and the rest of them are fine." Frida ground the base of her palm against her forehead. "All that aside, I don't see a whole lot of fungal activity out here."

She had a point. The lone bits of color among the bases of the reeds and mud were archipelagos of lichen or moss sparsely arcing around the edges of the standing water.

"So…" she sighed. "Given all that information, I do have—it's an idea. A little closer to vacuum leviathan territory than the seas of Europa. No offense," she added to Noah, and he shrugged. "Dr. Gashaw believes that Jibril's infection was likely brought on by spores blown in from an unsurveyed part of the local biome. A fluke, basically. And it's not that it doesn't make sense, but…"

Then both heels of her palms were at her head, digging on the line of her cheekbones and shoving her glasses up into the dense jungle of her bangs. Her speech fell into a well-worn muttering rut, a practiced rant about the postdoc research she'd done on fungal samples retrieved from the Kapteyn system, comparing the chemicals in its gossamer-threaded clouds to muscimol and psilocybin. Any time TerraCosmos sent a ship out that way, at least a third of the crew returned still sporting some degree of ego death by the time the launch base cleared them after landing. "Those folks got weird in the head, sure," she said. "But they never—ego death is a perception, not reality, and it's temporary. Just because you *feel* at one with the universe doesn't mean the universe is actually reaching out to your electrified meat sack. But Jibril…"

They waited for her to collect herself, quiet aside from the wind wending through the grasses at their backs. Even Irene's pen had paused, hovering above the notebook that had been braced open against her breastbone.

"It's one thing to hear the rest of them talk about all the out-of-pocket shit he knew. It's another to hear him—fuck, mention the girlfriend I had at uni by name and where we had our first date. So something else is going on here," she said, hurtling past that moment of vulnerability as fast as her mouth could take her. "If this xeno-organism can relay information like that across almost twenty years and trillions of miles, then it can also play a complicated camouflage game, right? That's not an unreasonable assumption to make?"

As Tau Ceti ascended higher, Frida tugging down the brim of the hat over her eyes, the humid air grew closer to a fully solid thing, heavy on their shoulders. The vertical edges of the stone reeds shone; their misting season had passed, but moisture still clung to them, finding nowhere else to unload in the marsh.

Sweat pooled at the small of Noah's back, just as it had so many days in Rassawek. *Unreasonable* was a word Abelard had banned from their conversations, whether in lab or office hours of official adviser meetings or chance encounters off campus when Noah caught him hugging a to-go box of pad se ew to his chest. *The data says this, so would it be unreasonable—* and Abelard would stop him there with a look, a knuckle rapped against the desk, a grating whistle.

None of that, he'd say. *None of that preemptive value judgment. What does the data say? Spare us the rest.*

"You're taking into account all the facts," said Noah. "And that's a pretty significant one. Why would that be unreasonable?"

"The implications. It's the… have you tried to talk to him, Noah? Have any of you? You'll have a different attitude once he reaches in and yanks out something you haven't thought about in ages. Something you maybe—I don't know, liked where it had been this whole time."

Irene frowned. "Frida…"

"Whatever. The specific section of the stone reed field Jibril went to is just over that ridge." She pointed off in the distance where the flat expanse of mud rose up, grasses bending against an unfelt push of wind. "We can head over that way. Maybe you lot'll see something we didn't."

Tentatively she pressed a foot into the soggy earth, and when it didn't immediately swallow her foot, she strode forward without any vestiges of caution. Irene followed behind her, and then, after a tense wince from Savannah, Noah hopped after them. Savannah gripped a bunch of the back of his shirt in her fist as they traveled that last hundred yards, and he didn't have the wherewithal to shrug it off, relay how anything underfoot didn't care about a buddy-system precaution. A spore was a spore, a virus a virus.

Still, Noah reached back at the odd angle, latched a hand around her wrist and squeezed, lingering. Her other hand clasped against the other side of his.

Soon the mud began to suck at their shoes, a gloppy suction splattering with every step they yanked from its grip. Their weights broke through the thin film that had settled on top, and the pits left by their footprints released a foul odor, sharp with sweet-rot. Noah's boots were covered in black slop up to his ankles.

"Good thing I didn't wear my slip-ons," Irene muttered.

"Glad not to ruin a favorite pair of socks?" asked Frida over her shoulder; she'd paused, adding an extra bit of wriggle to pull her next step free.

"You said the fungal roots went through his feet, right?"

Frida's foot shot up out of the mud with a low *slorp*; she flailed, the muck creeping up toward the top of her other boot, until Noah caught a strap on her knapsack. The upper half of her body laid nearly parallel to the ground. "Fucking hell… thanks." They both took a couple steadying breaths, and Noah's heart rate eased as Frida righted herself. "Anyway… you make a good point. Why risk it—"

A deep cry rattled over the far horizon where the jagged line of grasses and stone reeds jutted against the sky—it warbled like an echo caught in a chasm, pressed itself against Noah's eardrums, hummed and jittered.

Savannah wrenched another few inches of his shirt into her grip.

Breakfast had already crawled halfway up his throat. He focused on Savannah's hold at his back, the cloud of heat crowding his skin, the weave of the knapsack strap still pinched under his thumb.

Frida cleared her throat. "We should get back. I don't think this mud is, uh… it's not healthy."

Gingerly they shifted their stances in the sludge, rotating on the slow spit of their ankles until Noah could bunch up Savannah's shirt against his palm, until Frida pulled his shirt tight and sharp against his throat where she grabbed hold, until Irene could lay her eyes on the top of the *Amihaf* or the distinct glare of a trailer roof.

They trudged forward, waiting for the bellowing noise to rush up at their backs, though it never came. Even when they escaped the muck, hiking back onto the sandy soil, the four of them still held fast to each other, the shirts and belt loops and bags, until they could hear the rumble of the surf and the distance-smudged conversations of their colleagues. Once past the unofficial threshold of the base, they scattered—Frida to the lab trailer, Irene and Savannah toward the water, and Noah nowhere in particular.

The sky's usual gray tint had rolled back in since they first left the ship, and it cut down on the heat just enough that Noah allowed himself to crouch into a seat on the sand. Ahead, Savannah bent down to unlace her boots, recoiling from the odor; Irene leapt over that step, forged ahead into the shin-high waves, stood still with tired shoulders. Soon Savannah joined her. Nethuns had sullied their boots, so it could wash them clean.

One of the trailer doors squeaked, followed by footsteps too hurried to immediately discern how many people they belonged to. Two figures slid into Noah's peripheral vision, dull sheens of bronze and silver forcing an instinctive squint.

"Are you forgetting that Yonas and I are in a conference with Cairo University? *The* Cairo Univ—Abelard. I put research on pause to come here. TerraCosmos isn't going to want to spend more resources to send me back to

Europa after all this, and CU has their Europan Oceanic Microcosm. They won't..." Henri shifted into rapid French, Abelard following suit until it was a tangled jumble of syllables, noise melding into the normal buzz of the planet.

They ran on, long enough for Irene and Savannah to tote their clean but waterlogged boots up the beach, long enough still for Sanelle and Nomvula's boat to edge over the horizon.

"Let me say it again," said Abelard, suddenly switching back to English. "My mother's French has atrophied, you see, and I want to make sure you understand. I *have* to find the leviathan. It eats at me, Henri, like nothing I've ever—you've known me a long time, *mon frère*. You know I don't take matters of this magnitude lightly."

Henri didn't sigh, though his ConBod still went through the motions. "You're right. And that is why I am worried. A leviathan, so you say, destroyed your organic body, and that is reason enough for you to mourn. But what you have spoken on—that is not mourning. That is something else. I cannot—"

"You have moved on from your own calamity."

"I have traveled outside the Solar System, yes, but my two feet have been firmly on Nethunsan soil since we arrived, and I do not force my crew into an anti-asteroid vendetta—"

"I do not *force*—Noah!"

He did his best to pretend that he hadn't been eavesdropping, though it was likely a poor performance. Abelard beckoned him forward as Henri tried to meet him halfway, insisting that everything was fine, that the conversation was about over anyway—so Noah paused. An apology for the stench of his boots was already halfway formed before he remembered neither had the capacity to smell it.

Abelard lingered a few feet behind Henri's shoulder like a specter.

"Now I know *you* know your vacuum leviathans," said Henri.

"I'd like to think so."

Henri grinned, but Noah could only mirror him with the kind of smile toddlers managed when shoved in front of a camera. "You don't have to be modest. At Algiers 1…" He caught himself, sighed. "So. Abelard. Has clearly told you of his… oh, how do I put this… pet project."

Heavy under *pet project* laid all the questioning worry built up in Henri's brainware.

"He has, yes…" said Noah. "It, um—it…"

Slowly Abelard raised a single finger to his lips, pressed tight there against a creeping tilt of—it wasn't a genuine smile, nor did it have all the implications of a smirk, but the angle of it was wrong.

Hush.

This doesn't leave our doors.

Behind his eye, Noah caught the flash of his father holding the newly-adopted Major in his arms as his gangly limbs beat against the empty air. Gerard Starbuck's calloused fingers scratched behind puppy ears as Noah's nose was clogged with snot, eyes stinging, a heaving against a barbed knot in his chest that made him want to die.

Call one of your cousins if you're upset. Major's drool dripped down onto the exposed skin of his wrist as he cradled his delicate puppy head. *Keep it in the family.*

"We're smart people," Noah finally managed. "We can recognize hyperbole when we see it."

Henri raised one eyebrow, then the other, his finger stroking where a mustache would have drawn to a pointed end. "Dr. Starbuck—"

"It's okay." He reached forward to Henri's upper arm to grip it reassuringly like he'd seen his father do so many times around the lakeside downtown. This wasn't him. He fought the urge to yank his arm back—from the unfamiliarity, and then also the singe of heat from the metal plating under Henri's sleeve. "I appreciate your concern, but—it's, um, one of those things, you know? A group of people stuck together alone for a long time—"

"So it's a… joke?"

"I wouldn't say that." It spilled from his mouth in a rush. "'Joke' has a certain connotation, right? And that's not it. It's, uh… shorthand. We've all got our reasons for signing up for something like this, and that's what Abelard likes to say is his."

Henri's brow fell into a pinched furrow. Behind him, Abelard's finger was still held against his mouth; Noah caught his gaze long enough to see him nod once, slow.

"I mean," said Noah, forcing a grin to his eyes, "it's his own way of saying he's really glad to be back in the field after the accident. That's the best revenge, isn't it? Living well?" Before he could stop himself, a few nervous chuckles leaked from the corners of his strained mouth.

"*Inshallah*," muttered Henri. He pulled his arm from Noah's hold and circled back toward the trailer. Giving Abelard an extra few feet of berth as he passed, he made note of nothing odd, for Abelard had clasped both hands behind his back. At ease. Nothing to see.

The door clanked shut. Over the whistle of the quickening breeze and the surf it churned, Noah heard his name—Irene was waving him down on the far side of the base, pointing at something in the sand that Savannah was following in a crouch. He couldn't make out exactly what she was saying. Something curled against the inside of his ear, ringing sharper than tinnitus; he gestured that he was coming, turned his head, caught Abelard striding over toward the mess trailer. His ConBod's left eye flickered black, then to a dark static, then clicking back to normal, all within the span of a footstep.

"When we get back to Earth, we should go to the Summer Festival again." Noah, chin in hand, glanced up from his breakfast, staring across the table where Savannah was scrolling through one of the many spreadsheets Zainab dropped in her inbox. "I might face my fear of that swing ride."

"When you say 'we,'" she said, "is this you playing third wheel with me and Tracy, or do I need to talk sense into you?" She chewed at the end of her pen, attention still focused on the cells full of numbers.

"I'm not sure what you—"

"I will hack into your tablet and block Justin myself if you don't screw your head back on the right way. Okay?"

He physically bit his tongue keeping his retort to himself, a metallic tinge coloring the inside of his teeth. *Check my 'sent' folder. There's nothing there I wrote and sent specifically to him in—what, weeks? Months?* His inbox, of course, was another matter entirely, but he couldn't stop Justin from writing as much as he couldn't stop the *Amihaf* from barreling forward once Esmail engaged turbolight.

"Okay?" she repeated.

"Yeah, I get you."

"Good."

She moved the pen to the other side of her mouth, zooming in on a marked-up image taken from one of the base's microscopes—a sampling that resembled a brick wall more than even the most rigidly rectangular of Terrestrial plant cells. A yellow comment note sat on the far edge of the screen with an arrow pointing at an oblong organelle.

"The translation software can't read Zainab's handwriting," she muttered, tapping at the scribbled text. "They said something about this last night, but the only part I can remember is that they've been stuck on the issue for months…"

Noah leaned up from his seat to get a better look, as if that would suddenly give him the ability to read Arabic. It at least vaguely resembled the language, which was more than he could say about the cursive Cyrillic script he'd seen in Sergey's planner during grad school.

"Are those Zainab's notes on the stone reeds?"

Emerging up from the stairs, Omar approached the table. Dayo was close behind.

"Yeah," Savannah sighed. "Frida wanted me to follow up on a hunch, and Zainab was happy to have a second pair of eyes."

"I know the feeling," he said. "You need a translator for that, I assume?" He pointed at the note and then, not waiting for a reply, "I'm the only one who can read their handwriting. Drives Henri up the wall… ah, yeah. They think this structure here has some… angry? No, no, *magnetic* properties because of the detected iron content."

Their conversation quickly fell away into particulars, a sense of levity drummed up between them as Omar clarified the next couple notes in the file. As the excess of it pooled at their feet and stretched out on the floor, the space around Dayo provided a sudden stop. She locked eyes with Noah, straining against some invisible pressure digging into her back, the circles under her eyes dark like a starless night sky.

"Did you need something, Omar?" Noah asked.

"Oh—yes. Sorry," he added to Savannah. "Dayo said we ought to borrow you for a bit."

He had little time to ask for further details before they ushered him out into the oven of midmorning. The sandy soil of the path to the shore piled into the slippers they'd caught him in, the hem of his ratty joggers pressing into the dirt under every step. Neither Dayo nor Omar said a word as the sea spread across the horizon.

The path deposited them beside the medical trailer. Omar hopped up the short set of steps to the door, and Noah felt Dayo's hand on his shoulder, squeezing a reassurance.

Inside, Jibril kept his perch on his usual chair, condition unchanged. The mushroom cap loomed over the rest of his intact skull, the veil shrouding his face. The small table beside him held a neat arrangement of vials and kits, a tablet under a box of fresh syringes, but the rest of the trailer sat empty amid piles of clutter, dusty with neglect.

Each breath Noah took—this close to Jibril, this confined—rang in his chest like the peal of alarm bells.

"If this is about the, um—elephantine… y'know…" He pointed to Jibril. "… in the room, I'm not sure how much help I can actually be."

Omar glanced at Dayo, ceding her the floor, but she only chewed at the inside of her lip.

"I'll refrain from bad plays on idioms if that makes things easier," he said.

"Oh, hush," Dayo said, a little more life rising to her cheeks. "I just want you to look at something."

She nodded toward Jibril and pulled on a pair of gloves to maneuver him into a position more suitable for whatever she wanted him to examine.

"Omar, come hold his head for me. It won't stay how I need it to."

He quickly obliged, his own gloved hands soon cupping the base of Jibril's neck as Dayo continued to fiddle with the veil obscuring most of his face.

"Where's Frida and Yonas?" asked Noah. "Or did they already offer their insight?"

The two of them were holed up in one of the storage trailers on a consult Earth-side with Frida's colleague in Ychma who specialized in the xenobiochemistry of new psychoactive compounds, specifically in xenomycology. If Yonas didn't have answers and her own hypotheses had little data behind them, Frida had said, then Dr. Qori Jimenez was their best hope.

"I think Jimenez is the Abelard to Frida's you," said Dayo, "from what I could tell listening in. Anyway, come look at this. Look at his eyes."

Between the fingers of her other hand were more of the long tongue depressors they'd all seen her use that first day on-planet; each bit of wood slid into one of the fleshy lace borders of the veil, held it at the right angle for Noah to meet Jibril's gaze directly. The trailer's overhead lights shone across his face, dappled, highlighting patches of cloudy purples smothering the pupils like cataracts.

Just like the man at Ushuaia Station—Elliot, Elias, *something*. The smudges of unnatural color held the same shapes, though Jibril's were darker, an eggplant or indigo instead of the subtler lilac, and the warm wood-brown of his natural irises still broke through where the purple's edges had softened.

"The crystal shop guy. That's who you're thinking of, right?" said Noah.

Dayo nodded. "I'm no ophthalmologist, but I'd never seen anything like it before that pit stop and now—twice? With both of them just... knowing things—"

"You didn't mention this other guy was also…" Omar shimmied his shoulders for lack of free hands to wave about like he wanted. "Isn't that—"

"Elijah Tucker."

Jibril's voice croaked over the question, smothering it.

"Um… yeah," said Dayo. She drew back from Jibril's veil, motioning for Omar to join them a few feet further back from his chair. "I don't think we got his last name, though, did we Noah?"

"Nope."

Jibril's body, limp just moments ago, sat erect in the chair with a posture that would have made Gerard Starbuck proud. One of the violet-tinged eyes had a perfect gap in the veil to narrow in on a point in Noah's chest. A crosshair. The red laser dot in old movies before a rail gun tore through skin and bone.

"He was right, you know," said Jibril. "You've realized that, surely."

Noah and Dayo exchanged glances; he could see the calculations rattling off on the other side of her brow, all while his own thoughts returned heavy static. He wracked his memory for any detail of that encounter and only found dense knots of unease.

"Remember?" Jibril's neck loosened, head lolling back from the weight of the mushroom cap. "Never seen a bot with a soul, never ever, and he's taking you into the shimmering chasm of—" His head snapped back to attention so forcefully that the stalk wiggled in the hole in his skull. "Oh, this is where it all breaks down. What am I supposed to say about this chasm? I could call it God, but you could also call a regular hectagon a circle. It doesn't make it right."

That crosshair returned when Jibril refocused, training in on Noah until the trailer was reduced to the thin thread tying them together by their pupils. The rest of it darkened, murky under blotting blind spots.

Oh Noah—Jibril's voice reverberated at the base of his skull, repeating his name, then his deadname, devolving into a low hum that buzzed in his bones. *Noah and his false idols! We know this refrain, don't we?*

The heat hit him first.

The rest of the shore followed, shaky steps forward, one at a time with both Omar and Dayo grasping at his elbows to keep him upright. He caught the breaths he hadn't realized he'd lost.

"I'm fine, I'm fine," he said. "Just… hadn't had one of those moments with Jibril before."

"I'm sure that's all it was," said Omar, the sarcasm barbed sharp enough to break skin. "I know the drill. You don't have to explain to anyone exactly what he was referencing, but—"

"I'm *fine*."

Outside the trailer, remnants of Jibril's unnatural London accent hummed against his brainstem, the top knot of his spine, slipping down until the planet under his feet welcomed it home. Noah braced at the edge of a shiver, and the only thing he could get himself to do was shrug off Dayo and Omar's hands and set off down the beach.

It wasn't a dramatic departure. Sand didn't allow for the heavy, even type of stride that such exits demanded, but the grainy spray that jumped up with every step was satisfying enough.

"Noah. *Noah.*" Dayo caught up with him, latching her hand around his wrist and pulling him to a stop. "Let's slow down, okay?"

"Right. Slow. Okay. I just had someone speak directly into my brain so I don't know if 'slow' is something I can really manage at the moment… oh no." He spotted Omar's deepening frown where he stood behind Dayo. "That hasn't happened before, has it?"

Omar's mouth hung open for a few moments until he snapped it shut, bracing his hands at his waist. "No. Not in my observations."

Noah curled into a ball, his full weight pressing his toes into the sand like a pan fry. The imminent complaints of his knees loomed, but he could use the distraction, welcomed it, even. With the light blotted out, he fell through the dark behind his eyelids, the blank expanse of the universe—a vision of the future, when all the stars had burned out and gravity wells belonged to the surviving black holes, adrift on the cannot-bes. A man couldn't live with his brain so exposed, so leeched upon, and for so long. Telepathy couldn't exist. Language acquisition was not spontaneous. Anyone who knew his deadname still lived within fifty miles of downtown Erie.

Never seen a bot with a soul.

Whatever could be said about souls was out of Noah's reach. His chest panged, short and sharp: it was the sort of thing he looked to Justin to supplement, explain, having grown up religious even if he hadn't kept with it.

There was Esmail, too, but something about the dull light in his eyes the day before—

"—and I didn't have the time to get that Prana Tech certificate traveling between Ibadan and Mars every two months. Lockyer Base is needy."

"So what do you want?"

"Omar, we need some *help*. If everything else that comes out of Jibril's mouth is true, then we need to have a better idea what he's trying to say about Abelard."

For a moment, the only sound among the three of them was the surf, the wind, the clanking strain of the climate control hanging off the closest trailer.

"Okay. Let's—not here, okay? You want to come too, Noah?" The toe of his shoe nudged against Noah's hip, nearly offsetting his careful balancing act.

"Sure." He unfolded himself back to standing. "Where to?"

On the other side of the short cliff where Sanelle had brought out the boat was a narrow trail head that wove into the closest terrain to a forest the biome had on offer. The structures comprising the canopy and lining the bare strip Omar followed were tree-like in general shape, though the trunks were made of a shining black substance like obsidian, a blanket of spikes rounding the whole of it, branchless. They fanned out at their peaks, too far up to discern much outside how they blocked sunlight.

The trail split about five minutes in, and Omar led them down the fork carpeted by squelching, spongey lichen the color of rusted amber, which emptied out to a wide spread of a similar hue. A gust of wind from the sea whistled through the stony trees, rippling across the surface, giving it away as a pond.

"Algae," said Omar. "Not the same stuff that makes everyone sick. Zainab's explained the difference to me before, nutrient feeds and all that, but all I know is that they're different colors. The sea's algae is white when it's not blooming. Reminds me of…"

"Mold?" Dayo supplied after a beat.

"Yeah." Omar bent down and grabbed a handful of small stones, jiggling them in his palm like playing dice. "So, speaking of…"

He plucked one from the pile. It was a dark gray from damp, and Omar squeezed it in the intricate hold of his fingers like he was trying to wring it dry before flinging it into the pond. The film of algae opened up in a pop as it landed.

"I first met Henri on the *TCS Satet*. Barely spoke to him before that rock turned his skeleton into confetti." He chose another stone from the bundle cupped in his palm, rolled it along the edge of his finger, knuckle to knuckle. "At one point I had his blood splattered up to my elbows, probably right before he docked at Cernunnos Station. Some of the nurses there gaped at me as if I'd just come from a murder scene, and maybe I did, if you could pin that kind of agency on something as unthinking as an asteroid."

He flicked his wrist, and the rock jetted through the air. The pond swallowed it up with a collapsing gulp.

"I know what Prana Technologies says about Constructed Bodies. Consciousness transferred from body to brainware-powered machine. Like I told Dayo," he said, glancing at Noah, "I've got the specialist certification for ConBods. I understand the science, but..."

"But?" Dayo pressed her mouth into a thin line.

Another rock flew from Omar's hand. "I don't buy all of it."

Plonk.

A flat rock sat along the surface of the sandy soil a few inches from the toe of Noah's boot. He stepped on the end, angled it up against the mold it had dug for itself until he could easily pluck it from the dirt. "Something like this would be better if you're trying to skip them," he said.

"I know," said Omar.

"What do you mean," Dayo said, "by—"

"Not buying it? Well..." he sighed. "For all the progress we've made outside Earth, there are still things we don't know, Terrestrial-side. The origin of consciousness, for example. Prana Tech likes to say it's solved, that they know how to work with it and manipulate it, but…” The next stone was slightly flatter than the previous one, but the toss sent it spinning on the wrong axis.

Plonk.

“One of the few ‘trade secrets’ left in the world. Public-sphere hypotheses still hold that consciousness arises from the brain’s predictive takes based on —you know, perception of the outside world, interoception of our own bodily processes, that sort of thing, all in the aim of keeping ourselves alive. Until brainware was invented, the idea of a machine having consciousness was out of the question. So now—”

“Right,” said Dayo. Her frown deepened as he considered the next rock in the queue, little more than a pebble. “Brainware is able to reproduce that based on all the sensory mechanisms in the rest of the ConBod.”

The pebble whizzed through the air and fell into the water with a *plip*, barely disturbing the cover of algae. “So someone in a Constructed Body has consciousness. They’re sentient, sapient, everything that would legally classify them as a person. But that’s not the issue. There’s—okay…”

All the rocks Omar had gathered thudded to the ground, and he turned toward Dayo and Noah holding up his two pointer fingers close together— close, but not touching.

“Prana Tech says that ConBods give the otherwise fatally-injured or terminally-ill a means of continuing life. They have all their memories, their personalities, even the way that they learn and problem solve, however flawed. It’s all uploaded, right? Copy-paste, and then everything is tested eons past the point of reasonable doubt. *Years* of testing. We know how it goes.” He held Noah’s gaze as he said this, keeping the pause in place between the tips of his fingers.

"So, what?" Dayo sighed. "You think the process is flawed?"

"Flawed? *Flawed?*" Omar snatched the flat rock Noah had been idly stroking with his thumb, flinging it across the pond. It bounced and jumped too quickly to keep count, leaving circles of murky brown to track its path. "If consciousness depends on a brain, or on brainware, how do they guarantee there's continuity? The consciousness of Henri's organic brain and the consciousness that you two met—that's separate. It's a mechanical clone, not the same one I met on the *Satet*. There is a point when both exist, when the tests for the Constructed Body have met their mark, and the plug is pulled on the other.

"Henri the man is dead. Abelard the man... *is dead.*"

Of course, there was the talk about Jibril, about Elijah, all their focus on souls, and Omar shrugged it away on the grounds that he only argued on that kind of spiritual matter with his rabbi. Debating the question of souls in Constructed Bodies was only as useful as their ability to define what the concept of a soul even meant, as medical professionals steeped in the latest 28th-century science. Eventually it all drowned out into muffled nothings, leaving Noah to sit in the dirt, picking at the other flat rocks around their shoes until they pulled at the worn edges of his fingernails enough to draw blood.

Abelard was dead. Abelard awaited them at Camp Ilunga. This wasn't what Schrodinger's thought experiment was about, but it was the best way for Noah to internalize what Omar had relayed—alive and not, dead and not, some intermittent space where that fabled cat called home.

"What does this have to do with what Jibril's said, then?" Dayo pinned a sizable flat rock in the bottom V of her first two fingers, thumb tapping along the damp-dark side. "And not just today."

Omar shook his head. "I don't... none of us knows. There is so little we know about any of the life on this planet. They've put on a good act," he said, glancing at Noah. "You don't hear them talking at dinner about the latest in a line of setbacks and inexplicable data. Sanelle's worked alongside Nomvula ever since she first signed on with TerraCosmos, and she's never seen her so lost trying to understand that weird little eel. And that eel isn't playing at being clairvoyant."

He and Dayo stared at each other until he broke, bending down to grab another rock without inspecting its dimensions. He threw it at an odd tilt, and the short, flatter edge slid an inch of water clear of algae before sinking below the surface.

"I know that's not helpful," he said.

"You're right. It's not." Dayo was suddenly standing beside Noah, and she reached a hand down to help him to his feet. "Day after tomorrow, Abelard leaves with us and you don't have to worry about splitting resources for a problem that was never really yours to begin with. It's fine," she added when Omar looked like he was going to protest. "You've got... I'm not jealous of the challenge you have with Jibril."

Noah brushed the dirt from the backside of his joggers as quietly as he could, as not to snap the strained cord pulled between the two doctors. On the hike back to base, he slid into the second position, careful not to trip on a root as he dug the sharp end of a canine into his tongue to stifle the muttered indictments against TerraCosmos and all the other institutions back on Earth. Shēngdì, Camp Ilunga, the *Amihaf*—all struggling, too far away, seemingly, for anyone under the favored sun to lift a finger.

"I do wish we could help. Or knew how to." Dayo, the head of the line, paused a few feet short from where the trail emptied out to the beach.

"Frida's good, but—"

"A week is a week," said Omar. "That's no time at all."

Releasing the hold on his tongue, Noah waited for the tangy, ebbing pain to give way to something useful. He had nothing, just the phantom hand squeezing his lungs too tight for the words to form. The muscles along his lower back cramped in time, just another piece set to ring when the other alarms inspired a hopeless lack of action.

"Did you hear that?" Dayo thumbed over her shoulder, hopping forward another few steps to get a better look at the shore.

"What should I be listening for?" asked Noah, but she waved him quiet.

"I heard Jibril," said Omar. "Okay, yep, just checked the time—he's due for a grounding—"

Omar cut himself off as Dayo started jogging toward the base. The two of them ran after, following her out into the open, jumping down to the beach, and only then absorbing the scene fraying apart at the base of the lab trailer's steps.

At the center, Jibril sat under the shade of his cap and veil, his grip on the chair's arms turning the skin on his knuckles taut-white. To his right— Abelard, hands spread and held wide of his head, Frida and Nomvula and Savannah shouting over each other as Esmail crouched tight, plugging his ears. To his left, Henri stood frozen, mouth agape.

And then, at his feet, Quinn struggled to right himself, arms shaking as they propped him up out of the sand.

"What else would you have me say?" said Abelard. "I didn't see him. It was absolutely, entirely an accident."

Frida threw away all pretense as her hands curled into claws on either side of her head. Her knees tossed up a wake of sand as she dropped beside

Quinn, tilting his chin up so she could start her version of an examination. Dayo dashed up to join her, the rest of the spectating base offering a patchwork recap—Jibril needed his grounding, and Yonas had coded his own reference program that Quinn wanted to discuss, and Abelard had tripped.

Just tripped. A simple thing, a misstep. And he'd knocked into Quinn, who fell forward and took a faceful of Jibril's cap.

"It's in all likelihood entirely fine," said Henri, though he fared poorly at pushing back against the worry lines trying to crease his synthetic skin. "All of us here have been exposed to him regularly… and we're still intact. Mr. Kaiwhakatere has nothing to worry about."

Having nothing to worry about was always a lie, regardless of circumstance, and it left open so many dark corners for other troubles to hide.

When Noah glanced at Abelard, he found his eyes already staring him down, heavy and blank, the angle of it digging a knuckle into the soft flesh under his throat.

EIGHT

DINNER WAS LATE AS the *Amihaf* left Nethuns in the shimmering wake of its turbolight jump. Avoiding another bout through the Leroon Disk only required a few extra calculations on Irene's part, and their next destination—the Gliese 1061 system—was close enough that those extras were simple.

The menu that night, determined by the rotation set before Jupiter had disappeared into a pinprick, relied on mimeo arctic char, mixed greens, and a heaping portion of rice. Three-quarters Irene, one-quarter whoever else could wrangle the raw rice the mimeos belched out on command—the latter was usually left for either Dayo or Esmail, and both of them had other matters yanking at their earlobes for attention.

So it was 2130 IST before the eight of them sat down for dinner, seven with plates and Abelard watching, grinning without the extra wariness that prickled the hairs at the napes of their necks. The conversation jerked and stuttered forward as if they'd just met each other, halfhearted ribs about al dente rice that only received shrugs in return, inquiries about the spice rub on the char that died before the punctuation landed. Just the clinks of forks on plates and an aversion to looking the head of the table in the eye.

In the trough of one of the lulls, Esmail's stomach gurgled. His fork pierced through the fish on his plate, leaning into an angle that started to cleave it in half. He'd nibbled around the greens, instead fixated on Quinn beside him; he frowned, tried to puff away a strand of hair that had pulled loose from his bun.

And Quinn: his eyes hadn't left his plate. His helping of the rice found itself shaped into a square by his fork, the greens smashed along the bottom edges in a limp, wet pulp. He stared at the finished product, motionless aside from a steady wave of breathing that rolled through his shoulders.

"Quinn, *azizam*—"

"His hemograph readings have been normal since we left," said Dayo, mostly to her own plate.

"*Astaghfirullah*," Esmail muttered. He covered his eyes with his hands, pressed hard, then quickly tapped the tips of his fingers against his brow. He shifted toward Dayo, the hinge of his jaw pausing its flexing pulse. "I know that. Thank you. I was going to ask if there was something else he wanted for dinner instead."

"You won't offend me, by the way," Irene said. "If that's what you're worried about."

Quinn shook his head. "Nah, mate. I just don't think I'm hungry."

"You haven't had anything since the morning before you—" Esmail stopped himself. "It doesn't matter. You still need to eat something."

Across from him and Quinn, Dayo glanced up, a wince tugging at her face. "His blood sugar readings in the hemograph were—"

"I don't care about the hemograph!" Esmail's fist slammed down on the table, catching the edge of his plate and flinging his uneaten food into the air. It sailed in an arc over his head and onto the floor behind him with a damp splat. "I'm sorry. I'm sorry." He hurried to collect it all into a spare napkin from the table.

Quinn stooped to help him, murmuring too low for anyone other than Esmail to even guess what he was saying. They retreated to their bunk after the mess was cleaned, Savannah having already stacked their plates under her own. With their door shut behind them, the rest of the table rose one by one to claim whatever minute task under the greater umbrella of dishes was still available. Each migrant to the galley shifted their limbs around the mess table seats as if bumping into them would bring an electric shock and send the ship's oxygen supply alight.

Soon only Irene and Noah were left with Abelard—who maintained his grin with a plastic stillness.

"It's the rule about the cook not doing the dishes, correct?" said Abelard, and Irene nodded. "My family had the same system growing up. My parents must have as well. They treated the idea like the sun rising in the east, just the way things were."

Again Irene nodded and she snuck a glance across the table to Noah. Her dark eyes swallowed the light overhead until it reflected as a mere pinprick.

Abelard's head began to swivel toward him, but he hopped up before it could properly land, slamming his knee into a sharp edge of the metal supports.

"Are you okay?" said Irene.

"I'm fine," he said through a muted wince, mouthing the same thing to Savannah as she checked over her shoulder at the sink. "You have another dish towel for me?"

They did, for a time, until Frida and Dayo pointedly asked the rest of them to leave without saying as much, the deniability barely plausible. Abelard had disappeared from the floor's common areas, having returned to his bunk, or the lab, or wherever he was so fond of hiding on the small ship. Whatever Frida and Dayo wanted to discuss alone, Noah wasn't yet so curious that he looked for a reason to stay, so he followed Quinn and Esmail's lead back to his bunk.

It was more disheveled than usual, with his comforter in a tangle on the floor and a steep hill of clothes blocking most of the bathroom entrance. His tablet laid on the pillow, lit with a long list of new email notifications to pile on top of the rest he'd let accumulate during the stint on Nethuns.

"Fine… I'll dig out," he muttered.

Most of the messages he could delete or mark as read without opening— heat cancellations for summer session classes, the provost's official comment on some incident in the larger Monacan region, calls for conference papers. He fired off a couple reminders that he was off-planet to the graduate students pinging him for after-hours lab access and skimmed the alert of a new citation of his work, frowning to himself when he saw the journal was in a language unavailable in the translation software.

Which only left him with a handful out of the original couple hundred—two handfuls, really, one each for his parents and Justin.

He opened the most recent message from his parents first, just to get it out of the way. The tablet whirred against his lap as it caught the embedded images downloading from the closest relay, loading in thin strips, a preface to the rest of the email. The first showed the two of them on a great expanse of overgrown grasses and wildflowers, the black-crusted remnants of a domed building far in the background. They held up a flag Noah mildly remembered from history class. The color scheme was the same as the more recognizable design, but the stars in the top-left corner were fewer, arranged into a circle.

He swiped away from the message text before he had the chance to catch his mother trotting out terms that would have curdled conversations even centuries ago. He didn't need to see it for himself. He knew it was coming, a history of histories left to stain their whole home with its odor. Their home and, later, his—the force of instinct letting him forget the silence he'd learned to fold into could never extend protection past himself.

On the other side of his bunk door, Frida's footfalls plodded down the hall. Moments later, Dayo followed, her own steps broken by an early pause, assumedly at Esmail and Quinn's room. No knocking sounded before she continued on.

Quinn's fine, he reminded himself. *The hemograph says he's fine, and Abelard said it was an accident*—but that hadn't been in question, that last part. Anyone could succumb to clumsiness, Constructed Body or not. Not every well-worn rut had to play at determinism.

Sighing, Noah pulled up Justin's most recent email, a short note half an hour old comprised only of a photo, aside from the auto-inserted signature block. It loaded more quickly than those from his parents, apparently attached at a lower resolution.

Subject: wish you were here

The image had been clipped from his tablet, a short passage highlighted in pale yellow that cut off after a semicolon with no way to check after the footnotes hinted at by the tiny, floating numbers. A publication on Catastrophe-era literature from the way it referenced econihilism alongside nations that had faded into dust-cushioned history eons ago—but a few lines in, he spotted it. A reference to a two-episode plotline in *Deep Space Nine*.

Noah hit the button to dial Justin before he had a chance to sense the grin splitting his face in two, and the line connected with signs of it still pinching at the corners of his eyes.

"You're extremely predictable. You know that, right?" Justin flipped a couple stray locs out of eyes from where he sat at his desk—what used to be Noah's desk. The room behind him, hazy through blurred pixels, was familiar but rearranged. "I don't hear from you for weeks, but drop one allusion to classical science fiction—"

"First of all," said Noah, "this *is* work. I do actually have responsibilities between planets."

"Sure, sure." The window behind his tablet setup cast his face in the dewy blue light that harkened the coming sunrise. "Are you going to tell me what that reference meant or what? There's a kid in one of my seminars who might be a bigger nerd than you, God's honest truth. Ze is going to have my head Tuesday if I don't bring it up."

"You can watch those episodes without a whole lot of extra context, you know."

Justin drew his face up in an exaggerated frown. "Can I really? I don't know—"

Laughter rose from Noah without him noticing. He'd seen the episodes on the Bell Riots enough times that the added distractions lurking in the ship couldn't pull his thoughts apart into threads—prescient contemporary takes on the economic woes of everyday people, with little worry to spare for the whistling kettle strung up inside the ozone.

"Compelling," said Justin. "You might get me to watch an episode yet—"

The door to Noah's bunk slammed open.

He jumped. His hands pounded into the thin mattress, sending Justin's face onscreen into a free spin until it landed at an odd angle against his knee.

Savannah stood in the doorway, her own tablet clutched to her chest. "You're on speaker with Tracy," she said as the door slid shut behind her.

"Uh, likewise?" Noah stretched his back as he readjusted the tablet against a mound of pillows. "It's Justin," he clarified.

Tracy made no effort to hide her drawn-out grumble.

"Oh. Um…" Savannah's face pinched in frustration, but she shook it out. "That's fine. Scoot over."

"There isn't that much—"

"*Scoot.*"

Eventually they settled themselves with their backs against the metal hull, legs tucked beneath them instead of letting them dangle off the side. Noah glanced over at Tracy on Savannah's screen—the same early light streamed in from the apartment's one good window in the corner, stifled by the surrounding trees. The sterile glow of a desk lamp lit her preoccupied efforts to pull her hair into a ponytail, the odd tics of her brow perfectly legible only to Savannah.

"Justin was just asking me about a reference he didn't get in a paper," said Noah.

"It had to be *Star Trek*, right?" Tracy asked, and Justin laughed.

"Wait." Noah held up a hand. "Who said it 'had to be?'"

For a moment, even with half their number held in tablet screens and the tight vibrations of turbolight sizzling at their backs, they could have been talking over each other in line for the Ferris wheel at the Summer Festival.

"Anyway," said Noah as the bustle settled. "What was the big emergency?"

"'Emergency' is a strong word," Tracy said. "TerraCosmos wouldn't be interested under any circumstances, let's put it that way."

"Still could be an emergency, by that definition."

Justin tilted his head, the tenuous connection stuttering the image. "And what is that supposed to mean?"

"You're not TerraCosmos, are you?" said Noah. "Why worry otherwise?"

"What's been going on up there?" He readjusted in his seat, and in the new position, freshly-creased worry lines got caught in the shadows. "You said Cousteau's been weird, but…"

"There's that fungus mind-reading guy from the planet you just left. Right?" Tracy said. "It's been a few days since you mentioned it, babe, and I'm not entirely sure I didn't make it up."

Justin's eyes nearly popped out of his head. "What? Noah, turn the tablet so I can see her."

"I don't want to see you. Things are fine as it is."

"Y'know, it would only take me ten minutes to walk to your—"

"I am *not* letting you in my home—"

"Fine," Justin sighed, a pout pulling at his mouth that Noah knew in the rational part of his brain, however stress-addled, was purely performative. Just for him, like he could foresee when Savannah would turn her full attention back to her wife.

"I'll email you," Noah mouthed, and his stomach twisted into a complicated knot when Justin winked in reply. It could have just been a glitch in the display, a momentary buffer as the relays flung code across the impossible distance. But also—he knew how Justin winked, the exact timing of his eyelid, how the other eye twitched in sympathy. There was no mistaking it.

"Anyway," Justin said, cutting through the fog. "I'll let you three deal with whatever the issue is by yourselves. I'd really just wanted to tell Noah the good news face-to-face."

In three semesters' time, he'd officially be in a tenure-track position with the Rassawek English department, and the bewilderment lingering at the edges of his face was the genuine article, only overtaken by the excitement. He rolled one of his golden loc cuffs between his fingers as he outlined the details, what the semesters in the meantime were going to look like, how he would finally get to design and teach the class of his dreams.

"It also means I'll still be here when you get back," he said. The flush tingeing his cheeks was subtle, a rusty wine-red under the deeper brown.

"Good to know." Noah grinned at him.

In his peripheral vision, Tracy rolled her eyes.

Something off-camera caught Justin's attention, and he excused himself in a hurry. A tonnage of strain dissolved from Tracy's spine as soon as the disconnecting blip sounded from Noah's tablet.

"Ugh, finally," she said.

"What—"

"You got us in the divorce." She added belated air quotes. "I consider it my duty as your friend to loathe your ex, even when you don't."

"I appreciate the sentiment," Noah said. "But you really don't have to."

"Out of all the people in the galaxy that I'm not married to, you're my best friend," Savannah said. "Can you blame me?"

"But I never told you what happened! The biggest piece of it was my fault!" He took a couple deep breaths. "And maybe… I… I might want to fix it when we're back Earth-side."

The footsteps outside rushed back from the common areas, a low thud landing against the wall.

"Really? I mean—sorry," said Savannah. "If that's—I'm glad." She patted his knee with two solid taps as Tracy forced a grin.

The conversation tracked away from anything he could contribute to, leaving him with the outburst to turn over in his hands. Surely they could have worked through their problems, worked past everything that metastasized in the burnt rhubarb, if that one day with his parents hadn't been such a cowardly display. They were both adults, both steered by good heads —it didn't have to be insurmountable, but Noah had pushed it there as his father's screeds dropped unchallenged.

Only a little bit of magical thinking was required to picture an alternate version of the *Amihaf*, one where he and Justin were still together and Justin, without a single brain cell oriented toward the sciences, was allowed to come along. Noah could have returned from that last venture into the Lulal jungle, blood splattered across his face, and been met by something other than a silent, empty bunk. He could have faced each new troubling event without his thoughts tangling up in a whirlpool, just by having Justin sitting beside him.

And maybe that was unfair to Justin. Likely unfair. He was more than what he could do for Noah, crisis or not, but that didn't change how all the barbed variables in this mission had kept him unmoored since those first odd moments still inside the Kuiper Belt.

He missed him. He was twelve lightyears away from Earth, seventy trillion miles, and he *missed him*.

That was forgivable, wasn't it?

"What was that big emergency you busted in here about?" he asked, cutting through the subject of the moment.

"I'd had a zoology question for my draft, but…" Tracy glanced toward the wall clock, then swore under her breath. "I'll email you later, Noah," she said, pushing away from the desk. The chair slid past the shoe rack she'd been reaching for and she shuffled her feet to drag herself back. "The Udayars wanted me to walk their dog while—"

"Who?" Savannah's question went unanswered as Tracy ducked out of frame to tie her shoes, talking to the vertical face of her shins. "Hon, who are the Udayars?"

"They live across the hall? Gala and I—oh, right." The top half of her head popped up over the desk. "Moved in after you zipped off planet." After a couple hurried assurances that the couple and Savannah would love each other, Tracy ran off with a promise to call later, the air kiss cut off mid-frame.

With the room suddenly quiet again, Noah listened for any more movement in the hall; nothing aside from the usual hums and bumps of the ship stood out. There were a hundred reasons someone could be lurking after the de facto lights-out—needed a mimeo, forgot something at the mess table, anything.

"Do you mind if I hang out in here a bit longer?" asked Savannah. She'd pulled up a list of files on her tablet and was fiddling with the button on her favorite pen that switched the ink nib to a stylus. "I had some stuff I wanted to look over, and—"

"So do I," he said. "And it's not like you need an excuse to come over anyway."

"First of all, it's late and you can get fussy."

It was a line she'd used many times, and protesting only proved her point. "What's on deck for the illustrious Dr. Brown tonight?"

She tilted her screen toward him—it was split between her English recreation of Zainab's notes and a spreadsheet whose basic formatting she'd standardized during her dissertation. "Pattern hunting."

"A hunch?"

"Kind of."

Her free hand took up a stray coil of hair that laid across her forehead, stretching it taut and then winding it methodically around her finger.

Noah ducked his head toward his own tablet to hide his grin. Every one of Savannah's haunts at Rassawek had witnessed her like this at some point in the program—mostly the earlier years, when the time-swallowing focus came without the bruise of hazmat suits and lab quarantines and a joke during the keynote address of the European Xenobotany Conference.

When he peeked at her screen again, she'd scrolled up high enough for him to catch the column headers, a familiar set of titles. "That's the Chironese fern data."

"Yes."

"I seem to remember someone insisting after her defense that she was never going to think about that fern ever again."

Savannah's face shifted to the beginnings of three different sentences, finally setting her tablet to the side to face Noah directly. "And you know what's funny? My hunch has to do with the spore sacs that almost ruined everything." She laughed to herself as her gaze drifted over Noah's head, to the far corner of the bookshelf where Spock sat in quiet observation. "A couple questions are still... hm. When we get back, I wonder if they'll let me handle the samples again."

"You were never banned to begin with."

They locked eyes, waited. He raised his eyebrows, and she shifted back toward her tablet with a huff. "You know what I mean. And didn't you say you had your own work to do?"

Noah was three pages into a twenty-year-old article by Chen Yuxuan on theoretical organism structures when Savannah's arm looped with his own, her head resting on his shoulder.

The *Amihaf* woke the next morning to Quinn confined to the med bay.

No one aside from Dayo and Frida was allowed inside out of what they called an abundance of caution, but what the rest of them understood as a level of common sense they hadn't seen exercised on Nethuns.

Breakfast was a strained affair, as if everyone was afraid to accidentally inhale some pathogen Quinn released before his isolation. Or perhaps Noah was projecting. Whatever development had landed Quinn his new bunk assignment was not public knowledge; Dayo had taken her coffee to-go, while Frida and Esmail each hunched over their toast to stave off if not the attention of the rest of the crew, their voicing it. Frida's hold of her back was a tough shell with spikes. Esmail merely wanted to curl into a dense point, pop out of existence.

It was into this tableau that Abelard entered, his Constructed Body approximating a warbling whistle. Oblivious. He headed straight for the galley, the knives balanced on the edge of the sink still bearing smears of butter. He began to clean. Clinks of silverware rang in Noah's ears like emergency alarms. Across the table, Irene winced.

"I've got a good feeling about today!" said Abelard.

The faucet stream hissed as he rinsed what was available. The water ran on and on and no one at the mess table had anything to offer up in reply. They did, however, look to Noah, one at a time.

"What about?" he managed.

"Revisiting some readings from the *Khonsu* probe." He dropped the couple knives he'd been washing into a basket attached to the drying rack. "Those anomalies TerraCosmos couldn't explain back in the day… I've got some new ideas. Just something to chew on while we're in transit, really. Nothing more."

Noah nodded. "Sounds… interesting."

"It really is!"

At one end of the table, Frida pressed her thumb into a section of her toast, breaking through the crust with a crunch. At the other, Esmail plugged his ears with the inside of his wrists.

"Why don't I help you go through them?" Noah hopped up and practically leapt across the galley to the sink, prying the sudsy plate from his fingers. "We can spread out downstairs in the lab. Where do you keep your tablet in your bunk? I can go fetch—"

"*No*—I…" Abelard settled himself almost clunkily, as if he had forced an application restart. His hands came to Noah's shoulders, an airy sort of gentle, and pivoted them away from the sink. "That sounds like a lovely idea, but I can't in good conscience allow you to rummage through my bunk."

Noah waited for a clarification, but Abelard continued to gaze down at him, warm despite the metallic chill radiating from his forearm. In his peripheral vision, he caught a blurred glimpse of the mess table: empty, plates stacked neatly at one end.

"Fine by me," he said. "You go set that up, and I'll finish these dishes."

When Noah arrived at the lab, a thin sheen of chalk dust hovered over the center table, threatening to sink into the folds of his pruned fingers. The tablet sat on a spare stool, all but forgotten as Abelard reconstructed the star system at the center of the probe's mission. Every science class' units on astronomy and the history of space exploration highlighted it in the curriculum: the modern equivalent of the *Voyager* series, the first clear photos of an exoplanet's surface, the standard of data collection for any star TerraCosmos would encounter in future endeavors. *Khonsu*'s readings were nearing their three-hundredth anniversary, but that hadn't stopped them from starring in recent citations of groundbreaking research, from astrophysics to xenopathology.

"So what are we looking at?" asked Noah.

"The TRAPPIST system, of course." Abelard struck a long line under the circles representing the star's seven planets.

"I know that—"

"Ask specific questions for—"

"For specific answers," Noah finished. "I know. You *know* that I know."

"Reminders rarely hurt!"

"Right."

He pulled up a stool opposite Abelard and studied the rendering of the star itself. A thick arc rose up from the edge of the circle, brushing against the innermost exoplanet.

TRAPPIST-1-b, as it was first called. If it had earned a proper name since Noah's middle school science project, he'd never encountered it.

"Is that a solar flare?" Noah pointed toward the stray arc.

"Indeed it is," said Abelard. "During *Khonsu*'s third fly-by, the star had a burst of radiation. At the time, the probe was relatively close to exoplanet

B…" He added a crude drawing of a satellite beside the planet. "We only know about the flare because instruments back on Earth picked it up. *Khonsu* later detected increased radiation levels on exoplanets C through E, but none on that closest one, and none directly with its own instruments."

Noah caught Abelard's unblinking gaze, or the facsimile of it. Toward the bottom edge of his left eye, something sparkled, like he was watching a migraine aura creep into someone else's vision. He shrugged it off as a trick of the light, maybe a new way his body had learned to sense it coming on in himself. The longer the silence dragged on, the more certain he became that an hourglass was bleeding out sand until his head would split open; but until then, the silence was his responsibility to solve, taking the information Abelard gifted and leading them forth into the inquiry together.

Not a new task with Abelard, but the acrid taste in his mouth colored it so.

"It's safe to assume that the irradiated exoplanets weren't directly lined up with TRAPPIST-1-b's orbit," Noah said, clearing his throat. "So that leaves some… object—phenomenon?—*something* preventing the radiation from reaching it and the probe." He sighed. "Probably not a giant slab of space lead. That would've been in the report."

"And the subject of a great many TerraCosmos commission, no doubt," said Abelard.

"Well…"

The answer he wanted Noah to land on and embrace glowed until he could only squint against it, reducing any alternatives to illegible smudges. He chewed at his lip, bought himself a precious few extra seconds.

"Wells are for water," said Abelard.

"I know."

"Drink up and let me know what that good head of yours is thinking."

"I'm thinking," Noah said slowly, "that as much as you want it to be vacuum leviathans, there are some issues with that theory."

"Leviathans? That's quite the assumption."

"The last six months have given enough reasons to put this in the category of an educated guess." He watched as Abelard gently set down the nub of chalk. "Anyway—if this *were* a leviathan, that would mean that its body was either incredibly dense or that the base element of its biology is based in a heavier element—germanium, tin… uh, well… lead, to keep going down that family. And!" He threw up the first fingers of both hands to cut Abelard off before his brainware could compute the command to open his mouth. "In either case, given how big one would have to be to block an entire exoplanet from radiation, the mass would have thrown off the system's gravitational fields. There were no readings of irregular orbits."

Abelard only grinned at him, his hands clasped over a spot against his stomach where a slight paunch of old age had started to show on his organic body.

"What?" He tossed up his hands. "What is that look for?"

"You're not taking into account the radiation data you've acquired outside of *Khonsu*."

His first thought landed on the spreadsheets recently sent from Eber. "You mean from my dissertation?" he asked after a moment, and Abelard waited another long beat to nod. "Those were all deep-space readings. The circumstances are… the number and type of variables alone—"

"Noah." He slammed his hands on the table. "I trust you. I have always placed trust in you. Can you afford a bit more on my behalf? We're going to find a leviathan on this mission, and it's for you as much as it is for me."

The shimmering fuzz at the corner of Abelard's eye hadn't dissipated, and when Noah squeezed his own eyes shut, the pattern wasn't burned into the dark—as good a sign as any the effect wasn't his to bear. Not in that way.

"You plan on hauling back a leviathan corpse to TerraCosmos?" he said. "What, rigged to the back like a trailer? Sounds exactly like the kind of scenario turbolight engineers have accounted for. I'm sure we'll be able to return to the Solar System before—"

"I think we should resume dialogue on this when you're feeling more open-minded." Abelard swept his tablet into his arms and marched out of the lab without even a thought of a glance back. An arc of chalk smeared across his drawing, rendering *Khonsu* and the sunlit edge of TRAPPIST-1-b a disaster zone.

Noah swallowed the thick stone that had settled into his throat as he wetted a rag to clear the table. The ruts this moment rolled over were already worn deeper than they needed to be. So the specific feeling of the rock was already halfway to being forgotten—so what? He still knew what to do, stretching his shoulders back into a proper posture and letting himself dig into some manual task, this time the circular orbit of his hands returning the lab bench to its neutral slate.

Soon Abelard's diagram of the TRAPPIST system had been reduced to a mere suggestion of chalk, but other sections clamored for Noah's attention. Various flutes and beakers crowded around the open sinks, storage cabinet doors fought to click shut against the current arrangement of their contents, and Noah was starting to isolate the strange underlying odor keeping just out of reach of description—a small refrigeration unit at the back, previously unnoticed, warranted some slice of his time.

It was simple work, or at least simpler than the data analysis Abelard had hinted at. Reorganization didn't require basic math, much less the most rudimentary xenobiochemistry. He could busy himself here, outside the cyclical churning afforded by every other option on the ship. Straighten the microscopes, rinse the glassware, air out the fridge, don't spare an extra millisecond for concerns recorded in earlier relevant mission logs or the sharp edge to Abelard's departing remark.

Hours passed. His motions fell back into a rote pattern from his undergrad years at Dionde:gâ University, assisting the grad students and techs clean up after the leads hung up their lab coats for the day. Every time Noah paused to stretch or rinse out a rag, he would jump finding himself staring at a blank wall, no porthole offering a direct line through untold lightyears to a building over eight centuries standing and the three-river confluence just beyond.

He hadn't spared Dionde:gâ this much thought in years.

A pointed stomach pang grounded him back in the present. He didn't bother checking the time—lunch was on the immediate agenda regardless of the hour —and shuffled out of the lab and toward the stairs, mentally flipping through the available leftovers in the galley fridge. If he were lucky, there might still be some akara left from Dayo's last meal duty rotation. He could almost smell it—

A loud thump rose from behind the med bay door, followed by a agonized groan.

Noah froze at the foot of the stairwell, froze further to a new, impossible point hearing another groan—from the cockpit.

From Esmail.

Irene, at least, was there with him. Noah could have seen inside if he turned his head, but even listening in came too close to overstepping a boundary, even with the open door. Whatever Irene was saying to him was low enough to keep that border intact, between themselves, and Noah remained where he stood only to take some comfort in Esmail not being alone.

Before long, the whole first level of the ship grew quiet, and Noah let himself start up the stairs, stopping again when Esmail gave a loud sigh.

"Your cousin… how could you bear it?" he said.

"I don't know if it's a matter of 'can' or 'cannot.' You share space with it, until—"

"Until you don't?"

Irene said nothing for a moment. "He'll get through this." Another beat. "If your hair's still overstimulating, or—I can give you a trim… yeah? Give me a sec to grab some scissors."

She'd squeezed past Noah on the stairs before he could say anything, only leaving a lingering warmth where her hand had briefly held his arm.

"If it makes any difference," Dayo said, rubbing the corner of her eye, "I wouldn't be asking if I wasn't desperate."

She barely voiced the last word. Hugging her stomach, she'd corralled Noah and Savannah at the end of the mess table farthest from the lounge. Esmail sat at one end of the couch with his legs tucked up under him, glazed eyes scanning a tablet.

"I don't care that you're not physicians. We need bodies. We need a bigger breadth of xenobiology on call." She held her hands open, presenting the unstated conclusion.

Savannah rapidly clicked the pen in her pocket. "It's not that—I just—okay, backspace. The thing is," she said, "I know myself, and that's the kind of situation where whatever help I can provide is immediately canceled out by everything else." When Dayo didn't immediately say anything, she barreled onward: "You heard about the fern incident, right? The first thing I did when I realized I'd fucked up wasn't hyperventilate or anything. I just threw up on my shoes. Med bay's not big enough for that."

Noah grasped her shoulder before she offered up any more details. "I can corroborate."

"Okay." Dayo stared at Savannah, then at Noah, as if she were waiting for a similar unspooling of an out on his end. "Okay," she repeated. "Let me grab a coffee and then we can—I can brief you."

The mimeo seemed to take eons longer than normal to brew up a single mug of black coffee, leaving Noah to drum up untold numbers of potential nightmares waiting inside the med bay. Quinn with half of his skull gawking blood, torn open with some equivalent of oyster mushrooms. Quinn with white fur crawling over his pupils. Quinn with a thick paste of slime mold gumming his teeth shut.

Extreme, yes, but justified. Jibril's progression took time to build itself up to the breaking point, but as far as anyone at Camp Ilunga knew, he also hadn't taken any piece of the fungus up the nose.

Dayo led him down to the lower level, winding down the narrow spiral of the stairs with one hand on the rail and the other tipping the coffee back in a harried chug. Despite everything, her footing never faltered.

It wasn't until they were at the med bay door that she remembered she'd promised a briefing.

"Let me get this out how I'm used to, all right?" She waited for his nod of acknowledgement, taking another swig of coffee and a deep breath. "Patient is cis male, endosex, forty-one, no significant chronic conditions or surgeries outside of wisdom teeth extraction. Patient is currently presenting with hypertension, ocular discoloration, and a variety of neurological and cognitive symptoms ranging from abnormal reflexes to psychosis. Hypertension suspected to be caused by issue in the adrenal glands on the basis of the known origin of the pathogen and elevated adrenaline levels."

Noah felt himself shift just to the left of his physical body and back again as he digested each technical term on a stark delay. Dayo's stare bored into him with enough force to cause dents before he could search his memory for the definition of *adrenal*.

"Hey."

He met her eyes with a grimace. "I don't know if I caught all that."

"That's fine," she said. "Let me worry about his endocrine system. You help Frida with the pathogen."

"Dayo…"

"I'm scared too." She opened her mouth to continue, but whatever she was about to say stayed firmly put.

The door slid open. Noah was greeted with a frenzied clutter shrinking the already-cramped space—boxes of supplies strewn across the counter and scattered underfoot, equipment carts askew against the wall, the lone chair upended and draped with a wadded-up medical gown. And in the center of it, at the impasse of the long side of the gurney, Frida fought to keep Quinn from standing.

"I've gotta—where's Esmail, I've gotta tell him—"

"You are *not* leaving this room like this—"

"Got backup," said Dayo, sliding the coffee mug beside a box of gloves and crossing the room in two steps flat. "Quinn, listen to her. You've got to lie back down—"

The two of them strained pushing him to horizontal, Dayo leaning on his shoulders and Frida flung across his knees with her full weight; as they laid him flat, Quinn found Noah's face, the whites of his eyes laced with plum webbing. One of them drooped, trailing after the path of a tablet stylus Frida had kicked in the struggle, while the other stayed locked ahead.

"Um—"

"Noah," Frida said through gritted teeth. "Can you—"

"Is that new?"

"Fuck—yes it is—"

She reinforced the pressure on Quinn's legs as Dayo shouted for Noah to grab what he'd misidentified as a stylus; it was the hemograph's swab wand attachment, and she directed him to stick it up Quinn's nose.

"*Quickly*," she said. "We can only hold him still for so long."

Noah hopped through the mess to the side of the bed. Frida and Dayo could keep Quinn down, but they couldn't stop his squirming altogether. "How far up do I shove it?"

Behind him, Frida grunted, readjusting her weight across a larger portion of Quinn's wriggling legs. "Don't *shove* it, one, and don't go so far up to— Quinn, cut it out—don't dig into his brain."

Up deep, but not too deep, and swing the wand around in three full circles —that was all they needed, Dayo clarified.

This close to Quinn, the webbing in his eyes was all the more apparent. The threads he spotted across the med bay were the thickest, but gauzier tendrils spread in the gaps, through blank stretches of white and around the inroads of veins.

Noah braced himself for Quinn to fight the wand, but just as the tip disappeared, his body stilled. His errant eye swiveled toward the back corner of the room, blocked from view by Dayo's frame, and he bared his teeth in a wide grimace.

"Okay, we're good," said Dayo. She rose from her hold on Quinn and plucked the wand from Noah's hand, heading straight toward the hemograph on the counter. Docked on one side of the device was the swab's corresponding attachment, and Dayo stuck it in a subtle hole along the bottom to complete the reading.

Frida took an extra couple moments to shove herself off Quinn's legs, her feet hitting the ground unevenly and threatening to roll an ankle. "We've been trying to get that culture sample for hours." She spotted Dayo's mug amid the mess on the counter and stepped past him to steal the now-tepid leftovers.

"What's…"

He couldn't untangle his thoughts long enough to say much more than that, and Frida met him with an unreadable glance over the lip of the mug that landed heavy on his chest.

He was brought there to help Quinn. He couldn't begin to know how to help Quinn.

He'd started mentally reciting old sets of flashcards and mnemonics from biochemistries both Terrestrial and xenological—the steps of glycolysis, basic polymer structures, sulfuric nucleotides. Nothing that could illuminate the basest processes lighting up the narrow gaps between neurons, or the discoloration seeping its way through Quinn's most visible parts, or the electric spritz that would allow one eye to loll about on some unnatural impulse.

The first graduate-level lab Noah had at Rassawek had handed him embryonic Europan eel worms to work with. Even within the same star system, their genetic data expressed itself far outside the known quantity of

DNA. Predicting how they would react to non-sterile lab conditions, much less the variables of Terrestrial agents, was haphazard guesswork. Asking him to treat an esoteric pathogenic fungal agent was little more than handing him a piñata blindfold and wishing him luck.

An orange blur passed in front of him—Frida joining Dayo around the hemograph, beckoned by her frustrated muttering in Yoruba and hand smacking against the side of the device. They kept their voices low, huddled closer with their backs to Quinn, likely out of habit. Noah turned back to the bed and found Quinn staring at him again, both eyes working in tandem.

"Ger—no, Noah. Noah," he said, hoarse. "Come here. I think you'll… you'll get it. Esmail would get it, but I don't see—ha, well… I don't see why you wouldn't either." He reached out his hand, and Noah waved it away, tiptoeing around the mess.

There was a lucid shine to his eyes standing this close, even through the stark lines of purple. Quinn could have been talking his way through the latest breakthrough in the ever-persistent logging problem or arguing with Frida at one of the fronts of their verbal war—logic underpinning it all, even if his blinking now tilted more toward the drunken end than the sober.

"What's going on?" Noah murmured.

"Can you really not sense… it's everywhere, right? It's obviously—there's so many that are… parallel? But—no, they're parallel *and* perpendicular, and everywhere. Different axis."

Noah couldn't fend off the confusion furrowing his brow, and Quinn mirrored him. "Who or what is 'they?'"

"It's… it's… you're you and you're not, right?"

"What does that mean?" Noah crouched down closer to Quinn's eye level, where he laid against a starchy pillow. "Are you talking about alternate dimensions or something?"

"No, no—that's not it at *all*. No, no, no." He pinched the bridge of his nose, his fingers slowly coming to press on the corners of his eyes, wrenched shut. When he met Noah's gaze again, some of the purple lines had burst. The color drifted over his eyes like watercolors, a fine-threaded current sinking into the open void of the pupil.

"Help me understand, then."

"I don't know how to break it down any further. You're you, and you're not, just like Esmail is Esmail and also… next. It's the same thing."

Noah could only stare blankly at him, and frustration drew his whole body taut. The blipping monitors attached to the bed picked up in tempo as Quinn wound tighter.

"Hey, hey—you're fine." Noah placed his hand on Quinn's arm, squeezed. He was lying of course, and this was the kind of situation where he wasn't any good at it—when it mattered, closer to life-or-death than not. And when his hand landed on Quinn's skin it ran so hot that he thought his palm might burn; still, he kept it there, the attempt at reassurance.

"Not as worried about that as you lot are."

He arched his back, stretched his arms. Noah's hand stayed put as the skin shifted underneath. By his elbow, a few inches beneath the border of his half-sleeve tattoo, sat a sharp splotch of mauve, radiating more heat than anywhere else nearby.

"Esmail's worried," said Noah.

"That's why I want to talk to him. He's—*e hoa*, I love him more than anything in this galaxy or the next, and I know how he takes this sort of thing. I can't stand knowing he's facing it alone. I've got to talk to him. I'll know what to say to him even if I couldn't explain it to you. Esmail's different. He gets it. He gets *me*." Quinn paused, laughing to himself, and another thin thread of purple popped open in his left eye. "He gets all of it, understands it better than anyone…" His words slurred into quiet, leaving Noah's knees crackling tinnitus-loud as he stood.

He needed to sit down. A real chair. A lightness overtook his head, not enough to send the room spinning. Not yet. This was the before, the thin gaps of space in his skull filling with something like helium that would tug his body up until there was nothing left to ground him. No floor, no ground, no walls.

As he fell into the seat, it all caught up with him at once: the noise as he righted the chair amid the mess, the bright burn in his lungs. He sucked in a breath. And again. He folded himself over, pinching the nausea valve shut against the snapshots of the possible coming days flooded his imagination. Quinn, his self further devoured; Esmail, sick from grief, and still the crew would have to alert his sister—

"All right?"

Noah sat up. Dayo studied him, frowning.

"I guess. Whatever that means. I'll be fine," he added, cutting across the start of a wince. "Is there an update?"

She motioned for him to join them on the other side of the room, where Frida gripped the hemograph with white knuckles. The reading for the nasal swab had returned, though that status came with a heavy asterisk. The screen displayed all the information about the fungus that such a test could discern— what Frida had been most interested in dug into the xenobiochemistry, specifically the genetic material. The molecule's general shape as well as the individual monomers that comprised it could predict a significant amount of the xeno-organism's basic biology. There were patterns, Frida said, which Noah backed up with a fervent nod.

But—"Look at this," said Frida, and she shoved the hemograph under Noah's nose.

The screen displayed a model of the fungus' genes. Noah blinked, and the image glitched. When it cleared, he immediately spotted two new monomers distending the ropy structure.

"That's… interesting." He met their expectant gazes and reached desperately for something more substantive. "Is the hemograph malfunctioning? I just wonder," he added quickly, "because if the genetic material was actually reconfiguring itself so radically, the organism wouldn't be stable enough to stay alive."

He glanced back at the hemograph to study the new diagram closer, but the screen had scrambled itself again, half static and half a mosaic of broken images from the device's larger memory—a hand, the bulb of a classical analogue thermometer, a translucent red exclamation point spliced four ways. The collage stuttered and righted itself. A cousin of Terrestrial DNA displayed this time, except with a quadruple helix instead of the normal double. The monomers were based in a mix of silicon and carbon, nothing close to familiar.

"Fungus is weird, as a rule," said Frida. "But that weird is still within the parameters of accepted biological theory."

"Maybe if we got a sample from another part of his body…" Dayo continued murmuring to herself as she approached Quinn's bedside. "Quinn… Quinn. *Òré mí,* can you focus up here? That's it, on my face…"

Noah and Frida crept up behind her as she gestured for Quinn's attention. His one eye was again swirling about independently, toeing the edge of rolling fully to the back of his head; his other was rapt.

On Dayo's other side, Frida swallowed an uneasy groan.

"Quinn, do you know who I am?"

"Yeah, yeah… Dayo. Dr. Oyekan."

"Good—hey, keep at least one eye on me, okay? All right." She sighed, stretched her neck. "Is there anywhere else on your body that's started feeling off since we first checked you in? Physically, I mean."

"I think my foot—something's not right."

The three of them peered down to the other end of the bed in unison.

"Which one?" asked Noah.

"My foot's stuck all the way in Venus. It's set to start hopping across the sky. So hot it's numb…"

Searingly-hot feet was a start, but not the kind of symptom they could configure the hemograph to read without stopping at an Earth-side medical depot. Dayo's attempts to realign Quinn's focus sputtered and failed; he instead spoke up at the ceiling, to the walls, the empty spaces over their shoulder in Māori with a feverish fervor, and his errant eye showed the white of it fully, tints of violet bleeding in at the edges.

"Wait."

As soon as Noah opened his mouth, Frida and Dayo had already crowded around him. He held up a hand to carve out enough distance for him to breathe and nudged Quinn's arm over with the pressure of a single finger. The grayed lilac blot had already spread, ducking under and through the lines of his tattoo with mottled arms.

"What about this?"

Dayo swore. "It's not good, but we can work with it."

The extra hemograph plug-ins were stored in the far cabinet, and Dayo plowed ahead through the obstacles of mess. The metallic clicks as the different add-ons were swapped out sounded like reloading rail guns from pre-Catastrophe action movies.

"Okay. You take this," said Dayo, shoving another wand into Frida's hands. "And Noah—you've got to hold him still on your own. Punch biopsies are outdated, but on Natocke Station, it was between a more state-of-the-art module and restocking syringes."

They slid into position as Dayo fired up the attachment—this close, it was impossible to hide the chipped veneer and flattened corners against the newer central device, and when she kicked on the connecting port, it threw out a whine pitching up toward the inaudible. One of her hands held it steady as it stabilized, the other contorting itself into finger gymnastics to prep the bi-modal suture pen.

"Frida, rub your numbing wand over the discolored area and two inches on each side until I give the word. Noah—"

"Yeah, I'm on it." His hands were small. One could barely wrap around even half of Quinn's bicep, but he made do, leaning his shoulder into the muscle.

"Good." She tucked the suture pen behind one ear and took the hemograph in both hands, positioning one end over the blemish. One eye pinched shut as she hesitated over millimeters of difference in her aim. "Frida, on the count of three, pull your wand out of the way."

"Just say when."

Dayo counted down. Frida yanked her hand back, and the hemograph module landed on Quinn's skin, clacked, sent him into a spasm of pain. Noah's legs strained as he tried to leverage more of his weight to keep the arm still; and when Quinn calmed, Noah lifted his head in time to catch Dayo shoving the hemograph into Frida's arms. The suture pen descended to the bloody hexagonal chasm, first threading the skin back together and then, when the tender edges were close enough, cauterizing the gap in a thin fit of smoke.

The hemograph whirred and whined processing the slab of flesh, underpinned by Quinn's groaning.

"What was the point of this thing, then?" said Frida, the numbing wand listing in her hand. "A lot of good that did—"

"Would've been worse," Noah said. He stretched out his arms after standing upright, putting a few extra inches between him and the bed.

"It can always get worse, can't it?" she muttered. The wand clanged against a metal tray atop the cart beside her, the grip suddenly slack.

The hemograph whined further, and Dayo grumbled. The module processed samples slowly, being so old; she was going to read the results as soon as they popped on screen, so help her heavens surrounding. The mystery would fall apart, and Quinn would be fine. They could send what they'd found through the relays to Camp Ilunga, and then Jibril would be fine too. *One nightmare at a time*—her muttering devolved into that one phrase, repeated.

And Frida—her fists balled up so tightly at her sides that they'd started to shake, and that same dark flush of red crept up her face, drowning out her freckles, and she screwed her eyes shut like that would keep it all from boiling over into open air.

"*Fuck.*"

Noah jumped out of the way in time to avoid the unceremonious shove Frida would have gifted him otherwise. She took his place near the head of the bed, crouching to eye level with Quinn, her small hands gripping creases into his shirt sleeve. With one eye glassy and the other spending more time staring at the inside of his skull than not, Quinn didn't acknowledge her.

"Listen," she hissed. "You may be a knob, but that doesn't mean you get to roll over for some piece of shit fungus. If anything was going to be the end of you, it was going to be me, first of—" She met Noah's gaze over her shoulder. "I'm exaggerating, obviously." She sighed, biting her lip. "C'mon... I still haven't fought you on the Neogallish New Wave. I was going to make you so fucking angry—whatever. Just lay there, I guess. But I'm going to save your fucking life. If only because it'll drive you up the wall." Her hands twisted more of his sleeve into her fists, white-knuckled. "And Noah, I don't want to hear it."

"Hear what?"

"Exactly." She stood, her shoulder check landing closer to his elbow as she rejoined Dayo with the hemograph. The two of them huddled around the screen, and Frida's arms wound around her stomach in a constricting embrace, pulling the loose fabric of her shirt flush against her back.

The results, when he maneuvered to the other side of Dayo, boasted at least a functional confidence the glitching nasal swab could never hope for—the hemograph's main screen displayed the genetic polymer in a lower resolution, but the image remained static. Dayo and Frida combed through the middle ground between Terrestrial meningitis and xenomycological theory, hoping to stick on some kernel that could propel them out of the rut.

And then Noah saw it.

Another glitch.

"It's done it again," he said, pointing around Dayo's arm. "The gene diagram—it... did you not see it?"

"Not this time," said Dayo. "What did you see?"

"It wasn't as severe as before. The whole image obviously didn't collapse, but a slice of the polymer jumped out to the left, and it was clearly part of some other biomolecule just based on the shape."

Frida ran a thumbnail over the arc of her eyebrow. "What the… what is going on with—wait a second."

"What?" asked Dayo.

"Noah—my camouflage theory…could this be how it hides?"

"As in…" he said. "It's not a tech glitch? It literally changes its genetic makeup on a whim to fit its needs?"

Dayo's brow folded in thought as they all chewed over the idea, the plausibility, the potential implications. The whole of the *Amihaf* seemed to fall silent—

Noah's face slammed down into the med bay floor. He winced against the bruise bleeding against his cheekbone as he clamored to the most basic of sitting positions to survey the room—Quinn had held onto his spot on the gurney while Dayo and Frida glued themselves to sturdy medical equipment or cabinet doors. Around them, the ship groaned directly against the sensitive layers of their inner ears.

Just as suddenly, it stopped.

"Everyone okay?" Noah called.

"Physically, yes," said Dayo. She recalibrated her center of balance, flattening out the wrinkles in her yellow sweater as she went to check on Quinn. "I won't presume to speak on anything else."

"Another fucking problem…"

Frida stormed her way out toward the foyer, and Noah rushed after her. Gathered there already was Irene and the specific chord of Esmail and

Savannah's crosstalk echoing down the stairwell. The door to the cockpit remained open over Irene's shoulder.

"To start," said Irene, "I want to stress that we are not in any immediate danger."

"How much work is 'immediate' doing in that statement?" Frida's voice cracked, tilting higher than any of them had heard from her.

"Frida… I should know better than to ask, but—"

Irene cut herself off as Savannah and Esmail wound down the steps to the foyer.

"Know better than to ask what?" said Dayo. She leaned against the jamb of the med bay's half-open door, her frame blocking any view of Quinn or the larger room.

Caught in the middle, Irene looked between Dayo and Esmail with her usual reticence, but the longer her silence held, the tempered calm shuddered and wobbled.

"What is it?" Esmail said. "If you need to ask about Quinn, you can do it in front of me. I should know anyway, right?" He jumped as Savannah put a hand on his arm, then leaned into it.

Irene nodded. "Is… would Quinn's condition… allow him to help me troubleshoot the navigation computer?"

"Absolutely not," said Dayo.

And at the same time, from Frida: "What the fuck does *that* mean?"

The ship's rumbling rose and fell with another metallic groan.

"Can I see him?" asked Esmail, quiet.

"Maybe tomorrow." Dayo wrung her hands. "We'll just have to see."

"Irene." Frida approached her slowly. "What is wrong with the navigation computer?"

The mask crumpled in the single motion of her face widening in a grin, all teeth, aching to stretch wider, finally spilling out in a peal of laughter that rattled Noah's own tenuous hold on his composure—his and everyone else's. Irene's shoulders shook and she was halfway to doubled over, then pulling herself back, forcibly erect, the tears in her eyes a sharp white glare under the lights.

"What's wrong with the… I don't know! That's the problem," she said, catching her breath. "I did as much troubleshooting as I know how to. What I do know… we're not headed to the Gliese 1061 system anymore."

Noah's throat closed against a sudden lump. "Um… where *are* we headed now?"

"I don't know!" Her arms spread wide, hands rolled into fists. "I can't get the computer to display the new vector! It could be somewhere! Or nowhere, one of those infinite lines through space that doesn't intersect a thing—"

"Over my rotting corpse." Frida ducked under one of Irene's arms and into the cockpit's antechamber, where Quinn had set up his own troubleshooting station months ago. His laptop was still there, the ship's system plugins idling in the side ports. Frida scoured the edges for the power control for a few seconds, cursed, and shoved it aside to claw open the service panel. It swung across the full arc of its hinges and into the wall with a clang. "This is the main hub of the ship's computer-whatever, right? I've fixed my tablet dozens of times."

The rest of them scrambled in the foyer—Esmail slipping over to the abandoned laptop, Savannah swallowing her anxiety to dash to the med bay, Irene ducking back into the cockpit to check on the navigation computer. And Noah, joints suddenly gummy, forced his legs through it to take him to Frida's side. His head spun with too many thoughts to effectively focus on them all, so he narrowed on one, the most immediate worry: his minimally-acceptable grades in computer science, the worn path from his Rassawek office to the IT department.

He situated himself just behind Frida as she assessed the scene. At eye level, a large service screen waited for input, its background a pastel orange. Above and below the screen sat a server chassis, each thin blade distinguishing itself with a blinking green light, each flashing without any sense of unity, like pre-Catastrophe footage of fireflies.

"It seems too easy to just type 'navigation computer' in that tablet," said Frida. She glanced at Noah for a second opinion, but he could only shrug. "Whatever that other problem Quinn cared so much about clearly needed to bypass it—you got it to turn on?"

Esmail, sitting cross-legged on the floor, froze with the laptop balanced between his knees. "I—yes? I've seen him use this for years. I still might not be able to actually log on. He has three or four different layers of security—" The laptop chirped a quick lilt of notes. "Oh!"

"What?" Noah said.

"I didn't know he'd…" Esmail blushed trying to hide a smile. "He set up bio-recognition for me."

"Lucky us," sighed Frida. "See what you can find that's decipherable to the average person."

With a thumbs-up, Esmail dove into Quinn's files. His fingers clacked away at the retro physical keyboard, fading more into the ambient noise of the *Amihaf*'s bow as Frida turned to fix Noah with an expectant glare.

"You ever wrangled something like this before?"

"Not in the slightest."

"Great. We're equally lost." She prodded the screen with her thumb and a digital keyboard rose from the bottom. "Easy enough. And I know I just said this wouldn't lead to anything but what else do we have?" She began to type *navigation computer* into the search bar.

"We should be able to see if it's connected properly this way," said Noah. "I think."

Frida hit enter and the results page was as empty as the vacuum beyond the hull. "This might not be a bad sign. This might not be bad—Irene! Does the navigation computer have a fancy longer name or model type?"

She poked her head outside the cockpit, frowning. "Not really. It's technically an 'astronavigational vector computer,' but no one's called it that since TerraCosmos announced the first prototype. And models are named numerically."

Again Frida swore, smacking out a new search: *show me the connecteddevicees yuo bloodyp iece of sht.*

No results.

"Did that, uh—"

"No, Noah, it didn't help." She ran her hands through her hair. With a reset to the starting page and an empty prompt bar, she tapped the search icon; the bar lined itself in red. "Thought that might've taken us to a master folder library. Fuck."

"I've got something!" Esmail typed out a few more lines on the keyboard, and then the panel screen flickered—gone was the search bar and plain orange, now replaced with a projection of the laptop's current display. About two-thirds of the screen was taken up by program windows, hiding the photo Quinn had set as his wallpaper.

Or, hiding most of it. A nature scene, likely in Aotearoa, peering down from a mountaintop, all browns, to the sharp teal oval of a lake below. Only the bald crown of Quinn's head and the rightmost quarter of Esmail's were visible over a window. Quinn's hand curved against Esmail's hip, warm. Esmail's smile-folded crow's feet gave away his concealed expression.

Noah couldn't bear to look him in the eye.

Instead, he skimmed through the information: one window listing all of the devices connected to the *Amihaf*'s central server hub, the other the system firewall's home screen.

"This is fantastic," said Frida, "even if I have no idea what you did."

"Ah." Irene had soundlessly snuck up behind them, positioning herself in the empty space above where Noah and Frida's shoulders met. "That makes sense—this main server's troubleshooting system is in TerraBase, but the deeper internal workings are all in another operating system. No wonder you were having problems."

"I thought everything used TerraBase," said Noah.

"Everything the average person deals with," said Esmail. "The other has been around for centuries and is… well, as much as TerraCosmos doesn't like to admit it, a better host for this kind of work."

Frida pinched the bridge of her nose, tilting her glasses. "I thought you didn't know anything about computers."

"*I* don't," he said, "but Quinn's always used me as a sounding board, and I pay attention when he's having a moment."

"So you know what he knows," said Irene.

"Well, no… I know a vague idea of what he knows. Probably a *lot* of misunderstandings about what he knows. Not at all the same thing—"

"It's going to have to do," Frida sighed.

Esmail chose a spot beyond their heads to stare at. His hands flexed in and out of fists, fingers fluttering in their usual way as they curled into his palm. "It's—let me show you." He used Quinn's laptop to pull up the list of core systems. Slotted between the third backup life support manager and the fuel recycler was an item simply titled *ASTRONAVCOM*.

"And what's that?" Irene pointed at the text. "Does it take you somewhere else?"

Esmail clicked on it and the window opened another page, the top listing the specs of the device, and the rest various graphs of real-time data—or at least Noah assumed as much based on the labeling. The fields stood stagnant, barren under the large red font heading the section.

Status: Unknown.

"Can we get in through the back door?" Irene said, hurrying to kneel behind Esmail. "The only training we get on this is done through the beast itself."

"I don't know. I don't... I don't know what troubleshooting with one of these things means. Or really even with this." He motioned to the laptop. "There's a button here to try to repair the connection to the central servers —"

"If we do that while we're on a turbolight vector, is the ship going to explode?" asked Frida.

"Nope." Irene pointed over Esmail's shoulder toward the advanced settings option tucked into the corner.

"But—"

"I can explain later."

It would have been better if their many attempts were closed off behind the sleek gray back of the laptop, a mystery that could cup a shallow bit of hope for the next moment, or the next, or the one after that when their eyes would pop wide, alight with surprise and relief at the fix spreading open before them. Instead: Noah and Frida watched the screen mounted into the wall as the cursor pressed onward, trying option after option, receiving nothing but pop-up error messages. And watching was the only thing they could do.

Ages into the fruitless troubleshooting, only a minute had passed. Ninety seconds, at most. A hand landed at the crook of Noah's neck, squeezing in a way that told him the body at his back could only be Savannah.

"How are things over here?"

"Hard to say," Noah murmured. "How's the med bay situation?"

"Stable."

"No throwing up?"

"I did very well, thank you." A pleased grin spilled over into her voice, but he doubted she let it show. She adjusted to rest her chin on his head, then tapping Frida on the shoulder. Whatever she mouthed to her was met with a resigned shake of her head.

"Well…" Irene jumped to her feet and strode toward the screen in the wall, where the navigation computer's page had just expanded to take up the whole of it. "We did figure out one thing, at least. The vector we're currently on is directed so far past Gliese 1061 that it will put us outside the bounds of what Project Khepri covers."

The ship's normal hum seemed to grow ten times as loud as they processed Irene's assessment.

"How far outside?" asked Esmail. "A couple lightyears? Or is it… deeper space? Project Aker deep?"

"I don't know." Irene shoved her fists in her jacket pockets. "The data we have access to here is partial. That still narrows down possible destinations by a lot, if it's actually sending us to a system instead of…"

The great vast middle of nothing.

"And I do think it's aiming at a system," she added.

Frida had saddled up beside them, squinting at the scant bits of data Esmail had helped them dredge up from the depths of the processor. "How can you say that with any confidence?"

"I guided us safely this far."

Whatever reply Frida had lined up against her teeth instead flushed across her face, crossing cheekbone to cheekbone.

"I think," said Esmail quietly, "that she was hoping there was some room for you to be wrong. So we could be... *not* on that path."

"Has... shit, I hate to ask this." Savannah's grimace pressed against the top of Noah's head. "What about Abelard?"

The last thirty-six hours flipped through Noah's head. He hadn't seen Abelard since his sudden departure from the lab the previous morning, huffing about leviathans and the *Khonsu* probe, and on a small ship, there were only so many places to hide from the other seven members aboard. A few moments passed before Noah realized Frida and Irene were staring at him.

"I haven't talked to him today," he said. "We all know he spends most of his time between systems in his bunk, anyway."

"I saw him briefly this morning.' Esmail's head ducked down as he absently picked at a cuticle. "But it was just to grab something from the mimeo in the galley. He said something about... resetting his system."

"Is that a thing?" Frida cocked an eyebrow, met with shrugs and muttering about how only Dayo would know for sure.

Noah sighed. "It's probably safe to say he doesn't know."

Something about the way Irene could meet his gaze—betraying not one mote of substance churning on the other side of her skull—still conveyed, at the very least, the depth of that churning, the shape of it, an aspect that couldn't readily be put to words. It was that way that her eyes met his now, and Noah knew that whatever she said next would hit his throat like a vise.

Irene nodded to Esmail, and the window of data from the navigation computer minimized, leaving the firewall's home screen—but it wasn't the home screen. The thick green menu tabs along the top were the same, but the bulk of the page held a zoo of quarantined intruders.

Or rather, intruder. Singular.

The file's icon was hemmed in by a black border with a thin red line running through the center, the program's highest level of containment.

"I'm not at Quinn's level of expertise," said Irene, "but I do know that TerraCosmos ship systems have one kind of external interface, the communication relays—and the security architecture there is the most stringent I've ever seen."

Savannah shifted so her cheek rested on the waviest section of Noah's hair, her arms wrapping over his shoulders in a hug whose looseness was carefully calibrated to not squeeze too tight against sensitive stretches of the throat, or force her to cradle her elbows in a way that would shine on the snarled tangle in her stomach.

"Is that"—Frida pointed at the laptop—"not an external interface?"

"Okay, yes," said Irene. "When I said 'external' I meant relative to the ship as a whole."

And then Irene was back to staring at him, and this time, he could see through the veil of her apparent stoicism to the plaintext hunched underneath.

If the file couldn't have come from outside the ship, then it had to have come from within; and the reasonable suspects among the eight onboard—

A bright wave of nausea created against the back of Noah's tongue. He shuddered against it, and Savannah pulled back to check on him, just far enough for him to slip out of her embrace. It didn't have to be true, despite the logic. Of course viruses and their ilk couldn't force themselves into existence within a system. Of course the relay security would unravel any malignant files ping-ponged through their arm of the galaxy. He suddenly recalled Quinn's earlier hypothesis, the file as remnant, a thought that now couldn't settle into sense.

So: of course someone would have had to thrust the infection in themselves.

Noah removed himself from the closing knot of conversation, into the foyer. Over the clamor, Savannah noted how the file—identified as FDL.exe—couldn't have possibly caused the trouble with the navigation computer since it had been in quarantine. He reached the bottom of the staircase, and Esmail fought to be heard as the other debates ran on—he'd heard Quinn muddling through this just before they landed on Nethuns, and regularly that muddling would concentrate at a dead end. The file may have been named FDL.exe, but *exe* was not the file extension; the actual extension could only display as hollow rectangles, illegible in both operating systems no matter the configuration adjustments.

"That quarantine might be useless?" Savannah shouted.

One blink later and Noah found himself facing the second-story lounge. The bunk hall was a step lighter than a solid black-dark, the shadows sharpening into the outlines of doors the closer he grew.

A sliver of light shone out from the far end, the back corner. Abelard's bunk with him in it. Awake, presumably.

Another blink and Noah was in the dark, knuckles already smarting from pounding on the door.

"I'm afraid now's not a good time," Abelard called from inside.

His arm dropped to his side, bruises welling up warm under his skin. "It sure isn't! Which is why we need to talk!"

"Trust me, it's quite—"

"Open the door."

"Noah."

"*Open the door.*"

The door slid open a few inches, enough for exactly half of Abelard's face and body to block Noah's view into the room. The half of the grin under his mustache relaxed against the technicality he'd taken advantage of.

"Thank you." He straightened his back, tilted his chin up to meet the half of Abelard's gaze he could see. His father's voice hummed low at the base of his skull—*if you're so determined to be a man, you need to stand like one.* Sudden flop sweat chilled under the ceiling's air circulator, and he hesitated. One moment, and then another to mentally curse the first. If he could stand calm before his tirading father, then this shouldn't have been such a large jump.

He took a slow, solid breath. In, out.

"Something's wrong with the navigation computer. It's got us way off course from Irene's vector to the Gliese 1061 system."

Abelard's mouth pulled to one side in thought, completely behind the border of the door. "That's quite a development." He made no move to imply he had something else to add.

"We're not having any luck fixing it," he said, carefully handling each word. "I know this mission is important to many people, Abraham and Eber included. The university's standing with TerraCosmos would be affected if things here… went wrong."

"To be completely forthcoming, Noah, I don't see how that is any of our business."

"What—our department depends on TerraCosmos for most of our funding, and there are countless graduate students and faculty whose research would fall apart without that. They're the only reason any of us are on this ship or have this field to work in at all! And you want us to say *who the fuck cares* to them when something's malfunctioning? Not to mention our *lives*—"

"I don't think I've ever seen you so worked up." Abelard brought a hand to his chin, as if he were merely remarking on a curious sample under a microscope.

"*Abelard—*"

"You recall what I said to you in the lab," he said. "Keeping an open mind? This is a fantastic opportunity for an exercise, see. Our vector may no longer be taking us to Gliese 1061, but must that mean that matters aboard have 'gone wrong?'"

"Yes!" Noah's voice cracked at a pitch he hadn't been able to reach since his voice dropped. "The bases on those two exoplanets are expecting us. We don't know where the new vector ends—is it a system we'll reach in our lifetime, is there a habitable exoplanet there, does our path overlap with a black hole's gravity well…"

All of the possibilities pressed down upon him like the ship's gravity modulator had dialed up its settings. His shoulders sagged, and the voice of Gerard Starbuck in his head couldn't shout loud enough to pull them back up.

"Noah…"

Abelard's hand shot out of the door, grabbing Noah's arm at the elbow. His thumb found the crevice in the bone and dug against the ulnar nerve—pain rolled into the joint, numbness spreading down toward his hand. Noah tried to curl his fingers into the fold of Abelard's shirt mere centimeters away, but they moved on delay, slowing as the Constructed Thumb tested how far it could press into that soft valley of sinew.

"Noah," he said again. "You were always so smart. Surely you are smart enough to know better."

His knees wanted to buckle, but he fought, propping himself up in a wavering middle ground that gave Abelard another few inches of height. "Don't you know better than to be threatened by me?" he hissed through the pain. "What can I do against your ConBod?"

Abelard's thumb shoved deeper for half a moment before his grip broke, letting Noah fall to the floor. He stared down at him with a blank expression that held no suggestion of emotion, as if the crew at Njord Station all those years ago had simply forgotten to install that brainware package.

"If anything," said Noah, pulling himself to his feet, "you should be wary of yourself."

The light leaking into the hall around the door and Abelard's frame held as Noah dragged his uncooperative body toward his own bunk. As his hand reached the door handle, the hall slipped back into that thicker darkness.

The *Amihaf,* shuddered around him once again, rattling at an unfathomable velocity into a wide, terrible unknown.

NINE

"DAYO, I TOLD YOU. I'm fine! Really!"

"If you want to have even a chance of me believing that, at least let me do a basic exam."

"Do you not trust me?"

"I trust the fact that just last night you were incoherent—talking to me like you were my baba, and with a completely purple tongue—"

"That's clearly not happening anymore, now is it?"

"Fine. Show me your tongue."

"Of course. Just a…"

The med bay door slid open, and Noah jumped out of Quinn's way with hardly a second to spare. His clothes still clung to the wrinkles they'd developed while hastily folded in the corner, and a shiny blot of scar tissue sat under his tattoo, but otherwise he bore no sign of his xenomycological psychosis four days after it had set in.

Quinn ascended the staircase, and Dayo huffed after him, hemograph tucked under her arm. "This is a small ship, and I know where to find you!"

His feet disappeared beyond the stairs, pulling her to a halt, with a sigh that devolved into muttered Yoruba.

Whether it was the right move or not to interrupt her like this was irrelevant in the face of the deep ache pulsing in his bones. Four days of Quinn's stint in the med bay was also four days along the mystery vector far flung from TerraCosmos' stated agenda for the ship; and at night, whether he'd woken up at an odd hour or simply hadn't fallen asleep at all, Noah would recalculate exactly how fast on this brave new route they were going, unfathomable distances in the time it took the mimeo to brew a cup of coffee. All in the wrong direction.

"Dayo…"

She jumped, grabbing the collar of her blouse. "Noah—is it eleven already?"

"I can come back. Flexible schedule… nowhere else to be."

Her free hand propped itself on her hip as she surveyed the ship's foyer and, over Noah's shoulder, to the cockpit's antechamber. Esmail and Irene crowded around the laptop to attempt another few rounds of troubleshooting, now frozen awaiting Dayo's next edict.

"No," she said. "I already made you wait long enough… Esmail!"

He leapt up and stumbled to a stop beside Noah. "You called?"

"You can take your time, you know." When he didn't offer anything other than his usual warm grin, she continued, "Please go check on Quinn. I'm— what he's claiming doesn't line up with any accepted theory of medicine, and —"

"Right," said Esmail. A rosiness colored his cheeks as he tamped down the spread of a wide, splitting smile. "I can do that, absolutely. I'll be—"

"Careful, yes?" Dayo put a hand on his shoulder before he could dash for the stairs. "He claims he's healthy, but I haven't been able to verify it myself."

Esmail laid one of his hands over hers, guiding it down so he could clasp both of hers between his own. "I understand."

"I can't have two patients like that."

Dayo marched back across the foyer as Esmail ascended the stairs, motioning for Noah to follow her into the med bay; he glanced at Irene hunched over the laptop, thumbnail digging into her chin. There wasn't time for her to look up.

The mess in the med bay seemed less like it had been addressed than a tornado had torn through and simply rotated the clutter into new formations. Quinn's gurney still had the sheets, one corner of the fitted set having sprung free by the wall. A sickly grayish-purple blotch the size of a melon curled over the edge of the mattress.

"Here." Dayo shoved aside a small stack of boxes and a wrinkled medical gown, revealing a stool. "Sit."

"Biohazard?"

She paced up and down the length of the countertop twice, suddenly remembering the hemograph was under her arm. "I'm throwing it in the airlock once Frida cuts out that stain. Everything in my gut—hers too—is screaming to let it meet its end in the vacuum, but…" She sighed. "Part of her is still curious, and if that sample could help us treat the pathogen, Hippocrates would have a case about violating that oath of his. What can you do?"

Noah shucked off the flannel he was wearing over his t-shirt to allow better access to his arm. The bruise Abelard had left this time hadn't spread like the one from Shala, instead concentrating around the joint like a jacket's elbow patch. Once the hemograph obtained its blood sample, Dayo pulled up a seat on an overturned waste basket and gently stretched his arm to its full extension.

"Now that it's been a few more days, the blood tests can help me rule out any further damage," she said. "I don't like that he got you in the same arm again." She turned his arm so his palm was facing up, and he flexed his fingers. The ring and little fingers were hesitant to respond. "You said he dug in here?" She lightly tapped at the center of the bruise, and he nodded. "Have you had any numbness in your hand?"

"Just the first day after, and it wasn't constant."

"Around these same two fingers giving you trouble?"

Noah nodded again, and Dayo set off on another mumbling monologue. The hemograph, tucked against her foot on the floor, chirped with completed results. She scrolled through the readings, biting at the inside of her cheek, and got up to dig through the cabinets. She stooped behind a rolling cart of supplies, so Noah could only go by sound alone—more grumbling in a language he didn't understand, a few glassy clinks against the floor. She reemerged pinching two glasses in the crook of one elbow, while the opposite hand clutched a half-full handle of clear liquor. When Dayo set the handle down on another nearby tower of boxes, Noah got a better glimpse of the label—the same bottle of *pisco* Frida had dug out of her bunk the night they left Ushuaia Station.

"It's still morning," said Noah.

"Morning is relative. Do you want a shot or not?"

"If it's doctor's orders…"

"I'll write a prescription." She balanced the two glasses on top of one of the more stable stacks of the nearby clutter, spilling only a couple drops pouring between them. "Here."

Noah took the finger's worth and held it at eye level. "To frontier medicine."

She twisted the glass in her hand, examining how the softened octagonal edges and cloudy patches distorted her fingers. "It is, isn't it?"

"We don't have to toast to it if—"

"No." She readjusted her grip, raised it just enough to tap the rim of Noah's glass. "Might as well."

Noah tossed back his shot on her cue, the herbal flavor sinking hot down his throat. The mixer from that first night had diluted it more than he'd realized, and he suppressed a shudder. "I'm okay," he said, catching Dayo staring with one raised eyebrow, hemograph in hand. "Been a while."

"Right. Well..." She nodded toward the hemograph. "Confirmed my suspicions. The nerve is bruised. It'll take up to six weeks to mend itself, but there's still a chance of complications lingering past that window."

After a couple last-minute examinations to check that she hadn't missed anything more serious, she cleared him to return to the tension-thick atmosphere of duty awaiting him in the rest of the ship. The door shunted open to an empty foyer, Frida flicking through a document on her tablet perched at the bottom of the stairs, hunching her shoulders at an increasingly steeper angle whenever an odd noise rang out from the floor above.

"Dayo's free," he called.

"Fantastic." She slapped a couple buttons on the screen and a strained version of the satcall's ringing audio trilled from its speakers. "Qori wanted to talk to her directly, and it was starting to get too late, Ychma time..."

As she disappeared into the med bay, Noah surveyed the rest of the bottom floor—the lab sat dark, empty, and Irene had spread the work station around the maintenance panel around into the cockpit, where she buried her head between two tablets and Quinn's laptop, occasionally reaching to adjust some setting on the actual navigation computer. Upstairs was nearly as empty, save for Savannah at one end of the mess table. Esmail and Quinn had presumably retreated to their bunk.

Abelard, presumably, still had not left his.

Noah took a seat at the upper end of the materials Savannah had papered the table with, a handful of screens holding down the edges of paper copies sporting speckled russet stains from the Nethunsan sand. He didn't need to say a word for her to start talking, more of a mental monologue stretching in the open air for the first time, his own role as the audience an afterthought. A possible connection between Jibril and Quinn's fungus and the stone reeds— she couldn't shake the idea, not after that odd moment they all had out in the marshes. She'd pulled up the translation of Zainab's work beside her own notes on what she'd overheard from Frida and Yonas, lost hours and sleep to the archives of the couple relevant journals she was subscribed to. One tablet held a long email thread between her and Camp Bachelor's geologist, Luz Matapang.

But her monologue eventually slowed, falling under a new pall of focus that suggested he not linger.

His own bunk was in an even worse state of disarray than he'd registered upon waking up. He shoved aside the piles of junk with his foot as he crossed the short distance to his bed, flopping onto his back. Something dug into his spine—Spock, who must have taken a transporter from the shelves to the knotted folds of his sheets. He held the figurine by the ankles after he fished it out from under him. It stared down with its missing pupils and ear tips worn down to a more human curve.

"What am I supposed to do?" Spock fell backwards against his stomach as he ground his palms against his brow. "I know you'd just say something about logic… how am I supposed to *wield logic* against the forces of some psychic xenofungus and—whatever is wrong with Abelard? Hm?"

Noah propped Spock back up on his chest, this time holding it by the waist. Of course the plastic itself wasn't going to answer, but if the last six months had taught him anything, it was how quickly the wide breadths of the impossible could flatten into the everyday, something to slot between brushing your teeth and waiting on the mimeo coffee.

So he focused on the figurine's empty stare, the straight cut of its bangs and the pointed tips of its sideburns. Surely Leonard Nimoy's warm bass could reach through eight hundred years to deliver an epiphany. Literally, figuratively, whatever made the message stick. Jibril al-Khattab knowing his deadname, among so many other things, burst the walls hemming in expectations.

The only voice that came to Noah was his own, a faint whisper he directed not toward Spock, but the ceiling beyond. "Okay… Abelard cares more about finding his vacuum leviathan than our assigned mission. The navigation computer has malfunctioned and is shooting us who-knows-where. A virus got in the ship's system and may be able to breach containment." He glanced toward Spock, but the vacant stare was too expectant, tripping up the step-by-step plot of his thoughts. "It's probably safe to say the virus *has* escaped, and it would follow that the navigation computer's troubles stem from that. If we stop the virus, then we could fix the navigation computer, but the only person who can do that is—"

Noah sat straight up, sending the figurine tumbling to another oblivion among the sheets. His chest seized with an icy burn at the center that oozed outward, hollowing out his breath. The flickering still frames of memory played back in slow motion from the beach at the edge of Camp Ilunga—Quinn in the sand, a divot of Jibril's cap carved out, Abelard claiming an accident.

Feigning.

He'd been planning this.

Wherever they were headed, the vector was pointed at Abelard's best estimation of a leviathan den.

"Fuck."

He briefly considered what Spock would do upon such a realization, or anyone on the *Enterprise*; but he couldn't help but sense himself shrink, as if he were once again a small child trying to carry something far too hefty for his size. Whatever a Starfleet officer would do was out of reach.

He could spring into action later.

Now, he just wanted to sleep.

Noah had an entire three seconds after waking before he remembered what had sent him running into the arms of unconsciousness in the first place.

"Ugh." He kicked his legs straight from the curled tuck they'd assumed and heard a solid thunk against the floor—Spock, newly freed from the sheets.

He swore under his breath as he retrieved the figurine and replaced him on his usual shelf, and he swore again as he spotted the time. It was already inching toward the late end of the afternoon, and the rest of the ship's activity wasn't offering any hints by way of noise.

After splashing his face with a few handfuls of cold water and changing out of his shirt stale with sweat, he slipped out of his bunk and into the common area. Only then could he hear other members of the crew, all on the floor below and far quieter than they would be if something wasn't looming over their heads.

Descending the stairs, the conversation pulled itself into focus—though it was less of a conversation than Frida straining to keep a monologuing rant under a certain volume, her neck craning to stare Quinn in the eye.

The sight was almost a relief.

"—and I know I've no formal medical training, but medicine is still a science, Kaiwhakatere, so me saying 'this is shite' still counts as my professional opinion." She ran a hand through her hair to punctuate the point, though the effect was lost once the rest of them noticed Noah's arrival.

"Where did you go?" Savannah asked, an arm outstretched to hook him to her side in the crew's larger huddle. "We thought the worst."

"Just my bunk. It's not a big—what do you mean, the worst?"

No one answered him, instead falling back on whatever discussion Frida's blustering interrupted. Everyone was involved, no matter if a laptop was cradled against their chest or a hemograph was emitting its typical processing hum. Too many threads wove out in too many varying directions for Noah to keep up, at least until Esmail ducked through the throng to settle beside him, opposite Savannah.

"I think," he said into his ear, "someone had an anxious thought about airlocks. But it's fine now!"

Esmail pulled back to give him a small grin, personal, and Noah pushed himself to return it. He pushed himself further when his gaze dropped to the stretched scoop collar of Esmail's sweater, where inside the curve of his shoulder sat a lopsided purple blot. Noah tapped at Savannah's hip until it drew her attention out of the debate of the hour.

"What?" she mumbled.

He tried to motion to the spot with his eyes alone. "Esmail's neck—"

"Oh fuck, it *is* contagious—"

In an instant, the entire foyer congregation turned to face them. Dayo caught it first, rushing up to Esmail and tilting his head to better inspect his neck. "Esmail," she said, "have you noticed anything else like this anywhere on your body?"

"Um…" His face folded open with a grimace. "That's not a fungal mark."

"What do you m—"

"This is Quinn's sweater." He waved one of the arms. The sleeve ran past the ends of his fingers by a good few inches. No one said a word. "He's my husband," he said slowly.

Dayo stepped back, narrowly missing the toe of Irene's boot. Her hands clasped together under her nose, praying not only for the right words for the situation but for the collective fate of everyone on the *Amihaf*.

Under her gaze, Esmail's grimace deepened.

"We got it," said Dayo.

"I wasn't sure." From the inside of the sleeves, he started to bunch up the extra fabric in his fists, pulling the trailing ends into a crumpled, truncated stump. "I had been so worried, and—"

"You said you'd be careful! We don't know how or if it can spread." As if she could sense Quinn behind her opening his mouth to protest, she held up a hand to silence him. "Follow me." She marched across the foyer toward the med bay with Esmail close behind.

Before Frida could dig back into Quinn with renewed vigor, Savannah uncoupled herself from Noah and planted herself between them, asking after some point tangentially tied to the design of her latest novelty t-shirt. And just beyond them, Noah watched the med bay door slide shut, Esmail's embarrassed flush outshining everything else on that side of the ship.

"Always something." Irene settled into Savannah's spot beside him, gazing curiously at the blank face of the door. "You said you were in your bunk?"

Noah bit the inside of his cheek hard enough to draw blood, the oncoming swears absorbed into the tangy flood of copper on his tongue. Abelard falling out of his attention had been more peaceful than he ever could have imagined.

"I, um—" He jerked his head up toward the bunk hallway, where Abelard remained holed up. "I think our circumstances are a little more dire than we thought."

"Oh. *Oh.* Okay." A short high whistle snapped the others' attention her way. "We need a secure conference."

Seconds later, without a word, the five of them piled their way into the med bay as Dayo pushed back with talk of privacy standards and the room's lack of space. Other options were suggested, from the cargo hold to the lab, but Dayo's foot remained solid at the boundary she'd set.

"Can it wait until the exam is over? It's the matter of Esmail's rights as a patient," she said. "Not where we are."

"I don't have anything to hide," said Esmail.

"That's not the point—"

"*Look.*" Frida had climbed onto a stack of boxes, taller than everyone else in the room as her knees dug into the edge of her perch. Even without the added height, the whip-crack of her outburst would have achieved the same result. "We're all here. Let Noah say what he has to say."

They all turned to him, waiting. The hemograph beeped over the *Amihaf*'s engine.

He explained the web he'd drawn connecting the various pieces of their trouble. The hemograph, under it all, seemed to chirp louder at the worst moments possible. As his account drew to a close, the quiet awaiting him, all their thick and heavy stares, sank into the weight already condensing his stomach into a painful lump.

Savannah was the first to react, hands splaying across her face in cover.

"Please don't tell me you *just* realized this," said Frida.

"I—what?"

"All of us already put two and two together," Dayo said. "And with you knowing Abelard better than any of us—"

Noah's cheeks burned and he fought to keep his head up. "I was trying to deal with things as they came, okay? I'm not always the best at putting together a cohesive picture under stress."

"Are you—that's what a doctorate *is*! How did you survive grad school?" Frida didn't give him any time to answer, instead redirecting the question to Savannah.

"My arguable stupidity aside," Noah said loudly, and the chatter dimmed. "What are we going to do about it? Knowing what happened the last time Abelard met a leviathan, I'm not thrilled to be rushing toward one this uninformed."

The seven of them held the question in their hands, wrung between squirming palms or balanced at the mute end of a pen or simply left to hang on the crooks of limp fingers. The hemograph beeped once, then trilled. The test was complete; Esmail was fine. Quinn's tensed shoulders eased.

"What if there's nothing?" Savannah said. She stared at the corner of one of the medical carts, pen held close against her chest like a sword. "What if there's nothing we can actually do? If we can't regain control of the ship, then we're going to end up wherever Abelard's pointed us, leviathan or no leviathan. Or…" The undertone of her skin turned a wan and sickly green. "…multiple leviathans."

Esmail raised his hand, then pointed at Quinn. "We decided the ship problem was because of the FDL file, right? Quinn's better—"

Dayo and Frida made no effort to stifle their questioning whines.

"Fine," Esmail sighed. "He's not bedridden, and he can have a conversation that makes sense. Let him look at the problem!"

Quinn nodded his support. "I was on my way to figuring it out before all this, and it's why I made myself better in the first place."

"…right, sure." Irene folded herself onto a nearby sturdy box. "Regardless of fungal interference, I'm sure Quinn can do it. But also… Abelard got the virus into the system once already without being detected. We can't rule out backups of this thing stored on his personal drive."

Abelard, as Savannah and Noah were quick to point out, was the most hopeless of Rassawek's faculty when it came to computer science: he could hardly stand up a research database on the university servers without crashing another department's archival storage. The idea that he coded it himself was absurd—but, Quinn wondered aloud, how did a ConBod's nature as a sapient computer translate into how they interfaced with unthinking systems that comprised everyday life? ConBods could be customized to the extent of the end user's imagination—

"I'm not concerned with how he accessed the system quite yet," said Dayo. "If it's so unthinkable that he coded a virus, then…"

Quinn frowned. "Unthinkable before the accident. What I meant was—a brain made of brainware might have a better sense of computer engineering."

"I don't think so," she said. "The neurology unit in medical school wasn't any easier because my brain was flesh and blood. More likely that the doctors who uploaded him gave him some crash course during his ConBod orientation."

Savannah sighed. "None of this matters if we can't wrangle the—"

Clang clang clang.

Nobody moved.

There was only one person available to knock.

Clang clang clang.

"Must have missed the call for the all-hands!" Abelard's voice was muffled through the wall.

As Noah took in the rest of the crew, he couldn't help but stick one foot back in English class, an early year of high school, an old novel whose idioms that arrived at the present day in illegible tatters. *Deer in the headlights* was once a cliché, at least in an age of personal vehicles and intact ecosystems; Mx. Delgado explained it the best xe could, but only now did Noah fully understand.

Clang clang clang.

There was a moment where the seven of them in the safe pocket of the med bay seemed to take a breath, a deep thing into some collective lung; but as they all took that breath, they also knew that they couldn't hold it forever, that the door would have to open.

Noah stepped forward. At the touch of his hand, the door slid open to reveal Abelard, looming taller than he should have been, the bald dome of his head just shy of the jamb.

"I trust everything with my crew is all right, Dr. Oyekan."

The hemograph she'd been holding slipped from her hand, landing on the floor with a clatter. "I do like to cover my bases, especially at times like these."

Abelard's grins hadn't always been visible under the shadow of his mustache; the Constructed Body did little to change this, and all they had to go on was a gentle tilt of his head, or the way the synthetic skin of his cheeks bunched up under his eyes.

Catching the corner of his mouth inching past the bounds of his mustache now—the air soured..

"That is an excellent quality in a doctor," said Abelard. "Any scientist— any person, really." His display eyes took stock of the room, the bodies tucked into the cramped space amid the mess. Each of them earned a spotlight under the weight of those digital pupils, seconds that stretched toward infinity like an orbit too close to a black hole.

They landed on Noah last, the left eye twitching the iris in half, shunting to black, and righting itself in the time it took to blink. He met it dead-on, recalling suddenly that the ConBod's real eye sat higher, at the center of his brow—and that the angle of his head meant he had been looking beyond him, all of them, now to Dayo or Esmail or some other part of the room, whatever his true goal had been.

"So!"

Abelard's head twisted ever so slightly for the ConBod's camera to focus on Noah. "So, *indeed*, Dr. Starbuck."

He could deflect. He knew how to do this, how to fight the clot in his throat and pose that redirection—*what were you saying to Mom at dinner last night about the new lakeside restaurant, did you want to go over that*

Khonsu *probe data again.* He'd registered all the ways a mouth could turn under the cover of facial hair, beard or no beard, in every stage of graying; he'd cataloged all the possible moods that could prompt them.

His mouth opened. The words were already half-formed. And in an instant the med bay exploded with movement—Irene hurtled under Abelard's outstretching arm as Frida slid past the narrowing space on his other side, Dayo scooping up the hemograph from the floor while putting herself between Abelard and Quinn. Noah froze until Savannah and Esmail appeared at each of his elbows, the three of them pressing forward until Abelard was no longer able to absorb the empty space of the doorway into himself. He tumbled onto his backside, a metallic clunk muted by his khakis.

The bottom of Frida's shoes disappeared at the top of the stairs. Savannah sprinted after her, long legs closing the distance as she bounded up the steps three at a time. Esmail followed suit, slower, checking over his shoulder— Dayo was guiding Quinn out of the med bay in an arc, her back to his chest, chatting with Abelard like it was any other average day. Noah hastily scanned the bottom floor for Irene. He couldn't find any sign of her, any indication of which direction she'd headed.

There was a bump behind him, then the stomp of stumbling steps; he whirled around and saw Irene just having exited the lab, a fire extinguisher hugged to her chest. She dashed across the foyer, and Noah tailed after. The spaceshield still held the shimmering spread of the turbolight vector flinging them into the unknown. The navigation computer chirped and whistled. Irene grumbled under her breath in barbed Inuktitut, glaring at the blinking lights and displays in the wall as her grip around the cylinder hardened.

Irene brought the sharp end of the extinguisher's base down on a central panel of the navigation computer.

Whock. And again, harder—*whock.* The metal started to buckle against the extinguisher, bits of red paint streaking off in the crevices.

"Irene!" He ran forward. "What are you—"

"*No*—keep back!"

Raising the cylinder above her head, tilting her whole back into the arc, she slammed it into the computer with a sick crunch. Sparks zipped out of the open pockets around the paneling, broken pieces of wire and snapped chips tinkling to the floor like loose change.

The screens on the wall darkened.

"What the fuck was that for?" He gaped at her, digging for something else to say. Past the spaceshield, turbolight ran on, as strong as ever—maybe stronger, if the navigation computer had kept the ship's helm steady all this time.

Irene stepped past him to the main console, between the pilot and navigator's seats, one hand weaving through a complex set of menus and the other hovering over a lever orbited by a set of red buttons. A bead of sweat rolled down her neck.

Her preternatural stillness overtook the rest of the cockpit until all Noah could hear was Dayo and Quinn talking over each other in the foyer, the irregular frantic thumping of feet overhead. The still-fritzing computer, the whine of the console's processor, the denser rumble of the engine under the cockpit floor—it was all muted. It was muted, and he was frozen, and once again he hadn't taken even a second to account for—

"Abelard." He whipped his head around, scoping out the foyer through the slim lens of the door. "Where's—"

"Grab onto something," said Irene.

"What—"

A face full of hair, bruised elbow crashing against a flat face of the console —and then he was thrown back. One of Irene's bony shoulder blades drilled into a nerve on his chest that hadn't healed properly after top surgery, and the pain soaking through the rest of his body got an added electric jolt.

Irene rolled off of him and onto her knees, reaching a hand down to help him sit up. "You need more than a half-second warning next time, I take it."

His spoken language wasn't fully back online. He tested his already-injured arm and ground his teeth through the pain, but none of it was the steep stabbing of a broken bone. Irene appeared mostly intact, aside from a sheen of sweat and a welt on her forehead.

Behind her, the starscape was static, deep black with the dotted field of stars.

"You stopped us."

"I didn't *want* to break it," she said, sitting back on her heels. "There were… three—no, five other ideas I had before this one. But there's only so much you can do with a forced hand." In one fluid motion she rose to her feet, again offering a hand to pull Noah to her level.

Noah approached the spaceshield, taking care not to agitate the new odd twinge in his knee. For all his life's work was oriented toward the so-called final frontier, he didn't have the discerning eye that could orient himself within their local arm of the Milky Way. The splatter of light facing the *Amihaf*'s bow was hard pressed to differentiate itself from what watched over Mars.

"Turbolight vectors can be entered manually," Irene said. "We're not stuck, but it's not going to get any easier after this."

Overhead, Frida's muffled voice rolled in the cadence of curses.

"Shit…" He peeled himself out of the narrow space at the console, throwing a thumbs-up in the air as Irene called for him to be careful, and in the foyer, Dayo had already pulled Quinn back into the med bay. He sped as quickly as his knee would allow. The pinching ache faded with every step winding up to the second floor.

The pain burst open as soon as his first scan of the common area found no sign of Abelard. He caught his weight on the other just in time to keep him upright.

And then he spotted Frida, flanked by Savannah and Esmail.

Wads of blood-splattered napkins from the galley arced a ring around the three of them; Esmail and Savannah each held another reddening wad against the underside of her nose. Frida leaned her head back against the table, revealing smeared streaks of blood drying a dark rust across her neck.

"If you're wondering why I'm sat on the lounge floor," she said, nasal through the plug, "don't worry, because it's far more dramatic than it seems."

Esmail jerked his head around. "Is everything okay?"

"Yeah, all in one piece." He limped over to the galley sink for a cup of water and brought it over outside the ring of soiled napkins. He dabbed a clean corner of one of them in the cup and started to wipe away the worst of the dried blood. "Irene forcibly regained control of the ship, so that's what that was. We're out of turbolight for now."

"*Mashallah*," Esmail said. He pulled the napkin back half an inch, and another few globs of blood leaked from Frida's nostrils. "*Ay*, even my sister never had nosebleeds this bad." He patted around the floor in search of something fresh and, finding none, refolded the one in his hand so the remaining white patches sat on the outside.

"I *am* wondering about this," Noah said, "but less about why you're on the floor and more about…"

Frida grinned, highlighting a thin rivulet of blood coloring the edge of a canine. "When we get home, the official story will involve a fist fight. Slamming my face into Abelard's reinforced titanium-whatever breastplate when Irene did her thing—sure, it's the true sequence of events, but it doesn't capture the spirit of the moment. Who's to say a fight wasn't imminent when we were yanked off that vector?"

Holding up a fistful of thick wires, her grin widened. More red dribbled between her teeth as she relayed how she'd broken into Abelard's bunk—the bed immaculately untouched, an entire wall's worth of inner workings exposed. Homebrew alterations, bright purple and green wire insulation running from odd ports in the wall down to the floor, nearby piles sturdy enough to support the weight of a Constructed Body. The FDL file had few other means of ingress.

It was one mystery solved—a suspicion confirmed—but not a solution that would rub soothing circles into their backs when the clocks eventually called them back to bed.

0630 IST. The only light in Noah's bunk glowed from the tablet leaning against his thighs in bed, blocks of text on a plain white background. An email saved locally in his drafts, waiting for the relay symbol in the corner to turn green again, reconnect him and the rest of the ship with the wider network of humanity.

Frida noticed the blackout first. Once her nosebleed clotted and Dayo had given her the clear, she'd all but dragged Quinn by the ear to her own tablet to conference with Qori Jimenez on the nature of his supposed recovery. *No one, not even you, can just will themselves to get better, not like that.* And before Quinn could follow the script and jettison them both into another fight, the tablet sang its alert.

Irene's positive spin called their collective disconnection an extra data point, one less variable in the manual lassoing of astronavigational math she'd have to contend with. Seventeen lightyears from Earth was the minimum they were facing as the ship idled in the latest stretch of nothingness —not insurmountable, but far from ideal. The rest of them took the news with nothing else to add, as if it hadn't been delivered to them at all.

The rest of the day pressed on. Abelard didn't reappear. Little by little, as the hour aboard the *Amihaf* mirrored Cairo in its deepening, each of the crew revealed what they thought could be a passable bedtime. Savannah couldn't fool anyone and knew it, disappearing just after 2000 IST. Noah lasted until 2145, passing out fully-dressed as soon as his head hit the pillow, and woke with a start at exactly 0554 like he'd downed four cups of organically-brewed coffee.

And thus: the email.

To Justin, of course.

Savannah didn't have to know.

He reread the last sentence he'd added: *The dream I had last night was new, but part of me was aware that it was a dream, and it was also trying to tell me I'd seen this many times before.*

Justin's voice leaned into his ear, talking through an idle chuckle about some seminal Catastrophe-era novel out of Hanoi that had—and here was where the illusion of his company flaked apart, because Noah's brain offered up words like *theme* and *motif* and *subtext* at the same time, combined into a garbled block of noise with no meaning at all. The voice persisted. Justin had brought up this novel a few times before with how it handled dreams and the intersection of histories, the specifics of which had long been lost in those unplugged cavities in Noah's memory.

The dream itself held tinges of Justin too, scenes cribbed from his favorite historical fantasy archetypes, smoggy streets and interlocked cogs with oily magic-laden stains. There was a body, a bare thing with thin coiled tubes and uneven checkerboards of plating forming the contours of pectorals and abs. The original brass had been smeared with grease, dulling the natural golden hue. Steam hissed from the narrow seams between segments. Bones strained, whined, snapped. The machine squeezed and squeezed until blood joined the grease, and Noah's dream-knees shuddered and crumpled under the pain— pain that was immediate and pain that expanded to take up the whole of his life span, and he knew that this moment was one he would never escape.

Until he'd jolted awake under the tangle of his sheets.

His fingers tapped in a flurry against the tablet keyboard. *I can't find the line that separates naiveté from paranoia.*

The date display in the corner claimed that it was nearing the end of July on Earth, the point at which Rassawek turned from a sauna to an oven as the city counted down the last weeks before returning undergrads tested the capacity of the train station. Justin was likely neck-deep in planning that first class in his new tenure-track position—sitting on the floor of the living room, orbited by a ring of books on the threadbare carpet Noah had salvaged from a back alley downtown. He'd be grumbling over whether the value of a text outweighed how much time it demanded to be properly taught, undoubtedly worried that one wrong choice would tarnish him in the eyes of the administration forever.

How do you talk yourself down from the worrying? Noah typed. *How do you know if it's warranted? I think I know, but I somehow find myself always on the wrong side of that line, like I've crossed it sleepwalking.*

I wish you were here—backspace.

I wish I'd found that line before we—he couldn't even finish the sentence.

He powered down the tablet and tossed it to the foot of the bed, curling onto his side. This end of the ship was quiet, any potential goings-on taken to a far side of the level below. Still, he strained to listen for any thumps or knocks that would betray activity from Abelard's bunk at the end of the hall.

Nothing. His gut pulled itself in opposite directions, the poles on the furthest sides of that line he kept hunting for. It was fine and it was a terrible sign. It portended brighter days ahead and it promised doom.

He pressed his eyes shut and waited for sleep to return to him, shuttle him forth to a less miserable morning hour. A haze settled over him, obscuring whether he'd actually dozed off, but when he glanced back at the wall clock, it only read 0704 IST.

"Fine," he sighed. Rolling out of bed, he didn't bother to change out of the rumpled clothes he'd worn the last twenty-four hours. The lounge and galley were both empty as he waited for the mimeo to churn up a coffee, the aroma's artificial tinge barely registering.

The foyer's lights were dim when he reached the bottom of the staircase, a lone chunk of light beaming from the cockpit. Noah squinted as he shuffled closer, leaning against the jamb of the antechamber. Between the pilot and navigator's seats, Quinn sat with his laptop still wired into the ship, while Esmail and Irene had contorted themselves into their respective posts.

"Hey." Irene ripped a page from her notebook, holding lines of densely-scrawled math in Quinn's face. "Can you run this dot product? My tablet is still running the Thorn condition on those Lorentz transformations from an hour ago."

"You got it. Just curious… how long would the nav computer take to do that?"

"Don't remind me," she muttered.

"My curiosity is totally sincere." Quinn glanced up from the laptop to the wall of dead screens, jumping when he caught Noah loitering. "*E* Noah, how long were you standing there?"

"Just got here, don't worry."

"I wasn't," he sighed, turning back over his shoulder. "Irene, is that a one or a seven?"

She frowned. "It's a two. See?"

Noah stepped around the outer edge of the cockpit toward Esmail's seat as the two of them hashed out Irene's handwriting and was greeted with a yawn that audibly popped the joint of his jaw.

"*Shab bekheyr*—or…" Esmail checked the clock on the console. "No, *sobh*. We must have missed the sunrise." His grin turned into another yawn.

"Did none of you go to bed?" But Noah already knew the answer before he asked. It was easy to forget that Esmail was almost ten years his senior, but the lines creasing his face were sharper under the sleepless light of the cockpit.

"I think Quinn took a nap at some point, but… wait—I'll be back!" His limbs sprung free from as he leapt up from the chair, hopping over the ends of Quinn's legs to, Noah assumed, see to his prayers.

Noah settled into the empty seat. From this vantage point, he could see both Quinn's laptop and Irene's tablet screens—some windows held fast under the processing spinner, and others he couldn't begin to decipher. Both systems whined. Cooling fans aspired to sopranos. In one of the smaller portions of Quinn's screen sat the firewall program with FDL.exe still nominally behind the quarantine border.

The debate over Irene's handwriting showed no signs of easing, so Noah looked out toward the starscape. The only sign that this was the same starscape he saw when they last dropped out of turbolight was an arc of bright blue-white stars directly in front of the nose of the ship.

"Your tablet's still on the local network, right?" Quinn asked. "Just LAN-drop me the vectors. That way I won't accidentally kick us into a nebula."

A minute later, the laptop chimed, and Quinn settled into a focused hunch, transferring the data into the system's native calculator.

Esmail returned just as Irene's tablet screen resolved into an answer, the gray-tinged window rousing itself from its calculating slumber. "It finally finished!" he said, leaning over the back of her seat. "Good news?"

Her tablet echoed his laptop's chime, the figure popping up in a new window. She hummed to herself. "I'll need to look this over more... something here isn't consistent with..." She waved toward the starscape without glancing up.

"Is all that going to tell us where we are?" asked Noah.

"Oh, no. I figured that out not long after you went to bed. This"—she tilted the tablet screen toward him with its dense grid of vector matrices and odd notations—"is trying to figure out the safest route back into relay range. It's pissing me off."

Noah felt his eyebrows fly up his forehead before he could stop them. "Is it?"

"I just said so, yes." Her mouth thinned, barely fighting off a frown. "My math isn't wrong. My physics isn't wrong. I've done thousands of calculations just like this by hand and I checked it twenty times before hitting compute." She untangled herself enough to sit forward over the console, a fist slamming down onto a bare section between data displays. "Something isn't right out there!"

Bleep-bleep-bleep.

The four of them turned toward the dashboard, staring.

"I've never heard a ship make that noise before," said Quinn. "And I've been on a lot of ships."

"Did I break something?" Irene muttered.

Bleep-bleep-bleep.

A blinking blue light toward the top of the console caught Noah's eye. "Does that mean anything to anyone?"

Suddenly Esmail was beside him, tapping at his shoulder for him to cede the pilot's seat, which Noah gladly did. "I forget everyone else hasn't spent most of their careers on freighters. That," he said, fiddling with one of the screens before him, "is an incoming message from another ship."

"This far from a relay point?" Quinn nudged himself forward between the two seats, and Noah repositioned himself on the other side of Irene.

"It's not from a relay. This is direct, ship-to-ship. The *oldest* of old school." He knocked a knuckle on the screen and a projection appeared on the spaceshield, blocky green text against the black starscape.

Each of the three TerraCosmos divisions' emergency codes, followed by what looked like coordinates.

None of them said a word.

"Didn't expect to see this many people up so early, but Abelard—whoa." Savannah skidded to a stop in the cockpit's doorway. "I didn't know there was a screen there. When did this come in?"

"Just now," said Noah. "What were you saying about Abelard?"

"He's out of his bunk. Making a mess in the galley in the name of a crew-wide breakfast."

"Hm,'" Irene said.

"Can't say I'm thrilled about it either." She reached behind her head to contain the cloud of her bedhead with a couple thick ties stored on her wrist. "We're going to look into this, right?"

"Could be a trap," said Quinn.

"By *who*?" The bands snapped into place, leaving Savannah full use of both arms to fling to her wide wingspan, fingers splayed for emphasis. "This isn't *Galactic Legions*! We can't be so far from Earth that we'd need to start worrying about space pirates using stolen codes." She turned to Irene. "How far are those coordinates?"

She flipped back a few pages in her notebook, holding her tongue between her teeth. "At average intrasystem speeds, two hours at most."

Savannah nodded to herself, a deep maroon tinge spreading under her freckles that Noah could pin as self-consciousness, the sudden-onset variant. He crossed the distance between them and grabbed her hand, angling it out of sight from the others. Her flush began to fade.

"Might as well check it out," he said. "If we landed out here, someone else could have too."

Unspoken in the looks aimed his way was the assumption that he would contain whatever was unfolding upstairs, the crashing pans masking the breadth of conversation and footfalls beneath it. He accepted the terms, leaving them to hypothesize further about the mysterious ship on the other side of the message.

The galley was a wall of noise and heat and sizzling butter so solid that Noah recoiled half a step, nearly sending him backward down the stairs. And at the center of the action—Abelard, one hand poking a large spoon around a skillet and the other's fingers stretched around three eggs.

Noah paused. He could just as easily withdraw back down to the cockpit or the lab, or slink into the darkened hall of bunks, someplace where he could continue to try to ignore the ache that gripped at his elbow and knee whenever his muscles so much as twitched. On cue, his little finger tingled into numbness.

Screw it, he thought. There were six other people on the *Amihaf* counting on him to occupy their de-facto captain.

"What's the occasion?" he called, forcing a curious smile when Abelard turned around. "A birthday, or—"

"Noah! Thank the encompassing heavens, I was *just* wondering how I was going to keep watch over the pancakes without burning anything else. Come, come, grab a spatula!"

All of the available counter space was taken up by bowls and pans all holding ingredients fresh from the mimeo.

"You didn't answer my question."

"Does one need an occasion for the most important meal of the day?" Abelard set down the spoon in order to offer him the closest spatula with a flourish. "Seven-eighths of this crew still need to eat!"

Abelard wasn't going to concede the point; Noah took the spatula from him, stepping out of the way as the newly-free hand shot forward to grab a carton of some small, dark fruit from behind a mixing bowl—blueberries, one of the few foods mimeos had always failed to reproduce in a way anyone found edible. The soil-grown batches were so expensive that Noah couldn't think of a single time he'd ever tasted one.

"There's no way you brought those from Earth," he said.

"Why do you say that?"

Because it's been almost seven months and no produce lasts that long."

"We have a freezer. It's over here, right where it's always been."

"And it's never been full enough for someone not to have noticed the blueberries."

He caught Abelard's eye over the carton. The synthetic skin at the corners of his eyes crinkled in their old patterns, his mustache folding along the lines of a smirk Noah had seen so many times before the disappearance, and a knot in his stomach untangled even as some invisible pick dug into his elbow.

"If you're putting this much effort in, I don't want you to ruin it with mimeo blueberries," he said, finally turning away with a sigh. "What are you using them for, anyway?"

The berries poured out of the carton with muted plops, piling atop the thick batter in the bowl below. "Don't tell me you've never had blueberry pancakes!"

"Should I lie, then?"

Shaking his head, Abelard tutted under his breath and swapped his handful of eggs for the spoon. With the sort of care he'd reserved for handling xenomicrobe pipettes, he folded the batter over the heap of berries, the slow repetitive motion dispersing them evenly in the mix. Only one of them burst in the process, staining the creamy surface with a splotch of purple.

He tried not to think about Quinn, the similar blots in the whites of his eyes.

Abelard wasted no time in scooping the batter across Noah and into the pan on the stove. The popping butter he'd heard upon arrival had already burned away to dark freckles.

"When the whole surface is full of bubbles, that's when you flip," he said, nodding to the spatula in Noah's hand.

Part of him wanted to protest that he knew at least that much about pancakes, if only in theory. But he swallowed his pride, watching the batter solidify at the edges. All the while, Abelard talked—not a lecture or a monologue, but leaving enough empty pockets for Noah to chime in should he have felt the impulse.

The blueberries, as it turned out, were indeed soil-grown, kept in a personal deep-freeze pod packed into his luggage for a special occasion and thawed just last night. Abelard had connections around the habitats where they had originally grown wild and had made a resurgence—it was where he grew up, a hundred miles straight east of Pitawbagok, which Noah knew as Kaniatarakwà:ronte and his father refused to call anything but Lake Champlain. The blueberries were just starting to take root when Abelard was a child, left to wander around the woods surrounding the family cabin.

"I had no way of knowing they were some sort of luxury item until I left for school—oh, flip!"

Noah jumped and grabbed at the handle, holding it still to wriggle the spatula into position. The other sides, once turned, were only a few shades too dark.

"*Maman* would make these with me on special occasions," said Abelard. "Birthdays, holidays, a good test grade... sometimes she found her own reason. 'Oh, *mon chou*, the sunrise was so beautiful today'... I heard that one quite a bit."

Not knowing what else to say, Noah simply nodded and studied the pan for any signs of burning. He knelt closer for a better look, a dark sweetness rising up from the metal. He righted himself, found Abelard sticking a plate under his nose, and deposited the first batch in a lopsided stack. A lumpy pat of butter landed in the empty pan with a splat, another three rounds of batter settling into position soon after.

"I realized," Abelard said, considering the rest of the materials on the counter, "there is much about you outside of the 'lab,' as it were, that I don't know. For all the time we spent together on campus before my little accident, and even now… so tell me."

Out of the corner of his eye, he saw Abelard turn toward him, that same grin warming his face. Noah bent down toward the pan to inspect the bubbles, a reasonable excuse to avoid meeting his gaze directly. "Tell you what, specifically?"

"Oh, I don't know… did your family growing up have any special meals like this?"

Noah bit his lip, passing it off as a tic of concentration as he flipped the pancakes. One landed on the curved inside edge with a short smear that browned to a crisp in seconds. "Um…" He tapped the flat end of the spatula against the shard of batter, breaking it off from the pan before it could burn. It softened on his tongue, tasted of toasted butter. "Not really."

"Not even one tradition?"

If there was any tradition behind the front door of the Starbuck family apartment, it was how quickly Noah could make himself disappear whenever his mother moseyed to the kitchen in the early evening or his father carried a plate of mimeo meat to the grill on the balcony. Innocuous remarks that would be met with a pointed frown or sigh at any other time of day, when the oven and stovetop sat cold, suddenly were prone to combust—and that would be the whole night, his father waking the next morning with a raspy throat.

"No," said Noah.

"What about—"

"I'd rather not talk about it," he mumbled.

"That's perfectly fine. I didn't mean to pry." He aided Noah with the next batch in silence, offering the plate, spooning the batter, taking another pass at the counter with the eggs back in his palm as if he were trying to decide how best to use them.

Another nine were added to the stack as the process became rote; moving the plate even an inch threw the soft pieces of the tower into a terrible wobble.

"Would you mind if I broached a different subject?" Abelard asked. He scraped at the last dregs of batter in the bowl, swirls of purple remaining without any chunks of fruit, and poured the dribble evenly on the three still cooking, smothering the burgeoning bubbles.

Noah motioned to go ahead, watching in his peripheral vision as Abelard took the bowl to rinse in the sink.

"Did Dr. Tuuluq relay our current coordinates?"

"To me personally? No," said Noah. "She said she'd figured it out, but I didn't think to ask."

"Well… I do think you will recognize them." He nudged the faucet on to its highest setting, a dense beam of water hissing against the side, and he paid no attention to the level rising closer to his Constructed arm.

Noah's mouth latched onto the first letter of his response as his brain scrambled to catch up. "Why?"

"The University picked up those readings, did they not? The kind that were so similar to your dissertation data?"

His body constricted on itself, suddenly cold, and the pancake he was flipping landed halfway on its neighbor, their raw-batter sides fusing into some approximation of a Mobius strip.

"That's all right! We have more than enough to feed everyone already," Abelard said. "But yes, the readings—once I knew what to look for, it was just a matter of finding my proper, oh… configurations."

"How did you even know about those readings?" Later Noah would have the capacity to reckon with how starkly his voice had shrunk, how, in a flash, he stood in the *Amihaf* in the curled, defensive hunch of himself young enough to still don clumsy braids.

"I know everything the ship knows." His lips curled up into a smile, revealing the full array of his teeth out from under the shadow of his mustache. "It really is amazing what these Bodies can do."

The water rinsing the batter bowl had filled it completely, spilling over into the sink, and still Abelard stared and smiled and infected the sweet aroma of the galley into a sour rot.

Steps tramped louder from the bunk hall. Two sets, Dayo trailing just behind Frida.

Abelard snapped back to normal. In a single movement, he switched off the sink and presented the breakfast offering with a bit of choreographed fanfare. "Best of mornings to you both! I do hope you're hungry!"

Noah forced himself to eat with the rest of the crew as they all assembled, even as the coveted blueberries turned to sand on his tongue.

By late morning, the inner workings of the *Amihaf* had settled back into its normal flow. Abelard slipped into his bunk when no one was looking his way, and the rest of them opted for being as far away from said bunk as possible. Taking objective measurements would have directed them to the far corner of the lab or the cargo hold, and since no one had taken a post there, Noah surmised the distance was more emotional than physical. With Irene and Esmail at their respective stations in the cockpit, the other five of them claimed parcels of free floor at their feet, spilling over into the antechamber.

Also at play, Noah guessed, was a meld of curiosity and well-founded anxiety about what laid at the end of the mystery message's coordinates. The ship had drifted enough during breakfast that Irene wanted to recheck a few figures before setting Esmail loose at the helm; her new calculation had put them at the site just before noon.

With that issue, all there was to do was wait.

But elsewhere—

"What does that mean, knowing what the ship knows?" Frida frowned as she flipped through a file on her tablet. "This thing isn't sapient, much less sentient—right?"

She glanced up at Quinn, who had claimed his old spot by the service panel. *Obviously,* he mouthed. He rolled his eyes once she'd returned to the screen in her lap.

"I clearly don't know how he could manage it," Noah said, "but the simplest explanation is that he got access to the comms terminal and used that to wiggle into my email."

"Wiggle?" Quinn said. "Quite the technical term."

Noah shrugged, resting his head against the cockpit's entrance jamb. "It's also probably safe to say he's got ears where we'd assumed. Less super-hearing and more… bugging."

The others grumbled to themselves, tapering off after a few moments.

"It's better to know than... well, not to," said Esmail after the quiet had shouldered back in. His hands hadn't left the yoke since Irene gave him the heading and all its accompanying caveats.

He was right, and they all knew it. What they would trade for peace of mind in the moment would circle back to sever their Achilles tendons in a jump scare of poor timing. They had a chance, at least, of yanking their feet out of harm's way, knowing that the harm was another passenger scuttling about the ship.

As Esmail continued to guide them through the pocket of empty space, they each returned to their preoccupying subject of the hour. Frida and Savannah buried themselves in xenobotanical and xenomycological papers, while Quinn dug further into the mystery surrounding FDL.exe and tried to avoid Dayo's continued monitoring of his condition. Noah's hands, even holding his tablet with his own article drafts, felt empty. His best contributions laid in trying to predict Abelard's next moves, but even with everything that he was able to amass and hold in his head, too many loose threads were left to dangle, unable to prop up even the weakest hypothesis or plan of action.

Only Quinn made any headway, most of which he narrated as he teased through his thoughts out loud. The FDL virus—or whatever it was—had been behind the infamous logging problem from the beginning, the discrepancies arising when it tried to cover the evidence of its activities. Now that he knew where to look, he could observe the act in real time, cursing interspersed with more grumbling questions about the still-illegible file type extension.

Savannah caught Noah's eye over the top of her tablet, a concerned tilt to her brow that he mirrored. The more Quinn uncovered about FDL, the further outside Abelard's capabilities it became.

Bleep-bleep-bleep.

"What was that?" Dayo said.

"New message coming in," said Esmail.

By the time the text was displayed against the spaceshield, they had all squeezed around his and Irene's seats for a better vantage point.

TCS HATHOR CALLS TO TCS AMIHAF FOR VIDEO-GAM.

"The *Hathor*?" Irene pulled their tablet from its spot on the console and reflexively brought up a search engine, tensing as the error page reminded them of the current predicament. "Isn't that one of the Project Aker ships?"

"I think so," Quinn said. "I heard they're Delta-class too. Real swanky."

"If it's so swanky, how the fuck did it get in so much trouble?" Frida had crouched between the seats, elbows pinned on their armrests. She smacked the back of her hand at Esmail's arm. "What's this video-gam thing they're on about? Did their spell check break too?"

"No, it's a real thing! It's a ship-to-ship video call when there's no way to dock together for something in person." His explanation was picking up speed by the word, his free hand making tight circles in time with the acceleration. "It comes from a really old nautical term, actually—"

"Great, cool, not sure how or why you know that."

"I know a lot of things."

"That you do. Which," she added pointedly, turning to Quinn over her shoulder, "is fine."

Within minutes, one of the daubs of light in the starscape expanded exponentially relative to its neighbors; a dull pinprick bloomed into an oblong stretch of gray, eventually solidifying into a ship three times the size of the *Amihaf*. Along the side in black, the TerraCosmos emblem sat beside the *Hathor*'s name in the Latin and Arabic scripts as well as Mandarin characters.

Littered around the *Hathor*, as if in orbit, were swathes of broken ship debris.

"I'm guessing this is probably not what you want to hear," Esmail said quietly, "but proper video-gam protocol says the captains of both vessels should be present."

Noah stared down at his shoes as the weight of six pairs of eyes turned in his direction. It pressed in on him, suffocating—what did they want? For him to step up and pretend to be captain? To march up to the bunk hall and bring Abelard into the sliver of the galaxy they'd carved out for themselves? An impossible choice, bearing down with an impossible pressure, until—

"I'll go get him."

And he did. Two knocks on Abelard's bunk door, and it opened to a full view of the room: a bed unslept in, a wall panel ripped open from its bearings. Noah said *video-gam*, and Abelard traipsed his way down to the cockpit, sidling into Noah's empty position in the larger tableau.

As the spaceshield screen dialed the *Hathor*, Noah nestled himself into a thin bit of space between Irene's seat and a particularly crunched-up panel of the broken navigation computer, where she met his gaze with her usual inscrutable stare. He made the motion of a deep sigh without the actual breath of it, and then the gam connected.

The grainy video showed a Black man with short-shaved hair haggardly adjusting his posture to something that would befit a TerraCosmos captain. "Ahoy to the *Amihaf*. My name is Antonio Gardiner, and on behalf of the…" He sighed and forced an overly-cheery grin to his face. "On behalf of my crew still aboard, I welcome you to the *Hathor*."

Abelard made a move like he was about to speak, but a crash rang out from behind where Antonio had based his center of operations—not the *Hathor*'s cockpit, but some other nook of the ship where he'd jury-rigged the connection.

Another series of clanging, clattering noises overtook the audio, collapsing what did make it into squeaking metallic bolts of static. Antonio shouted something over his shoulder, half-muted from the ongoing din, his voice becoming unintelligible mid-word; a few sentences passed before Noah registered he was speaking Spanish.

"I would apologize, but…" Antonio adjusted the device acting as the camera. "I don't doubt that you understand the circumstances. It's—" The image on-screen zoomed forward to a close-up of his deep brown eyes, then back out. "*¡Santo dios!* As I live and breathe, and you do so again—Abelard Cousteau!"

Behind him, a voice shouted, "*Ken eres?*"

"Antonio, I am delighted to see you again! And as the captain of a TerraCosmos shop—I can't say that I'm even a little surprised." Abelard spoke with a warmth that broke through the facade Antonio had cobbled together, teasing out something far more genuine. "Captain Gardiner here was one of my students during a summer research program on Titan," he added for the benefit of the *Amihaf*.

"A long time ago," Antonio said. "I wish you'd caught us at a better time so I could at least ask how you're not dead, but there's no time—"

The source of the other voice popped into frame from around the corner, eyes wide at the sight of them on the other side of the screen. Antonio must have been sitting on a spare crate with the way she bent down for a better look—her olive skin was dotted with grease spots, her hair grown out just enough from a buzz cut to hint at some yet-indecipherable texture. "I take it back. We got our… shiny armor… I don't know the English phrase."

"Knight in shining armor?" Esmail supplied.

She shrugged, shoving Antonio aside to give her room to sit down. More black spots ran down her tank top, not from grease, but charred bits of fabric left over from some sort of burn, likely electrical if the sparks and pops down the hall were any indication.

"Esther de Castro, our Chief of Operations," said Antonio. "She and I and Jhony…" He glanced at her, and she tersely shook her head. "I—okay. Okay. So—Esther and I are the only ones still… we're the only members of the *Hathor* crew that I can confirm are still alive."

The *Hathor* had been stranded apart from its sister ship for going on three weeks, too far from the *Meret* for direct ship-to-ship comms and too far by lightyears, as the *Amihaf* was well-aware, to depend on the relays. Both their intrasystem and turbolight engines sputtered and died when prodded. All life support was functional, but the water recycler had started to leave a worrisome aftertaste.

No one asked him and Esther to elaborate; none among them wanted to be the one to risk implying a hunger to witness the details of their suffering with a careless inflection or improper grade to their grimaces. But they were curious, by nature and through empathy and also out of a hazy instinct that this was in the interest of their self-preservation, so when Antonio began the story of the *Hathor*'s last three weeks, they looked anywhere but his eyes.

"We were prepared for the mission to have bumps," he said. The only thing Project Aker's planning teams could predict with any certainty was that the schemas they'd spent years—entire careers—constructing would have to withstand the wracking forces of interstellar physics. Just over a year ago, the *Hathor* and the *Meret* launched from the tarmac at Cape Guacara to blaze a route to the Polaris system, four hundred and fifty lightyears from the clouded border of Earth, the most ambitious feat of exploration ever attempted. At normal turbolight speeds, such a journey could take up to two years, but no turbolight engine had ever remained at full tilt anywhere close to that long; and the burden on the astronavigators to accommodate hundreds of lightyears' worth of variables in a single vector calculation was simply too great.

Instead, they mapped out a series of shorter vectors between Earth and Polaris, gaining familiarity with the various strings comprising all the physics in play. On the return trip, with a fuller knowledge of the path between the two systems, they would be able to pick the best spots to deploy new relays, extending humanity's communication capacity to new heights.

"In theory," Esther said.

"It's… I still don't know if I believe what I saw," Antonio said.

To Noah's left, strained upholstery groaned under Abelard's tightening grasp, digging in over Irene's shoulder.

"What did you see?"

Abelard's question was an innocent one, an utmost deniability hovering close overhead. It was a deniability applicable as soon as the *Amihaf* was left behind. Outside the bounds of the airlock, on Earth or Natocke Station or floating in the empty icy bounds of space, there existed enough room for it to contort into something that didn't rumble with a terrible hunger.

"As I said," Antonio sighed. "What I saw—that's determined by how I made sense of the visual input. What I saw might not be what—"

Esther rolled her eyes, snapped something at him under her breath.

"I've been reminded that this sort of study is for a later date."

The upholstery groaned deeper, enough for Esther to narrow her eyes through the screen as Antonio continued on. The *Hathor* and *Meret*, after completing their last lull between turbolight vectors, had traveled in their tandem formation less than two lightyears before matters truly started going awry. Sure, the *Hathor*'s internal plumbing system had been acting up, but Esther had pulled a member of the ops team from the *Meret* during the last pause to investigate the situation. And when the two ships were suddenly ripped out of turbolight, there may have been an accusation of the plumbing work shorting out the engines' power grids, but a thirty-second inspection once everyone got back on their feet dismissed the idea.

Not an inspection of the *Hathor*, but a glimpse out of the porthole toward the *Meret*—at that point, the other ship was still within visual range. The back half of the *Meret* had crumpled like tin foil, debris spinning in the vacuum off the leftover momentum, failing electrical conduits baring themselves in death throes. Most of the *Hathor*'s systems had been rendered nonfunctional, but at least the body of the ship was still intact.

The crew scrambled, cramming the halls in frantic sprints in every direction. Antonio threw ping after ping after ping to the *Meret* as Esther herded the rest of the ops team to run more thorough diagnostics, as a pair of the physicists aided the doctor—Jhony—to the med bay.

"I've wondered if he should have been here at all," said Antonio. "This mission had too many forays into the unknown for someone of his age, with the chronic issues he had…"

"It was his choice to come," Esther said—not to Antonio, but the *Amihaf*. "This mission, and then retirement. It… went wrong. He knew what this was."

"Jhony was the one who first noticed it, even with that pipe sticking out of his leg." Antonio squeezed his eyes shut, tighter and tighter, and he opened them again, the glossy reflection of the light there sharper. "The three of them passed a porthole, and Jhony made them stop. And do you know what he said?”

The stars have gone out.

Others abandoned their tasks to crowd around him and when there was no more room, they hurried toward other viewports toward the starscape, a few pressing in beside Antonio in the cockpit.

The shouting started up not long after. Jhony wasn’t wrong, was the issue—peering out of the narrow scopes of the *Hathor*’s portholes, the crew only found a deep black devoid of any signs of light, as if the ship had been plucked from its path and deposited in some extra-dimensional pocket removed from the rest of reality.

“In the cockpit, I made myself take a moment to really look at what was beyond the spaceshield,” Antonio said. “And yes, most of it was a void. Terrifying. But at the edges, the very bottom and top of what I could see, there were still a few stars. Something was just blocking everything in between.”

In any other circumstance, the thrumming in Noah’s gut would have belonged wholly to the incredible leap forward in the focus of his career. Survivors of an encounter who could actually put words to their memory, assembling graphs and long series of numbers into a shape, a hue, an action —on Earth, he would have run outside into the hot Rassawek sun and shouted up and down the street with an unspeakable thrill. Now, he fought to keep the blueberry pancakes from rising back up his throat, burning with acid.

“It was a short peace,” said Esther. “Antonio called to the *Meret* eight, ten times very quickly, and then…” She mimed an explosion.

“Nothing blew up,” said Antonio quickly, and Esther sighed. “But…”

A split second after the last of the pings, something—either the entity blocking the starscape or another strange force rearing up from the ether—swatted the *Meret* aside, jettisoning it into the distance with such force that it was little more than a dim star by the time they could blink. A dim star, and then nothing.

The entity then slammed against the *Hathor* again. The craft's atmospheric flight wings snapped off, the electrical systems stuttered, and Antonio's hold on the crew slipped out of his hands as if they'd been oiled. Esther delivered Jhony to the med bay, hooked him up to the right devices through his strained instructions, and reemerged into the main hall of the ship to find Antonio staring at the status screen of the ship's bottle shuttles.

All had been deployed.

The starscape had returned to its former brilliance.

"They all wanted to chase after the *Meret*." Antonio spoke toward a far corner off-screen. "That, or whatever attacked us. I couldn't stop them."

"And you haven't heard from any of them since?" Savannah asked, and Esther shook her head. "I'm so sorry."

Antonio ran a hand over his hair. "We tried to find them, but the bottle shuttles don't have the same tracking beacons the ships do. The weirdest part... we told you the *Meret* is still in range, but it's also stationary somehow, which—"

"I told you a hundred times," said Esther. "Our computers are broken!"

Their argument slipped into Spanish, layers of talking over each other. Irene, eyebrow raised, caught Frida's eye where she knelt.

"He thinks the inexplicable physics can be explained away by leviathan influence—we're all on the same page there, right, that it's a leviathan?—and she's not as prone to such flights of fancy," she whispered.

The two of them kept at it, and the crew of the *Amihaf* waited, those outside the language barrier trying not to tense up whenever certain names and cognates floated to the surface. TerraCosmos. Leviathan. Names that they could only assume were from the crews of the *Hathor* or *Meret*, names of people who may or may not have been dead.

Eventually Esther stood, made like she was going to leave, then pausing to turn back toward the camera. "*Guay de mi*… it was nice to meet you. I hope we all live long enough to return to the Earth." Her grin was pained, and as she trudged down the hall, her fist flew out to ram against the paneling, collapsing a wrinkled stretch of metal further into itself.

"Antonio," Quinn said. "Our ship can't dock with yours, but is there anything else we can do to help? Not to state the obvious, but you're in some dire straits."

"Well…"

The *Amihaf*'s console trilled with its triple bleep, a corner display popping up with a set of coordinates. Irene scribbled the figures into the margin of her current notebook page, then laying out a series of equations with enough Greek variables to make Noah's head spin.

"That is where our readings have put the *Meret*. I don't want to wait until Esther gets our engines functioning again to check on them if we don't have to. And…" All at once, his posture collapsed, head in his hands. His entire body seemed to take a breath, hardening, until all the pressure leaked and he could bear to unfurl himself again. He stared straight at Abelard, a plea already coloring his brow; Noah saw himself there, but not in any way he could readily articulate. It just made his chest burn.

"Dr. Cousteau… Abelard…I remember very clearly what your specialty was. You shared so much with me those late nights on Titan. Please, help us find our crew that went after the being that attacked us.”

The effort it took for the *Amihaf* crew to stop themselves from staring at Abelard outright strained in the air, pulling taut into a high whine. Esmail didn’t heed the memo; his back popped as he turned, earning a wince on both sides of the screen.

“Oh, Antonio.”

The tone wasn’t right. It churned at the bile rising from Noah’s stomach.

“We cannot help you.”

He reached forward, his ConBod pressing down on where Frida sat with its unrelenting metal, and slammed his fist on the button to disconnect the gam. Almost immediately, the bleeping started up again. No one moved, aside from Abelard straightening himself.

“Don’t answer that,” he said, like he were describing the weather. “Mr. Rostami, Dr. Tuuluq—take us away from here. I’m certain Dr. Starbuck has a collection of nearby sectors where we can travel next in pursuit of our quarry.”

Again, no one dared voice a reply.

“The timing is less than stellar,” Abelard continued. “Something is acting up in the space where my hardware meets the brainware, and I need to run a scan—in my own quarters, Dr. Oyekan. I have the equipment.” He’d held up a hand toward her to stave off an impending interruption, but Dayo hadn’t stopped biting the inside of her lip long enough to even open her mouth. “You might be tempted to fly elsewhere, engage with other limping ships, but I will most certainly know if this occurs, and—though I hope it never comes to this —there will be serious consequences. So!” He clasped his hands together under his chin, beaming. “Do take care. I will see you tomorrow morning.”

The bleeping had stopped, Antonio's hope only fueling him so far. Even the engine held its breath as the crew listened after Abelard's footsteps: across the foyer, up the stairs, then overhead to his bunk until they finally settled. Still the silence held.

Sometime later, whether it was five minutes or a half hour, Savannah cleared her throat. "We're not going to do that, right?" Her voice was small, barely a murmur, but they heard her as clearly as if she'd shouted.

Dayo held up one finger and wove her way out of the cockpit, disappearing up the stairs. A few minutes passed and she hopped back into her old spot, breathless. "He's already hooked up. I recognized the noise through his door." She spoke at normal volume, and half of them shrank back. "There's no way he could hear us now. Everything goes offline in those scans."

"Those sectors he mentioned," Esmail whispered. "That's what was in that email Noah got, right? If he could hear us in that meeting—"

"He hacked my email, not the meeting," said Noah. "And he'll probably be able to see where we've gone after the fact, so…"

Esmail looked like he was going to say something, but instead hugged his legs against his chest. Quinn laid a hand on his shoulder, where it slowly traveled up until his whole palm held the weight of Esmail's head.

"'Consequences'… hm." Irene cracked the spine of her notebook, laying it flat on the latest page above a series of console switches. "I can get us to the *Meret*. I've also recorded the *Hathor*'s coordinates. If we can't help them ourselves, we can at least send their statuses and locations to TerraCosmos once we're back in range of the relays."

Frida snorted under her breath. "Right, like they'll make the effort to come fetch these guys when they've been ignoring Lulal."

At first, it seemed like Irene was going to ignore her, but every time her hand connected with a piece of the dashboard, whether it was a knob or button or some part of a touch screen, the force increased tenfold, until finally the course was set and her knuckles held the buds of bruises. Esmail took the yoke and steered the *Amihaf* on the calculated path, and only then did Irene turn toward Frida.

"Do you know how many Delta-class ships TerraCosmos currently has that aren't involved in Project Aker? One." She snatched her notebook from the dashboard and flipped it to a blank page in her lap. "They require so much more material to manufacture than something like the *Amihaf*, or even the freighters. The money they spent on recycled scrap and newly-mined ores... even if they don't care about the people, they're still not going to leave all these resources to waste away in the void."

"They can shell out more money to the African Mining Board," Frida said. "They haven't exactly shown much restraint there historically—"

"Sure." There was a venom under Irene's single word and it nipped Frida's rebuttal quiet. Noah peeked at what her pen was scratching out on the blank page—a mountain valley broken into a chasm, skeletal hands stretching up from out of frame, hasty suggestions as the ink scrambled and rolled into shape.

He stared at the edge where the hands sprouted, the suggestion of the arms attached to them extending to where they could never exist. Open air, off the paper. Only hinted at. He couldn't help but wonder after the news article Luz had skimmed about TerraCosmos' dwindling resources, the lobbyists in the Arctic, the mysterious emblem Ikemba had relayed to Dayo; and as Irene added enough hands in the drawing to cover the chasm completely, he wondered how much of the unsaid in her terse *sure* tangled with the roots of those others, if they were simply one large mass.

No estimate was given for how long it would take them to reach the *Meret* with intrasystem speeds, but everyone assumed it was enough time to pick away at something during the wait. Dayo pulled Quinn aside, asking what he knew about brainware—she had an idea, and if she gave him a disconnected tablet empty of anything valuable, could he transfer the FDL.exe file to it? The two of them headed toward the med bay, and then Frida wanted to go check up on some of the fungal samples in the lab, until finally there were only four in the cockpit, their attentions straining in different directions, ready to collapse.

Savannah approached behind Noah, draping her arms over his shoulders, and rested her chin on his head. The familiar pressure settled the skittering under Noah's skin. "I miss the engineering library," she murmured.

He wrapped one of her hands in his, or at least the best he could, given the difference in height.

"So..." Esmail said, cautious. "I assume we're all fine with those consequences he threatened?"

"How could it be any worse than what he already had planned?" Irene's pen carved ruts into the paper as she added detail to the mountains, veiny layered rocks and snow-capped crags overlooking the scene below.

"I guess you're right."

Three hours passed before the *Amihaf* found itself in a sparse field of debris, the concentration ramping up the further Esmail steered them on Irene's path. Sheets of metal, broken recycling tanks, bundles of wires and burst seat cushions and tattered burnt bedsheets—they maneuvered around the tight spaces, dull thuds sounding down the sides of the ship when they clipped a corner.

And sometimes, not so dull: something metal scraped along the starboard side, and Esmail whipped around with a wince. "That's fine right?"

"Esmail—"

Savannah's shriek snapped them all back toward the spaceshield.

A body.

No time to veer the *Amihaf* out of the way. They approached it somehow slower than the rest of the debris. They could take in the missing arm, how the severance bit wide enough to crush part of the rib cage. The bloating stretched the skin like an over-taut balloon, bruises discoloring the whole of whichever *Meret* crew once resided within.

Whatever Noah should have felt, alarm or revulsion or sorrow, didn't knock him in the stomach. A numbness overtook him as the body neared, finally thumping against the spaceshield and rolling off, out of sight, another few thumps fading down the length of the ship until all they were left with was their own warm, intact selves and a greasy smear along Irene's side of the cockpit.

"Fuck." Irene tossed her notebook to the floor.

"Sorry," Esmail said.

"There's no way you could have avoided that, even if you'd been looking," said Noah. His voice rubbed raw against the back of his throat, almost foreign.

"Sorry," he mumbled again, hands tighter on the yoke. The *Meret* had started to expand into view, just off to the left of where the *Amihaf*'s nose had been pointing, and he guided them there without a word.

"I'll…" Savannah shakily made her way toward the foyer. "I'll go let everyone else know we're almost there."

Her reappearance was announced with the irregular patter of her clicking pen. Dayo, Quinn, and Frida filed in behind her. They were too relaxed for Savannah to have told them about the body.

"That thing really got hammered, didn't it?" Quinn said.

Antonio's retelling hadn't left much up for interpretation, nor had it carved out any extra room for embellishment. Where the *Hathor*'s aft had extended several dozen yards behind the wings, the *Meret* ended in a knotted wall of scrap metal, a dense cloud of debris hovering in its orbit.

"We can call them, right?" Dayo glanced between Irene and Esmail.

Irene reached toward the appropriate buttons once she noticed Esmail had barely acknowledged the question. "Please hold."

Bloop-bloop-bloop—the dialing tone pitched lower than the incoming chime, and they waited in silence as it rang once, twice, three times without any answer.

"I hate to be the one to say it," Frida said, "but there might not be anyone —"

The screen in the spaceshield fizzled to life, a sweaty man appearing before them wearing a tattered shirt with the arms of olive coveralls tied around his waist. His billed cap read *MY SHIP IS OVER THERE*, with no arrows to indicate direction.

"Breaker, breaker, roger, hell, this is the TerraCosmos Ship *Meret*," the man said with a twang. "Cap'n Coleridge speaking. Who the blazes might you be?"

"The, um…" Noah startled himself, unaware he'd decided to speak. "This is the TerraCosmos Ship *Amihaf*. We just came across the *Hathor*, and—"

"They say anything about Zak?"

"Who?" said Irene.

"Zak! Zak! He's one of mine! He ran over to help Tony on an issue with their shitters."

"We didn't—"

"He's my freakin' nephew, man." Coleridge knocked his palm against the side of his head. "If I make it back to Earth, how am I supposed to tell my sister her kid is lost in space?"

The *Meret*'s cockpit looked to be about the size of the *Amihaf*'s, but refuse and debris from their recent encounter melded into the paneling, drawing the walls in closer until all Coleridge had at his disposal for pacing was a narrow aisle amid scrap.

"It's not fair to y'all, I know this," he continued. "I don't even know why you're out here. Can't be on purpose. And there's nothing you can do, I know that too. How's a Gamma-class ship supposed to dock with a Delta-class? Now, we Deltas, that can be tip-to-tip." He brought the ends of his first fingers together, a grin curling up behind them. "Not that we and the *Hathor* ever had to go that route. Nah. Now, though—whew, probably. Our airlock jetways were fine enough 'til now."

"Captain Gardiner, he…" Noah fought to clear his throat, but whatever had lodged itself there was not inclined to move. "He only confirmed statuses for himself and two others. We didn't hear anything about a Zak—"

"Aw, hell, he ran off with the rest of them, didn't he? Saw those bottle shuttles break off the hull before we drifted too far…" He paced down and back along his narrow walkway, and then flung his hat into the shadowed cover of the main hall. "*FUCK.*"

"Um... Capt—*Cap'n* Coleridge..." Esmail probed. "I'm sure there's something we can—"

"Yeah, there is one thing y'all can do. Get out of here." Coleridge's hands splayed across a row of broken dials on the dashboard, leaning close to the lens. "I mean it. I don't have any idea what hit us, but it left me with a few concretes: whatever it is plays with the limits of what's natural, and everyone else on my ship is dead."

He swiped debris from the pilot's chair and collapsed into the seat, which tilted at a broken angle. "You caught me right as I was about to space the last one. Galina Yurasova... she, uh... she liked to draw little pictures for the rest of the crew and tape them on the bunk doors. It was her first mission outside the Kuiper Belt. I hate to do it, you know. Spacing 'em. But there's nowhere else to put them where they wouldn't stink up the place before I get Earth-side. *If.* Heh."

Noah didn't reach for anything to say to that. He knew there was nothing he would find.

"I meant it: leave. Coleridge out."

The call disconnected.

The crew of the *Amihaf* collected themselves in a fog, drifting away to where they'd stashed themselves in the last interim. Words came haltingly, unsure, if at all; the only evidence Irene was actually speaking to Esmail was the movement of her mouth, and then she, too, slid past into the foyer, leaving Noah and Esmail alone.

Without the background shuffle of movement, Noah could hear Esmail repeating a line, deliberately enunciated, a mantra that slowly calmed his shaking hands. He lingered, and long enough for the Persian to cleave into individual words in his head.

Esmail's hands stilled, and he rolled his fingers around the yoke, if only to guide the *Amihaf* to a new corner of space to stall, away from Coleridge's final and solitary duties—though this came too late, the brutal demands of the vacuum slinging across the starscape the broken body of Galina Yurasova, already starting to bloat.

Night fell in the arbitrary fashion of deep space, signaled only by the steady march of the clocks. Midnight struck, and while his eyes stung with fatigue, Noah was at the opposite pole of sleep. Esmail's mantra cycled just under the normal stream of his thoughts—still without a translation, even after asking Quinn. He could name the poet, even question if Noah had heard Esmail correctly, but his Persian was simply too rudimentary.

"Esmail does love Forough," he said.

Spock blankly gazed down from his bookshelf perch, and Noah stared back. Without network connection, he couldn't look up who this Forough was, nor could he sink into the familiar cache of old *Star Trek* episodes. There was just the ceiling, Spock, and his incomplete article and email drafts to hurry time along.

It was a new reflex that kept yanking him back into wakefulness whenever his blinking grew too heavy. He wanted to pretend, for just a moment, that this was the deep-space mission that had graced his best dreams as a child. He would oversleep trying to chase the ending, and his father's voice would shake the walls admonishing him for missing the school tram, and for once he wouldn't mind. Sleep, though, would open the great maw of nightmares.

He rolled out of bed and lumbered into the bunk hall, then to the empty space where the galley, lounge, and top of the stairwell met. The ship itself was unusually quiet, the engines idle instead of churning to maintain the impossible speed of turbolight. Each step Noah took seemed to clang like a gong, liable to rouse the rest of the crew from their isolation.

So he hurried down the stairs. The TerraCosmos seal emblazoned on the foyer floor clenched at his empty stomach. His options were limited. Lab, cockpit, med bay—

Cargo hold.

No one would stumble upon him there.

It was colder below. The boxes and crates they'd used as seats remained where they'd left them after that after-hours huddle.

Noah knew little about the standard set of supplies afforded to TerraCosmos spacecraft outside their general shapes. Replacement parts for crucial flight and life support functions. Bulky emergency medical devices, including various accommodations should a crew member become disabled mid-mission.

But specialized equipment for spacewalks—everyone received that training. A crate with that label sat directly before him, the red triangle on the lid marking its contents dangerous. Ray-knives meant to cut through wires and sheet metal during ship repairs could turn deadly at pointblank range.

And they worked. They wouldn't have been approved for takeoff otherwise.

A finger tightening around the trigger, a white-blue streak of plasma.

It could be over so quickly. The synthetic skin and Constructed Skull melting around the heat, motherboards of brainware sizzling down to nothing. Another shell for the breeze to whip through in a howl, absent of anything to ground it.

TerraCosmos wouldn't have to know. This far outside the mapped dots of the galaxy, any number of accidents could break them—hadn't that been the lesson the first time Abelard met an end? Something could malfunction while he checked on the airlock. An acid from a xeno-organic sample could spill, eat into his active memory. He could wander off into the wilderness at their next exoplanet port of call, beyond any border where search and rescue could hope to recover him.

It was easy.

Abelard was offline, a target no one could miss.

The crew could think so much more clearly when the breath of his cooling fan wasn't brushing the back of their necks. Plans for Shēngdì, for Jibril, for the *Hathor* and *Meret*, they would rush out of them, a geyser blazing its first path to the sky.

And maybe that was too romantic of a hope. Maybe all he needed to aim for was ensuring the *Amihaf* wouldn't collapse into blood and scrap under his watch.

I've never killed—Noah stopped the thought before it could spool out to completion, letting his wobbling knees guide him to the floor. He pressed his forehead against the open ledge of the crate; it was cool, just like the surface of the freezer door in the kitchen he used to share with Justin, when the sun dipped out of high noon and behind the tree at the window. He leaned there often after advisor meetings in Abelard's oven of an office, even before he'd officially moved in. It grounded him. And sometimes, as it grounded him, he would catch the bulbous little body of an ant scuttling along the counter and crush it under the tip of his ring finger, staining it with the sharp odor of its insides.

That was killing—that and the spider Abelard tutted over, and an injured bird that had once hobbled in front of his speeding bike tire, and maybe, too,

Tristan, because if they hadn't been taken from Shala with his assistance then they never would have met that end.

But a human, a *person*. It was different, and it also wasn't, and also still— Omar's voice returned to him, close to his ear. *How can you kill him if he already died on Njord Station?*

But what about the rest of the crew? Did they not count as people? Was Abelard's monomaniacal quest not priming them to bleed out as the vacuum swallowed them whole?

Noah whacked his head against the edge of the crate, then again, and rose to his knees. He pulled out one of the ray-knives, assessed the weight tugging at his wrists, his elbows. It was a dense thing, deceptively heavy, and its material, one of those odd blends of metal and recycled plastic, was even cooler against his skin than the crate. Cool like a pre-Catastrophe autumn, cool like an unseasonable February night on the Rassawek campus, standing in the quad at the center of an undergrad dorm complex, as close as they could get to the historic observatory without the sky being brambled over by trees.

That was a specific night. Noah and Abelard, a stationary island amid the flocks of freshmen reveling in the chill—the greater Monacan region's power grid had failed just before sunset, and classes were canceled, and for the time in many residents' conscious memories, the Milky Way reopened itself across the blank dark overhead.

I know you're not any kind of astrophysicist, Abelard said. He pulled a device from his messenger bag. *This one star has been acting up over the last year, and maybe without the light pollution, we can get a better look...* The device was an adaptation of an engineering student's capstone project, fixing a small telescopic smart lens with a laser point system that would do away with the gap lost in translation when someone tried to point at a specific star using only their finger. *For the astronomer and their friends on the go!*

Abelard never mentioned the name of the star, or if he had, it was while his face was obscured by the device as it fought his attempts to configure it. The star was bright without dominating the pocket of black overhead, but its supposed antics never jumped high enough to breach Noah's surface knowledge of astrophysics.

And eventually—quickly—they devolved into a kind of show-and-tell. Abelard found the star system where a TerraCosmos rover had retrieved the tissue samples he'd used in his first publication, the star system where he and another researcher from Almaty spent the night amid prickly ferns and a language barrier after being separated from the group. Noah could only direct the device to a sector, an estimate; he never managed to locate the star system from his undergraduate thesis, but Abelard's attention was rapt. He hung on every word.

The earthy tinge to the air, hovering so close that he could almost smell it, dissipated in an instant. The *Amihaf* rushed back in with such force it was a miracle he didn't choke.

Noah stared at the device in his hands.

"I can't. I..." He sighed, and it caught in his throat with a growl as it slipped back into the crate. "Who am I even talking to?"

With the ship idling, there was a direction he could face that would lead to Earth if he followed the straight line across—and that was the sticking point, the billions and billions and billions of miles it asked of him.

He sat back on his feet, paused, and then untangled his legs until he could curl himself into a ball, arms pulled snug around his knees.

"This isn't what I wanted," he murmured into the tops of his thighs. And again, louder, "*This isn't what I wanted.*" An icy pulse of pain zipped down his arms to the twitching tips of his fingers. "I wasn't asking for much… I wasn't asking for anything."

The *Amihaf* met him with silence. He blinked away the stinging at the corners of his eyes.

When Noah took the stairs up to the foyer, he went with empty hands.

TEN

NOAH EMERGED FROM HIS bunk the next morning with the rest of the crew, having been roused by a repetitive and irregular banging coming from the mess table.

It wasn't clear who among them had read it as a wake-up call and who had assumed yet another piece of the mission had spun off in a separate crisis—mostly because they had no time to confer. The seven of them stood bleary-eyed, clad in sleepwear, hair running wild or hemmed in by silk scarves, yawning—and Abelard, fully-charged, beamed at them with the giddiness of a child on their birthday.

"Best of mornings to you all," said Abelard. "I do hope everyone has had ample time to recharge after the events of yesterday."

On the other side of the gathering, Frida mimed the particular bob of her head when she snorted derisively under her breath.

"At this point in our journey, I believe it is time to involve you all in what has, until now, been a bit of a solo project." He pulled out a tablet with a projector attached and laid it on the mess table. With a couple taps, it displayed a rotating schematic that was more words than useful detail or assembly drawings.

He took a moment to observe a full rotation. "You're probably wondering exactly what it is I've conjured up here. To be completely transparent, I'm not sure myself. The… *inspiration*, as it were, has not been forthcoming about all of the principles and logic underpinning the design, but I trust it."

Noah caught Savannah's eye from where she stood beside Frida. She mirrored the subtle furrow of his brow, and the longer those furrows held, the more the rest of the crew picked up on it.

"I think," Abelard continued, "that with the perspective of an additional seven people, all of them quite brilliant, this idea can become a tangible asset."

"You still haven't told us what we'll be using it for," said Dayo.

"Dr. Oyekan, I'm sure you can puzzle out the answer to the latter."

Frida crossed her arms. "I want to hear you say it."

Abelard swiveled his head toward her with the mechanical precision of a pre-Catastrophe animatronic. "But of course, Dr. Wick. W—I am of the utmost belief that this device, once built, will kill a vacuum leviathan."

As implied, the reveal was more of a confirmation than a surprise. What possessed Noah's attention, and also that of a handful of others, was what could be made out in the scribbled spinning spec file before them. A leviathan had ripped through the *Meret* and *Hathor* like they were gnats, and one had levied as much destruction against Abelard mere years ago—the hologram, at this stage of design, resembled little more than a bazooka with a dream.

"That's not to size, is it?" asked Quinn. "From what Antonio said, they're not exactly small—"

"It will suffice," Abelard said, a deniable sharpness coating his words.

"None of us is that kind of engineer," Irene said. "We also don't have the kind of raw material you'd need for this."

"We will make do." One of Abelard's eye displays flickered as he stared over them, arms crossed. "If Dr. Starbuck did not supply the proper coordinates after leaving Captain Gardiner, then we ought to adjust course before attempting anything else. I have a heading," he added as Noah made a move to speak. "Dr. Tuuluq?"

Irene wordlessly stepped forward to take the slip of paper he'd produced from his shirt pocket. She pinched it from his grip, barely holding onto the corner. "And if I don't?"

"I am the captain of this ship." His grin collapsed. A digital eye flickered again, this time a quick burst of static—easy to miss, though none of them had.

Irene turned on her heel and marched down to the cockpit.

Abelard was primed to herd the rest of them down to the lab in their wake, but extended some semblance of sense allowing them to get changed. The murmuring as they filed into their bunks stayed low, still unsure of the extent of Abelard's hearing. Savannah locked eyes with Noah from her door, teeth grinding without the buffer of her pen.

They were the last to return to the lab. Dayo had argued her way out of whatever duty this was, citing some medical standards none of them could reproduce when asked. Irene still held her station in the cockpit, and Esmail's services there had not yet been deemed necessary; instead, he kept to the back of the group, pacing in tight circles.

On the center lab bench was a rough pile of metal, all fabricated for purposes outside of a bespoke leviathan weapon. It looked as if Abelard had taken apart the furniture in his bunk for scraps, from the bed frame and faucet to all the screws that held them together. Though the pile took up most of the space on the bench, creating Abelard's vision still felt far out of reach. There was no way to deploy heat for any kind of metalworking given the ship's life support system, and even if there were, the amount of metal present only covered a third of what the haphazard schematics called for.

But Abelard had plans for it all, however impractical. There was a workaround process for metalworking without a forge or blowtorch. They could circumvent the mimeos' limitations on inorganic materials by using it for banned pre-Catastrophe plastics, the kind synthesized from petroleum, Abelard having hacked in to remove the restriction. Each individual's personal lack of engineering expertise was painstakingly accounted for— Abelard had poured over not only their professional backgrounds, but also academic transcripts dating back to secondary school. What Quinn couldn't configure with the electrical components, Savannah had aced in an undergrad physics elective. What none of the research team could discern about a metal's particular properties, Esmail had gleaned from hands-on maintenance work. Abelard salvaged them for parts, a reanimated patchwork corpse of an engineer's skillset.

It didn't seem to matter that, much like a reanimated corpse, their efforts were clumsy and imprecise. They left the lab each evening with the acrid stench of burnt plastic coating the air and gauze taped against the exit wounds of metal splinters.

Three days passed like this, and Abelard remained undeterred. If anything, he grew more eager by the hour. They had managed to construct a workable casing and the beginnings of the primary internal circuitry—far from functional, but to Abelard as miraculous as a newly-discovered iceberg.

The morning of the fourth day, Noah woke over an hour before his alarm, nearly blinded by the sparkling static of a migraine aura.

The thick curve of it looped across his vision, leaving only a small corner along the bottom right unobscured. He squeezed his eyes shut, and the aura held fast in the dark, parts of it winking between white and lavender. It had been years since he had a real migraine to this scale, but he still knew the path they took—at this stage, he had about half an hour until he could see properly again, half an hour until his head split open and turned his stomach inside out.

He didn't bother pulling on anything over the worn athletic shorts he'd slept in, shuffling out into the bunk hall while trying to aim himself at Dayo's door under the guidance of the one clear spot he could see. Two steps in, a clatter rang from the lower level, muffled enough that the med bay was a likely source. Likely, but not certain—Noah stretched a hand forward to where Dayo's bunk should have been and grasped at empty air, finding the jamb of an open door as he cast his hand wider.

So she was definitely in the med bay.

The maneuvering toward and down the stairs was a slow trudge. Odd noises drew his eyes despite better judgment. He found only the constant glitter of the aura hiding what he'd meant to focus on.

Thankfully, all the months aboard the ship had gifted him with an innate sense of the floor plan, and he was able to deposit himself at the bottom of the stairs without incident. The foyer posed more of a problem, but Noah forged ahead on his best approximation of a straight line. The clear patch of his vision came upon one of the sunbeams in the TerraCosmos emblem underfoot, and then a hand gripped his shoulder.

He tensed, yelped.

"Noah, it's me," said Irene's voice. "Are you okay?"

"Yeah, yeah…" he said, catching his breath. "Sorry… I can't quite, um…" He tilted his head so the free corner of his peripheral vision lined up with her face; it was blurry but welcome all the same. "Got a migraine coming."

She shifted toward the med bay and back, connecting the dots. "I won't keep you long, then." Her hand squeezed harder as she stepped closer. "In one day, we're going to hit Abelard's destination. It's in range of the relays. Queue up anything you need to send back home."

As soon as she released her hold, she strode up the stairs toward the galley mimeo or her bunk or—Noah's train of thought terminated there, the impending headache starting to ramp up with a low and steady pulse.

When he reached the med bay, the pain sharpened under the sudden influx of noise—monitors and hemographs and some other software in the tablet propped up on the counter. Noah angled his head to get a better view through the aura, but there were too many moving parts for him to focus on any one thing, or even pinpoint Dayo in the chaos.

"Another one!" Quinn's voice called from the back corner.

"Great," Frida's voice replied. "Just great! Bloody great—"

"Noah?" This was Dayo. This was her hand guiding him to an empty stool, the handle of a drawer pressing up against his back. "Please tell me you're not infected too—"

"No, no… migraine," he said. "I just need some migraine meds."

Though he couldn't see her through the aura, he could picture the way her shoulders sagged from the loosened hold she took on his arms. "That I can do, easy. Give me five minutes."

Her steps retreated toward the back of the room where the AutoChemist was embedded in the wall.

"Wait... 'too?'"

"Hold on." Moments later she shoved two paper cups in his hands, one with pills and the other sloshing with water. "Bottoms up."

Noah tossed them both back. The water chasing the meds couldn't stop them from sticking, a lump in his throat slowly descending into the pit of his abdomen. "What did you mean by 'too?'"

Even without the pills fully absorbed into his bloodstream, his vision had started to clear. Both the gurney folded out from the wall and a spare mattress on the floor beneath it were occupied—Quinn and Frida, folded into themselves, ashen. Tendrils of purple snaked up Frida's nails.

"What does it look like? This one relapsed," Dayo said, pointing at Quinn, "and... I thought we were careful." She frowned as Frida rolled onto her back, chin tilted up to catch a glimpse of Quinn on the wall gurney. Her eyes were glassy. "Popped up within seconds of each other, barely lucid."

"Are you—what about you?" Noah swung his head following Dayo's sudden dash to a back cabinet, a throb of pain rising in his temple. His own clock was ticking more quickly than he'd estimated if the actual headache wasn't waiting for the aura to dissolve.

"I'm fine," she said. "Taking better precautions. And I'd like to not risk anyone else more than necessary." She stepped around the still-standing pieces of clutter that remained from the first round, snapping on a module to the hemograph, pointedly tilting her head in his direction.

It was enough to assume she was telling him to get back to his bunk, even if the larger part of her face was hidden behind the aura still clinging to a corner.

"Dayo, Dayo..." Quinn whined. "You've got to tell Esmail—Esmail and Irene, they've both got to know. The ship is at the wrong angle. We're flying sideways. It's not how we're supposed to move. The axis—"

"Lay back, please," said Dayo. "Noah, what are you still doing here?"

Noah stepped closer, hovering in the middle ground between her and Frida. "If you need extra hands—"

"Not if your migraine is going to make you sloppy. Quinn," she said. "I need to check your vitals—"

It happened all at once—the full bloom of the migraine gripping behind Noah's eyes, Quinn's foot kicking against the inner recess of the gurney in protest, a clanging along the outside wall closest to the airlock, and Frida breaking into hysterics.

Though the crest of the ache dug deeper into Noah's temples, most of the noise soon subsided, leaving only Frida's giggling to cover the background hum of the ship. It was a terrible sound, not only because the giggling couldn't fold into her voice or person in any natural way. That was the most immediately unnerving piece, surely, but watching her violet-stained nails hug her folded legs against her chest, then dig into the thin skin along her shin bone until they bled—it didn't help.

The door to the foyer slid open.

"Pardon the interruption."

Abelard.

The sharp one-two of his steps, a precise heel-to-toe, crested the pain circling behind Noah's forehead to new heights, dragging waves of nausea up with it. Abelard didn't venture too far inside, but it was enough for Dayo to round on him with a barely-reined fury as she tried to put herself between him and her patients.

"You're not needed here," she said. "Go back to the lab. The rest of the available crew should be there before too long."

"Dr. Oyekan, if I may—"

"You may not."

Frida's giggling pitched wider, leaning closer to an outright cackle. Her nails clawed deeper, and Noah grabbed a half-unraveled bundle of gauze and medical tape on a nearby counter, dropping to her side to wrap the thin bleeding crescents before their reds turned violet. His throat spasmed against the migraine bile as he worked.

"You're going to be all right," he said. Repeated. It was the only bit of bedside manner he could find. A tube of antiseptic ointment bucked off the counter overhead, and Noah grabbed it, squeezed a translucent line down the shin he hadn't yet touched. His head pulsed at a beat uneven with his heart; he wrapped Frida's legs with gauze and he felt his own blood vessels tighten, threaten to burst under the pain. "You're going to—"

"Like this is the worst thing to happen to me," Frida said through her laughter. "You know none of my family would return my calls after? Even Naomi, and she organized that sit-in against the Nu-tories. Gauze is nothing, Starbuck. It's going to collapse before—haven't you been listening?"

Abelard made the noise of clearing his throat, and then the only sound left in the med bay was the odd beat of the lone monitor Dayo had managed to hook up to Quinn.

"*What?*" Dayo snapped.

"I was hoping to borrow Dr. Wick," he said. "Much of the damage my bunk recently sustained was at her hand, so I was thinking she could help me repair it." He craned his head to peer around the taller columns of mess, around Dayo and Noah, straight toward Frida's line of sight. "What do you say, Pip?"

She tensed under Noah's hands; he barely had enough time to scramble out of the way before she sat up, staring Abelard down with her own threads of purple wrapping around the veins in her sclera. "The fuck did you did just call me?"

"Oh, see…" Abelard rocked up on the balls of his feet. "I had a cousin growing up. Another ginger. Their nickname—it was…"

His train of thought skidded to a stop; Quinn pulled himself to his feet, shouldering Dayo and Noah aside until he was chest-to-chest with Abelard, using his extra inch and a half to his full advantage. "Rethink this."

"Mr. Kaiwhakatere—"

"You touch Frida, then you answer to me, captain or not."

"I wouldn't think that you're in the best state to be making such idle threats."

"This—" Quinn hissed, wincing against some unseen pain. "This is far from idle. It's active, even. You bother her, or Esmail, or Dayo, anyone—"

Abelard took a step forward, nudging Quinn back on unbalanced feet; a couple scrambling hops, and he tripped on his ankle, tipping back, arms spinning for purchase in empty air. Noah and Dayo rushed forward, propped him back up. Once again he stood flush with Abelard, lungs heaving with adrenaline and unable to nudge the immobile weight of the Constructed Body back even the slightest.

"I would like to see Dr. Wick, please."

"Sure," Quinn said. "And I also bet you'd like to see a coordinate sphere with six-path and… the tessellating—no, it's the inverse? Quadinverse?"

"You should get some rest, Mr. Kaiwhakatere. You're not making any sense."

Behind them, the monitors started wailing. Quinn's blood pressure and heart rate spiked, the grating chirps ramming a searing-hot pressure behind Noah's eyes. He dry-heaved as Dayo tugged Quinn back to the gurney.

"You don't look well either, Dr. Starbuck."

"Unrelated," he choked out after another gag.

"Both of you need to go," Dayo said. "Noah, go back to bed. Abelard, I'm banning you from the med bay. *Get out*."

The lighting buzzed the pain under Noah's brow at an angle asymptotically steep. He squinted past it, up toward Abelard as he surveyed Dayo wrangling both patients now, all of them his crew, all of them struggling, and his mustache twitched against the placid grin beneath. One eye display had gone solid white.

Noah steered himself where Quinn stood moments before. He curled both hands into fists and shoved them against the metal plating where Abelard's ribs would have been in his old body. It did little physically but strain his knuckles, his muscles. "You heard her."

"But I must insist—"

"I will throw up in your cooling fans. Move."

They both knew that Abelard's reflexes could stop Noah before he'd have the chance to properly aim and that whatever alloys Prana Technologies used for Constructed Bodies could easily withstand the acidity. Whatever made Abelard retreat to the foyer, then, wasn't the threat, but maybe the sight of it with the sweat beading across Noah's blanched face, his grinding jaw bulging along his temple—it spoke of desperation enough that something in him gave in to pity.

The med bay door closed behind them; Abelard veered back toward the lab as Noah dragged himself back upstairs to his bunk, eyes shut against the knives of overhead lights. Minor fumbling led him to the right door, and within a few steps he'd wrapped himself into a cocoon with his sheets.

Moments later, he untangled himself and dashed to his bathroom, upending the remnants of his last meal into the toilet. As he caught his breath, he snatched the wastebasket from under the sink to place at his bedside.

He settled into the mattress. The throbbing pain behind his eyes masked the aftertaste of vomit still lingering on his teeth, and history said he had at least another ten minutes until the nausea kicked up again. In the interim, he nestled under the comforter, forcing himself to ignore the low hum of the *Amihaf*, the constant reminder of how fucked they truly were.

There was darkness, and Frida's laughter that was no longer just laughter but also a bitter heaving sob, and only when Noah looked up, neck craning, could he see the stars. They were few in number, faint twitching blips of light. White-blues and white-golds too far apart to be a real starscape. More like galactic freckles, acne. A smattering of melanoma not yet excised.

He'd read about this, once. The universe was constantly expanding. Some posited that it might one day collapse into the singularly-dense point before the Big Bang, a rubber band snapping back into place. Others weren't so sure, more comfortable hypothesizing about the millennia before that potential threshold, when the last light from burnt-out stars had already reached us, the others still alive having flung themselves too far to be caught in the historical snapshot overhead.

His chest ached at the sight. Seven, ten stars left out of a swathe of thousands—how lonely.

His neck ached at this angle, and when he adjusted, staring out at eye level, the blank black rushed forward, tried to swallow him whole. It was the absence crushing him, and it was also the being that enveloped the *Hathor* and *Meret*, spirits and steel flattened under the same force.

The emptiness pressed into his skull. If he turned around, he was convinced he'd be staring into an abyssal maw, the depths drilling down into the central, originating point of the universe, and he would never be able to wrench his eyes free. Tumbling head first, lost forever. Just as the universe had become lost to itself.

Then the scene fractured—physically, a literal breaking, cracks spindling in all directions. One shot straight at Noah's heart. He dodged, or tried to. He didn't sense any pain, nor could he see any evidence of the crack when he checked back over his shoulder. Instead, the empty starscape, which had rendered itself a sheer plane, split along the webbing fissures. It cleaved on clean lines, rushing forward with an alien groan; and in the newly-exposed face was a radiant burst of stars and nebulae and pulsars, the night sky as captured by telescopes for centuries.

The web continued to splinter, unsatisfied. It spread around corners, chipping off a sliver of the starscape. The force flicked it toward Noah, spinning lazily on a Uranian tilt, until he could reach out and capture it between his fingers. Translucent, yet still gleaming at the searing-hot pricks held in this shaved-off piece of the universe.

Something behind him thumped. He tensed at the noise, pinching the sliver until the sharp ends broke skin. A thin trickle of blood ran down the side, dripping over the face and the heat within, sizzling copper burning the inside of his nose. It thumped again—

Noah woke with a start, tangled in his bedsheets. The *Amihaf*, he was on the *Amihaf* and it was just a dream, and what time was it—

He flipped himself over in the constraints of his bedding in search of the wall clock, and the blood in his head yawed to the opposite temple with a thick ache. The aftermath of an ebbing migraine digging its nails in as a last-ditch effort to stick around for an encore.

1307 IST. Early afternoon.

Somewhere on the lower level, the thump sounded again.

Piece by piece, the reality he'd left behind as the migraine took its course reasserted itself. For a moment, the throb of pressure rose, and he paused his untangling from the sheets until it passed.

He changed out of the sleepwear he'd stayed in after seeking relief from Dayo and the AutoChemist. The closest clean clothes his hands latched onto were an old pair of athletic shorts and t-shirt from the University of Dionde:gâ's *Star Trek* club his sophomore year.

As he descended the stairs, the thump's origin grew clearer: the lab, the corners of it furthest from the door. Until his head could bear a sharp swivel without any pain, Noah decidedly guided himself away from whatever was coiling into existence amid the lab benches, and then again away from the med bay, Dayo not needing any additional distractions.

So: the cockpit, its stillness beckoning.

Irene kept her focus on the tablet in her lap as he settled into the pilot seat, scrolling through walls of white-on-black text in the blocky font of code, pausing every few flicks of her finger to press on a string lit in grating yellow. A comment would pop up, she would read, and then silently slide past. Half an hour passed this way; Noah hugged his knees to his chest, testing the residual pain in his head about as often as Irene slowed on the highlighted text. Little changed, not that he'd expected as much so quickly.

He cast another sidelong glance at her, at the particular pretzeling that hemmed her limbs inside the confines of the seat. It was the kind of glance that leaned over the line into a stare, one that accumulated weight, but she didn't budge, didn't say a word. At least, she didn't say something out loud, not at that moment—he remembered suddenly the notice she gave in the foyer that morning.

Queue up anything you need to send back home.

Noah fished his tablet out of the pocket of his shorts. *Anything* encompassed more than a couple messages, each with its own flavor of urgency no less potent than the next. The projected deadline was fast approaching with his morning lost to the migraine. And in the worst case scenario—

No. He couldn't think like that. The *Hathor* and *Meret* were ambushed, unprepared. As far as Noah was aware, their crews' collective opinion on vacuum leviathans had aligned with that of Camp Bachelor, decidedly in the realm of myth. The *Amihaf* could at least anticipate what was coming.

Still—there was the issue of the deadline. He would write something to his parents, and he would write something to Justin, and that would have to suffice.

It would suffice, rather, as long as he could coax his brain into cooperating. Another hour trudged by, and the two windows of drafts remained woefully blank. He couldn't even bring himself to decide how to open either of them, typing out and backspacing variations on *dear* and *hi* and the space-themed salutation Joseph Ilunga himself had futilely coined in the earliest days of TerraCosmos. Noah would get a sharp earful the next time he spoke to his father if he began an email with that one.

Beyond that, he didn't know what to say, what reassurances would only bloom into more worry? His head started to ache, but it was a different sort of pain than a migraine, tracing along the back of his skull until it bundled around the base of his neck.

Sighing, he tapped on the window he'd designated for Justin's note. He simply needed to remove the cork of writer's block; he could pare it down later.

You mentioned the pie a while back, he wrote. *I've been thinking about it too. You remember the time I tried to make meatballs? How I thought I could make it work without going through the hassle of making breadcrumbs? I never can make dishes right on the first try. Something always goes wrong. The first time I ever made pie crust, I couldn't get it to stretch the full area of the tin without breaking apart. So what I'm saying is with the rhubarb, I should have known better.*

"Question."

"Answer? Potentially?"

Irene's gaze remained on the tablet, though she held up a hand as if her question came in a lecture hall instead of an errant ship's cockpit. "How much do you know about viruses?"

"Depends," he said, turning to face them. "Computer viruses? Not a clue. Biological—"

"That one."

"Right. Makes sense." His thumb rubbed circles into a resurging pang in his temple. Too many years had passed since his last time on the receiving end of one of Sergey's oral brainstorming sessions on xenomicrobes at the back of an off-campus bar. "I wouldn't want to give a lecture on the subject past the introductory level, but—"

"That's more than I can say. Come look at this." Finally she met his eyes, and the weariness there hung heavy. Once he positioned himself over her shoulder, she continued, "Brainware doesn't work like normal code, right? That's what makes it brainware and not software—it's script *and* playwright all in one. It follows, then, that trying to diagnose a problem in real time would be impossible. The 'source code' would change as soon as the Constructed Body registered any new sensory input."

Noah pointed to the blocks of code on their tablet screen. "So this is… not brainware?"

"No, it is." The brainware code was old, dating back to the first successful case studies Prana Technologies showcased to the public. A handful of papers were cross-published between computer engineering and medical journals at the time, which Dayo had downloaded for her personal edification in preparing for this mission. "One of the articles took snapshots of certain sections of the subject's brainware over a decade or so. Dayo highlighted some anomalies she noticed that the article doesn't comment on. She wasn't sure what to think, and with Quinn out of commission again, she named me the go-to for computer science, and…"

She threw up her free hand in a shrug.

"What?"

"Two classes fifteen years ago. Never covered brainware languages. All guesswork."

"Okay… okay…" Noah gripped at the corners of the seatback. "What exactly are the anomalies?"

Irene rolled back the code almost to the beginning. "Look here." She pointed to a specific line.

"What am I supposed to be paying attention to?"

"You don't need to know what it means. Just remember what it says."

She rolled through pages and pages to another code snapshot; it was nearly identical, save for the line she'd pointed out before. A set of brackets had descended on a phrase of the code, tugged it off to the side. The next freeze-frame arrived at a similar landing—identical code, an odd bracketed sample—but the bracketed piece had drifted down a dozen or so lines and had mutated internally. The timestamp dated it a month after the first snapshot.

"Do viruses do this?" Irene asked after she'd scrolled through further examples, the fifth iteration of the phenomenon hovering under their finger.

Sergey would know, wherever he was these days. Sergey had probably told Noah as much directly, either at a department function or in the hazy half-consciousness following their lone hookup early in the program.

"I really don't know," he sighed. "This is at the opposite end of the scale of what I usually work with."

Another thump landed in the lab, and she grumbled under her breath.

"Are you sure the article it came from didn't say anything about this?" he said. "Maybe—"

"Hold on." She switched windows to the actual text of the article, swiping until she hit the endnotes, and then farther still. "I don't think Dayo saw this."

Appended to the article was another short write-up, dated within the last five years and referencing a larger forthcoming literature review on early Constructed Body studies. She double-tapped to highlight a paragraph near the middle of the first page. According to the author, this study's subject was the only documented incident of brainware behaving this way, and the mutating blip of code was present just over the course of eighteen months before disappearing completely.

"Wait…"

The image resurged in a flash: Sergey squeezing the life out of a lime wedge at the corner of the bar, Savannah looking as if she hoped to rescue it from his chokehold, all while Justin stood on the receiving end of a practiced talk on a theory of the origin of viruses.

"It's not that viruses act like this," he said. "It's that they could *form* like this."

Irene whipped around so sharply that the tablet clattered to the floor, her eyes wide. "If what was in that code was a virus that didn't make it... and was the only one they'd seen..."

"And Quinn said malware has to be coded externally... this doesn't sound like something any operating system would be able to recognize."

"Or quarantine."

Another thump, this time quickly followed by the med bay door slamming open. Noah and Irene caught Dayo just as she veered toward the lab.

"For the love of—my patients need *sleep*, Cousteau, and you've been thumping for hours!"

She paused at the lab door to collect herself, or maybe just to catch her breath; Noah kept his distance near the center of the TerraCosmos emblem underfoot, and Irene inched toward the med bay, entrance still spread wide. From the half-lit shadows, Quinn and Frida stepped up to the threshold, peeking around the corner with a shade more lucidity about them.

Dayo tried to open the lab door and received a low buzzer of denial. Tried again, another buzzer, and then a spit of curses. "Abelard Cousteau, if you don't unlock this—"

The door slid open just as she'd raised her fist to start knocking. Abelard stood before her, hands clasped at his waist and beaming like this was a pleasant surprise. Dayo slowly took a step back, lowering her fist, and

Abelard seized the moment to survey the foyer, where Frida and Quinn had fully emerged.

"Oh, good!" he said. "Then we're all here."

He beckoned over his shoulder for Savannah and Esmail to follow him to the center of the foyer, and as he passed where Noah stood, the state of his eye displays wrested his attention away from the device being lugged from the lab. The right eye was split at an odd diagonal, one side normal while the other was overcome with static so reminiscent of migraine aura that Noah's temples pulsed in sympathy. The left, though—a grating blue had taken over, and what strings of text Noah could discern as he made eye contact hinted at the error screen of a system crash.

"Come, come," Abelard said. "Gather 'round."

They acquiesced with hesitant steps. Dayo stationed herself between Abelard and where Frida and Quinn stood—her concerned stare wavered between both poles, toward the unknown of their de-facto captain and what Noah could only assume was disbelief at their current state. The purple tinges and stains hadn't disappeared, though they had faded enough to not be the first thing anyone noticed. The only glaringly obvious sign that the two of them weren't operating at full capacity was how Frida gripped Quinn's sleeve like it was the only thing keeping her upright—and that Quinn was letting her.

Abelard waited for Esmail and Savannah to slip into the ranks of the circle, then stepping forward to gesture dramatically at the device they'd left at the center. "Behold! The missing piece in our quest to vanquish the mighty leviathan!"

Silence overtook the foyer as the rest of the crew visibly swallowed their most kneejerk responses. What they couldn't swallow rose up into their faces, the particular knot of a brow or chewed lip that hinted at the doubt kept at bay—Noah included. The instrument Abelard so proudly showcased was a misshapen, haphazard chassis of metal and plastic, stray filaments lining the outside edge like frizzy flyaways. At one angle, it could have been some kind of firearm.

"Does it work?" Quinn asked. "Was all that thumping the testing process?"

"I'm told it works just fine," said Abelard.

"Told by who?" Dayo looked to Esmail and Savannah, and they each shrugged. "By *who*, Abelard?"

He shuffled closer to the device, crouched down to examine it more closely, the tip of his fingers, tracing the edges. "The lead. The approval was there. Of course it will work," he murmured.

Esmail, stationed behind Abelard's back, shook his head even more adamantly.

"Hey." Irene crept nearer on the other side of the mechanism, balanced on one knee. She didn't reach out to a shoulder or elbow, as much as her hovering hand seemed to want to. "Dr. Cousteau, it's okay if you're not well. We can help you."

"Not well?"

"Yes." She watched as he continued to pour over the instrument with a rapt obsession. "It's not a foregone conclusion."

Abelard jumped to his feet without warning, his shadow enveloping Irene's kneeling frame. "We ought to mark the occasion."

The other seven among the crew reached for reassurance in each other's eyes, desperate, hoping above all else that something there could quell the brewing dread. And as the glitching screens of Abelard's eyes turned on

Noah, he expected his own dread to froth open into his chest cavity; instead came a numbness.

"Dr. Starbuck! You know Latin."

Noah cleared his throat, tried to find somewhere in the foyer to stick his attention that wasn't any of the others' frowns newly burdened by confusion. "Whether that has ever been true is… questionable."

"Your undergraduate transcript says you took six semesters' worth."

"That was the minimum for—what is this about?" His thoughts started to skid, stuttering from his tongue until the words caught traction again. "I don't think Ovid would have anything appropriate for this even if I did have a couple lines socked away."

He met Abelard in the middle of the circle, where Irene had knelt and since scrambled away. His arms held a frenetic energy the climbing pitch of his voice couldn't carry. His arms flung about, carving the circle wider, away from Abelard and the shattering grip of his fists.

"Of course I would not expect you to recite Ovid to us. You barely scraped a C in that class. No, no… what I'm after is a benediction."

Abelard gestured down to the tangle of metal and plastic at his feet with open palms, and slowly they rose toward the foyer's ceiling as if he were addressing the heavens on Earth, as if those heavens weren't straining the frame of the ship that held them safe against the vacuum.

A benediction—a blessing, that much Noah could guess. A blessing in Latin. Catholics, his brain supplied a beat later. Catholic Christians. Justin had been raised Christian, but not that sect, and he was long lapsed by the time he arrived in Rassawek, and Noah never quite learned Latin pronunciation in those six semesters because what was the point if it was a dead language, and wasn't that why he was there in the first place, because his father had seen his terrible Spanish grades and—

"I don't know," Noah murmured, half outside himself. "I don't know. I'm not—"

A blur, and then Abelard had the instrument in his hands, was shoving it into Noah's hands, a shared embrace of its cold dead body. The stray wires and edges cut into his palms, and as he tried to back away, Abelard stepped forward, pressing and pressing and pressing, and at each turn Noah readjusted, angling the nicks away from the clearest threats, but still they dug in. Again and again, again and again, until most of the device's surface shone through a thin, splotchy layer of red.

"This is good. This is good," said Abelard. "We don't have to baptize in any name. This is just as good—"

Noah's cheekbone slammed against the floor. The rest of the crew clattered to the ground behind him, sliding from the inertia as far as friction would allow. There was silence, and a growing chorus of groans, and then a chorus even sharper to overtake it—the pings and alerts of every tablet on the *Amihaf*, days and days' worth of emails and missed contacts landing in a single wave.

Some critical joint in Noah's body was sprained, but the layers of pain across the whole of him obscured any specificity. He pulled himself to a sitting position and turned toward the cockpit, the visible slice of the spaceshield offering a full view of a starscape out of turbolight.

Irene swore under her breath in Inuktitut.

"We, ah…" Abelard said, sighing. "We may have kicked up the turbolight velocity a tad for an earlier arrival. Their feeding on the radiation was—"

"Who is 'we?'" she yelled.

"It's no matter, Dr. Tuuluq—"

Quinn and Savannah latched onto both sides of Irene just as she was about to lunge forward. "We know about the FDL file. You can tell us. It doesn't have to be like—"

A flash of orange veered across the spaceshield, stabbing-bright, and the force of guarding their eyes against it buckled their knees. A strong-armed show of reverence, but Abelard remained standing, remained muttering to himself as he strode ahead to the cockpit, the best seats on the ship to catch the show.

Noah squinted through a thin sliver of his fingers against the flash. Each burst drilled into the parts left soft by the migraine, silent until his pocket started to chime—his pocket, the inside of Irene's jacket, the tables beyond the open doors to the lab and med bay. Every tablet, lit again in a flurry to remind them of the missed calls and emails and alerts, begging not to be outdone by the fiery storm of the vacuum.

With his back to the cockpit, Noah skimmed over the rest of the crew through the negative the last flaring burst, casting them all in a neon teal stain. "We're okay? Are we all okay?"

"I think so." Dayo had Quinn's chin grasped in one hand, the other holding down one of his bottom eyelids in search of something Noah would rather not know about. Not now.

Not when Esmail had buried his face in Quinn's back, and Savannah had curled herself into a ball, and Frida sat blank between them uncaring that shiny tracks of tears ran down her face for all to see, and Irene—

Bent over to avoid the bursts in their shifting tones of gold and bronze, she yanked her notebook from her back pocket and tore out the last page. Next came a pen, the nib slicing two lines across the center. Eye width apart, Noah realized as she brought the page to her face; a wince bloomed against the flashes, the flaws of her remedy, but she persisted. Kept staring, that wince opening up into curiosity.

"What is it?" he asked. He rose to his feet, his back still facing the cockpit. "Have you seen this somewhere else?"

"Not at all. It's…" She slapped a hand over her eyes, crumpling the paper across the bridge of her nose. "I can only make sense of it if there was an atmosphere, but…"

"That 'but' is doing a lot of work."

"How are you so calm right now?" She met his gaze over the line of their left shoulders. "I feel like I'm about to throw up and you're making *quips*?"

"What do you want me to do? What am I supposed to do to get space lightning under control and not short out our ship?"

"That's not what I meant, and you know it."

And Noah did know, but he couldn't bring himself to name it. "Just—make sure Savannah is okay. Please."

He didn't wait for her to respond, spinning toward the cockpit, elbow acting as a visor, marching ahead until the toes of his boots and the heels of Abelard's occupied the same frame. The flashes had begun to roll across the starscape, twisting ribbons jetting through the void. Noah could only steal glimpses of it—

Abelard, propping himself up with the pilot and navigators' seats, digging his fingertips into the cushions.

Abelard, encircled by strips of fire.

"Dr. Starbuck! Noah! My dear boy—what a sight, what a sight! Here we are at the precipice of our species. We will return to Earth as prophets, the enlightened! We've seen the unseeable, known the unknowable. What would a church be, then, but a false testament to the heavens? See, I understand now that it was for the best, how you couldn't bless our avenging scepter. What is an earthly blessing to the great expanses of creation and the means that can touch it? I now stand before these furious pops of impossible physics, impossible in my own right, and one of us should bow down. One of us should…" Abelard rolled the joints of his Constructed shoulders, fixing his gaze into the center of the blinding lights. "But it isn't going to be me."

The hum of the *Amihaf*, usually a rumbling bass, started to pitch up, as if straining against some unseen force. Noah's hand on Abelard's shoulder couldn't pull him from the fixed point the pinhole of his visual input had trained on. Still he tried to wrench him back, even as the thin slices on his hand split further open, red-raw skin stinging anew.

"No—*no!* We are not doing this! You're going to get us all killed!'" Noah clambered around the other side of the pilot's seat, leaving a splotchy red handprint on Abelard's shirt. "Hey—look at me!" He snapped his fingers before the lens hole in his forehead.

Abelard met his gaze with a swivel of his head that seemed unsettlingly independent of the rest of his Body. The eye that had been half static had fallen to it completely. "Noah… Noah, Noah, Noah…"

His voice descended into a grating tritonal split, smothering his natural pitch under the extra weight. He stepped forward, arm outstretched, again toward the bruise at his elbow.

Noah scuttled out of reach and slammed against the cockpit wall. The back of his skull lit up with the impact. No time to cede for it—his jostling steps sidled toward the door. Into the antechamber. Backwards into the foyer. Abelard pursuing, arm still reaching, Noah's name on repeat, chiding. More layers slipped into his voice until it rattled, metallic. He would have kept stumbling backwards had Frida and Dayo not caught him, one on each arm.

"This is your great final frontier, Noah." Abelard's hand retracted. "And what frontier was ever peaceful?"

Little reached Noah's ears outside of his own frantic breath and that of those beside him, behind him. And as Abelard waited, the staticked eye flickering into the blue error screen of the other, Noah realized his own were no longer straining against the orange flashing tendrils in the starscape.

Over Abelard's shoulder, through the spaceshield, there appeared to be no stars at all.

ELEVEN

"YOU SENSE IT TOO, then?" Abelard said. "It's here… it's *here*…"

In an instant he scooped up the device from the foyer floor and dashed back to the cockpit, stretching his Constructed Body to its limits craning his neck for a better view.

Even as Dayo and Frida's fingers coiled tighter into his arm, Noah was ten steps removed from the situation pressing in from all sides, a new depth of numbness that not only deadened his fear, but the capacity to do anything but watch it all unfold from where he stood. The rest of the crew spoke around him in a garbled distortion. His head throbbed, each pulse cresting higher than the last until he was ready to sink to the floor and let the aneurysm pluck him from the ship. But Dayo and Frida hadn't left him, and what words did make it through the miasma were Frida's, dipping into every swear she knew, and then Savannah was smacking him on the forehead.

"Come on," she said, pen held in her teeth. "Frida's got a porthole in her bunk."

Frida had taken the room at the far end of the hall, opposite Abelard, and the porthole overlooked the tip of the *Amihaf*'s bow. The bunks were never designed to hold more than three people at a time, and accommodations would not be made in the face of an emergency. They crowded around the piles of clutter dotting the floor, stared anywhere but the clumsy crocheted mushrooms acting as bookends on the shelves, and bit their tongues against the blank gaze of the worn teddy bear tucked under the comforter.

No one wanted to take point at the porthole. They pushed Noah forward.

The *Amihaf*'s second level afforded a small advantage in perspective— twenty feet could be swallowed by the galaxy in an instant—but crouching below the window allowed him to spot a meager speckling of stars beyond the leviathan's blackout, and the same couldn't be said when the attention tilted down. Though the data was vague at best, the tension along Irene's shoulders rattled loose—all of which, they figured, was a good sign.

"How far is that good going to take us?" Esmail murmured.

"One thing at a time," Quinn said, adding something in a lower whisper, inaudible. Whatever it was only distressed Esmail further; Quinn removed them both from the tangle of bodies at the porthole, conversation fading.

Again Noah bent down to study the visible stars; he focused on a brighter, yellow-white blip, the lowest one of the bunch, and squinted at the vast swathe of black below it for any sign of movement. A shift in the contours of the void, the slightest crest of the body blocking a stray ray of light, anything —but the view was remarkably consistent. Every assumption he'd made about the leviathans across his academic career was rearranging itself by the second. Remaking itself entirely.

"But you're still sick!"

Esmail's outburst turned all of their heads away, back inside the ship, Noah's knees tipping him to the floor.

"Darling—"

"You are. You are. It's still in your eyes. It's…" He grabbed Quinn's hand, gentle, and turned it palm up. Violet colored the deepest creases, branching out like tributaries of a river.

"One thing at a time. One thing," Quinn said, pointing through the porthole, "and then the next."

"But—"

"You feel fine, right? Yeah?" When he nodded, Quinn continued, "It's in your gums."

Dayo was between them before she had the chance to finish swearing. One look into Esmail's mouth, and the toe of her boot rammed into the bedside table. The tablet sitting at the edge slid toward the bed as she hissed in pain.

"Are you okay?" Esmail asked.

"I… yeah, Esmail… I'm all right." She looked to him, then to Quinn, then back again, and her face fought against whatever gravity urged it to collapse.

"Noah," Irene muttered beside him. "Do you have any idea of… anything?"

He bit into his tongue to block out the instinct to shrug helplessly. That was never any use. A set of steady breaths steered him from the stifling numbness, closer to where he could think more clearly.

"If we can get Abelard out of the cockpit," he said slowly, "then we might be able to fly far enough away to take a turbolight vector out of here."

"'Out of here' meaning where?" asked Irene.

He sighed. "Home?"

Outside the ship, something rumbled abyssally low, digging into his marrow.

"Ushuaia Station, at least," he added.

"I can calculate that. Room for error and all," Irene said.

With a modicum of direction, they were able to function at a base level of competence, the smothering black encroaching from the porthole merely one of several factors that needed consideration. While Irene sat against the wall to run the numbers, Savannah and Frida tore through the room for anything that had a chance of overtaking a ConBod.

"We have crates of ship repair lasers in the cargo hold," Quinn said, barely jumping out of the way in time as Frida dove to check under her cot. "Might not be anything else that could do the job."

"We're already banking on him being too caught up in that thing to eavesdrop on us here," said Noah. "Is it really such a good idea to sneak down the stairs?"

"Stairs are loud." Esmail's words were warped with his cheek stretched out by the end of Dayo's pen. "How's it looking?"

Dayo sighed. "For now? Not bad. But Quinn does have a point. Prana Technologies doesn't skimp on materials."

"*But...*" Quinn said. "It's risky. Miss, and you could fry mimeo wiring... blow a hole to the vacuum."

Candidates piled up at the end of Frida's bed—a shelf pulled out from the bookcase, a wrinkled old boot with its steel toe still caked in Nethunsan mud, a brick of a clothbound text on Terrestrial mushrooms with all the paint lost from the embossing.

"Put that one back," Frida sniped. "It's heavy but it's worth more than this ship."

Quinn snorted. "That's not true."

The pointed sigh caught in her throat. "Sentimentality is hard to measure. Still not considering it."

Toward the rear of the circle around the bed, Noah surveyed the room for anything they could have overlooked. Like the rest of the bunks, Frida's was mostly bare; the *Amihaf* hadn't made enough stops for anyone to start pocketing trinkets for decor.

"The bathroom," Noah murmured.

The door, at a right angle to the porthole's wall, stood ajar. He elbowed it open and stared up at the thick metal rod spanning the cubby of a shower—a thick metal rod with visible screws already wobbled a bit loose.

"Anyone have a screwdriver on hand? Or something similar?"

The others paused, turned in unison.

Savannah frowned. "What?"

"Obviously," said Frida, skirting between Dayo and Irene toward the bedside table drawer. "Phillip's head?"

Soon the shelf and boot had been swept off the bed, replaced by the rod. They stared down at it in silence.

"It's a bit short," said Irene.

"You have a better option lying around?" said Frida.

"It's not that. It's…" She picked it up at one end, stretching her arm out to its full length. "Abelard's tall, so he's got reach."

"And?"

"You of all people have never been in a fight before?" Quinn said with a laugh.

"I think we're all losing track of what's right outside *our fucking ship*," Savannah said. The words all crashed together, racing to the end, punctuated by the furious clicking of her pen. "Anyway—Quinn's tallest, but Quinn's just been sick and who knows when that's going to pop back up, because it already did once and that's precedent, so then it's just me or Irene and I don't want to volunteer anyone but also you can see what kind of state I'm in so do with that what you will." She gave a pained smile, glancing down to her shoes.

"Obviously no one is facing him alone." Esmail startled as all eyes landed on him. "Oh. Was it not obvious? Numbers matter. And there aren't rules against passing the rod between us."

Dayo frowned. "Aren't any rules at all."

"Well, that too," he said, hands bunching in and out of fists just under his chin. "At least that we know of."

They each took their turn to saunter down the spiral staircase, one slat down at a time, knees creaking at the sluggish pace meant to mute the metal's own brand of whining. Noah led the way, followed by the rest of the crew in ascending height order—except for Irene, armed with the rod.

They spread out around the edges of the foyer, creeping closer toward the center, and then toward the cockpit, as Irene approached, crouching, where Abelard stood. At each step she eased the rod over her head, primed to strike.

"...what a terrible, joyful hour!" His voice, more discordant, scraped against Noah's eardrums. "A terrible, joyful thing!"

Irene rose, pulled the rod another inch over her head—

"Dr. Tuuluq, please."

Abelard gestured to the spaceshield, the warped concave reflection.

Irene slammed the metal into the back curve of his skull with a startled wail —a dull clang, quick footsteps, and Noah threw himself out of the way, sliding back on a shoulder blade. He scrambled to his feet to see Abelard and Irene both gripping the rod, him rushing her back against skidding soles toward the service hall outside the lab. Where she'd made contact, a slab of synthetic skin had peeled away to bronze. The rod itself was merely dented.

"I'm quite disappointed," Abelard said. "So many smart people in my crew, and your best plan for mutiny is little better than a circus act!"

Frida reached him first. She launched herself onto his back, scrabbling until she found footing around his hips, shoving up to throw a hand over the camera hole in his forehead. Her other arm braced around his neck, and she proceeded to bang her heel into his side. "You bloody fucking—"

"Dr. Wick, this is most unbecoming—"

"Why don't *you* unbecome, you—"

Even with her holds around his head, Abelard still knocked the back of his skull into her face. She crumpled to the floor with a hiss, clutching her head. Dayo ran to her side, and Irene used the momentary distraction to drop her grasp on the rod. She ducked under Abelard's arm, and he ran straight ahead into the wall on momentum alone.

He dropped the rod with a clatter, rotated to face them.

They'd all charged forward without much thought as soon as Frida collapsed, and in the lull, they had reshaped their assembly—Frida and Dayo at the back, Noah at the point.

"Something tells me," said Abelard, setting his clasped hands under his chin, "that you were a primary *artifex* in this, Noah."

More Latin, and no more space to wonder about those specific motives. "I don't know about 'primary.'"

"Oh, Noah, that hurts. That truly hurts me." His hands, still clasped, swung down to his waist. "I trusted you. I showed you who I really am."

Outside the ship droned that skeleton-humming wave, too low to register as a proper sound.

Noah held up his hands, palms forward, and willed them not to shake. "We're just scared."

"Of what?" In any other moment, far away from here, the question would have read as sincere.

"The leviathan. You."

"Me?"

"Your actions have endangered us. Why shouldn't we be scared?"

"We have a plan, you know." Abelard stepped closer, arms open in a peace offering.

Noah didn't need to look over his shoulder to know the rest of the crew had backed away, further into the foyer. "Who—"

"Don't feign ignorance. I know you know FDL." But he tripped over the filename, not as an acronym, calling it *fuh-duh-luh*, a familiarity in the way the Constructed voice box hugged the syllables to his chest. "You know him."

"That's not you."

"My body made him. Why wouldn't he be me? And he's been in the ship for so long, cradling all of you against the perilous depths of the vacuum. You know…" Abelard took another step forward; behind Noah the crew retreated another few feet, and he swallowed the instinct to follow suit. "One might say that you owe FDL quite a lot."

Hushed murmuring rose from the crew. A lump closed up his throat—the next line wasn't coming to him, no sketch of grand strategy to guide the chess pieces. The lump widened. He couldn't swallow it down. One breath, the next, and the next, and he resolved to just try to keep them all alive for the moment to follow, on and on for however long it took to wrench them free.

"That may be," he said, strained. "Let's start over. Maybe… you and I can take the instrument you dreamed up, and everyone else can pull back as they see fit."

Abelard grinned, nodded, and before he had the chance to latch his hands around the device, abandoned by the wall, the other six of the crew scattered. Neither Esmail nor Irene made a break for the cockpit; it was a foolish hope.

But it wasn't to the cockpit where Abelard led him—instead, the pinhole camera between the error-blue eyes settled on the airlock.

The airlock was a tricky thing, unused on the mission thus far aside from the unfortunate incident with Tristan. The G-suits tucked into the wall remained as crisp and new as the day they were packed in Cape Guacara. Scuff marks left by their boots lined the nearby edge where the exit ramp unfolded beneath it, the only sign of activity in the nook. And why should there have been? What part of their duties required spacewalks if the ship hadn't been damaged?

So when Abelard cranked the handle to open the internal door, Noah nearly fell backwards over his own feet to put distance between them.

"Oh, Noah…" Abelard said, his entire body sagging. "Do you really not trust me?"

He cleared his throat. "I just… don't like airlocks."

"You have nothing to fear. The vacuum seal cannot open without the internal door being secured. See?" He stepped over the threshold, gestured to the cramped box of a room. The top of his head barely had an inch of clearance. "Besides, it has the most marvelous view."

The wall straight ahead, behind Abelard, was fully transparent, floor-to-ceiling, aside from a thickly-reinforced central seam of metal where the vacuum seal released. He'd seen the exterior of the airlock plenty while they'd been on-planet, but it had been opaque from that side, and there'd been no reason to inspect the area from the small viewport on the internal door.

Abelard beckoned him forth again, and this time he followed, trying not to pay much attention to the flap of synthetic skin bouncing to the beat of his excitement. The excitement, that bit was familiar, and Noah allowed himself to sink into it, just a hair, just enough to keep himself on the closer side of functional.

"When we set out from Natocke Station," Noah said, "you physically couldn't bring yourself to remember your first encounter with a leviathan."

"*This* leviathan."

Noah nudged the comment aside. "What about now? Do you recognize this?"

"I do." His arms folded across his chest, holding the device closer. "He was protecting me then, FDL was. He knew I wasn't yet prepared."

There was nothing he could say to that, not in this fragile detente. There was, though, plenty to say to himself, admonishments traveling months into the past for not taking the alarms as seriously as they warranted.

"Can you believe this, Noah? I feel as though we haven't had a chance to truly bask in what this means—our theory, right before our eyes! Could you have ever imagined we would be standing before a leviathan when you came to my office that scorching August day?"

Only after focusing intently on the black blankness before them could Noah begin to perceive the shape of the creature, where part of it arced up and inside another expanse of it, where a section bulbed in a regular pattern, narrowed to a point. The distinction didn't require even a blink for it to slip away; if he breathed wrong, the narrow line of dark-dark-gray withered, no better than a figment of his imagination.

"I couldn't have dreamed this, no," said Noah. "But I want to live long enough for it to matter."

Abelard tutted under his breath. "Do you not think I have a plan?"

"Do you not think I have a right to be skeptical of it?"

The tutting continued. He extended his arms, let the mystery device roll down to his hands, where he offered it up to Noah. "Do you want to know what this is?"

"I think everyone onboard does." He waited, and Abelard kept up the stare with a clear expectation for another answer. "You said it could kill a leviathan, so… does it shoot a laser or something?"

"Close. To a degree. And I was oversimplifying things." He tilted his head in a wink-nod, just as Noah realized his voice had narrowed back to one pitch, the one he knew. "You see—after we spoke with the *Hathor*, I knew my hypothesis had merit. What had they done just before their own misfortune? Coordinated the exchange of the boy who knew plumbing. And then I—"

Abelard ran on, but it was as if everything around Noah had been muted.

Before Abelard disappeared, he'd only transmitted half of the lecture to Sichuan University.

The rolling series of alerts and pings as the *Amihaf* re-entered the range of the relays played in his head.

"Radio waves?" he said finally.

"Exactly! Look there." Abelard pointed toward the tapering section of the leviathan, specifically the four bulbs at each of the cardinal directions from where they stood in the airlock. The bulbs were just as black as the rest of the body, save for a narrow sheen of gray curving along the edges, a reflection. "How large do you imagine those are, the eyes? Large enough for radio waves to count in their visual spectrum, perhaps?"

"You already know, don't you?"

"Well…" He winced playfully. "Yes. Forgive me if I'm still toeing my professional role."

"You don't need forgiveness for that."

Noah stepped closer to the transparent wall, staring ahead even as Abelard's face tracked his movement, blurred in his peripheral vision. Something between the angle of those glaring blue lights of his eye displays and the concentration needed to further discern the shape of the leviathan revived the last dregs of his migraine. The aura remained at bay, but stray pulsing jabs ran between his temples and the bridge of his nose.

"I do have a genuine question," Abelard said. "So they see radio waves— what would a relay look like with all that data bundled up and zipping by at impossible speeds? A collection of photons?"

"So… actually a laser, maybe?" As soon as the thought was out of his mouth, Noah wanted to kick himself. He couldn't be lulled this far off course onto a path so familiar. Nothing good laid at the end and he still found himself playing along. "If it is, satcall transmissions probably have an enormous beam diameter. I can't imagine that would be… well, a common sight."

Abelard's fuzzy figure beside him nodded, fiddled with the device. "I'd say the biggest surprise of all is that a TerraCosmos vessel wasn't intercepted sooner. Or…" His vocal system articulated a sigh. "I suppose before a few years ago we would have had no way of knowing." He continued on about one of the several disasters in the earliest survey stages of Project Khepri, the second mission to the Teegarden system, how the crew of the third found metal scraps in orbit around both planets and in its own belt of a graveyard around the star itself.

"The point is, Noah," he said, "is that they're sensitive to it." His hand latched onto a lever along the side of the instrument, a solid clunk sounding as it landed on the opposite end. Nothing stuck or whined to alert at some defect along the lines of what Esmail and Savannah had hinted at.

Noah spun toward him, leaving just enough room to keep up a patchy veneer of calm. "What exactly did you say this thing was actually supposed to do again?"

"Oh, I didn't. Funny how none of you seemed to catch on… just assumed that it didn't work." He laughed, shrugging. "You should know they're upstairs planning a second mutiny on your behalf. It isn't going much better."

"What?"

All at once—Abelard's eyes lit up in a blank white, and the heel of his palm slammed against a button along the device's underside, and Savannah came tearing down the staircase shouting Noah's name with two shower rods in hand and some odd parcel tucked into the knapsack at her back.

There was a beat, a silence that gave its total attention to all the particular chords of the *Amihaf*'s engine. A beat, and the inner surface of the leviathan's four bulbs clenched into a silver, a mote of a pupil still visible on the topmost eye. Noah cursed at Abelard, at FDL.exe, at the missteps that brought them there. The leviathan's low rumble dug in further, shivering into Noah's teeth, the hormone implant against his pituitary gland, the bruised nerves inside his elbow. Savannah fell to one knee at the center of the foyer. Abelard sang his ecstasies of discovery.

And the leviathan—a great maw at the center of the four eyes opened, a molten gold light gusting through the airlock and into the ship.

Noah's feet lifted from the floor.

He saw black.

When Noah came to, he was sandwiched between two terrible slabs of heat.

The deep bake of earth laid below, while above the humidity and sun pressed down with all the force typically attributed to dramatics. It was the atmosphere of Camp Ilunga, of Rassawek—but not quite. The particulars varied across the axes at play, rendering the almost-familiar almost alien.

He sat up, and immediately everything was wrong.

For one, he was on Earth.

And then there was the issue of his body.

That, at least, he was going to avoid thinking about as long as possible.

He had been deposited in what looked like a massive park—trees thick with age dotted the lawns between walking paths that connected a rail station on the far river bank and the massive, columned entrance of the building at the center of it all. Behind him stood pale crumbling plinths of concrete carving out a gentle arc, striping the bicycle thoroughfare at their bases in lengths of shadow.

He stared ahead at the building, wracking his memory: the long stretch of the facade facing him, the five stories of windows, the obtuse angle at which the next wall created the corner. The air shimmered in the heat, or—

One warbling opened a pocket to a cracked tarmac and the chugging spittle of early aircraft. As soon as Noah put a name to the sound, it vanished.

"What the fuck?"

Ice gripped at his chest despite the heat. The pitch was too high. So: no talking, either.

He went to hug his knees to his chest—reconsidered, and instead dug the heels of his palms into his eyes until they sparkled, until they could absorb the scream he was biting back, blood-sharp.

One breath, and another. One moment, then the next.

As the sparkling receded, the scene ahead of him twitched again to asphalt gridded with white paint, to a hoof-pitted oval scented by damp hay and animal musk—and finally to a tall figure offering shade, the sun casting its halo around the ends of a loosely-curled afro.

"*So* sorry to bother you, but you're the first person I've seen, and I'm in a bit of a situation—"

Noah knew that voice anywhere. "Savannah?"

"Wait a second." She knelt down to his level. "Holy shit. Noah… you too?"

He refused to pay any more attention to her face like this than was absolutely necessary; instead he focused on the worn knees of her pants crushing the grass. "The nightmare spared no one. Also—I don't want to—"

"Yeah, no. I agree."

She hopped up, hoisting him to his feet with a hand and a sharp tug. They placed themselves back to back, each of their hands laced together. Noah tipped his head against her spine, a further anchor as sweat dripped down the nape of his neck under his newly-long hair.

"Listen," she said with a sigh. "I don't want to shove the expert card in your face, but do you have any clue what the fuck is going on here?"

"I wish. I don't even know where on Earth this is supposed to be." He elaborated on the odd incongruent blips into his field of vision, and Savannah's lack of obvious surprise meant she'd faced something similar.

"It's Nacotchtank," she said finally. "I grew up in that building. My family had one of the units with a real window. Fourth floor on the best of the five sides, facing the river."

The humidity made sense, then. If Noah concentrated, he could smell the salt of the nearby ocean, feel the grit of sand in the dirt underfoot.

"So we could find your family?"

"Something tells me that's still out of reach."

He squeezed her hands, and she squeezed back, one sweaty palm against another. "Unfortunately, I don't know what else we can do aside from just standing here like this."

"How good are you at crab-stepping?"

Neither of them, as it turned out, was coordinated enough to not turn themselves into a spectacle. Had the park not been unnaturally empty, they would have attracted an audience on the concerned goodwill of strangers alone. Still: they never tripped or tilted so far off-balance to fall. They talked it through, even as Noah occupied a seeming falsetto and Savannah found the paths of her vocal training barely-worn.

"The yard always had something happening," Savannah said. She was leading them to the rail station, then onward to the building entrance. "I hate seeing it like this... a couple of neighbor kids taught me how to ride a bike just over there."

Her head tilted their combined frame off to Noah's right, toward the tree dominating that stretch of earth. There was the shade, the heat-blighted patches of yellowed grass, and in a particularly vivid circle of green there was another person, eyes angled toward the time-sanded obelisk rising tall across the river.

The crunch of Noah and Savannah's boots on gravel gave them away before they could introduce themselves first. The stranger's head swiveled back to them, holding a grin close to the chest until he could take in the full sight of their odd arrangement.

Once again there was a sense of familiarity. The stranger's grin grew, settling into the whole of his heavyset frame, the gold-tinged glow of his skin humming in the sun. "It's been so long since I've encountered another on this plane of things, much less two."

"So you're not lost?" Savannah said.

"Not in the sense you're thinking of."

Noah frowned. "In what sense, then?"

"Don't you recognize me? We've met." The stranger's grin spread wider, the white of his teeth gleaming under the midday sun.

The light fractured, cutting across the stranger's face in a steep diagonal, then jutting forth in a prism—the triangular side now inches from their noses, the adjoining facets shimmering and sheer and blooming with a starscape. And the stranger's face, so close now and split from the rest of him, turned sallow with a thick mushroom stalk craning out of his skull.

Two blinks, and the scene reverted.

"Jibril?" Savannah said, breathless.

"Surprise, I guess."

"I thought you didn't speak English."

"I... don't. Oh!" Jibril gazed around the yard, then back to Savannah, nodding thoughtfully. "Okay, yes. That makes sense... more sense than you two speaking impeccable Levantine Arabic. No offense."

"It's truer than you know," said Noah.

Jibril rubbed the end of his short mustache between his thumb and first finger, staring off at a collection of pigeons strutting around one of the more distant trees. A distinct line laid across the foliage, a border between the green and the bare, the dead side bearing scars of a lightning strike.

"This…" He waved toward the tree, the river. "I haven't been here or now before. Haven't had a reason to, you could say. Odd how they turned that into housing."

Against Noah's back, Savannah tensed, shifted. One of her hands left his, but only long enough to check her pockets—penless, undoubtedly.

"So," Noah said. "Are we not going to mention what happened a minute ago?"

Jibril frowned. "What do you mean?"

"The, uh—it was like something in the air broke? And you were here, and you were—"

"I didn't notice anything."

Noah pulled himself from Savannah's back just as she did the same, both to exchange one of the many questioning glances they'd perfected over the years. Their unspoken pact to perceive each other as minimally as possible in this state stood firm, but they plucked up the most important component pieces, excised the bits that never belonged.

So, no: Noah hadn't imagined it.

"I will say, though…" Jibril paused. He chewed at a hangnail on his thumb as he thought, and Noah suddenly longed to return to Nethuns and Camp Ilunga—but earlier, or in some other unfolding of events where Jibril hadn't become a xenomycology case study, whatever would have allowed them to know him without the hyphae carving through his brain.

"I will say," Jibril repeated," that if you're going to be traveling onward, you should expect some oddities and alterations. More than you've already encountered, is what I meant. I know those bodies aren't home to either of you."

They didn't return to their back-to-back arrangement, but Savannah still took Noah's closest hand in her own, squeezing so tight that Noah felt his pinky knuckle roll against its neighbor. Jibril grinned, and Noah returned it— and there was something else he wanted to say before they moved on, but behind Jibril, on the other side of a path, a dark shelled creature trailing a long stinger scuttled behind a tree. His balance wavered in the sticky heat, his foot scrambling to keep balance as he leaned, trying for a better look, and when his foot finally landed against the gravel, Nacotchtank had fizzled away.

Noah was alone.

He was alone, but the firm pressure of Savannah's hand remained. A jagged grid of gold and teal hemmed him in a cube. He glanced up—he saw himself hovering, his body contorted into some unnaturally steep arc, and then it wasn't himself. The body was of an older Asian man, hair sparsely streaked through with gray, his hand straining as it reached up toward some unknown. And then the unknown was another hand, followed into frame by Abelard, not yet bald. The scene froze before Abelard could reach the other man.

Chen Yuxuan. Alive and whole, but just barely.

One step forward, and the image dissolved.

Now he was outside, humidity clinging to his skin without the heat of high noon. Mountains darkened the northwest skyline. In the light straining through a second-story window, an even younger Abelard sat beside an equally younger Yuxuan, Mingyu across from them with her nose in a tablet. Their conversation flowed from Mandarin to English and back again, with pit stops in Wu, Hokkien, and—cued by the smirk curling Abelard's mouth—French. Yuxuan rolled his eyes, made a face with a finger hooked at the end of Abelard's chin; Mingyu raised an eyebrow, and Abelard's Mandarin fell past his teeth with careless tones.

He locked eyes with Noah across the distance.

The first thing Noah saw after the white specter clouded his vision was the warm mahogany of Savannah's eyes too close to his own. She was herself again, fully; a quick inventory revealed the same was true for himself.

"You with me?" she said.

"Yeah, yeah," he gasped, climbing to his feet. "Where did you go?"

"I was right here! *You* passed out as soon as we left—well…" Her head bobbed from side to side, chewing the wording. "As soon as Nacotchtank left *us*."

"Huh?—Oh."

The sun was setting over the Thames Bay, oranges wrapping around the spokes of islands dotting the water, ruined bits of history swallowed by its own hubris. Noah had never been to London, but he could hear the lapping of the waves nearby, around the corner of the building whose roof they'd taken as a perch, and the name of the neighborhood blipped into his head. *Tottenham.* Not that there was anything he could do with the information.

Across the street was a proud old residence, the centuries smudged across the stone as a badge of honor, a testament to its survival when so many others had not.

A window on the top floor swung open. A pane cracked with the timbre of old glass.

One tablet, and another, and a stack of books, and a ceramic blur of reds and browns flew past the sill—snapped, crumpled, shattered. They kept coming, with muffled shouts passing in waves behind the curtain of dark. They sat strewn across the sidewalk, into the road and its divot for the tramline. For a moment there was nothing, a nothing burst by the front door cracking into the ledge of the stoop.

Even buzzed short, even at this distance, the glaring shade of ginger humming over the new figure's skull could only belong to Frida.

"I hope they rebuild High Down just for Granddad and all his dirty money!" she screamed up to the open window. Her accent hadn't yet been cut through with Spanish and Quechua.

"She's just a baby," Savannah whispered.

Frida couldn't have been more than twenty years old. The way she held herself still latched onto the last peels of childhood yet to flake off, and the muttering echoing up to their rooftop as she salvaged her belongings was punctuated with more sniffles than swears.

"What is going on?" Noah wrenched his gaze up from the street. "We shouldn't be here—"

"Keep your voice down!" she hissed.

"Or what?" he said. "This isn't real! The leviathan is doing *something*—"

"Out of, I don't know, respect!"

When Noah turned back toward the street, the young Frida was staring back. She tapped the edge of her glasses—an electronically-augmented pair, he noted—and the green of her eyes swelled in the zoom.

"What are you doing here?" she called.

"What?" Savannah and Noah said in unison, peering over the edge of the roof.

"Both of you!" She shook the broken end of a lamp at them. "You're not supposed to be here!"

"Clearly, yeah," said Noah.

Grumbling, she tossed the lamp piece over her shoulder and into a bush. "Can you get back to the ship? It's going a little haywire, and Esmail isn't helping Irene fly the fucking thing—"

"Frida wait—" Savannah reached a hand down toward the street, not sparing a thought to the four stories between them, much less physics, dream or otherwise, that could have grabbed her by the collar to crack against the pavement. "Let us h—"

The world twisted itself up into black, unspooling into the pointed dry heat of Shiraz. The low skyline of the city spread out before him, and a halting English conversation had tucked into a nearby corner, shade-touched. Quinn and Esmail, new around each other.

"We need to go," Noah said.

Esmail laughed, full-bodied, and Quinn's hands rushed up to his jawline, kissing him against the warm stone wall, a first of many.

"How do we get back?" Noah gripped at Savannah's hand until she winced.

"I don't know—"

He saw Dayo struggling to hold an armful of comets all calling her name. Irene trying to weave a glowing thread of aurora around a spindle. He blinked again. Abelard was pressing his face into dry ice, a burning sort of cold; another blink, and he and Savannah strained to keep their last fingers hooked together on the edge of an event horizon. Another blink—

His head slammed back against the floor. All was silent, and then his hearing roared back, most of it carrying the sound of his clothes sliding over the TerraCosmos emblem in the foyer. As his eyes opened, a blur of browns butted in through the overhead lights, vague shapes he could identify as Dayo and Esmail, a hint of Quinn drifting behind them.

"*Alhamdulillah*, there you are."

"Ugh—where's Savannah?" Noah sat up, his vision swimming.

"She's fine," said Quinn. "Came to just before you did."

From the cockpit, Irene swore.

The hands holding him steady disappeared just as Dayo knelt in front of him, asking him to focus on the penlight, if this sort of thing had ever happened before, even once—

"What sort of thing?"

"Seizures," she said. "You and Savannah were both out at least a minute."

Closer to the cockpit, Quinn helped Savannah to her feet as Esmail rambled: the two-rod approach was supposed to be a distraction, a quick thing to draw Abelard into a more central part of the ship, and after Savannah had taken more than thirty seconds to signal for step two, that was when they found them.

"Just a minute?" Noah said. "Sixty seconds?"

"Yeah, why?"

"I…"

"Noah, what happened?"

Finally his vision stilled—he surveyed the foyer, where Esmail's rambling had shifted to Persian and shrunk to an audience of himself, where Frida sat pressed against the wall with nails digging into her scalp, where Quinn caught his eye with one that had rapidly clouded back up with violet.

"Where's Abelard?" He hastened to his feet, jellied knees pulling down to the floor on the first attempt. "He's still not—"

Without lifting her head from her knees, Frida pointed toward the airlock. The interior door had sealed shut, and a bald head with torn synthetic skin passed by the viewport. "Better to have him shut up in there than running around here, yeah?"

Her accent was the same as where he and Savannah had left it, wherever they'd gone; it seemed best not to mention it out loud.

"Noah." Dayo firmly placed herself between him and the airlock, squaring his shoulders to her so he had little choice but to meet her gaze. "What. Happened."

The border between plausible and the truly unbelievable fuzzed out into nothing. Here they were, still surrounded by a being of theory, still fresh from Jibril on Nethuns plucking knowledge out of apparent thin air. But something made him bite his tongue despite the insistent concern in Dayo's stare. Savannah could corroborate, unless he'd conjured up that version of her. Or Frida, but if Savannah had been a figment, the odds were atom-thin for anyone else. *It's nothing, just say it's nothing, a weird flash of images that left you quicker than dreams evaporating in the morning. She's not going to believe you and she's going to get angry and call you crazy for hours until it's midnight and you still have a test to study for—*

No, no. That wasn't right.

He came back to himself—again, a shorter distance than before.

"I think I understand how Jibril knew what he knew," he said, deliberate with every syllable. In the corner of his eye, Savannah nodded.

Dayo frowned, a new layer of worry sealing over her brow. "What does that mean?"

"Do you... um." The proper wording fought against his hands. "Are comets a significant thing for you?"

Immediately she put another few inches of space between them, eyes wide. "Fuck off."

"I—I'm sorry—"

"That's something between me and Ikemba. How—"

"It was really abstract! It wasn't…"

He couldn't breathe. Within the *Amihaf*'s foyer was also the condo in Erie, flashes of moments cutting across the left side of Dayo's body. Flashes that layered on top of each other, amplified into a single point white-hot with all the fury and hurt those walls absorbed across the years.

Then it was over. There was just Dayo, the distance she had closed between them, the hands at his elbows, the frantic heart slowing in his chest. "What are you talking about?"

"What do you mean?"

"You were going on about—you weren't making sense."

"Check him, Dayo!" Frida called from the corner. "Check 'em both! We're all goners."

She didn't bother with the med bay except to fetch the hemograph. Noah and Savannah stood side by side as Dayo took blood samples, peered into their mouths and ears and noses, rubbed against lymph nodes. The hemograph chirped, twiddled its figurative thumbs.

The blood tests ran longer than Dayo's exam, though he and Savannah didn't dare retreat to a perch on the wall. Noah looked toward the cockpit, toward Irene and her desperately-stretched stance trying to cover all possible bases at once, her palms slamming buttons and wrapping around levers while the console screeched and whined. The spaceshield still beheld the leviathan-born void.

"Nothing's fucking working!" she shouted. "If Abelard's got his fingers in the walls…" Her voice faded, a denser thing held close in her mouth.

The hemograph lit up with results, and Dayo pulled the grin onto her face as if she were stretched stubborn taffy, some flavor that turned Noah's gut. "Okay… okay," she said. "This is fine."

The ship shuddered.

"Dayo…"

He couldn't bear to keep eye contact as the grin melted. Back at the cockpit, the slice of the spaceshield visible through the doorway revealed patches of stars breaking through the black. He was starting to be able to discern the leviathan's movement in all that apparent nothing, ripples where the faintest flash of charcoal flexed and pulled like a muscle. He followed the path of one, lost sight of it when the creature's head loomed in from the right.

Its eyes were still pinched silver. The seam of its great yawning began to split, and gold like starlight shot ahead, spilled over its lips with a false gravity. Again, his bones hummed. There was a pattern to it this time, wasn't there? He stepped toward the cockpit for a better angle.

"Get down!" Irene shouted.

Noah hit the floor; Dayo had all but tackled him. Her cardigan shielded his eyes but the glaring maw-beams shone through the weave, orange against the back of his eyelids.

He counted as the rays burned his pupils to an ache, as he tried to bury his face into the crook of Dayo's neck for a mote of relief. On the other side of the foyer, Savannah whined, a slow ascending pitch ready to collapse into tears.

He counted to fourteen before it subsided, a light switch of a contrast.

"Hey, hey..." Quinn murmured from the other corner. "Savannah, it's all right."

"Where's her pen?" Noah called, but it was swallowed by Dayo's cardigan.

She rolled off of him, and they helped each other to their feet. "You didn't hit your head too hard, did you?"

"No, I'm okay. Thanks," he added. Just behind her heels was Savannah's pen, likely where it fell from her pocket the first time the leviathan had blasted the ship. He almost tripped over his ankles to return it to her, folding it into her empty hand as he slid on his knees the final few inches to her side.

"Sav?" He squeezed at her elbow. She hadn't tucked the pen between her teeth, instead just holding it against her lips, the dip above her chin. "Sav, you with us?"

Esmail spoke to her, then him, in rapid Persian, something rhyming, with a lilt of a song he wasn't keen to actually sing. Maybe another poem, in its entirety this time. Either way: Quinn reassured Noah that she would be fine, and Dayo was calling him back, the hemograph in hand; and caught between these two poles, once more he focused on the cockpit.

Irene.

Her shoulder blades stuck out, pressing up against her shirt as her hands dug into the seat backs for support. Her breathing hissed between grinding teeth.

Noah approached with tender steps. "Anyone check on you lately?"

"How much do you think it matters?" She drew in one long breath, her chest swelling to the upper limit of her lungs, and then she could finally look him in the eye. "I get us out of range of the leviathan and then what? What does Abelard attempt next?"

Something on the console chimed, demanding attention. She reached for it, her sleeve tugging up her arm and past the edge of a purple blot.

"Irene, your arm—"

His palm landed on the ball of her shoulder. They locked eyes as her hand switched the lever of the screaming monitor of the moment. Time slowed, molasses. The view of her fractured before him, twitch-tilted ninety degrees and back again with the sound of breaking glass.

The wall with the broken navigation computer had disappeared; instead the harsh lines of TerraCosmos engineering melted away into a gray sky and scrubby grassland dotted with shadows too distant to properly identify. A face stepped into view, a woman with Irene's nose and the same hold of her mouth when trying to remain stoic.

Irene stepped toward the opening, the reel it held playing in a choppy slideshow. She reached her hand toward the fuzzy boundary between the ship and the apparent Earth, the steely Nunavut sky close at hand instead of trillions of miles away.

"Hey." He rested a hand on her elbow, gentle, and she tensed beneath it. "Let's not—"

"Let's not what? Let me go."

"I'm not holding—"

"She's right *there*—"

The shimmering image had locked, a freeze-frame on her cousin as she stared down someone or thing unseen. Her voice rang in his head, mostly in Inuktitut, but the anger translated. It sang in his bones and made his ears run hot, scalding, hotter and hotter until Irene rushed forward. Noah caught her, just barely, and if he'd had an ounce more of his wits about him, he could have said something about this moment before them only playing at truth, a mirage.

Irene's fingertips were a breath away from the edge. "What can it hurt?"

He almost didn't hear her, as small as she spoke. "Irene… Savannah and I apparently both had seizures. Do you want a seizure?"

"You don't know—"

"Nobody knows anything! All I want is for everyone to make it home as intact as possible!"

Without warning, Irene stopped straining toward the gap, and Noah crashed back into the wall behind him. The edge of some display screen dug into a fresh bruise on his skull, a dull thing turned sharp. When he refocused his vision, Irene had turned from staring at the closing pocket over her shoulder to the lavender twists of smoke fizzling out over the fingertip that nearly made it through.

"You think we're going home?" Her eyes flicked to his from the thinning wisps. "You really think that?"

"You don't?"

She rubbed away what remained on her fingers, and then tugged down the collar of her shirt. Along the underside of her collarbone was a damp purple-black film that flaked off at the slightest touch, curling like mildew.

"Showed up while you were keeping Abelard busy."

"Irene…"

At that, she rushed him, grabbing his hand hard enough to rival Abelard. She twisted it so his fingertips stood right in front of his eyes. "We've all got it! Quinn and Frida and Esmail, and me and you and Savannah—Dayo didn't get a chance to give you your reading, did she?"

She kept on, increasingly erratic, jumping between languages too quickly for Noah to follow. Her grip tightened; Noah's vision narrowed, down and down to a point, the pale little half-moons at the quick, tendrils of purple carving out a river basin. Branch after branch, to the thinnest rivulets.

"When...?"

"Does it matter?" Irene was crying. "Try to tell me it matters."

"Timeline aside, all right? Timeline aside." His whole body rested airily on his skeleton, defying any sense of weight, and it sent the words rolling up his throat into the air, jittering. "Why would this keep us from going home?"

"Even if we can get out of range of this thing and hop a vector back, they'd never let us off the ship."

She was right. TerraCosmos quarantined returning ships for far, far less.

"We can still try," he said.

"One thing at a time." She shrugged out of his loosened hold, returning to the console and its array of lights blinking unfamiliar colors. "Abelard's still got the flight system locked, so we couldn't make the jump anyway."

There was more he had to say, but he couldn't render any of it audible, not now, so he heeded the cue. In the foyer, Dayo was guiding Savannah and Quinn through taking a blood sample with the hemograph, holding the bunched sleeve of her cardigan up past her elbow with the soft creased skin open and waiting.

Esmail sprang to his feet, landing beside Noah only to falter with what to do, opting after a moment to loop their arms together. The particular hold pressed the tablet in Noah's pocket against a corner of his joints. "Is she okay?"

"As much as any of us are, I guess."

"Good… well, not good, but…" He sighed. "I heard Irene talk about going home."

Noah glanced his way, caught his warm brown eyes, and he couldn't read anything there except an invisible hand, another connection to anchor them as the leviathan wove an eddy around the ship.

"Of a sort, yeah," said Noah.

"I've been thinking of a section of a poem." Esmail recited the couplet, the meter and rhyme bridging the language barrier. "Right—in English it would be… 'I'm drunk and you're crazy, who will take us home?'"

"Yeah?"

"Mawlana and Shams never had to face a vacuum leviathan, though," he said. "So… it makes sense that they're so calm about it."

Noah could only nod.

"I think it's the right question to ask at a time like this," said Esmail.

"What, 'who will take us home?'"

"Mhm."

Across the foyer, whatever reading the hemograph returned was unwelcome; Noah played back Irene's list of the crew who had been infected, and Dayo was the only name left off. So the list likely needed an update, and the list was moot.

"The only people who are going to take us home *are* us," Noah muttered.

"What was that?"

Everything in the ship rushed to cut off his reply.

Irene, shouting from the cockpit that the lock on the ship controls had lifted.

The grumbling hum from the leviathan, clenching at his throat.

The lab, draped in a mosaic of downtown Erie like shattered stained glass.

The floor underfoot, bucking them all into the air.

As their bodies flailed with twisting limbs desperate to find purchase that didn't exist, Noah's stomach flipped, then settled. The rush upward against gravity slowed and slowed, and there was the singular moment when he hung motionless, hovering, and the whole galaxy stood still. It was in that moment Noah spotted Abelard in the airlock's viewport, ranting to himself in a fast clip that Noah couldn't understand over the cresting bout of tinnitus.

What did leak through the thick door, though, was the tone, split again into mechanical stacked voices alien to Abelard's throat, Constructed or not.

Noah fell. Air whistled past his ears for those few short feet loud enough to drown it out, and for a moment he glanced back to the tilework of Erie in the corner, a jagged edge cutting down the middle of Gerard Starbuck's disdainful face.

He hit the ground with a wheezy punch of breath coughing up his tongue. Alarms blaring from all sides, screeching terrible things that could only spell a handful of words, none of them good. Irene was still shouting, this time for them to get to the crash seats in the cockpit's antechamber. She had one hand on the yoke, another urging the rest of them forward; Quinn, Frida, and Dayo hoisted each other past the threshold, and Noah tried to regain his bearings, but his ankle was sprained, and the bruised nerve at his elbow sent half his fingers cold and useless.

And beside him: Esmail, curled as small as he could go, heaving, hands over his ears, eyes squeezed shut, praying or reciting a poem or maybe a mix of the two. Maybe it was all blending together under the pressure of his palms against his temples.

"Esmail... Esmail." He reached to touch his shoulder, decided against it. "Hey, come on..." He knelt close, lowered his head as best as he could as the ship shuddered and wailed around them. "We've got to get us both into one of those seats, okay?"

Esmail's recitation continued, uninterrupted.

"Noah!"

He sat up. Savannah was headed toward them both as quickly as her legs could carry her over the tilting floor. "What are you doing?" he said. "Go strap in—"

"Fuck off, let me help." She slid the last stretch on her knees, murmuring to Esmail as Noah readied himself on the other side.

Something slammed into the *Amihaf*'s starboard side, quickly corrected by Irene at the helm. "It's not that I can't pilot this thing, but I'd like some help!" she yelled.

"Hey—" That was Quinn, and Noah looked up just in time to catch him unbuckling himself and moving toward the cockpit. "He'll get here when he gets here—"

Another slam, this time against the hull. A series of sharp snaps and pops rode the crests of the sirens right into their eardrums.

Esmail's recitations narrowed to a single word, but one of his hands latched around Savannah's, fingers woven together, and he let himself be guided first upright to his knees, and then to standing.

"You good?" she asked.

"Sure... yeah, yes," Esmail said, shaking his head. His left hand still covered an ear, better that than nothing, and he and Savannah only made it three steps toward the cockpit before turning back to Noah.

"Just give me a minute," he said. "I think I want to—"

"Noah." It was only one word, two syllables, but Savannah layered years' worth of warnings in it all the same. "Whatever it is—"

"Just get you both secured, all right?"

Commotion rose from the bow-end of the ship, and then Frida's voice vaulted over all of it: "Don't *tell me* you're doing what I think you're doing, Starbuck!"

Savannah and Esmail retreated, leaving him alone in the foyer, fists clenched hard enough to bury his nails in the barely-clotted cuts in his palms. He waited, and slowly, wincing, Dayo and Frida peered around the edge of the antechamber entrance where they'd strapped into their seats.

"What are you so afraid of me doing?" he said.

"There's no way to save all eight of us." The set of Frida's mouth warned against any argument.

He met both of their gazes, then turned toward the airlock.

Abelard last stared Noah down through the filter of error, the grating blue of code dragged down by malware. No human had malware, not in the most literal, one-to-one sense. Illness, parasites, its own processes turning on itself, yes. And maybe the accidental generation of FDL.exe rendered it closer to some Constructed version of cancer, and maybe it was another, wholly new thing; but it couldn't fully erase Abelard as he had inhabited the Body made for him as Njord Station flung around its orbit.

The glitching web covering the lab had shifted, leaving no errant eyes staring through the bridge there—yet the weight remained, and Noah tossed aside the growing protests from the bow as he navigated the bucking rolls of the floor threatening to drag the bruise on his skull a few hues darker.

"NOAH."

Irene. Her voice stretched high enough to break, and it pulled him to a halt.

"Finally," she said. "Obviously no one can stop you, but—ten minutes. You've got ten minutes, and then I'm venting the airlock."

He nodded, but she'd already returned her attention to the spaceshield, the navigation around the innermost wrappings of the leviathan, hoping that they wouldn't encounter the head.

The ship jolted, and Noah stumbled into the airlock's inner door. The rim of the viewport dug into his cheekbone.

"Abelard. *Abelard.*"

"Dr. Starbuck! You've returned!" He cracked the door open, his Body straddling the threshold while one hand remained latched on a wall handle in the airlock itself. It was a lean that put a great deal of faith in his shoulder's engineering.

"You don't have to do this, okay? We're going to get out of here. There's a crash seat with your name on it."

"What are you… no, no, Dr. Starbuck!" Every time he said his name, his voice split into more discrete parts, a clatter of machinery, only to condense back to three or four layers. "No, I never had the chance to tell you about part *two.* The instrument was only meant to attract and maintain its attention so at the precisely right moment, I could end it."

"What does that mean? What is that supposed to mean? What are *you*, like *this*, going to do to something like *that*?"

"What's the fun in spoiling the surprise?"

One of his eye displays stuttered like a wink, flicking between the blue error screen and dead gray glass.

"Can you really call it cutting edge," Abelard said, "if no one bleeds?"

Noah's palms stung as if they could hear those words themselves. "We can get you help."

"Whatever for?"

Even before his eyes started to sting, he heard his father muttering right into his ear. *If you're going to be a man, you need to learn not to cry.* A sudden pressure lit into his upper arm, just beyond the border of the bruise; he glanced down on instinct and found his father's disembodied hand latched there, collared by the sleeve of the navy suit he only wore for funerals.

"Dr. Starbuck?"

The *Amihaf* bumped and groaned around them, and hot tears spilled down his face, jostled free.

"Dr. Starbuck…"

Only two layers split his voice now. That was something. That could be something—

But when he glanced back at his eye displays, there was still the error and the excerpts of its warning text, and the other eye had dimmed to little more than a single crackle of power sputtering against all hope.

"When I heard you'd come back, even after Abraham brought up this mission…" Noah said. "Part of me still assumed there would be a future. We would fly back to Earth and both resume our positions at the xenosciences department, and… it wouldn't be like it was before, since we'd be colleagues, but we could still pick up where we left off. We could keep working on the leviathan theory and having meetings in our stuffy little offices…"

Abelard's face remained blurry no matter how quickly Noah tried to blink it all away. It obscured the worst parts—his position in the airlock, the dead half of his eyes, the bits of synthetic skin that had ripped past that initial tear—but he could pretend. Imagination only needed the tiniest germ to tangle kudzu into an autonomous knot of a thing, pressing and pressing and pressing until it forced its own kind of acceptance. Here, Noah could say the blurriness came from sweat. Rassawek was notoriously hot, after all. So they could be in Rassawek, the peak of summer; and if Noah's stomach clenched, it wasn't from a fear for his life, but hunger. Lunch was upon them, and they'd traipsed to the corner off-campus for bagel sandwiches amid gaggles of undergrads.

"We still can," he added, quieter.

There was a moment where Abelard simply stared down at him, dangling his smile between sad and something else Noah couldn't identify or didn't dare to.

"It can't be allowed to live after what it's done," said Abelard. "It ruined me, I'm—I see how you look at me, at us… FDL has revealed to me how to fix it. He's a prophet, you know. He is! Don't look at me like that!" His face crumpled in time with his fraying vocals.

"It's not a prophet. It's malware."

"Even if he is, wouldn't that justify this more? The only reason I'm living like this is because of this monster. Don't I owe myself that?"

Noah tried to step forward, but the phantom hand of Gerard Starbuck squeezed harder, held him back. The vision had materialized more of his arm, now halfway to the elbow, stained with the scent of his aftershave. "But is it what you owe Yuxuan, his memory?"

Abelard's unseeing eyes showed no recognition at the name. It didn't have to be like this. Nothing was completely lost where a choice still had room to breathe.

"You can't disappear again," Noah said. "You do owe me that."

His Constructed Body appeared to take in a life-giving breath. His eye displays returned to the setting that had greeted him in that conference room on Natocke Station, a first contact after the gaping vacuum of loss. And his smile now had none of the questionable undertones twitching under the machinations of FDL.exe.

"Noah… I—"

Metal crunched—not outside the ship where some limb of the leviathan slammed against them, but closer. The inner door to the airlock had clanged shut. Through the viewport, Noah found Abelard balanced on the very tips of his boots, head flung back far past the range of any organic body, the arm that had anchored him to the wall handle a tangle of bronze plating webbed through a torn shirtsleeve.

Ahead, on the other side of the airlock's seal, in the sea of starless black, was the ring of the leviathan's silver eyes.

When Noah tried to sift through the details of the moment later, he would pour over this series of nanoseconds the most—after the airlock vented, before the universe plucked the battered Constructed Body from the safer confines of the *Amihaf*. The vacuum was an unforgiving but not instantaneous force. In one terrible, brief instant, Noah was met with a head tilted back to its normal resting state with a skin-rippling grin readying itself for rapture.

He shone against the leviathan's background at first. Head over foot, white shirt and skin, gleaming bronze.

Noah flinched away as the great gorge began to open, pinches of gold breaking through in narrow beams, falling from the gaps of its lips in globs. His heart pounded in his ears, his temples, all the way down to his toes. Even shielding his eyes, near-migraine flashes of gold and indigo popped across his vision.

There was nothing he could do.

No—there was nothing he could do but watch.

He could play witness as Abelard Cousteau was reduced to a silhouette in a sea of gold and swallowed behind the maw forever.

His whole body shook trying to stay vertical. "You said I'd have ten minutes!" He didn't dare move from where he stood. As the airlock resealed itself, he spotted Abelard's hand still wrapped around the handle where the rest of his Body had ripped free. "Irene, you said it would be *ten minutes*!"

Another jolt rocked the ship. Beyond the airlock, across the whole of the port side, sprinkles of the leviathan's golden refuse remained. Noah waited for the kick into someplace else, a hallucination to splice a prism of a foreign starscape through his ribs and into the foyer. Nothing. Nothing except the gold winking out, and the silver of the leviathan's closest eye ebbing back to the edge.

"Noah, please!" Savannah's voice broke. "Irene's about to jump us out of here!"

"It's not so immediate," she said, "but—fuck, okay, yes it is—"

So Noah turned toward the bow.

Or: he tried to.

A hand was still attached to his arm—his father's hand, now extending to a shoulder, a torso, the rest of his body. Gerard Starbuck loomed over him, unnaturally tall.

"I'm no taller than I've ever been," the apparition said. "Of course you've forgotten. You haven't seen us in ages."

"Let me go. Please." Noah's voice shrank in his father's shadow. "It's—so much has... I—"

"'So much has,'" he said in a mocking falsetto. "So much has *what*, Noah?" His father's grip yanked him sharply forward. The prismed wall of the lab rushed to meet them, and then they were standing on the shore of Lake Erie.

"I hope you don't treat your colleagues with this kind of disrespect. Use your words."

If Noah clenched his teeth any harder, they would have cracked.

"Of course," Gerard said. "Nothing! Christ, you never learn. And I tried my best… I may have been hard on you, but you brought it on yourself."

Between their feet on the sand appeared the condo's welcome mat, Noah's empty duffel bag sprawled on top, half inside out—he knew that particular day. Coming home from school, a week from seventeen, hyping himself up to finally tell his parents he was trans. He'd seen the bag. Froze, remembered the state of the dishes. Next week, he could tell them next week—

"I didn't deserve it," said Noah. He stared beyond them both, to the lake lapping at the shore. His voice was still so small.

"I am your father." He yanked Noah up, forcing him to meet his eyes. "I was doing what was best."

"No you weren't—"

"Grow up. What, are you going to vent me too? Just like you vented your precious teacher?" Under the thicket of his beard, his mouth ticked up in a sneer. "If I go next, will you promise to let your plant friend go next? Sidney, Shiloh, whatever his name is—"

"Fuck you."

"I—how *dare* you—"

Noah strained every muscle in his body so tensely that he was sure something would rip. His next *fuck you* unraveled into a scream as he wrenched Gerard off his feet, fighting to keep his balance as the apparition's very real weight yanked him in tow. The hold on his arm broke as they both hit the damp, packed sand, and Noah rolled an extra step of distance between them.

Gerard leered from where he laid but did not move.

"Do you need me to say it again?" Noah stood slowly, brushing sand from his knees.

"You've always been a coward," Gerard said with a laugh.

The world around him faded into a void before it could rise to more than a single chuckle.

"No! No, you don't get off that easily!" He shouted more, repeating himself, repeating fragments, repeating nothing but a single peal of a note scraping his throat raw in the dense pocket of nothing. No echoes, no edges, just his perfectly-illuminated hands against the surrounding blackness.

He turned on his heel, preparing to run for it, just for the sake of trying something—but he wasn't alone. He turned, and his nose brushed against a surface of rock, warm like the Rassawek sidewalks in a summer twilight, extending endlessly above and below the plane on which he stood. He reached a hesitant hand out. Just before his palm flattened against it, the rock zipped away, still gargantuan, but Noah could take the whole of it in, just not all at once.

A planet.

A tangle of black with four silver eyes writhed over the crest of the northern pole.

"I almost approached you the first time you passed through, with your friend, but I thought better of it. The weather here is nicer."

Noah jumped, swiveled around looking for who spoke. There was no one, just more void enveloping him and the distant, hovering planet, until he looked down beside him.

The black sheen of their body stood out against the backdrop, the domed shell and long spine of a stinger.

"Tristan."

"That is what you called me, right."

"I…"

"Go on, sit."

So he did. The ground was cool against his palm as he lowered himself. Ahead, the leviathan unwound itself, silent, until it was one good lunge from nipping its own tail with the gold dammed by its lips.

"I think I understood you a little better there at the park, seeing you as you weren't," Tristan said. "We were even."

Noah glanced down at them, at their spindly legs adjusting one by one and then folding back under their body. Just one more question to jump into the fray trying to fight its way out—perhaps the least consequential of the bunch, but it fought until Noah swallowed it back. Instead: "Is this my imagination? You're dead, and also… talking?—or maybe not, because Jibril sounded like he was speaking English. And it seemed like Frida was…"

The planet and leviathan before them had turned the stifling empty space into a cavern.

"I'm just… very lost," he said, quiet, and then added, "Abelard is dead."

"I know." Tristan stretched up to the tips of their feet, holding themself there for a beat, and settled back. "Mighty Core, we never realized just how primitive your lot really was while I was still home. Even now, I'm learning new limitations of yours."

Noah's head spun. It was too much too quickly, and he was so young, and his mentors were dead or could feign as much at this distance with a simple ignored satcall.

"This isn't your imagination, by the way," Tristan said.

"Am I dead too, then?"

"You're called 'humans,' right?" When Noah nodded, they continued, "Humans must not be naturally attuned to this part of creation." One of their feet reached toward his hand, pointing at the rivulets of violet under his nails. "I can't fathom how you've managed to exist for so long like that."

"We're doing plenty well without it," said Noah. "We managed to travel to your planet, didn't we? Have your people ever left your homeworld? Have you even left that pond?"

Tristan laughed, and Noah gathered his legs to his chest, hiding his reddening face behind his knees.

"Pond? You think that was just a pond? Most of us live in the deepest depths of our planet, and there's so much we have yet to uncover about its mysteries. Have you met the heart of *your* world? Do you know its true name? Has it given you the ichor to approach it? I assume not, on that last point," Tristan said. "Or else you wouldn't have been so keen on mine."

A flash of light gleamed ahead; the leviathan's mouth pulled wide, drips of gold falling to the planet and landing with curling plumes of smoke. Below, another mass began to rise: two stone hands bracing to cup the planet's curve.

"Ichor… is it stored at the base of your stinger?"

"Of course."

So the venom was—"We don't have… what is it to you? What does it mean?"

More gold poured over the planet. It ran down in waves, burning. The hands met the surface, propped up by a second set wrapped around their wrists—a mirror of the miners' logo.

"It lets us in toward the heart. It's what lets us commune with the Core. I tried to tell you and Abelard after you kidnapped me. There was only so much I could communicate by tapping my hands when you ignored everything else."

"Oh."

The entire planet was covered in the molten gold, collecting under it in a spreading mass, crawling forward like lava flow. The leviathan's mouth gaped wider, and the two halves split further, four wings flared in the midpoints between the eyes; it slithered up, up, and then dove down against the planet's surface. Slices of rock, boulders the size of mountains, they splintered into a crater, deeper, until the whole thing began to crack down the middle. All the while, the stone hands dug and squeezed at the surface, ripping it apart faster than the leviathan could ever hope to, even as the gold melted its fingers like wax.

"I'm sorry."

"I know. I could feel it then, too. There's not a lot of good that does now, at least in this moment. Unless you take it with you."

"What, the guilt?"

"I don't understand."

"If I'm not taking the guilt with me," said Noah, "then what am I taking?"

The planet split in two, the halves blooming open with a rushing tide of gold flooding the plane ahead—frothing roiling waves, flecks of spittled foam, suddenly upon them both in a choking heat, slamming Noah's head back.

And back, further, into the cool surface of the *Amihaf*'s foyer.

"C'mon, man," said Frida's voice, soupy amid the blaring alarms. "If you don't get up soon—"

Savannah groaned. "Don't talk like that!"

"'M fine, I'm fine—"

"'Fine' my ass…"

The soupiness ebbed, and more alarms and whistled shoved in behind it. Frida and Savannah were suddenly dragging him into the antechamber.

"What happened?" Savannah asked. She buckled him into the empty seat beside her.

Noah could only shake his head, but she grabbed his hand once she'd latched herself in, squeezing everything into that space between their palms that she herself couldn't say.

From their seats, they had a partial view of the spaceshield, of Irene stretched thin between the pilot and astronavigator's seats. The *Amihaf* wove out of the way of stray tendrils of the leviathan's body whipping toward them. She only had one hand on the yoke, but that was enough. It had to be enough.

"Do you want to talk about it?" Savannah murmured.

Noah squeezed her hand back. The fungal violet had strands touching the untrimmed pale edges of his nails now, and he noticed a similar tinge along the vertical ridges of hers.

Irene swore, and the ship tousled them all in their seats. "Felt worse than it was," she called.

"Was that how it was all the time?"

There was an answer cobbling itself together for her, but ahead, around Irene's sweat-limp hair, burst the full starscape this spot in the galaxy had promised. The engine whined as they shoved the yoke forward, leaving the leviathan behind.

"With who?" Noah said. "Abelard?"

She frowned. "With your father."

He wouldn't let himself answer her, not even in his head. He couldn't answer her, but he could send the answer elsewhere—that answer, and others he'd sought, and all those he'd once decided to do without acknowledging. He pulled out his tablet, fingers shaking as he raced to beat a clock that might not have been ticking; the border of the relays' range wasn't a visible line in the vacuum.

"Are you seriously checking your email?" Savannah asked.

"Not checking," he said, ignoring the rest of the crew's bewildered commentary.

One message sat in his drafts, pre-addressed, half-composed in those late nights outside the bounds of the relays. He tapped to start a new paragraph.

Justin—you were right, before, when you ended it, but I want to try again. I think we can try again. I know it's too little too late, and you have no reason to believe me. Just know I want to try to be better. If that's the only thing I can—

The *Amihaf* banked sharply to the right, shunting the inside of the ship almost ninety degrees off from center; Noah juggled to keep hold of his tablet, but it slipped from his fingertips, shattering against the wall.

"Here's the deal, okay?" Irene yelled over her shoulder. "That thing damaged our engine. The fuel recycler is broken *and* it's leaking. There's a system nearby. Might be habitable. It's our best bet. This ship's only got so much turbolight left in it."

Irene broke her hold of the yoke to brace herself in the doorway. Dark circles lined her eyes as she looked over each of them in turn. "Of course, I may have miscalculated. If I did, and this jump rips us apart... it's been an honor."

She spun back to the console. One hand entered the coordinates for the vector; the other opened a channel for any nearby relay, the words spilling out of her mouth in a jumbled rush.

"This is the *TCS Amihaf* reporting to Cairo, Cape Guacara, Beijing, Kinshasa—anywhere," she said. "Abort Khepri. Abort Aker. We don't know what we're dealing with. They don't want us out here. If we—"

Without warning, the spread of turbolight lit up the spaceshield. The ship bolted forward at an unnatural clip. Something in the controls had broken, a limit released. Ahead and ahead and ahead, faster and faster until the whorls blurred into a single color, until they dropped out, the stars returning to pinpoints, and someone screamed. Himself? The scene through the cockpit twisted his stomach as it spun. They were all going to die. They were—

EPILOGUE

THE SOIL CHURNED UP by the long wake of the *Amihaf*'s crash was a garish goldenrod reserved on Earth for springtime florals.

It stank. Cakey clods of it seeped into their clothes after they'd hoisted themselves out of the wreckage—the port side of the ship and its clipped wing tilted up toward the sky, and just reaching fresh air was a feat. None of them had the energy to secure a clean landing, elbows and knees smeared with the sulfuric miasma.

As they gained their bearings, the idle chatter rose and fell, observations and questions and peppered bits of relief belonging to no one in particular. At least, all the voices sounded the same through the haze, through varying degrees of tinnitus or eardrums frayed during descent. How lucky were they all to still be in one piece. How incredible that this planet held oxygen in its atmosphere and didn't fry or freeze them alive at first exposure. How miraculous that they stepped out of the ship to signs of life.

The life in question spread out in the field now torn apart and littered with debris. Tiny spiraling tendrils, black and reedy, broke through the acrid dirt.

A grass, a fungus, something in between. The debate could be settled later.

The crash site had almost been a disaster. Behind the side of the ship where they'd gathered, on the side facing the vertical plane of the hull, the field extended, overtaken by a jagged ridge of mountains at the horizon. Less than half a mile opposite was the shore.

The *Amihaf* would have sunk—not like a stone, but worse. The heightened gravity would have seen to that, just as it wore at their aching, bruised muscles.

More questions—or, not questions, but wonderings they knew no one could answer, not right away, but it was something to cover the silence and the unfamiliar noises piercing the silence that they couldn't fathom thinking too hard about. Not yet.

So instead they wondered into existence a checklist to tackle when their shell-shocked heads stopped vibrating at that odd, fuzzed frequency where everything felt a little dreamy.

The base element of the planet's life. The chemical composition of the sea and its potential solutes. The length of a day, a year. The distance to the mountain range, what waited beyond it.

Time passed, but no one was counting. The air had started to cool, the clouds thinning to tease a glimpse at the impending night sky. The checklist's scope shriveled to the churned stinking ground swallowing the bow of the *Amihaf* halfway up the spaceshield. The scope shriveled, and they couldn't bring themselves to finish the thoughts out loud.

That hardly mattered. It was simply enough to fill in the blanks if someone trailed off wondering about the mimeos.

After sunset, no moon fought the spread of stars for the spotlight. Brilliant sprays of light, whites and golds and blues that reached down to the soil, plucking the ends of the grass-like life until their curls stood straight, tall enough now to brush their calves.

"Irene."

The first voice that asserted an owner. Dayo. It trembled.

"Irene, where are we?"

She didn't answer for a long time—not solely because she was scanning the starscape for the subtle signs she could read so well, but the warmth of her dark eyes held something that words couldn't touch and no one else could discern.

"I don't know," she said finally. "This wasn't where I was aiming."

The crew spent the first night back in the ship, huddled all together in the bunk hall with blankets and pillows pilfered from their cots. With the doors closed along the right side, there was room enough for all seven of them to stretch out—maybe not comfortably against the metal walls, but sufficiently. The temperature plummeted within hours of the last of them drifting off, and upon waking, they found themselves huddled around each other, arms flung over chests and over faces, left unremarked upon as they started to stir.

Outside, it was still dark. Noah woke the closest to the lounge entrance, so he slid himself toward the ledge formed by the new angle of the ship that hung over the door frame.

1342 IST.

"One more thing to adjust to," Frida sighed. "What's the over-under on the night cycle lasting more than twenty-four hours?"

A week ago, Quinn or Savannah would have told her to can it, but something about the way she grumbled in her typical tenor, chin tucked between a teddy bear's ears, left their barbs disarmed.

They assembled themselves for the first real day on-planet more quickly than Noah would have expected. Truthfully, he'd hoped they would have given themselves a little longer in their makeshift beds, allowed even a few more hours to waver in and out of consciousness before turning toward the stark reality outside the *Amihaf*.

It was quick work divvying up the items from the checklist. Quinn assessed the status of the ship, what parts were still powered and how long they'd stay that way. Savannah and Frida raided the lab for equipment to begin sampling the xeno-organisms covering the field, shoving some water-testing strips in their back pockets to use later on the sea. Esmail set off down the long trail the ship carved down the coast to retrieve useful debris. Dayo nudged her way into whatever work was undertaken in the moment, pressing the hemograph to skin while it still had power and could potentially be recharged, noting all of their new baselines relative to what she could recall.

Their bodies hadn't broken in the crash landing, but plenty else had—the ship's siloed server of medical records, for example. Noah's personal tablet whose screen had fractured just before the jump was found by the stairwell, snapped in half. So much relied on memory when they couldn't gauge if anyone was coping with a concussion.

Irene, amid it all, retrieved her pen and notebook from her bunk and dug herself in at the top of the mound the *Amihaf* had formed when it finally skidded to a halt. The black grass rooted there still lived, unrolling itself up toward the sky even in the thinnest portions of soil smothering the spaceshield.

Noah stood a ways off from the ship, shoreside. There was nothing clearly xenozoological to attend to, so instead he stared up at the stars, wondering what Irene was looking for.

At some point, his knees protested angrily enough to get him to sit on the damp, reeking soil. Dayo perched herself beside him later, just as the sun was starting to leak its glow over the horizon. She breathed through her mouth, a clearly conscious effort; if Noah were to have met her eyes, he knew they'd be stinging red, so he lingered elsewhere.

"Huh… everyone," she murmured, standing.

"Everyone what?"

"Look at your fingers."

Even the dim lighting couldn't hide the lack of violet streaking up from the nail beds. He sifted through the snapshots of the rest of the crew since they woke that afternoon—or whatever time the planet dictated—and the absence gleamed. The whites of Quinn's eyes were true to their name. Esmail's gums were spotless as he tried to lift their spirits.

The stars faded into the brightening blue of the sky, and though Irene closed her notebook, she did not descend from the peak of the *Amihaf*'s bow.

Noah climbed up to join her.

"Hi," he said.

"We're out of relay range," she said. "My tablet is the only one that isn't broken. I haven't told anyone."

"Anyone *else*, now. Technically." Somehow Noah wasn't surprised. If Irene hadn't been able to pinpoint their location in that first glimpse of the stars, the extra time fully analogue wasn't going to save them. It spoke to a system far flung from TerraCosmos' attention.

They sat in silence as the system's sun lit the line of the horizon in a bloody red.

"It's safe to assume we probably won't get off this rock," he said after a moment.

"No," she said. Her hand waved toward the fading stars. "It doesn't look good."

Frida and Savannah had wandered so far off that they were reduced to specks, a tiny smudge of orange and a taller smudge of brown hopping around some locus, invisible.

"Are you doing all right?" she asked after a few moments.

"Is anyone? I mean… I at least got to shoot off one message before it went to pieces. I don't know what can to say to any of them. Did you know Savannah and Tracy have been together since high school?"

"That wasn't…" Irene sighed. "That, we'll all manage together."

"So what were you talking about?"

"I'm not sure I want to say his name just yet."

Abelard.

The man who brought Noah into the academic fold of vacuum leviathans, the man who grabbed hold of their ship and steered it into the gaping throat of the beast, untheoretical. There was a time during Noah's doctorate when he would have insisted Abelard saved his life by guiding him to the path he'd blazed—the cutting edge of xenozoology, open space for Noah to practice feeling tall.

He reached with his right arm to scratch an itch by a torn patch of his jeans. The bruises twinged, needle-sharp, a flash of Abelard's Constructed Hand spread wide and rushing toward the chartreuse stain under his skin.

"I'll be okay eventually," Noah said.

"Eventually?"

"Shorter than it sounds. Promise."

Behind them, Dayo and Quinn rose out of the ship's exit, chattering optimistically about the battery life of the galley mimeo. Each of them took a deep breath of this mystery planet's atmosphere, reveling as their lungs held all those molecules tight, waiting for them to diffuse off where they were needed. The horizon bled more color, reds curling into pinks and saffrons, coloring even the shadows running about the fields under Frida and Savannah's feet.

It could be an honor, Noah considered, to live here and die here—a far stretch of humanity that, for once, landed someplace new and didn't unfurl into destruction. They could let the only sign of them be taken back into the heart of the planet.

(Abelard would have liked that, the version of the man Noah met that sweltering August day, years ago.)

In the distance, Savannah and Frida leaped and shouted in revelatory joy. Quinn and Dayo and Esmail gathered by the bow at the sound, faces bright. Irene jumped to her feet, offered Noah a lift as her boots started to slide against the layer of soil atop the spaceshield.

"They must have found something amazing," she said.

Noah took her hand.

Acknowledgements

Innumerous thanks to my first readers—Rourke, Ray, Sam, and Jeff—as well as so many others who listened to me yell about this story and offered encouragement over the last several years. Ray, in particular—thank you for fielding all my newbie questions about indie publishing.

Innumerous thanks and gratitude as well to Liam Stevens and Lara Kareem for their sensitivity consults and readings on Quinn, Dayo, and Esmail.

Helvetica Blanc—I'm obsessed with the cover you created.

It feels fitting to name some of the folks who made the science half of the sci-fi possible, laying a solid enough foundation so I'd know what questions to ask while trying to nail down How My Things Work: Mrs. Womack, Mr. Douglass, Dr. Gerrans. (Plus a special nod to all of my day-job colleagues who have explained basic computer science to me over the last eight years and will likely continue to need to do so.)

Lastly—the society this book envisions so far into our future, while far from perfect, was meant to be aspirational, and it feels far more out of reach than it did when I was first writing it in 2021. That doesn't mean that it *is*,

though, despite everything. Another world is possible, always. Land back.
Free Palestine.